# MANGA SHAKESPEARE™

# MUCH ADO
## ABOUT NOTHING

W9-AJL-571

*ADAPTED BY*
# RICHARD APPIGNANESI

*ILLUSTRATED BY*
# EMMA VIECELI

Amulet Books, New York

Library of Congress Cataloging-in-Publication Data

Appignanesi, Richard.
Much ado about nothing / by William Shakespeare ; adapted by Richard Appignanesi ; illustrated by Emma Vieceli.
p. cm. — (Manga Shakespeare)
Summary: A comic book version of Shakespeare's comedy about mistaken identities, games, eavesdropping, and unrequited love.
ISBN 978-0-8109-4323-0 (Harry N. Abrams, Inc.)
1. Graphic novels. [1. Graphic novels. 2. Shakespeare, William, 1564–1616. Much ado about nothing—Adaptations.] I. Vieceli, Emma, ill. II. Shakespeare, William, 1564–1616. Much ado about nothing. III. Title.
PZ7.7.A67Mu 2009
741.5'973—dc22
2009005872

Originally published in the U.K. by SelfMadeHero
(www.selfmadehero.com)

Illustrator: Emma Vieceli
Text Adaptor: Richard Appignanesi
Designer: Andy Huckle
Textual Consultant: Nick de Somogyi
Publisher: Emma Hayley

Printed and bound in China
10 9 8 7 6 5 4 3 2 1

ABRAMS
THE ART OF BOOKS SINCE 1949
115 West 18th Street
New York, NY 10011
www.abramsbooks.com

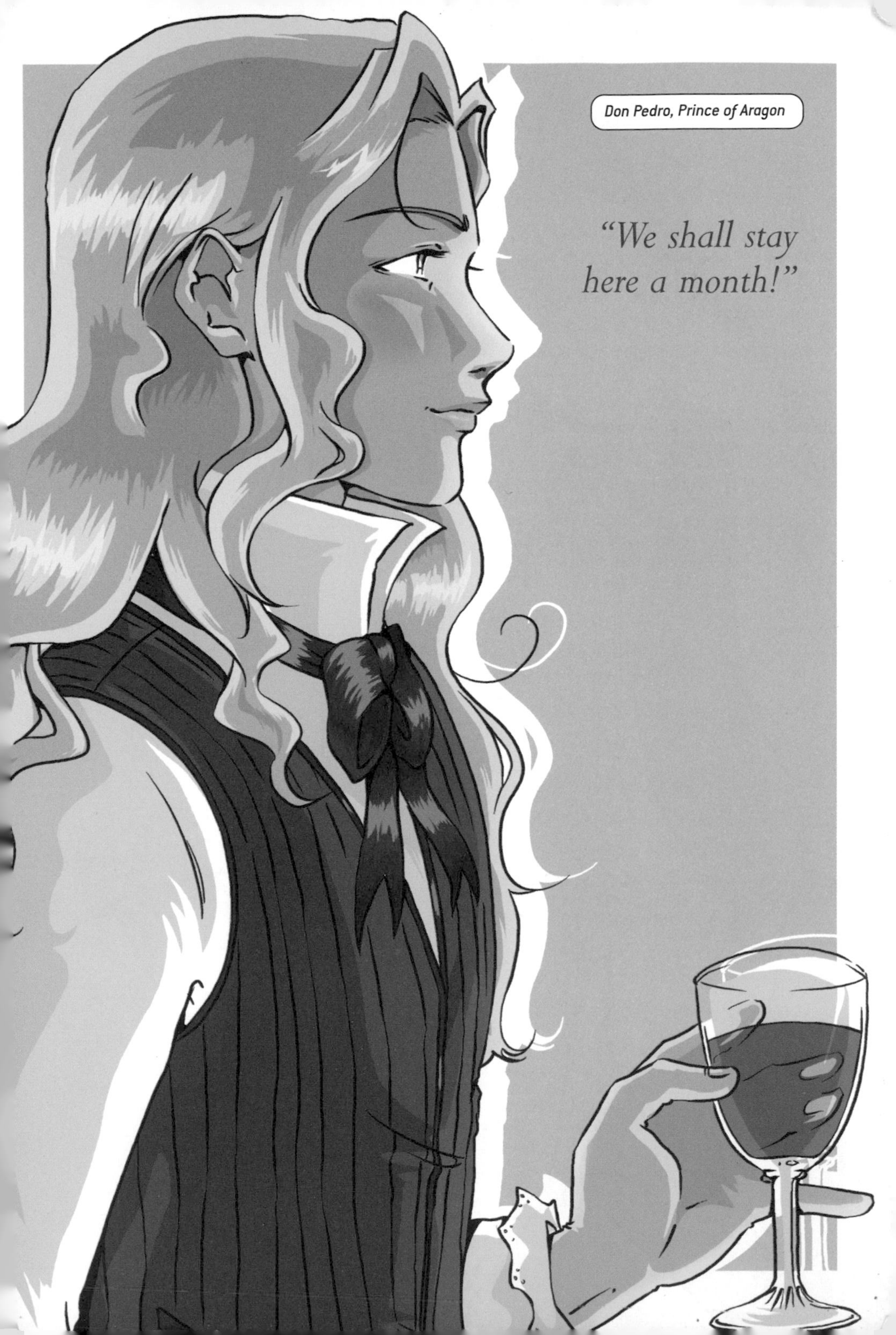
Don Pedro, Prince of Aragon
"We shall stay here a month!"

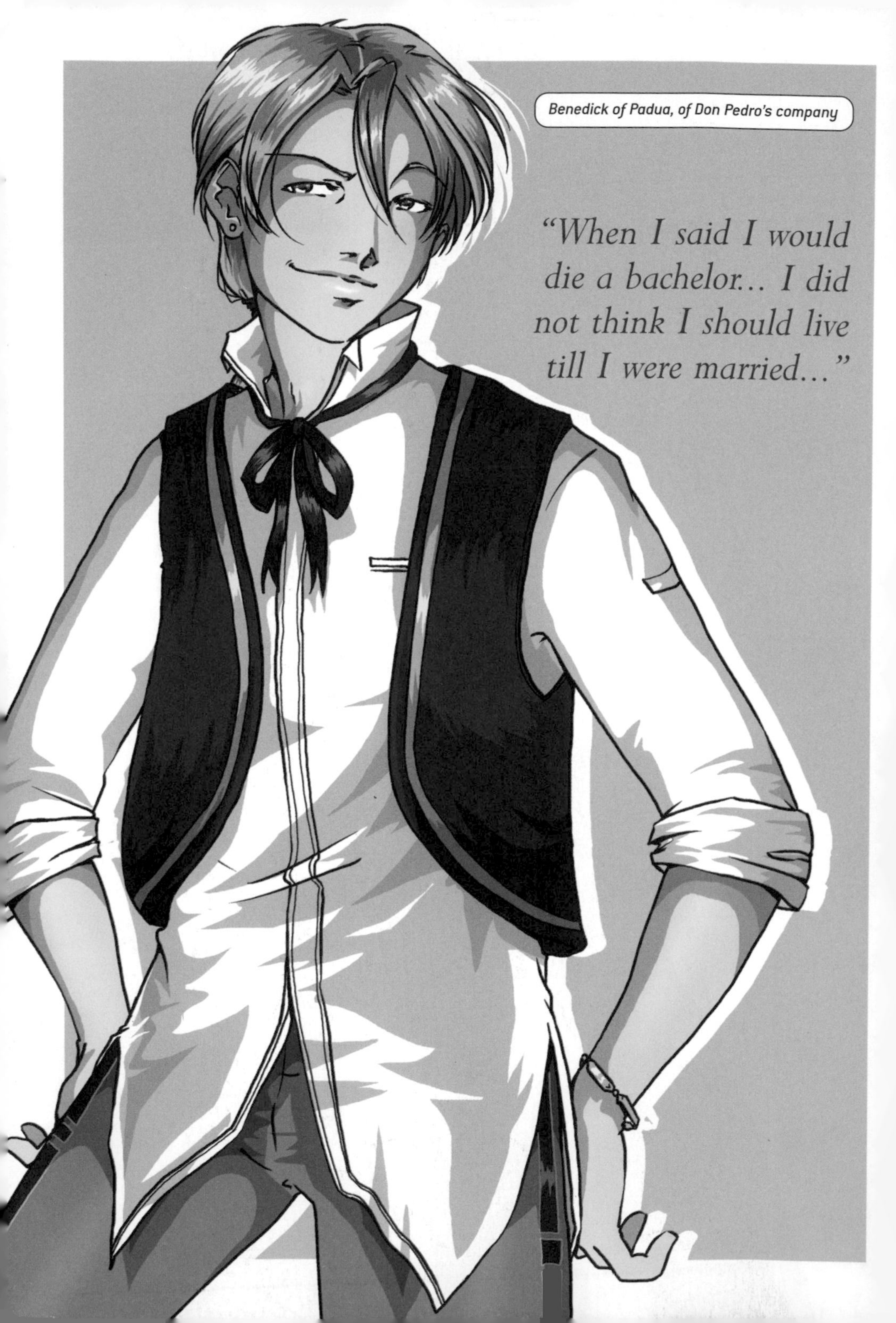
Benedick of Padua, of Don Pedro's company
"When I said I would die a bachelor... I did not think I should live till I were married..."

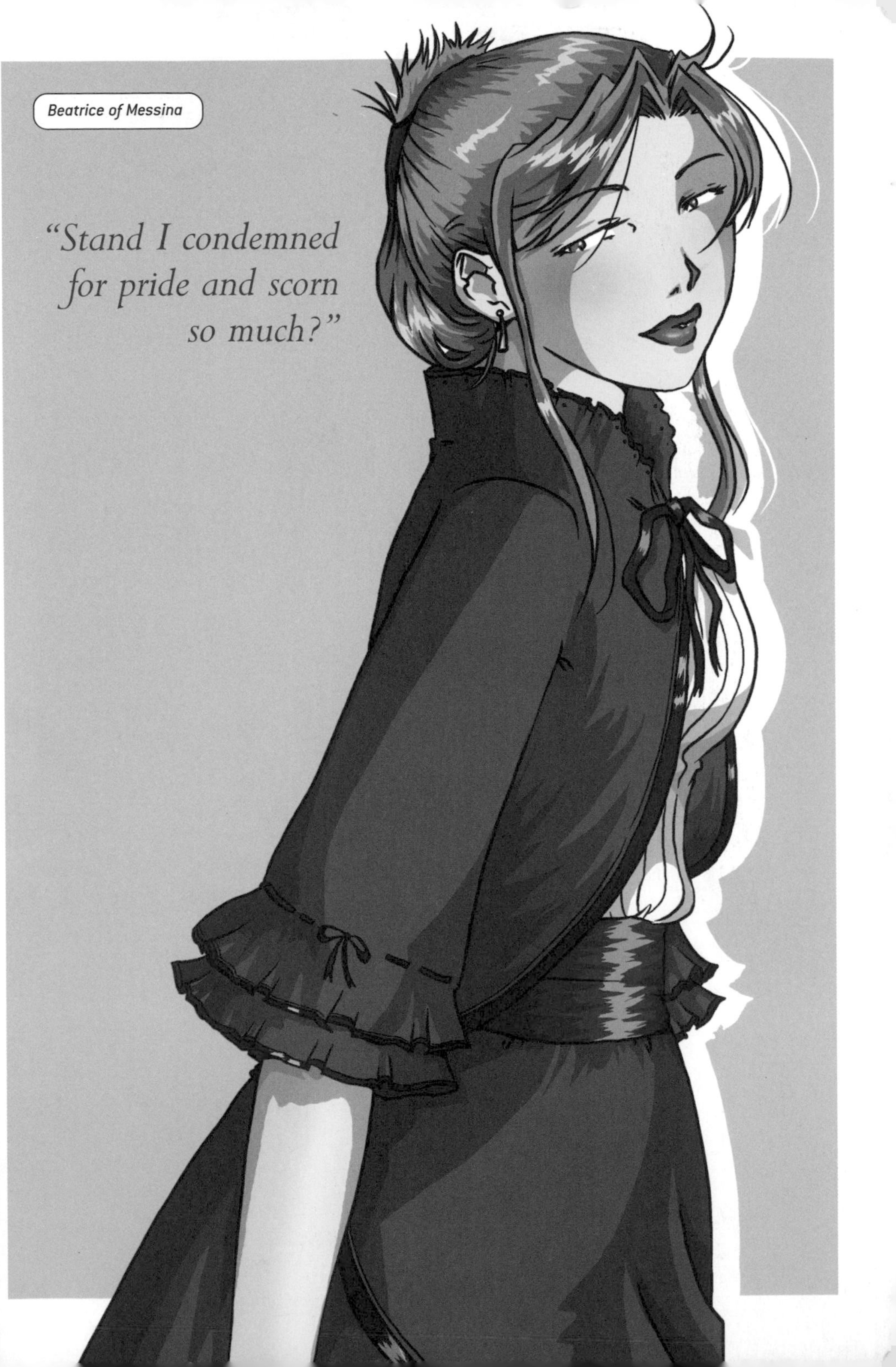
Beatrice of Messina
"Stand I condemned for pride and scorn so much?"

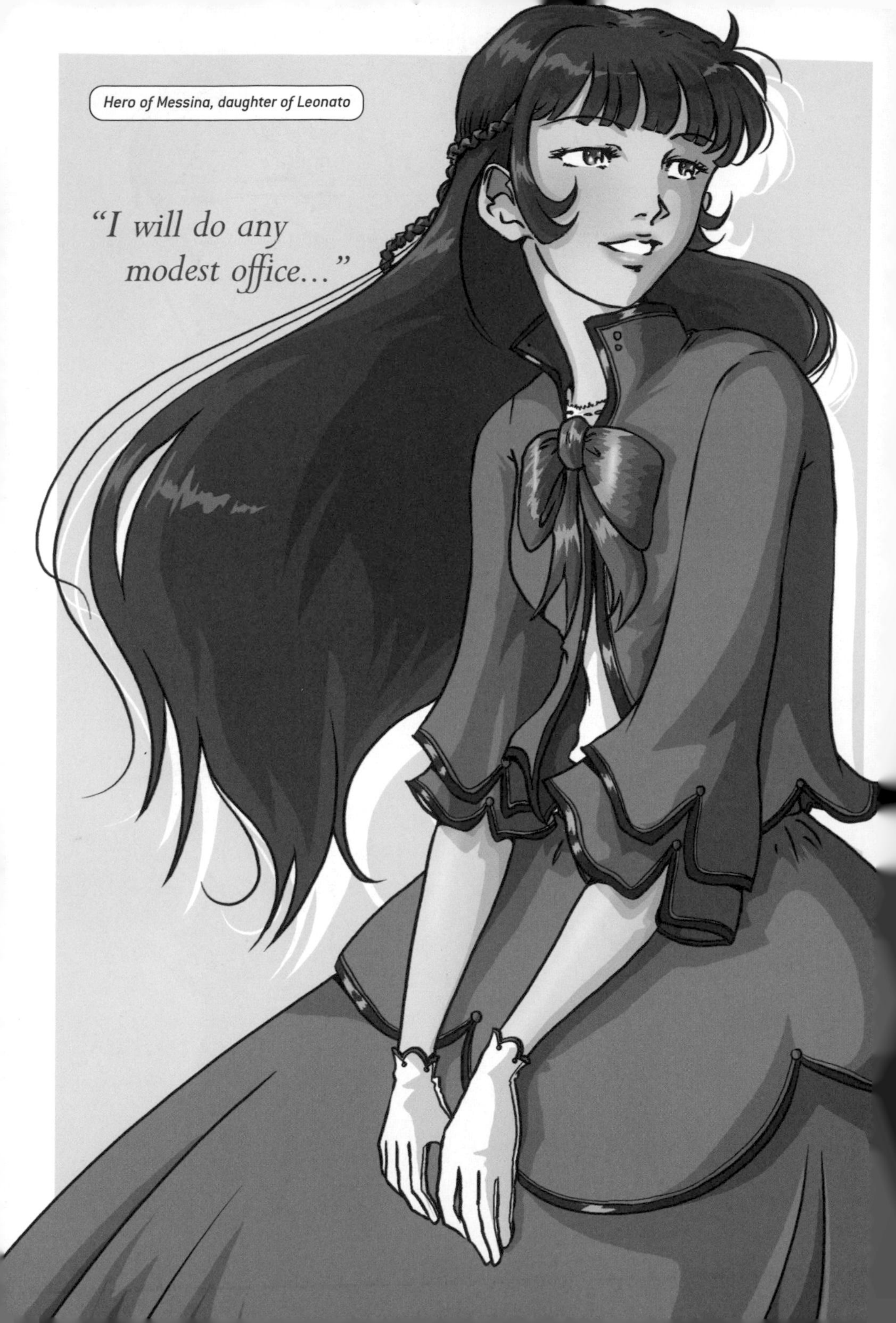
Hero of Messina, daughter of Leonato
"I will do any modest office..."

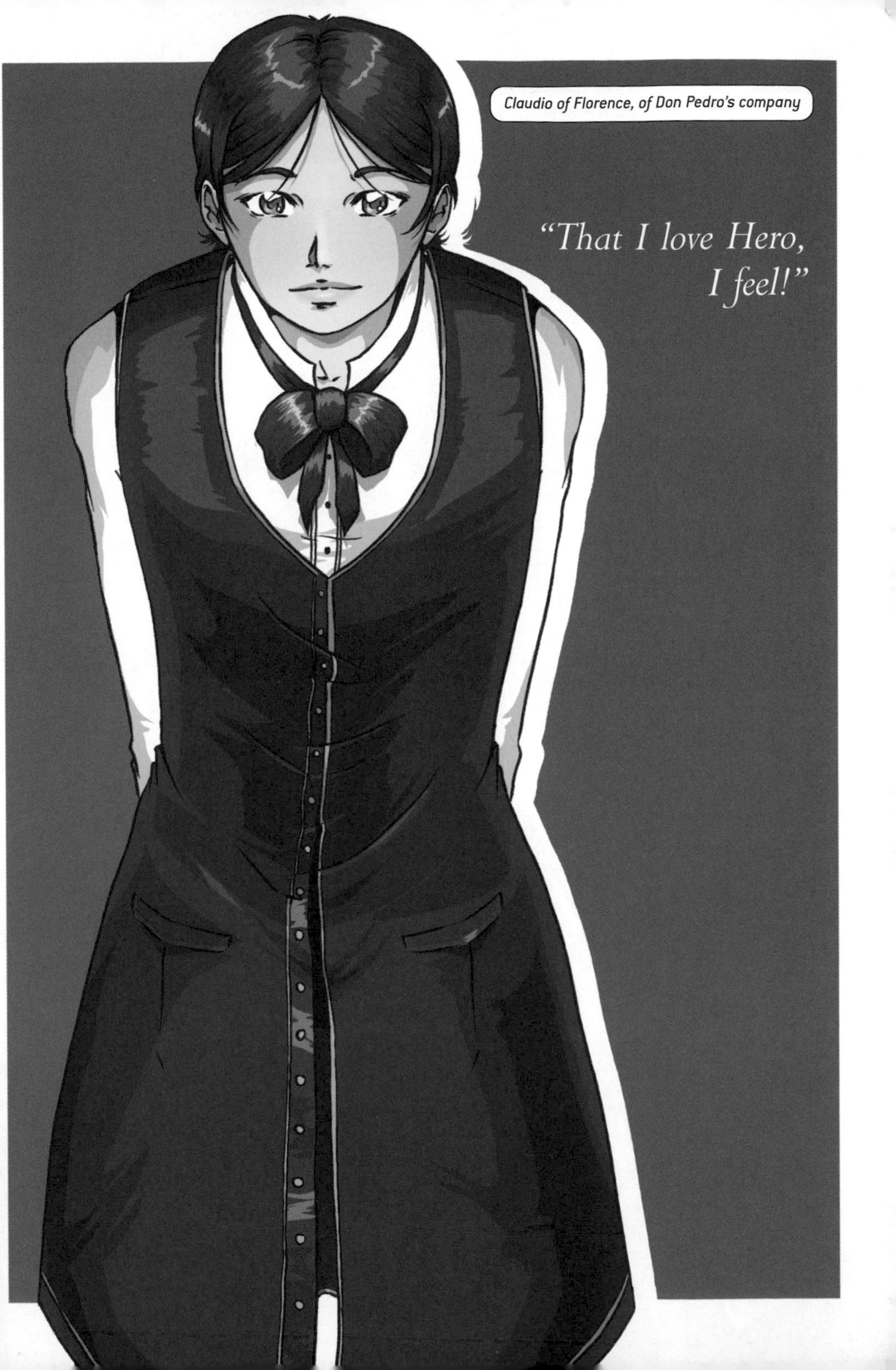
Claudio of Florence, of Don Pedro's company
"That I love Hero,
I feel!"

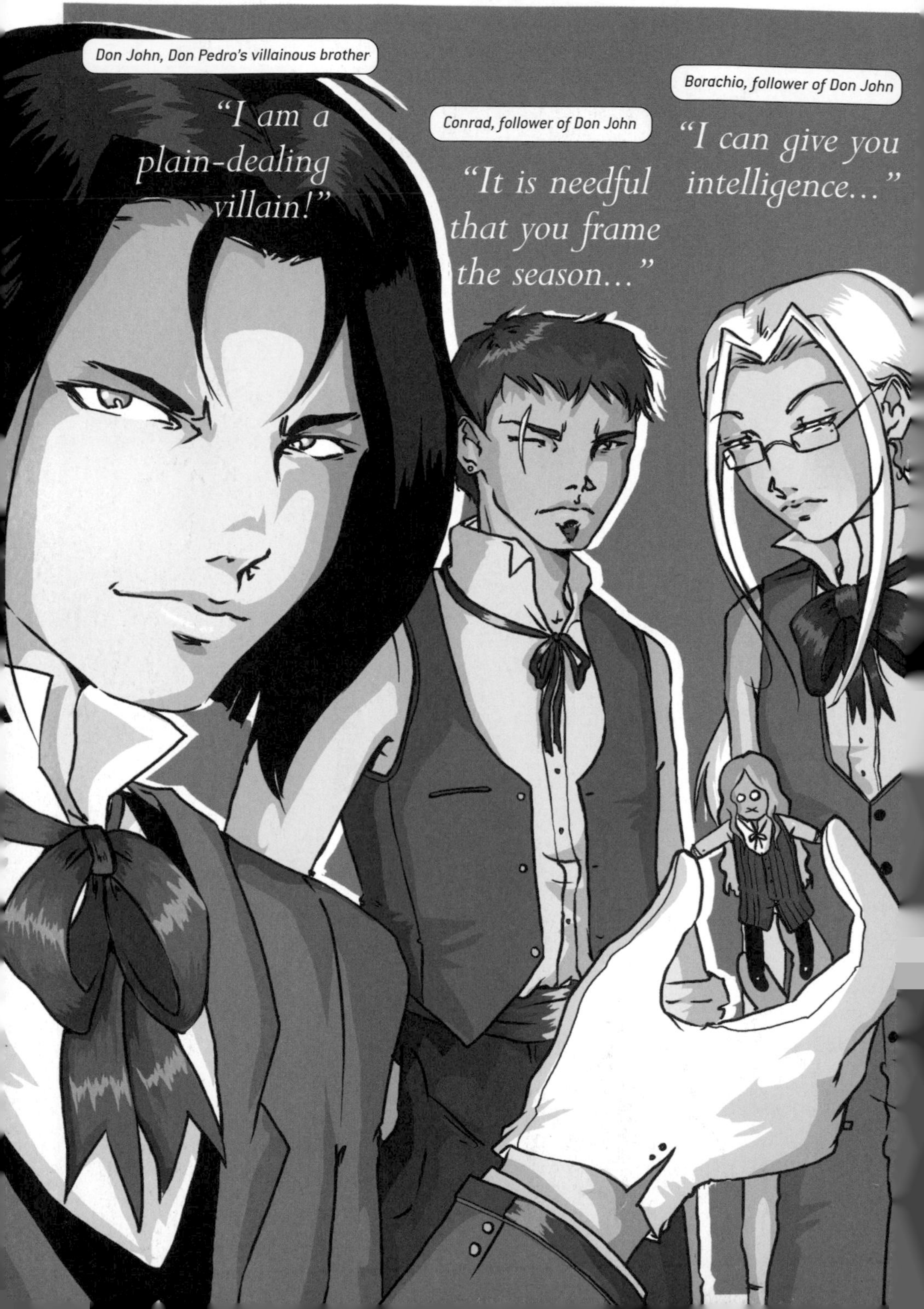
Don John, Don Pedro's villainous brother
"I am a plain-dealing villain!"
Conrad, follower of Don John
"It is needful that you frame the season..."
Borachio, follower of Don John
"I can give you intelligence..."

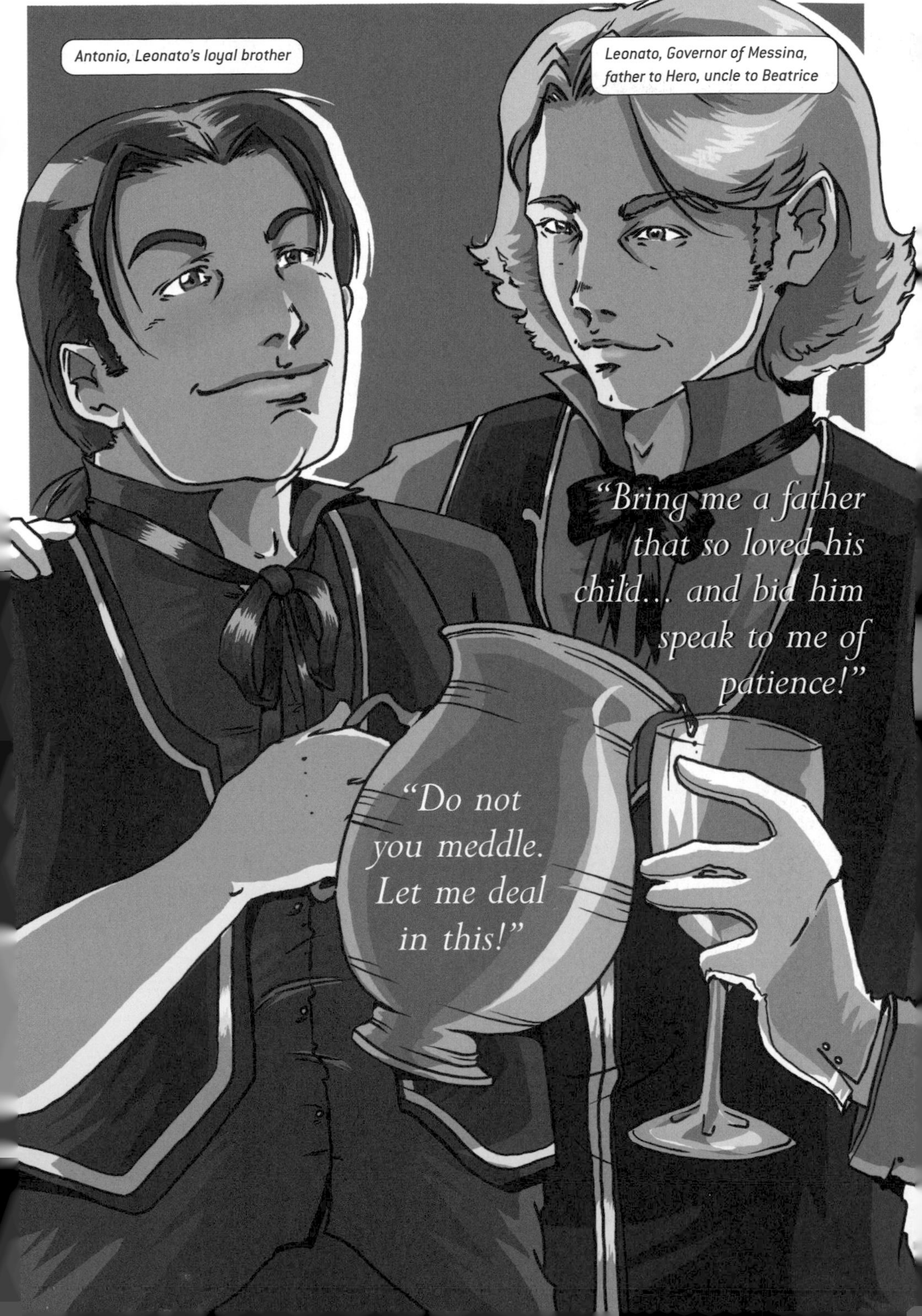
Antonio, Leonato's loyal brother
Leonato, Governor of Messina, father to Hero, uncle to Beatrice
"Bring me a father that so loved his child... and bid him speak to me of patience!"
"Do not you meddle. Let me deal in this!"

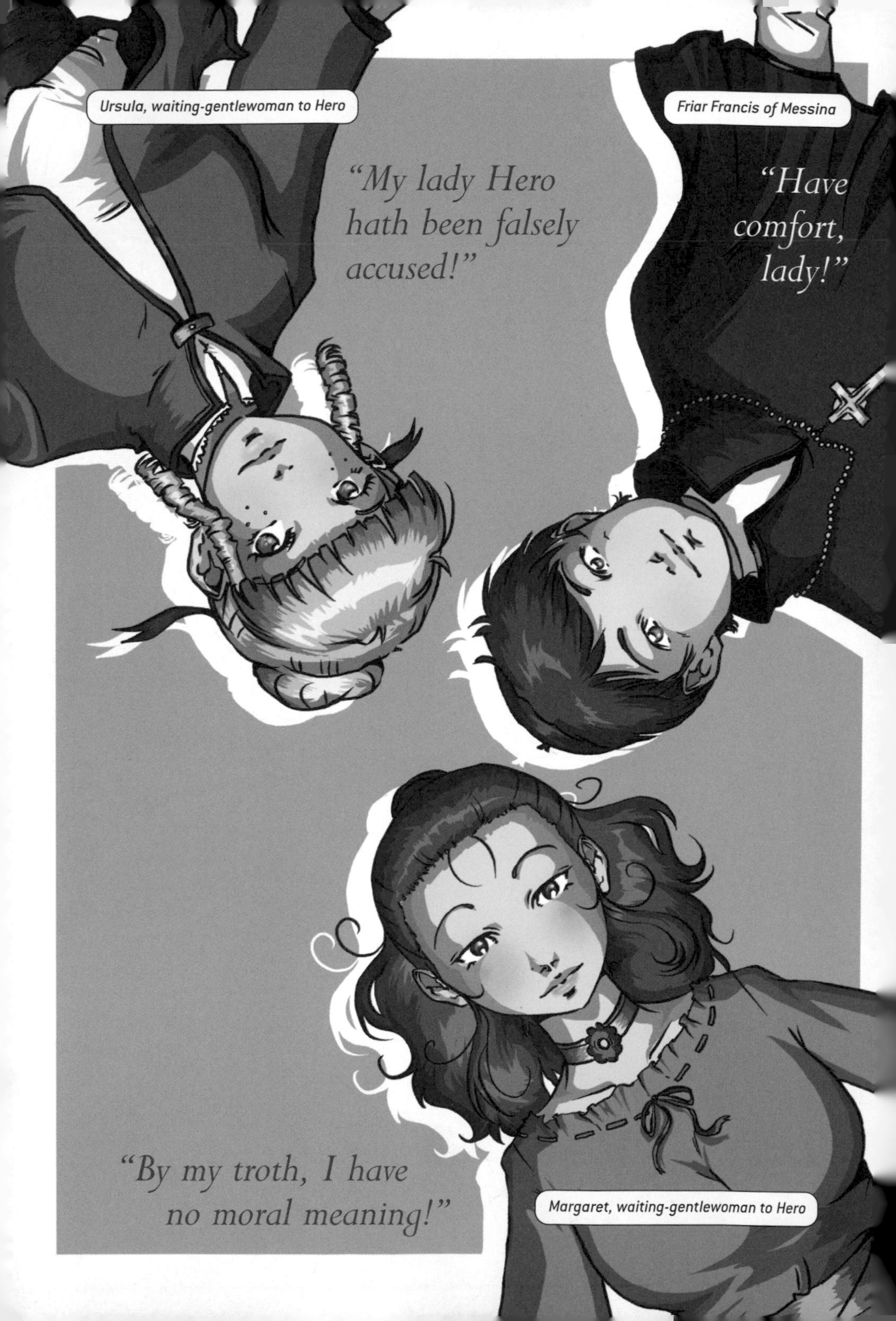
Ursula, waiting-gentlewoman to Hero
"My lady Hero hath been falsely accused!"
Friar Francis of Messina
"Have comfort, lady!"
"By my troth, I have no moral meaning!"
Margaret, waiting-gentlewoman to Hero

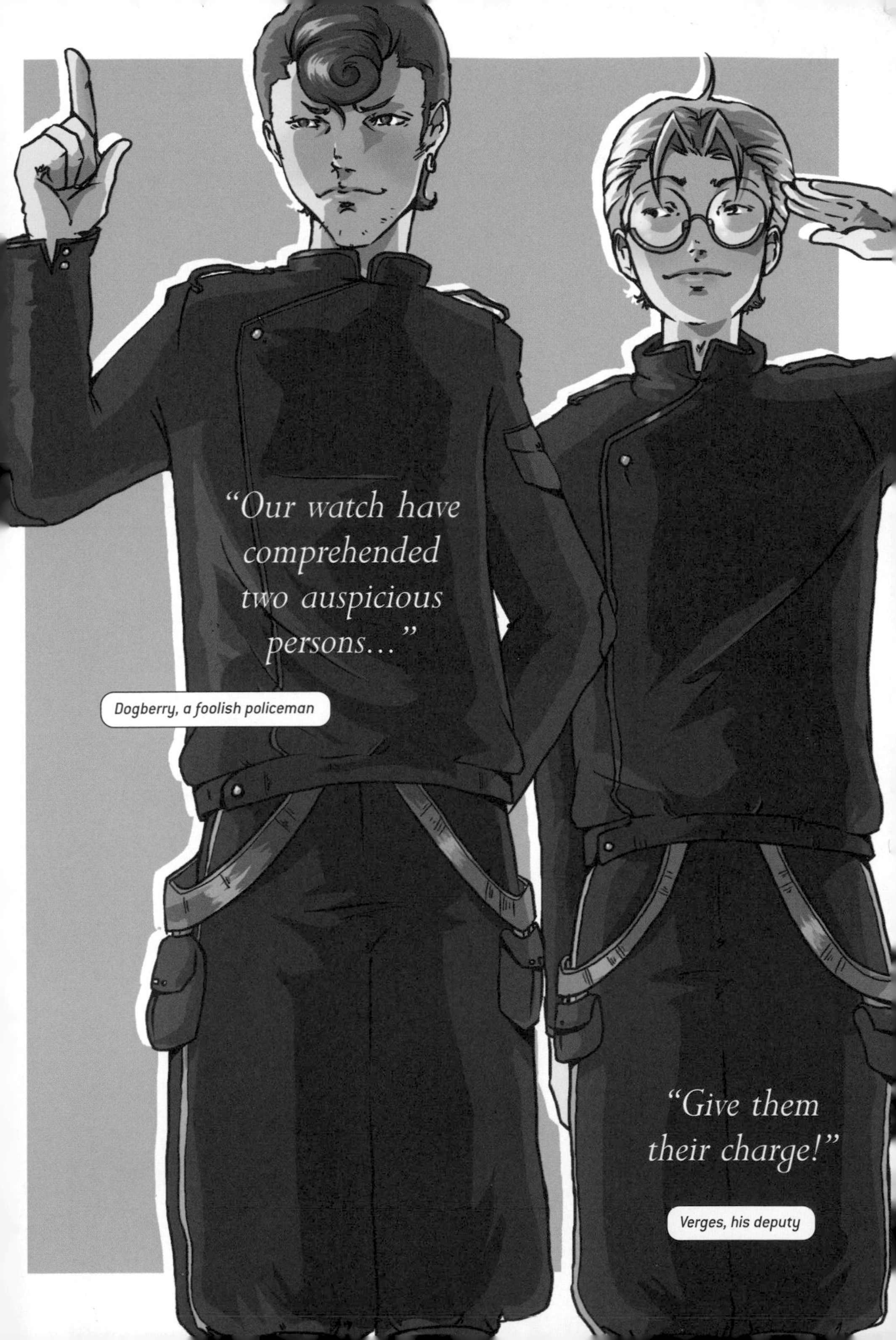
"Our watch have comprehended two auspicious persons..."
Dogberry, a foolish policeman
"Give them their charge!"
Verges, his deputy

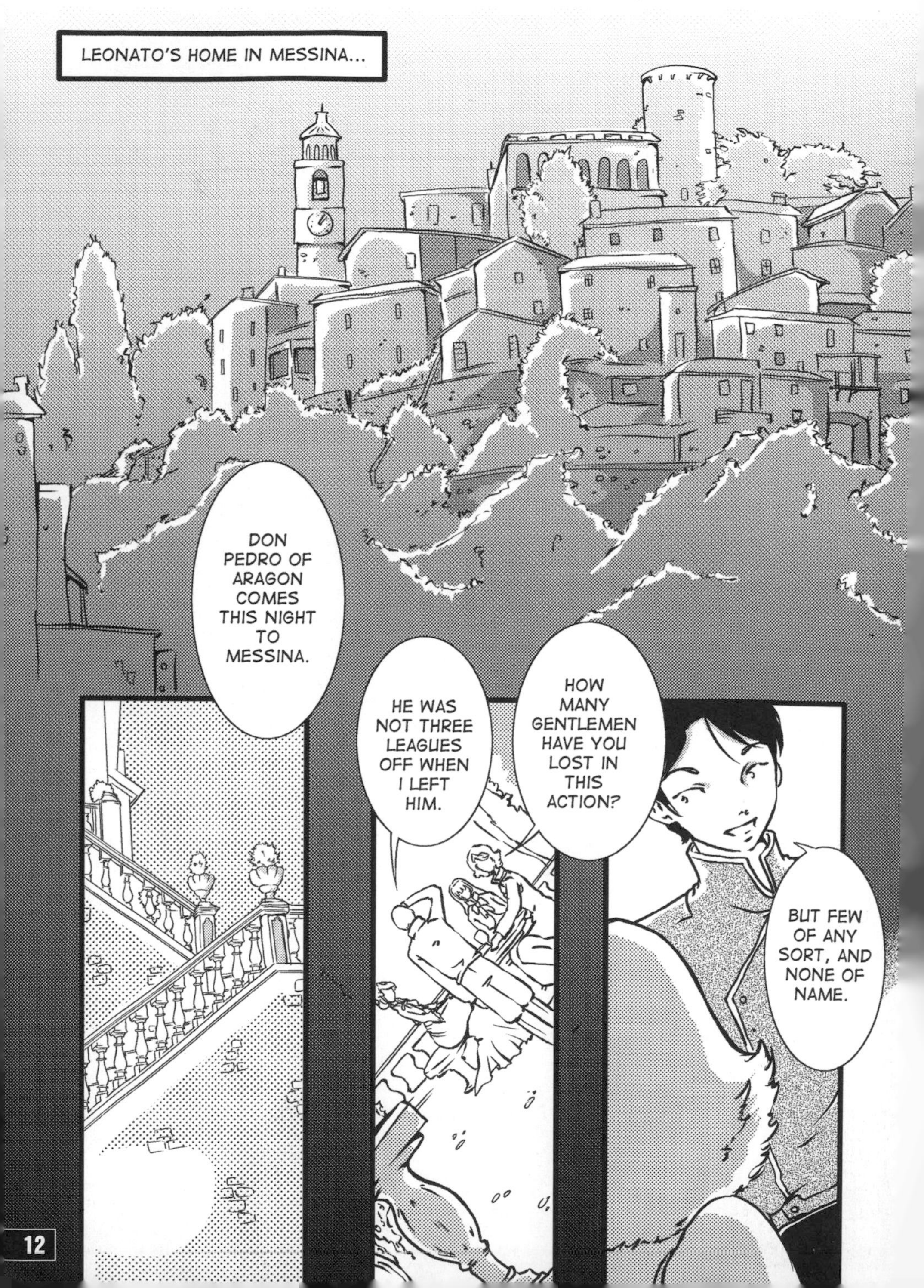

LEONATO'S HOME IN MESSINA...
DON PEDRO OF ARAGON COMES THIS NIGHT TO MESSINA.
HE WAS NOT THREE LEAGUES OFF WHEN I LEFT HIM.
HOW MANY GENTLEMEN HAVE YOU LOST IN THIS ACTION?
BUT FEW OF ANY SORT, AND NONE OF NAME.

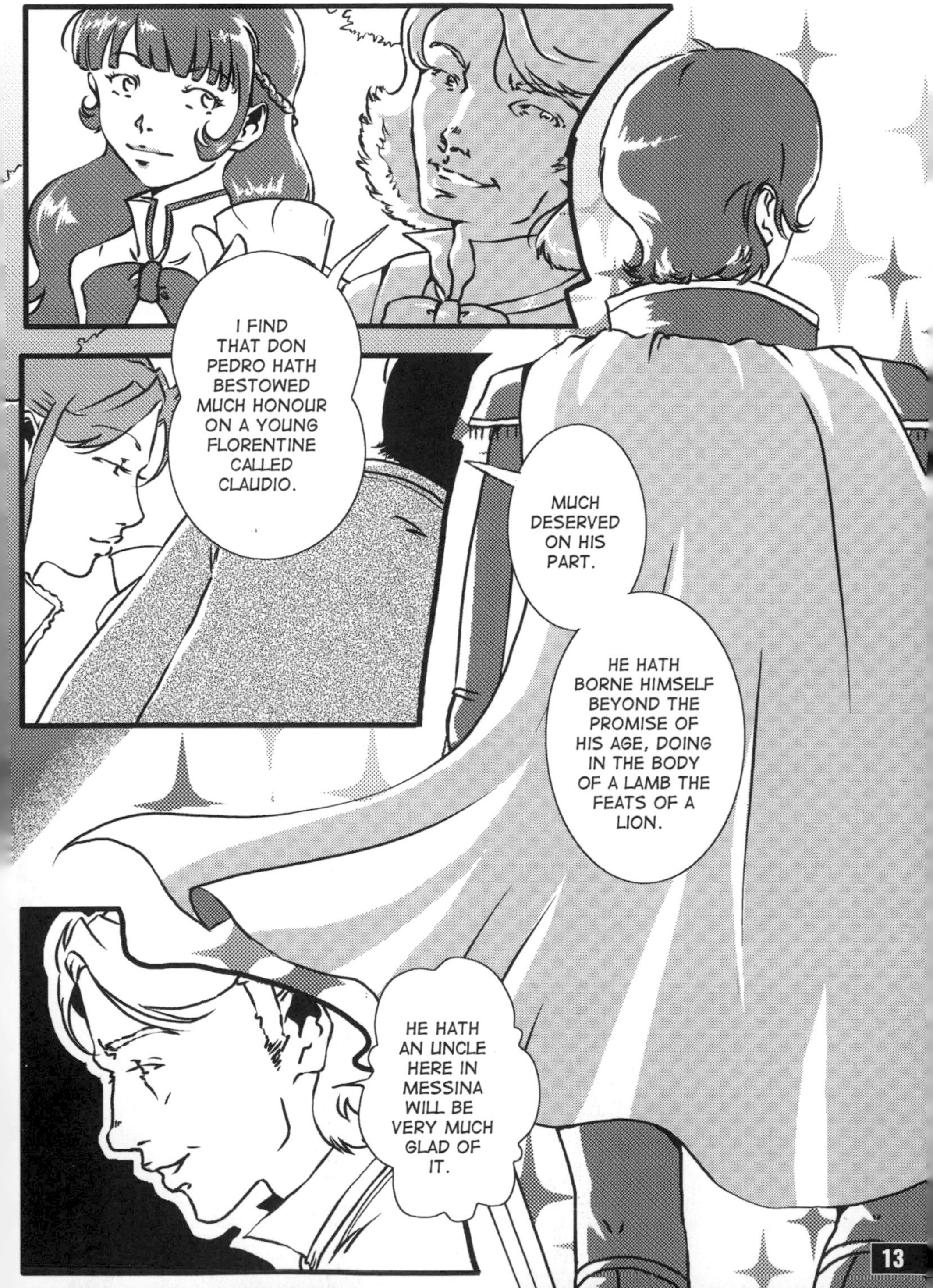
I FIND THAT DON PEDRO HATH BESTOWED MUCH HONOUR ON A YOUNG FLORENTINE CALLED CLAUDIO.
MUCH DESERVED ON HIS PART.
HE HATH BORNE HIMSELF BEYOND THE PROMISE OF HIS AGE, DOING IN THE BODY OF A LAMB THE FEATS OF A LION.
HE HATH AN UNCLE HERE IN MESSINA WILL BE VERY MUCH GLAD OF IT.

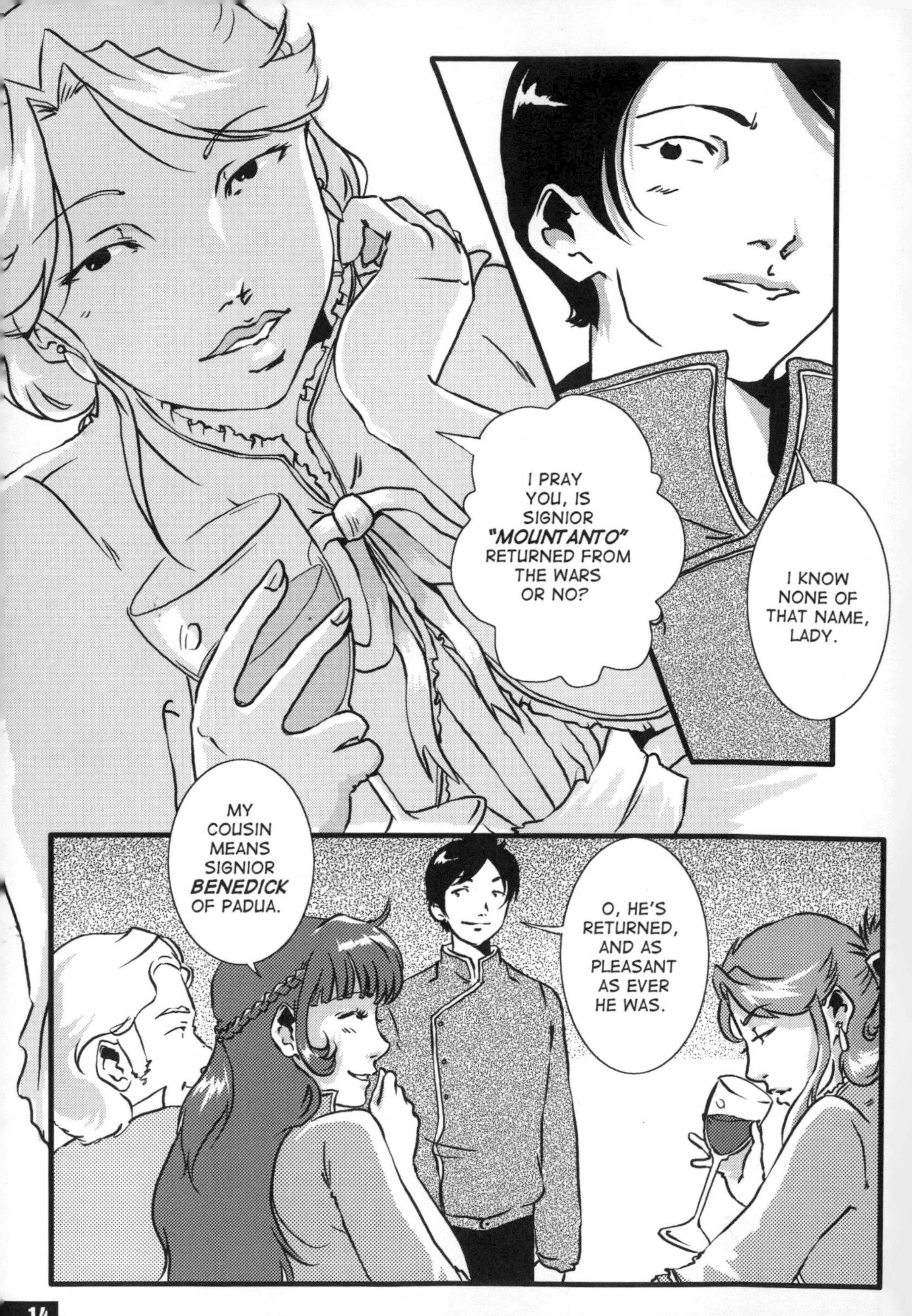
I PRAY YOU, IS SIGNIOR "MOUNTANTO" RETURNED FROM THE WARS OR NO?
I KNOW NONE OF THAT NAME, LADY.
MY COUSIN MEANS SIGNIOR BENEDICK OF PADUA.
O, HE'S RETURNED, AND AS PLEASANT AS EVER HE WAS.

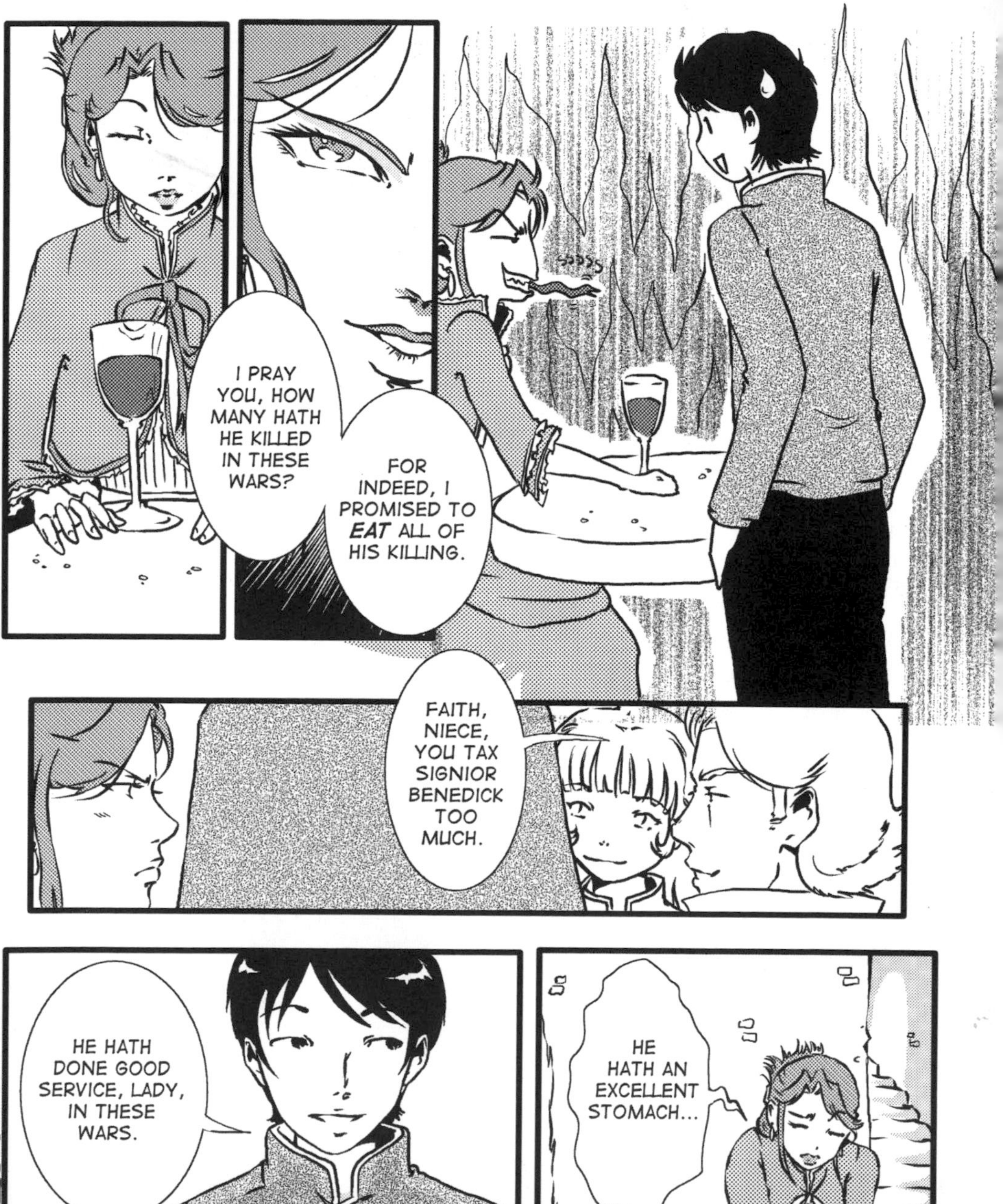
I PRAY YOU, HOW MANY HATH HE KILLED IN THESE WARS?
FOR INDEED, I PROMISED TO EAT ALL OF HIS KILLING.
FAITH, NIECE, YOU TAX SIGNIOR BENEDICK TOO MUCH.
HE HATH DONE GOOD SERVICE, LADY, IN THESE WARS.
HE HATH AN EXCELLENT STOMACH...

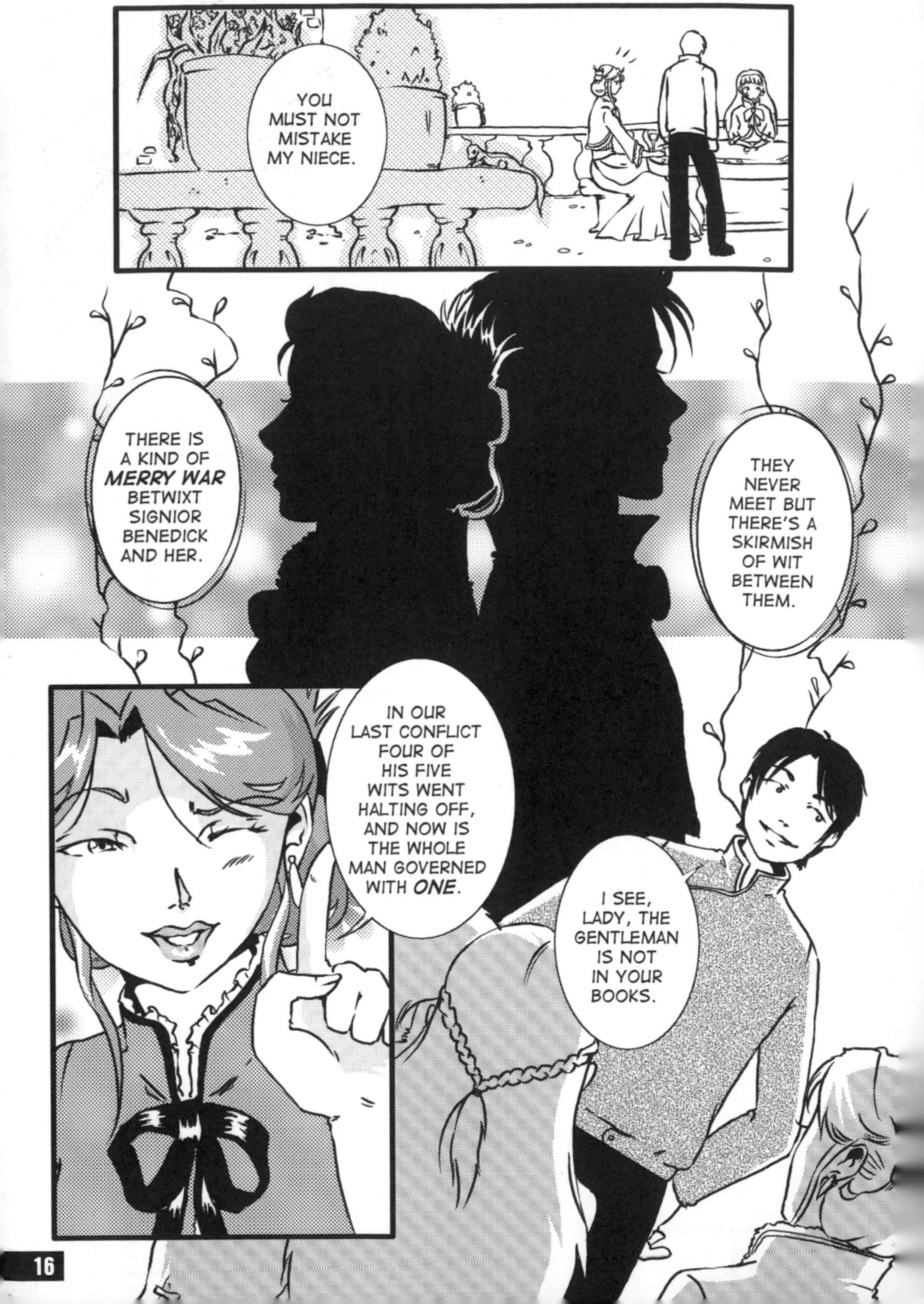
YOU MUST NOT MISTAKE MY NIECE.
THERE IS A KIND OF MERRY WAR BETWIXT SIGNIOR BENEDICK AND HER.
THEY NEVER MEET BUT THERE'S A SKIRMISH OF WIT BETWEEN THEM.
IN OUR LAST CONFLICT FOUR OF HIS FIVE WITS WENT HALTING OFF, AND NOW IS THE WHOLE MAN GOVERNED WITH ONE.
I SEE, LADY, THE GENTLEMAN IS NOT IN YOUR BOOKS.

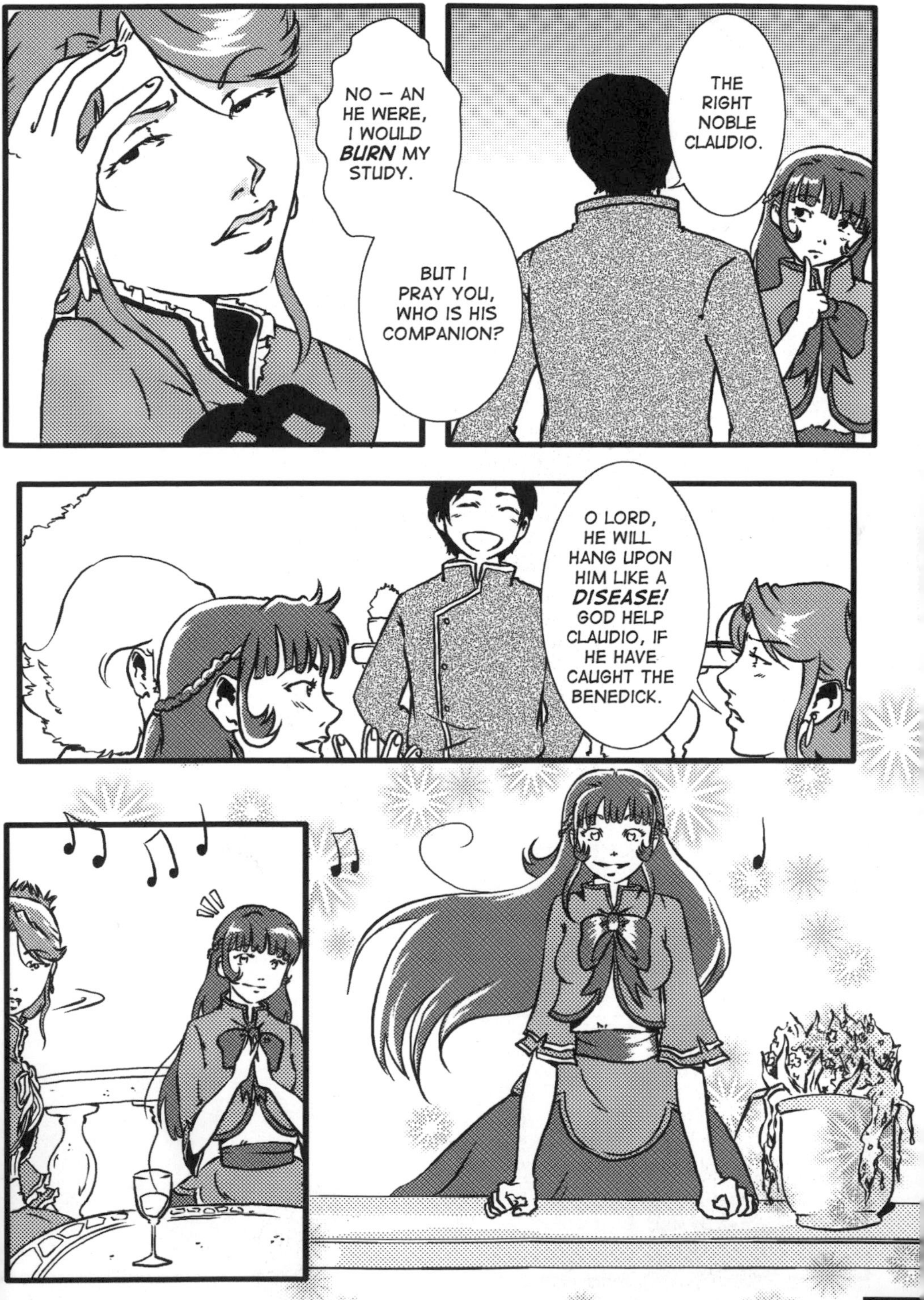
NO — AN HE WERE, I WOULD **BURN** MY STUDY.
BUT I PRAY YOU, WHO IS HIS COMPANION?
THE RIGHT NOBLE CLAUDIO.
O LORD, HE WILL HANG UPON HIM LIKE A ***DISEASE!*** GOD HELP CLAUDIO, IF HE HAVE CAUGHT THE BENEDICK.

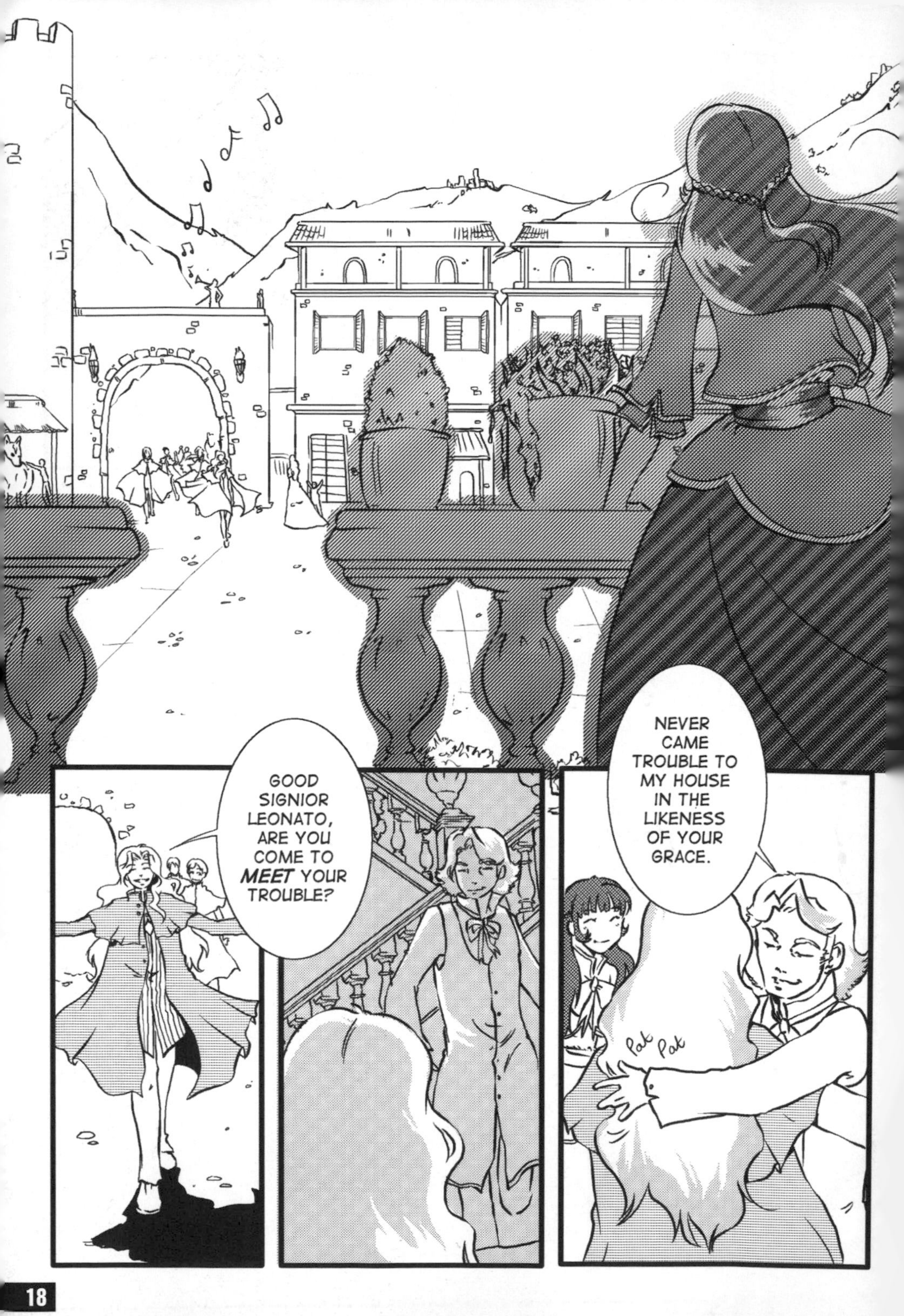
GOOD SIGNIOR LEONATO, ARE YOU COME TO MEET YOUR TROUBLE?
NEVER CAME TROUBLE TO MY HOUSE IN THE LIKENESS OF YOUR GRACE.
Pat Pat

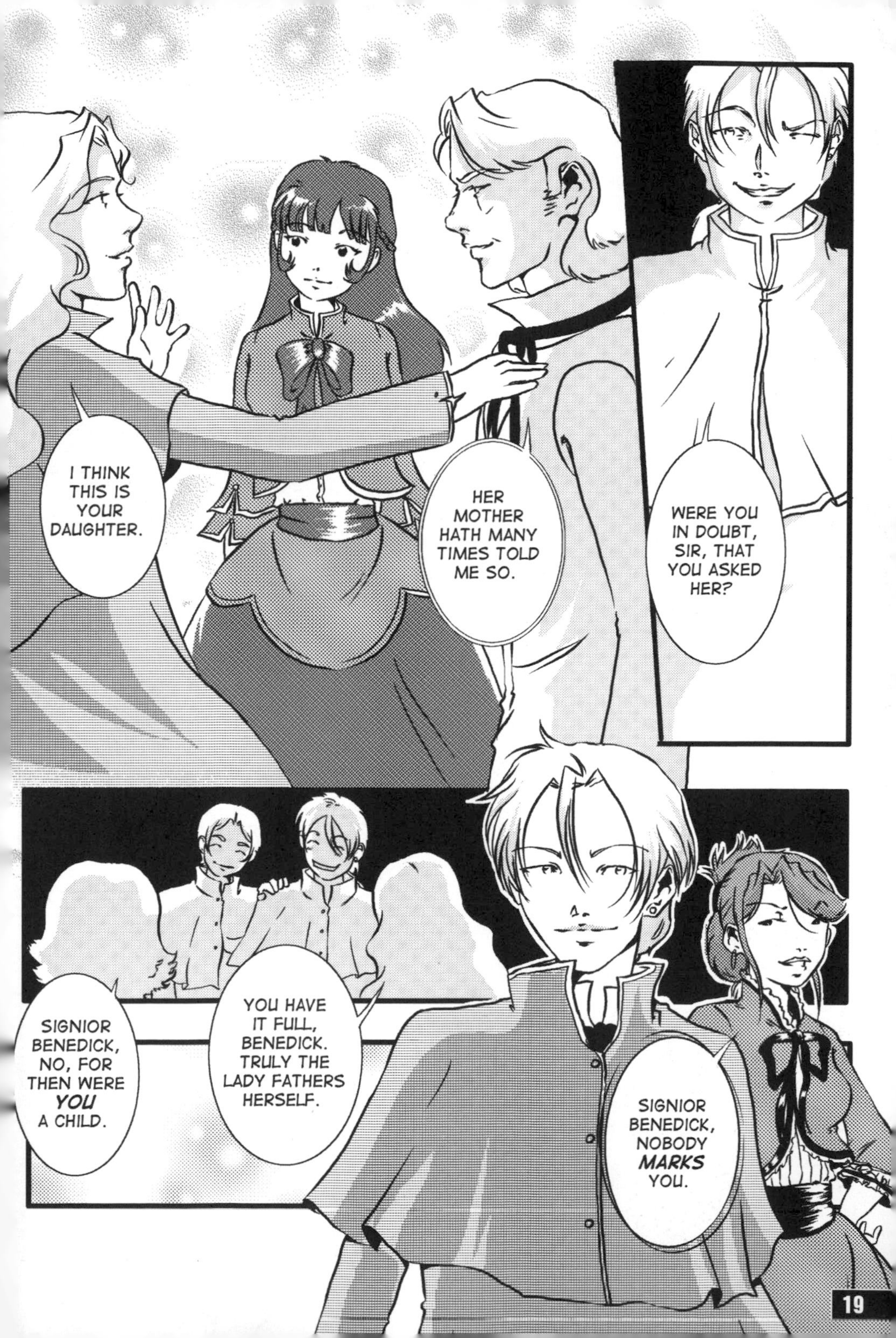
I THINK THIS IS YOUR DAUGHTER.
HER MOTHER HATH MANY TIMES TOLD ME SO.
WERE YOU IN DOUBT, SIR, THAT YOU ASKED HER?
SIGNIOR BENEDICK, NO, FOR THEN WERE ***YOU*** A CHILD.
YOU HAVE IT FULL, BENEDICK. TRULY THE LADY FATHERS HERSELF.
SIGNIOR BENEDICK, NOBODY ***MARKS*** YOU.

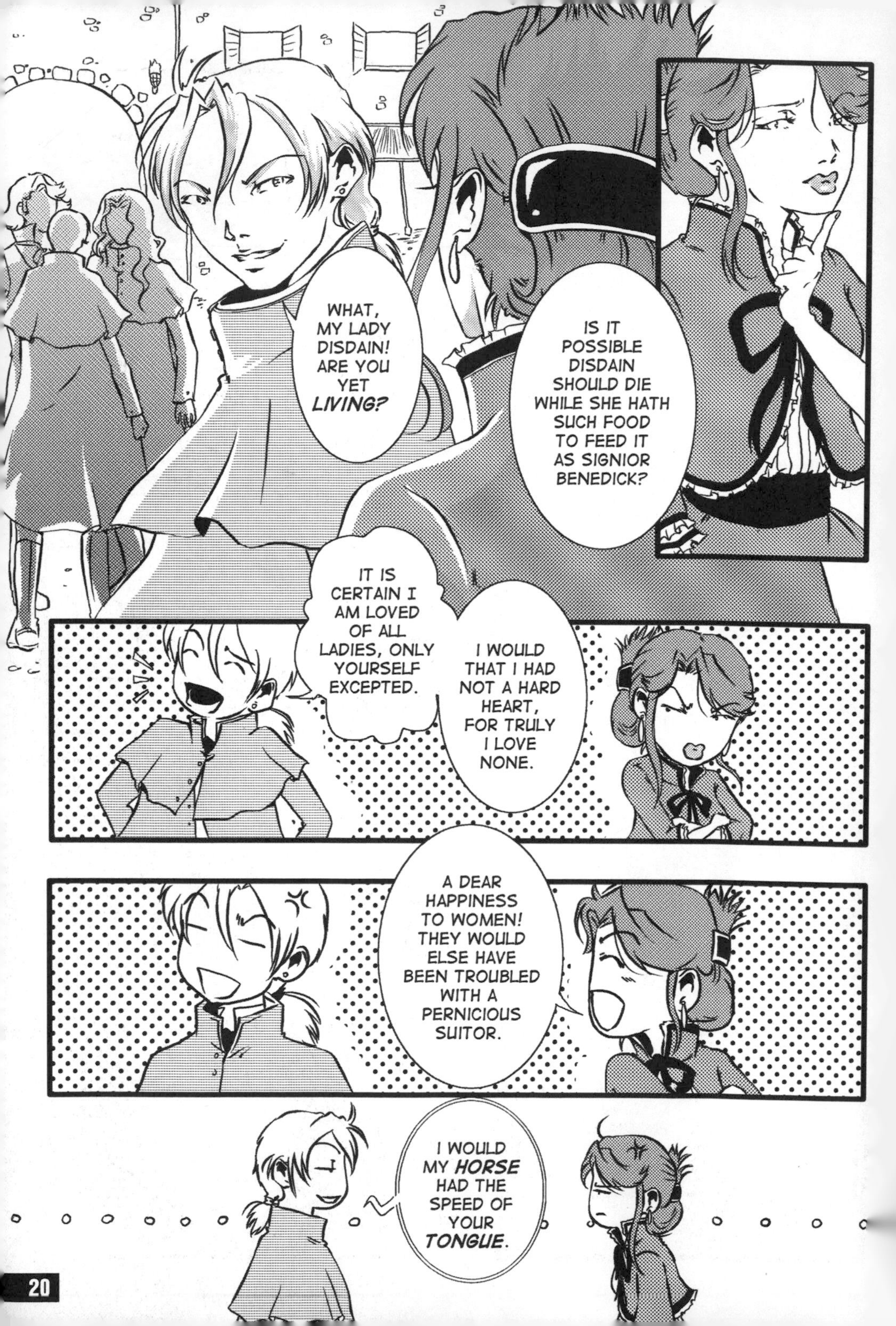
WHAT, MY LADY DISDAIN! ARE YOU YET *LIVING?*
IS IT POSSIBLE DISDAIN SHOULD DIE WHILE SHE HATH SUCH FOOD TO FEED IT AS SIGNIOR BENEDICK?
IT IS CERTAIN I AM LOVED OF ALL LADIES, ONLY YOURSELF EXCEPTED.
I WOULD THAT I HAD NOT A HARD HEART, FOR TRULY I LOVE NONE.
A DEAR HAPPINESS TO WOMEN! THEY WOULD ELSE HAVE BEEN TROUBLED WITH A PERNICIOUS SUITOR.
I WOULD MY ***HORSE*** HAD THE SPEED OF YOUR ***TONGUE***.

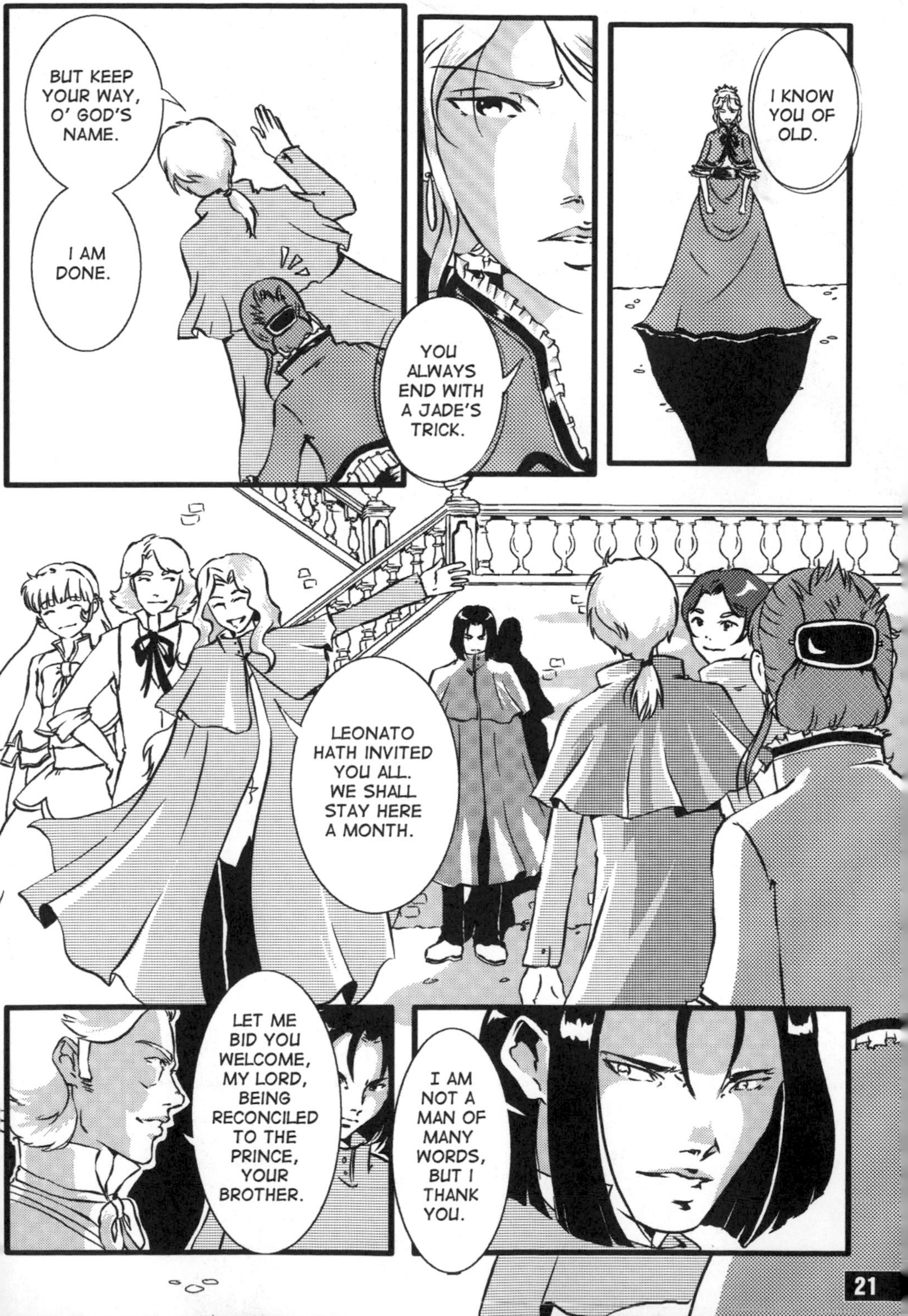
BUT KEEP YOUR WAY, O' GOD'S NAME.
I AM DONE.
YOU ALWAYS END WITH A JADE'S TRICK.
I KNOW YOU OF OLD.
LEONATO HATH INVITED YOU ALL. WE SHALL STAY HERE A MONTH.
LET ME BID YOU WELCOME, MY LORD, BEING RECONCILED TO THE PRINCE, YOUR BROTHER.
I AM NOT A MAN OF MANY WORDS, BUT I THANK YOU.

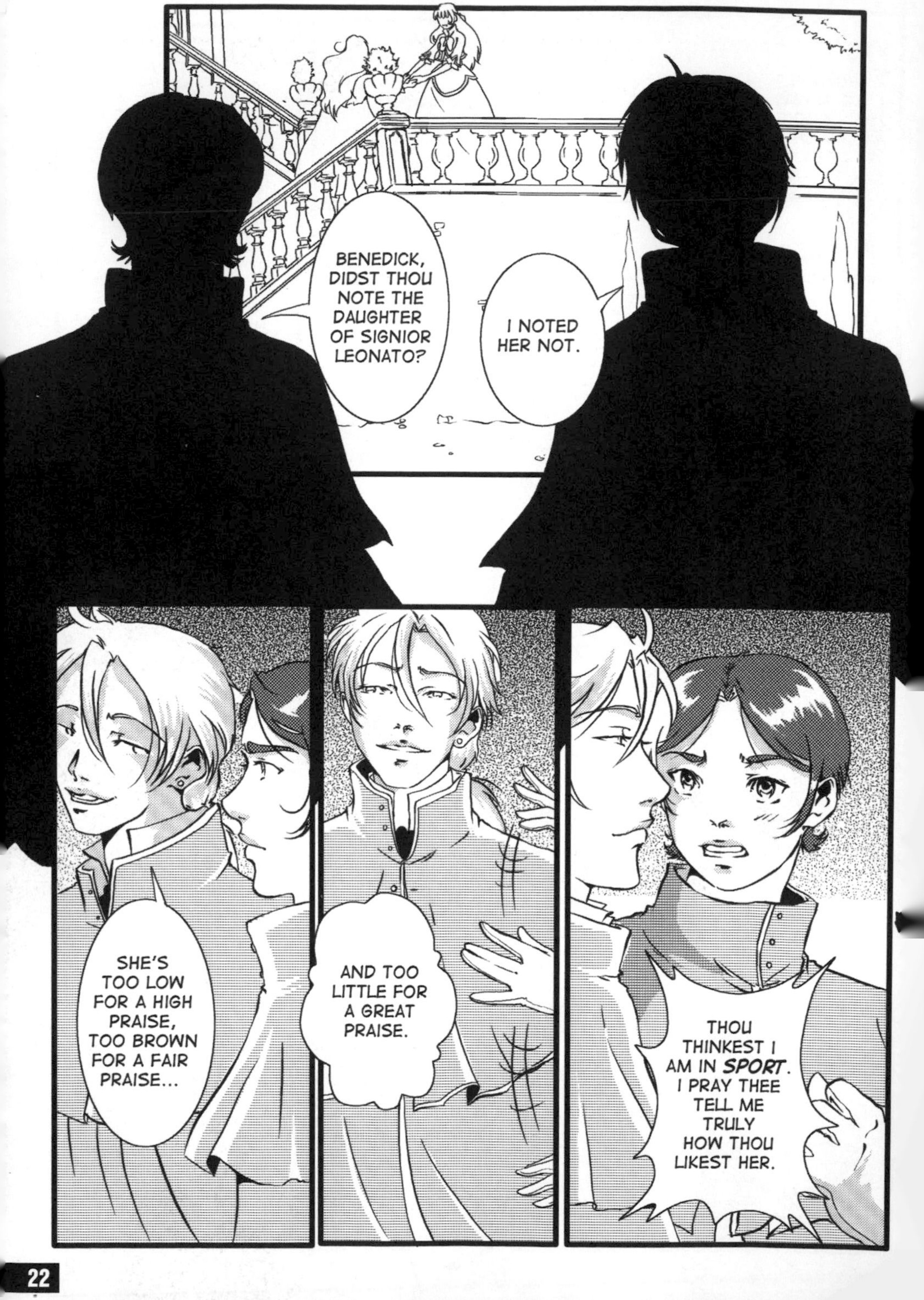
BENEDICK, DIDST THOU NOTE THE DAUGHTER OF SIGNIOR LEONATO?
I NOTED HER NOT.
SHE'S TOO LOW FOR A HIGH PRAISE, TOO BROWN FOR A FAIR PRAISE...
AND TOO LITTLE FOR A GREAT PRAISE.
THOU THINKEST I AM IN *SPORT*. I PRAY THEE TELL ME TRULY HOW THOU LIKEST HER.

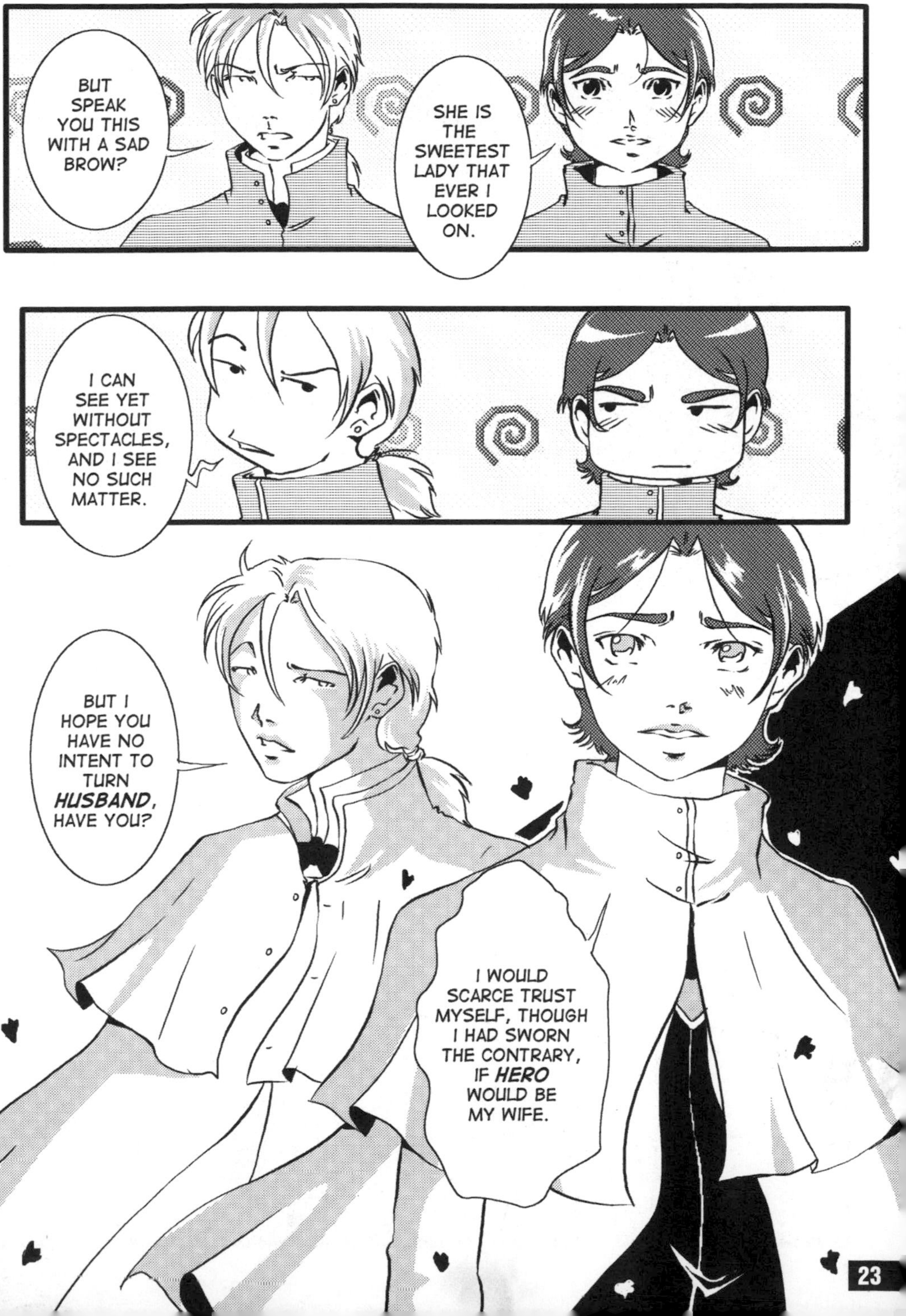
BUT SPEAK YOU THIS WITH A SAD BROW?
SHE IS THE SWEETEST LADY THAT EVER I LOOKED ON.
I CAN SEE YET WITHOUT SPECTACLES, AND I SEE NO SUCH MATTER.
BUT I HOPE YOU HAVE NO INTENT TO TURN ***HUSBAND***, HAVE YOU?
I WOULD SCARCE TRUST MYSELF, THOUGH I HAD SWORN THE CONTRARY, IF ***HERO*** WOULD BE MY WIFE.

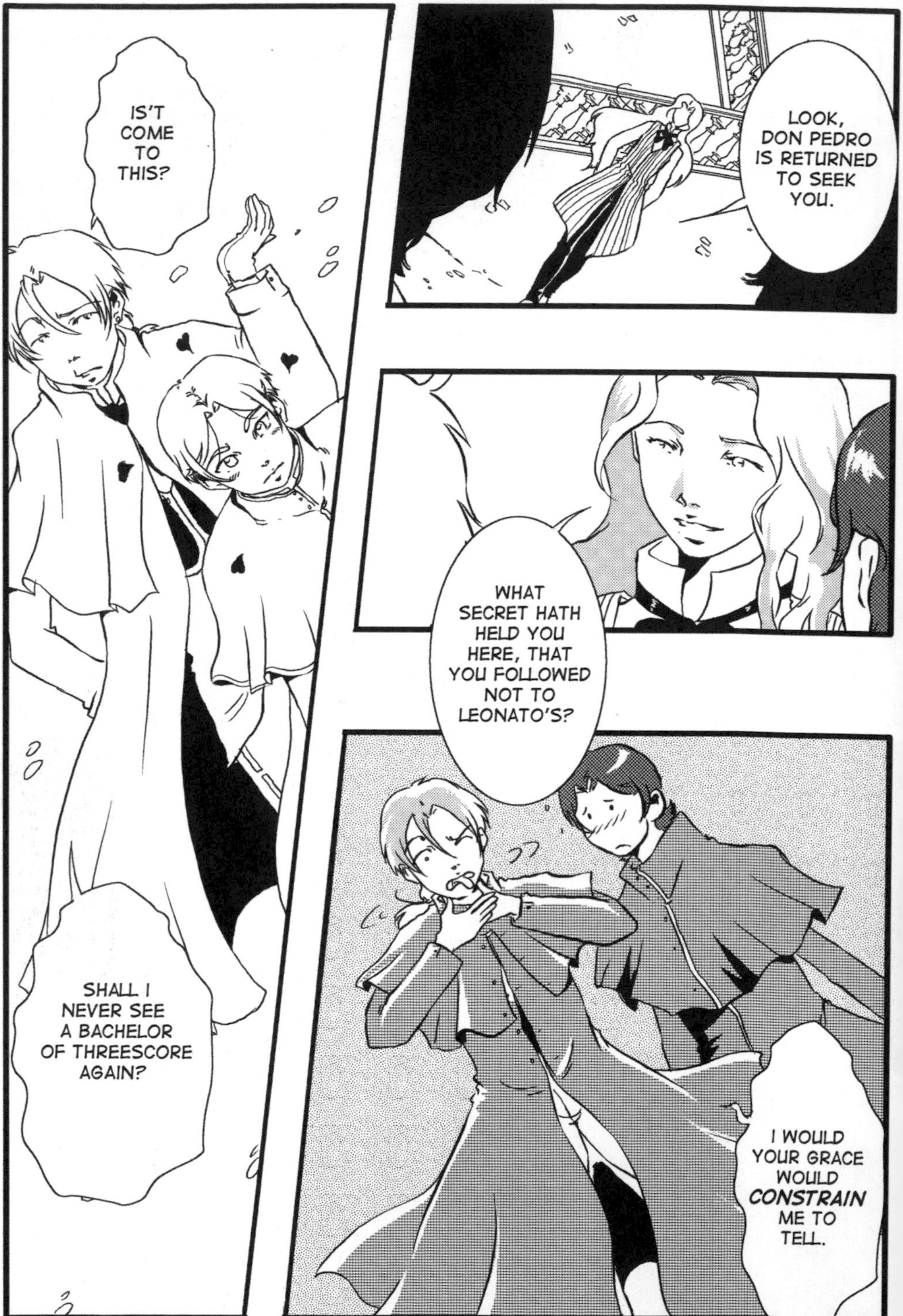
IS'T COME TO THIS?
SHALL I NEVER SEE A BACHELOR OF THREESCORE AGAIN?
LOOK, DON PEDRO IS RETURNED TO SEEK YOU.
WHAT SECRET HATH HELD YOU HERE, THAT YOU FOLLOWED NOT TO LEONATO'S?
I WOULD YOUR GRACE WOULD *CONSTRAIN* ME TO TELL.

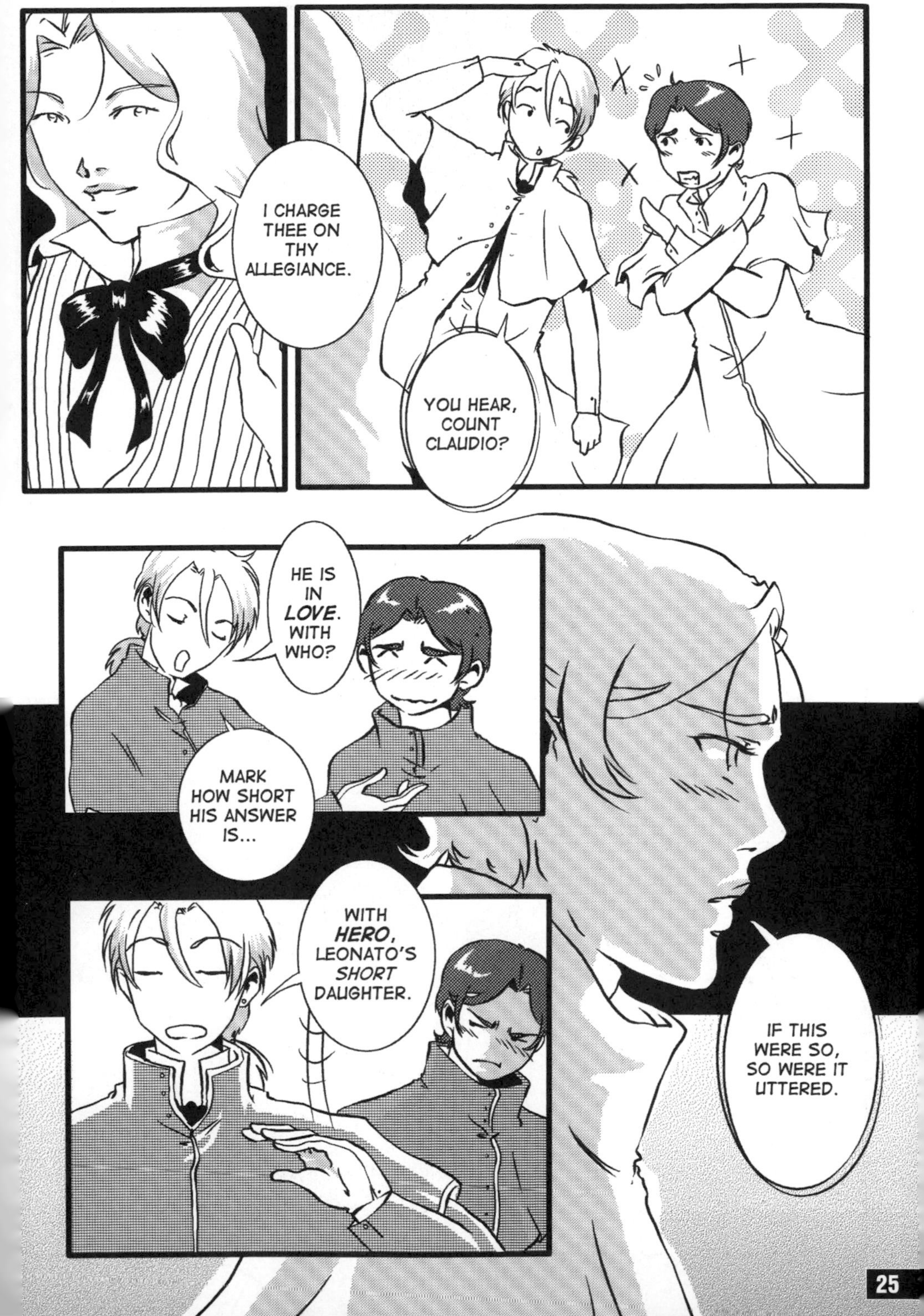

I CHARGE THEE ON THY ALLEGIANCE.
YOU HEAR, COUNT CLAUDIO?
HE IS IN *LOVE*. WITH WHO?
MARK HOW SHORT HIS ANSWER IS...
WITH *HERO*, LEONATO'S *SHORT* DAUGHTER.
IF THIS WERE SO, SO WERE IT UTTERED.

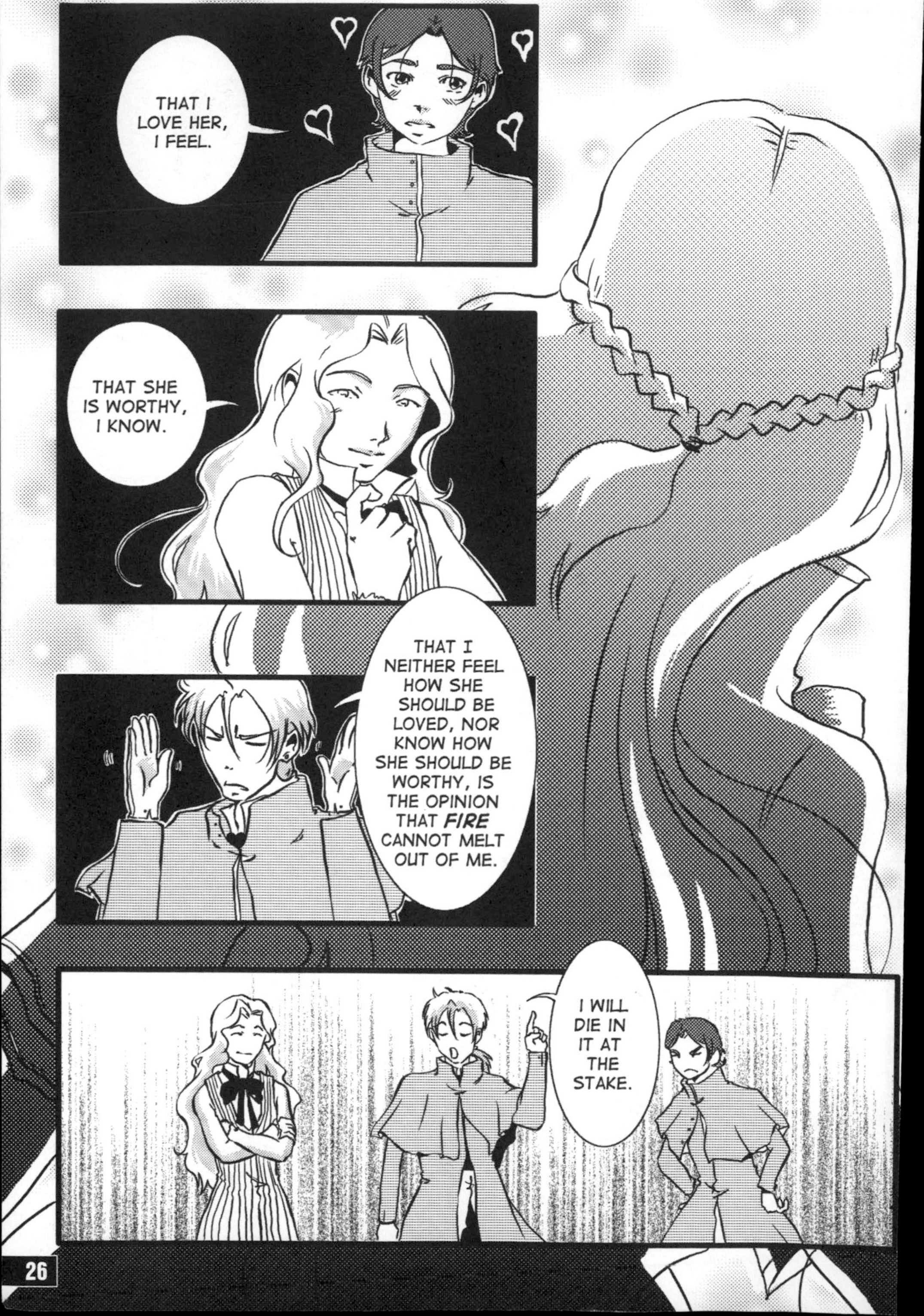
THAT I LOVE HER, I FEEL.
THAT SHE IS WORTHY, I KNOW.
THAT I NEITHER FEEL HOW SHE SHOULD BE LOVED, NOR KNOW HOW SHE SHOULD BE WORTHY, IS THE OPINION THAT FIRE CANNOT MELT OUT OF ME.
I WILL DIE IN IT AT THE STAKE.

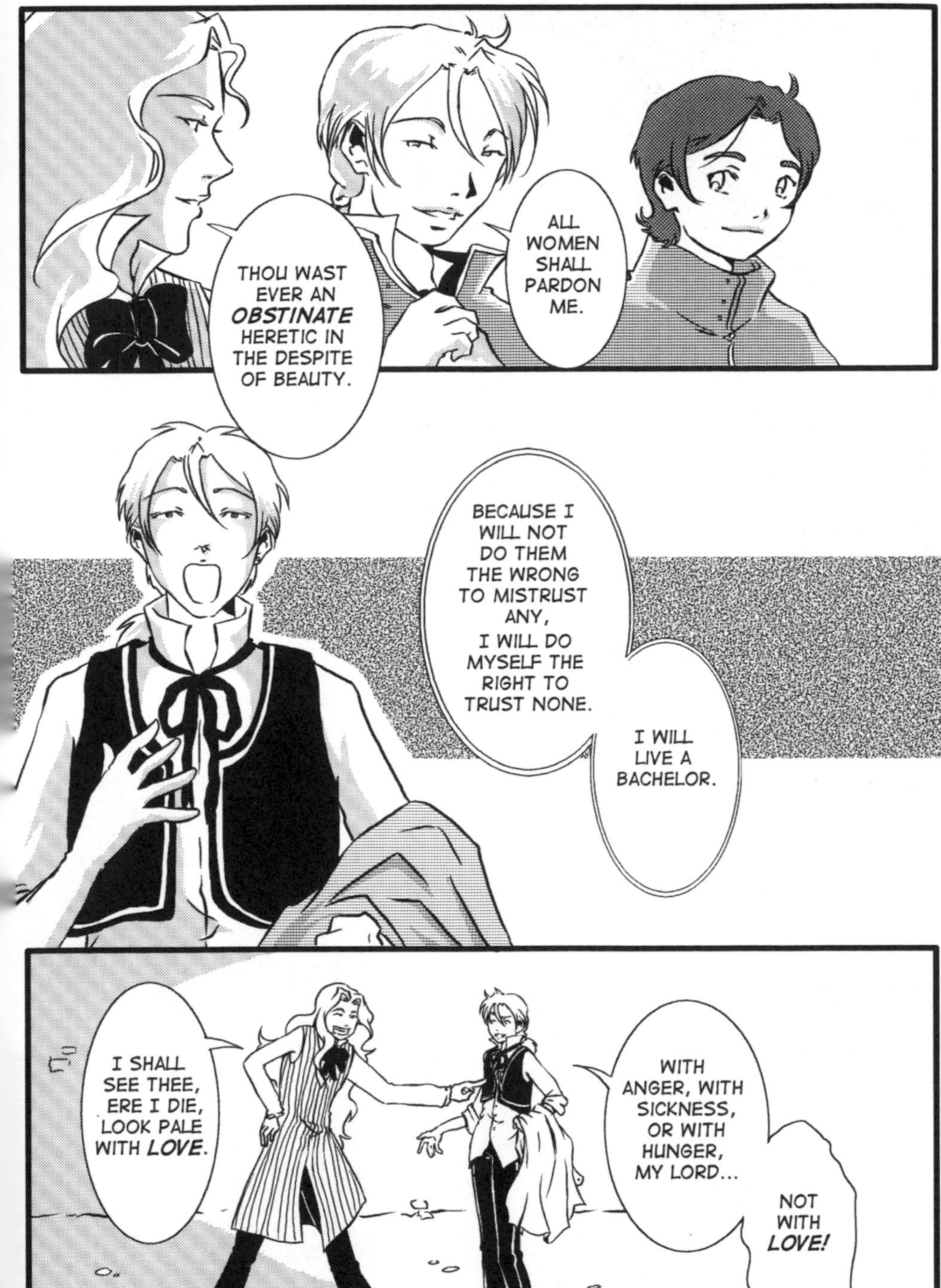
THOU WAST EVER AN OBSTINATE HERETIC IN THE DESPITE OF BEAUTY.
ALL WOMEN SHALL PARDON ME.
BECAUSE I WILL NOT DO THEM THE WRONG TO MISTRUST ANY, I WILL DO MYSELF THE RIGHT TO TRUST NONE.
I WILL LIVE A BACHELOR.
I SHALL SEE THEE, ERE I DIE, LOOK PALE WITH LOVE.
WITH ANGER, WITH SICKNESS, OR WITH HUNGER, MY LORD...
NOT WITH LOVE!

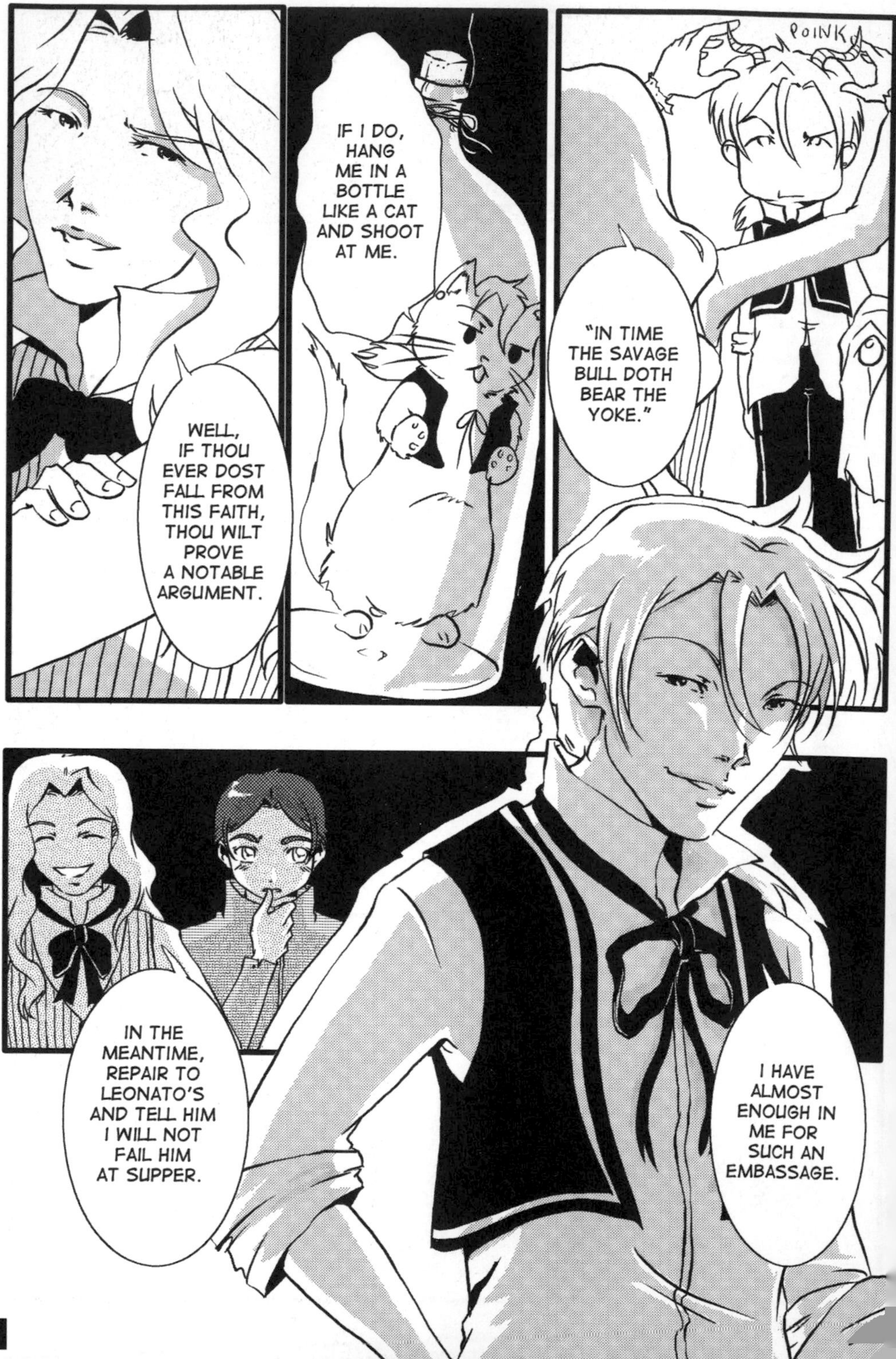
WELL, IF THOU EVER DOST FALL FROM THIS FAITH, THOU WILT PROVE A NOTABLE ARGUMENT.
IF I DO, HANG ME IN A BOTTLE LIKE A CAT AND SHOOT AT ME.
POINK
"IN TIME THE SAVAGE BULL DOTH BEAR THE YOKE."
IN THE MEANTIME, REPAIR TO LEONATO'S AND TELL HIM I WILL NOT FAIL HIM AT SUPPER.
I HAVE ALMOST ENOUGH IN ME FOR SUCH AN EMBASSAGE.

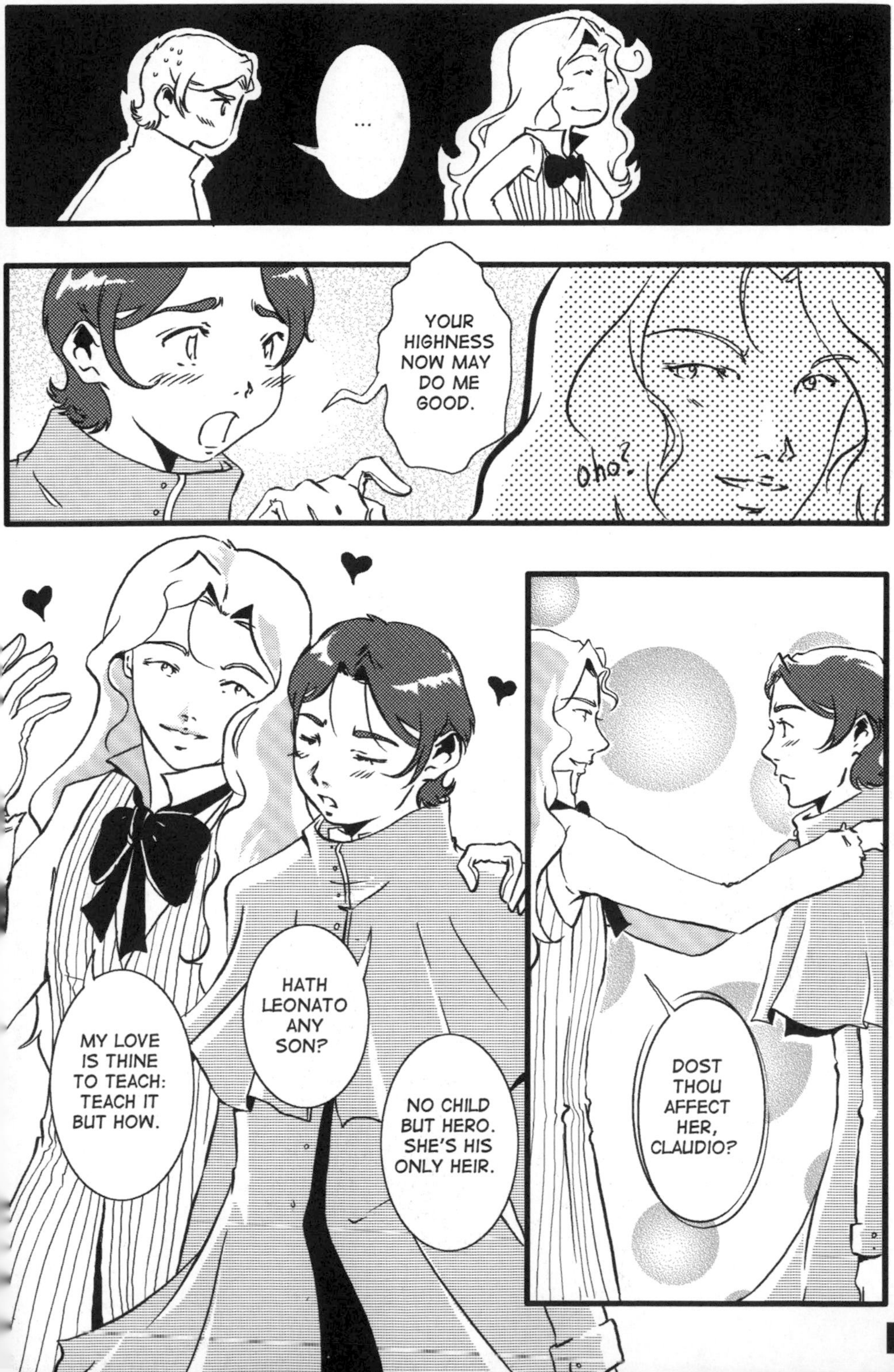
...
YOUR HIGHNESS NOW MAY DO ME GOOD.
Oho?
MY LOVE IS THINE TO TEACH: TEACH IT BUT HOW.
HATH LEONATO ANY SON?
NO CHILD BUT HERO. SHE'S HIS ONLY HEIR.
DOST THOU AFFECT HER, CLAUDIO?

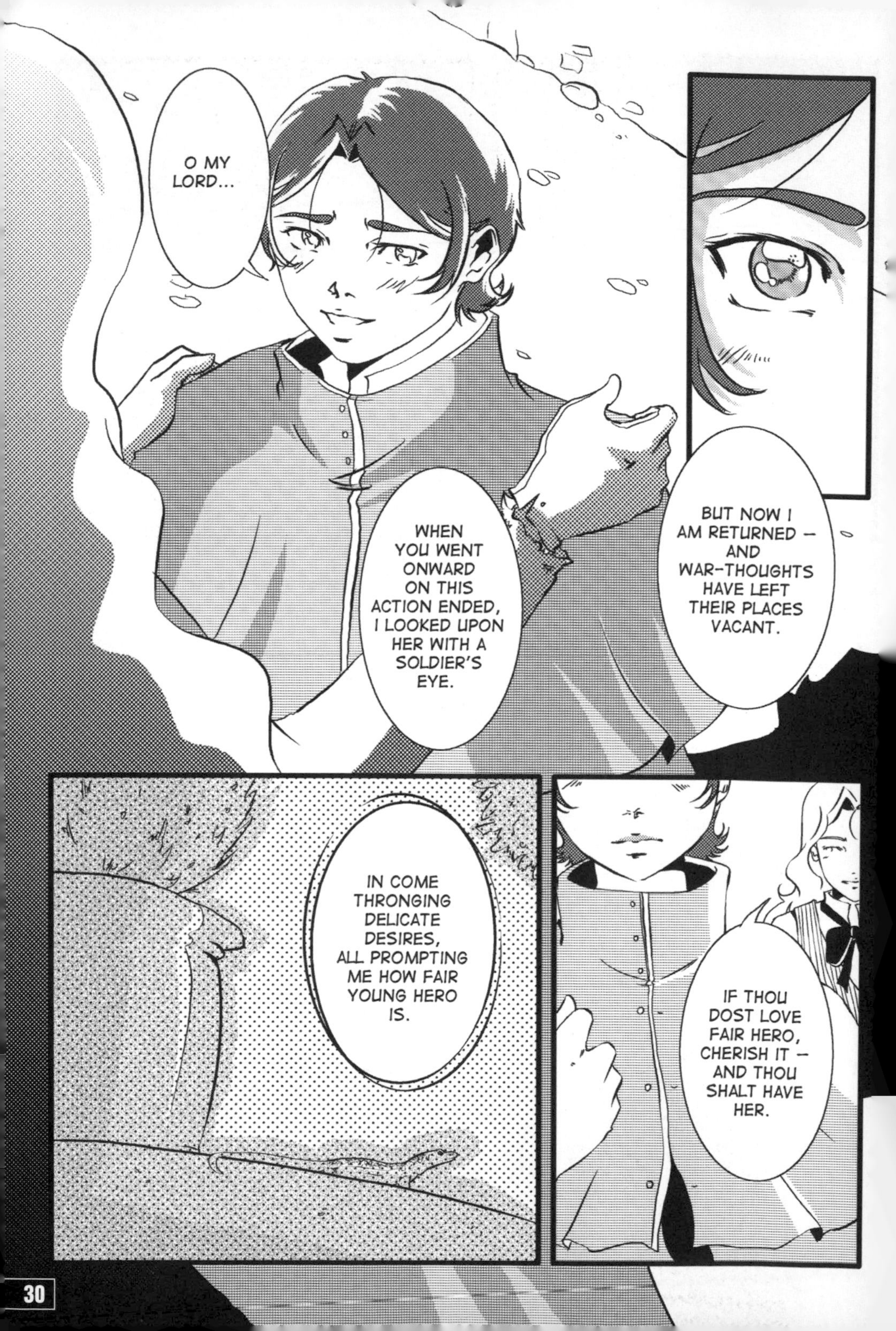
O MY LORD...
WHEN YOU WENT ONWARD ON THIS ACTION ENDED, I LOOKED UPON HER WITH A SOLDIER'S EYE.
BUT NOW I AM RETURNED — AND WAR-THOUGHTS HAVE LEFT THEIR PLACES VACANT.
IN COME THRONGING DELICATE DESIRES, ALL PROMPTING ME HOW FAIR YOUNG HERO IS.
IF THOU DOST LOVE FAIR HERO, CHERISH IT — AND THOU SHALT HAVE HER.

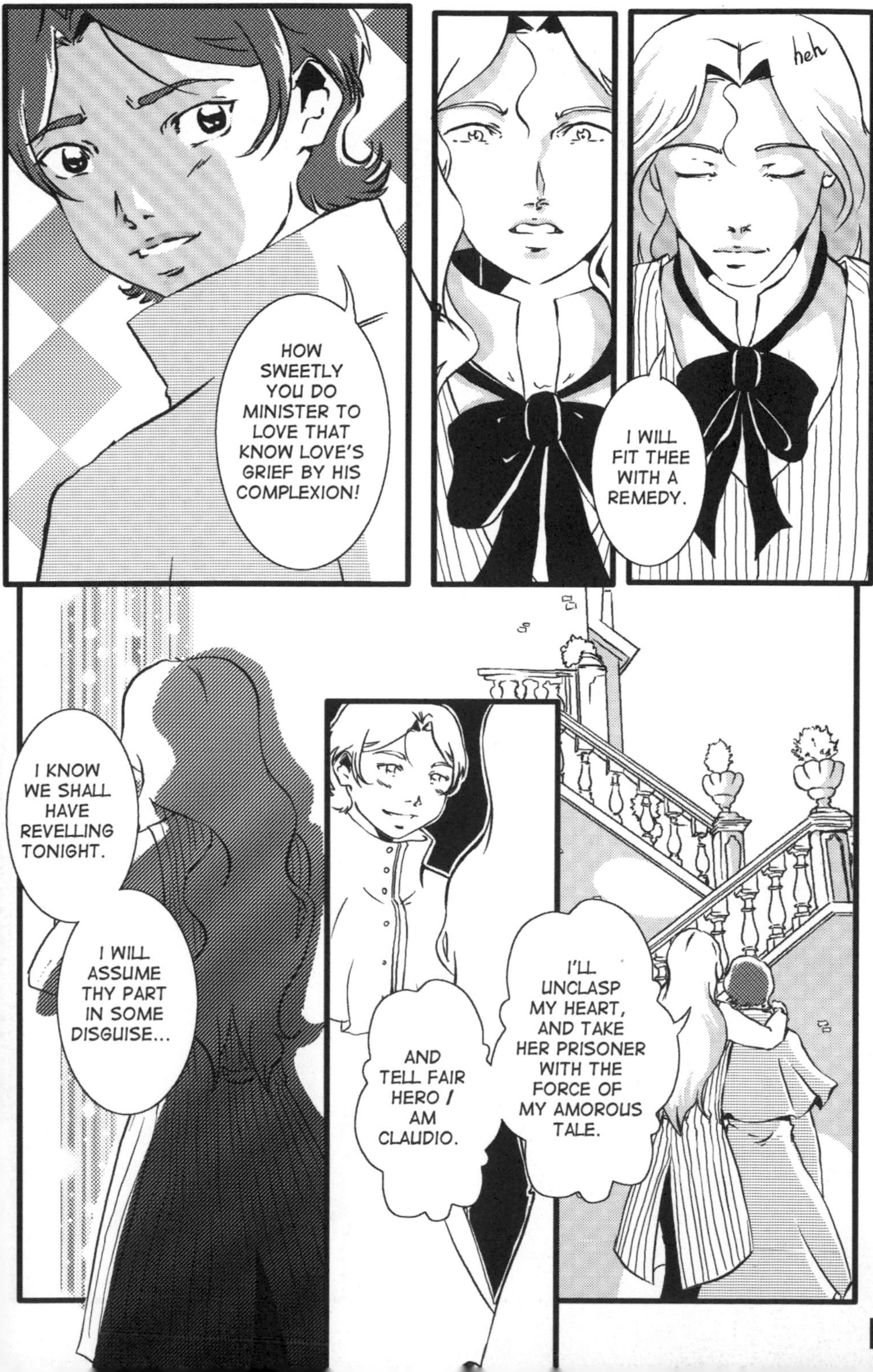
heh
HOW SWEETLY YOU DO MINISTER TO LOVE THAT KNOW LOVE'S GRIEF BY HIS COMPLEXION!
I WILL FIT THEE WITH A REMEDY.
I KNOW WE SHALL HAVE REVELLING TONIGHT.
I WILL ASSUME THY PART IN SOME DISGUISE...
AND TELL FAIR HERO I AM CLAUDIO.
I'LL UNCLASP MY HEART, AND TAKE HER PRISONER WITH THE FORCE OF MY AMOROUS TALE.

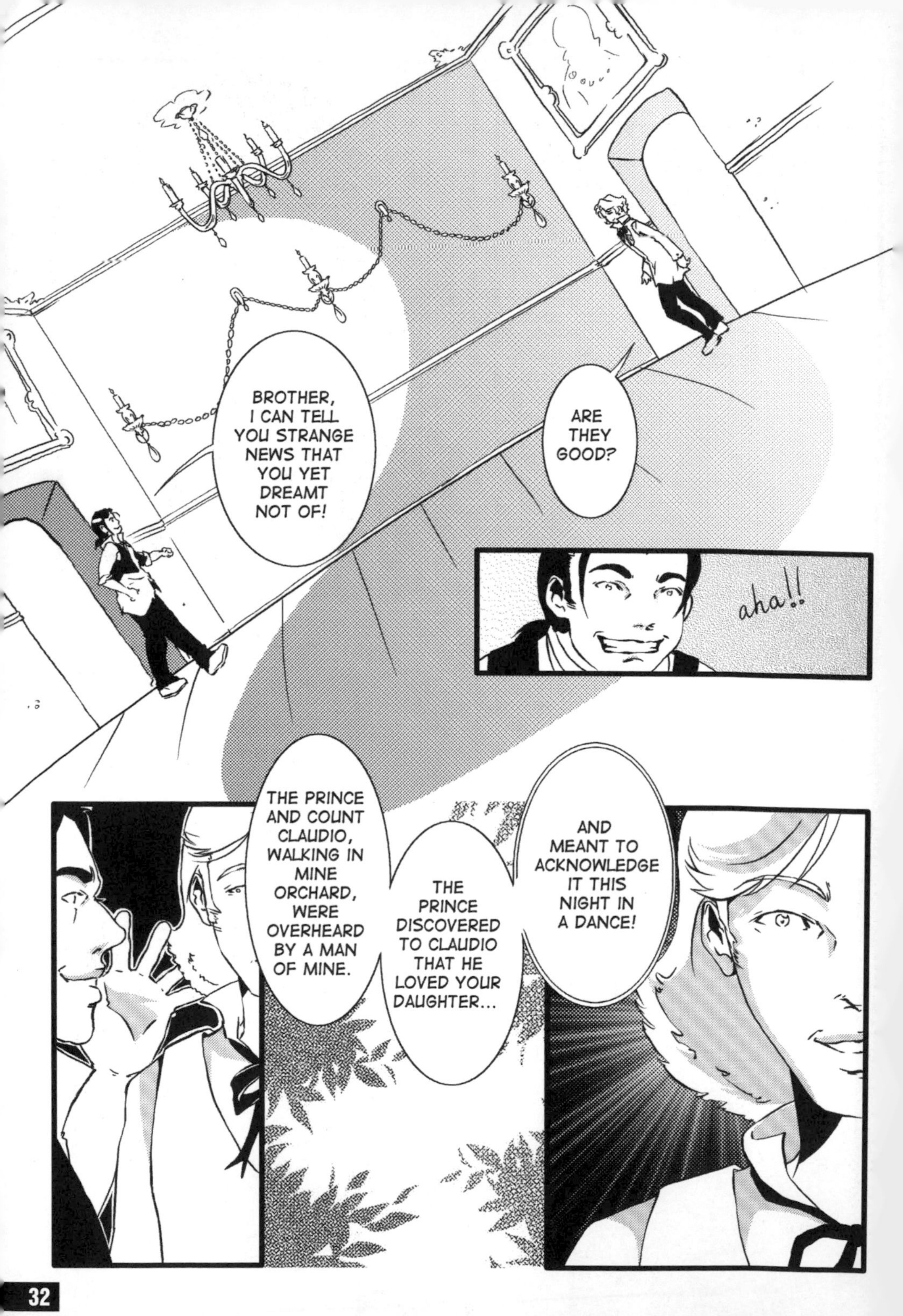
BROTHER, I CAN TELL YOU STRANGE NEWS THAT YOU YET DREAMT NOT OF!
ARE THEY GOOD?
aha!!
THE PRINCE AND COUNT CLAUDIO, WALKING IN MINE ORCHARD, WERE OVERHEARD BY A MAN OF MINE.
THE PRINCE DISCOVERED TO CLAUDIO THAT HE LOVED YOUR DAUGHTER...
AND MEANT TO ACKNOWLEDGE IT THIS NIGHT IN A DANCE!

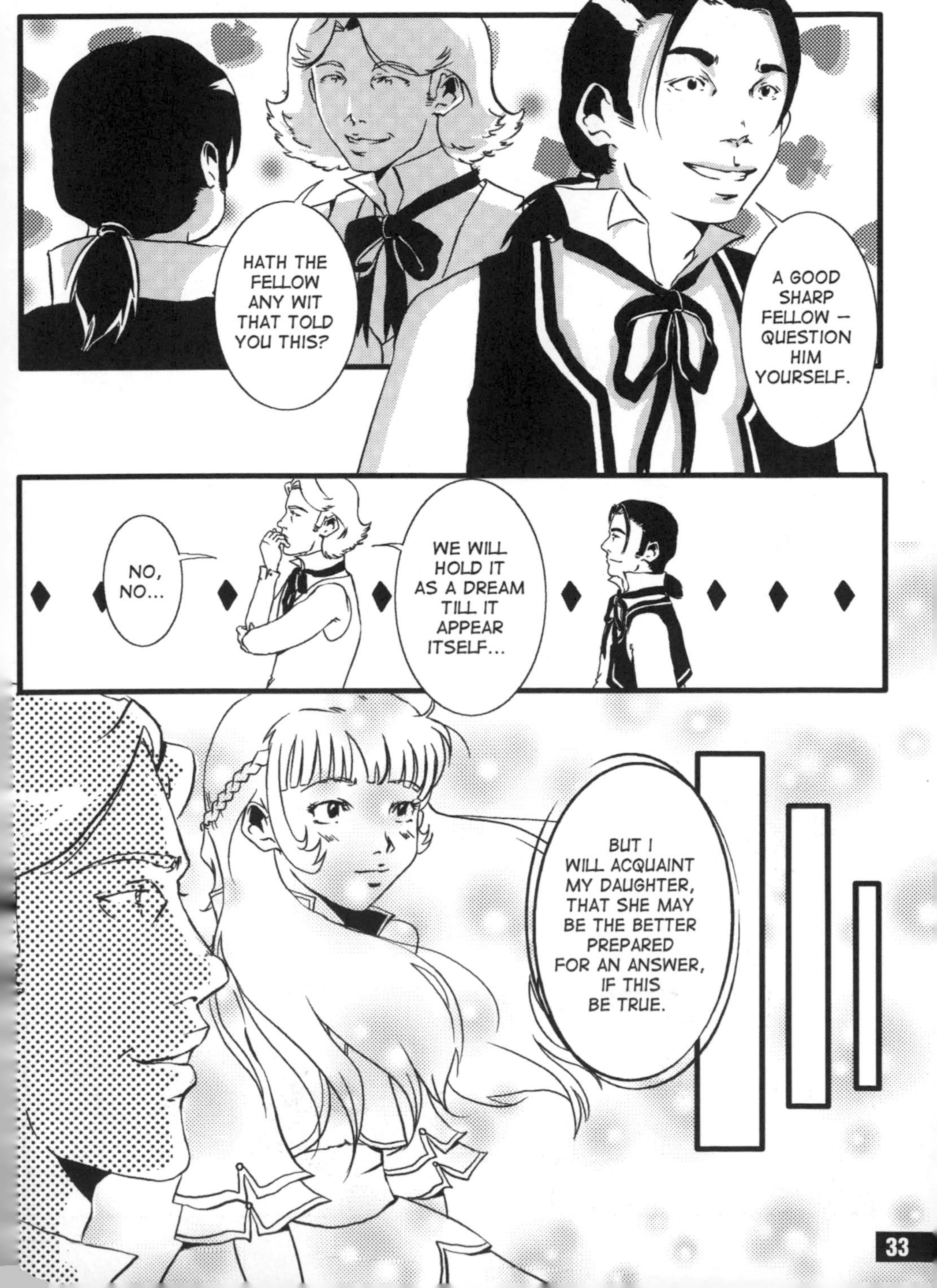
HATH THE FELLOW ANY WIT THAT TOLD YOU THIS?
A GOOD SHARP FELLOW — QUESTION HIM YOURSELF.
NO, NO...
WE WILL HOLD IT AS A DREAM TILL IT APPEAR ITSELF...
BUT I WILL ACQUAINT MY DAUGHTER, THAT SHE MAY BE THE BETTER PREPARED FOR AN ANSWER, IF THIS BE TRUE.

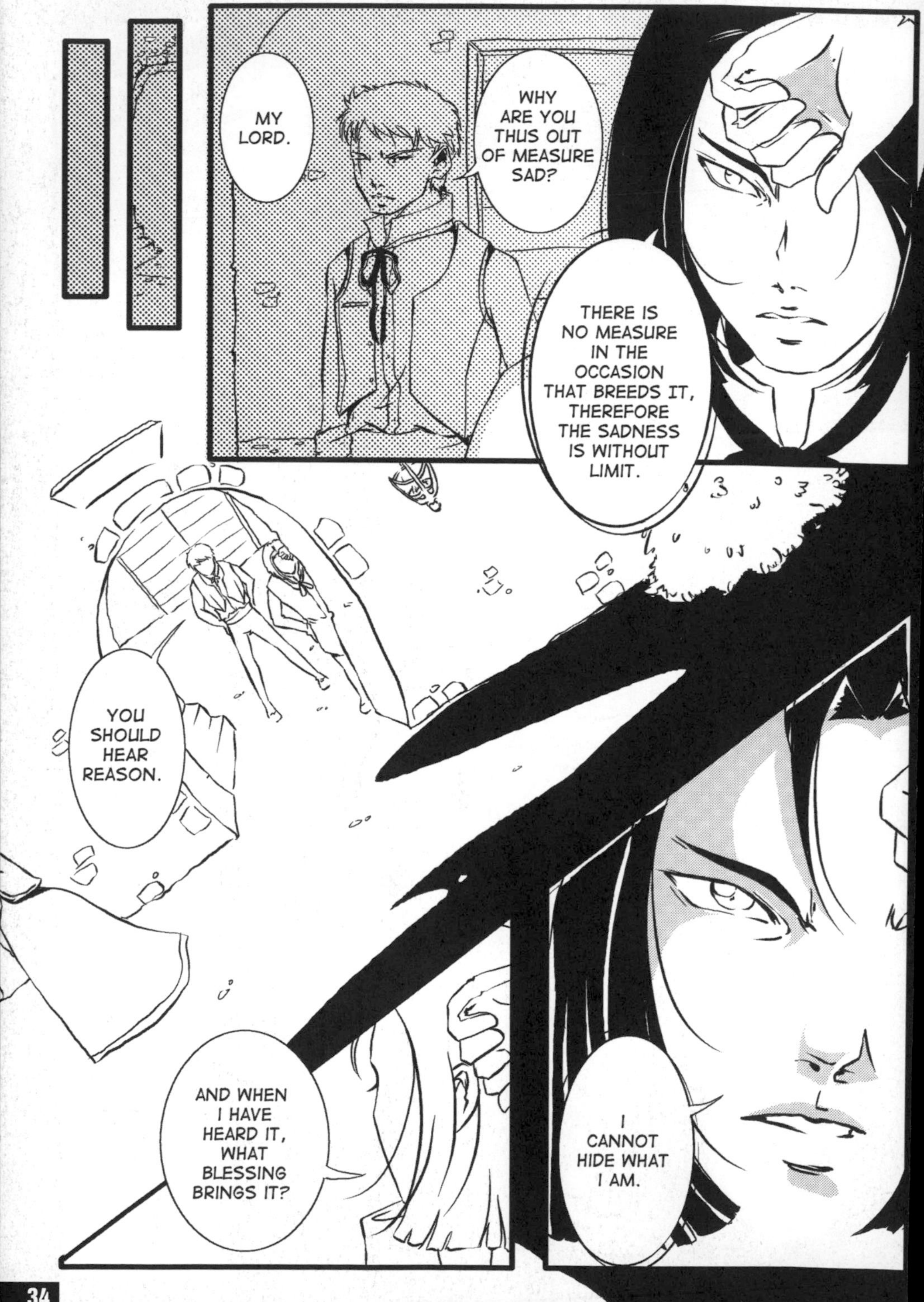
MY LORD.
WHY ARE YOU THUS OUT OF MEASURE SAD?
THERE IS NO MEASURE IN THE OCCASION THAT BREEDS IT, THEREFORE THE SADNESS IS WITHOUT LIMIT.
YOU SHOULD HEAR REASON.
AND WHEN I HAVE HEARD IT, WHAT BLESSING BRINGS IT?
I CANNOT HIDE WHAT I AM.

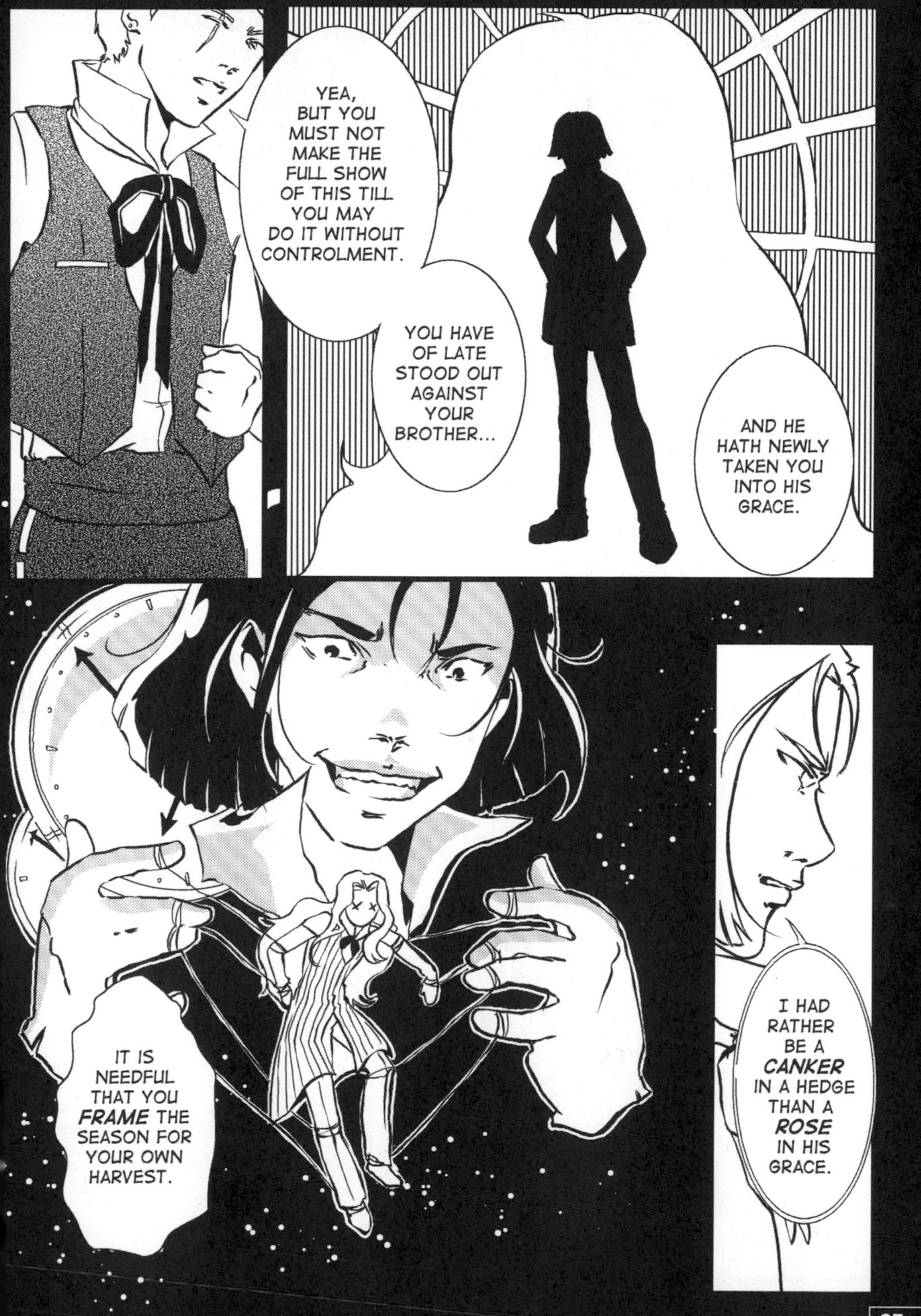
YEA, BUT YOU MUST NOT MAKE THE FULL SHOW OF THIS TILL YOU MAY DO IT WITHOUT CONTROLMENT.
YOU HAVE OF LATE STOOD OUT AGAINST YOUR BROTHER...
AND HE HATH NEWLY TAKEN YOU INTO HIS GRACE.
IT IS NEEDFUL THAT YOU *FRAME* THE SEASON FOR YOUR OWN HARVEST.
I HAD RATHER BE A *CANKER* IN A HEDGE THAN A *ROSE* IN HIS GRACE.

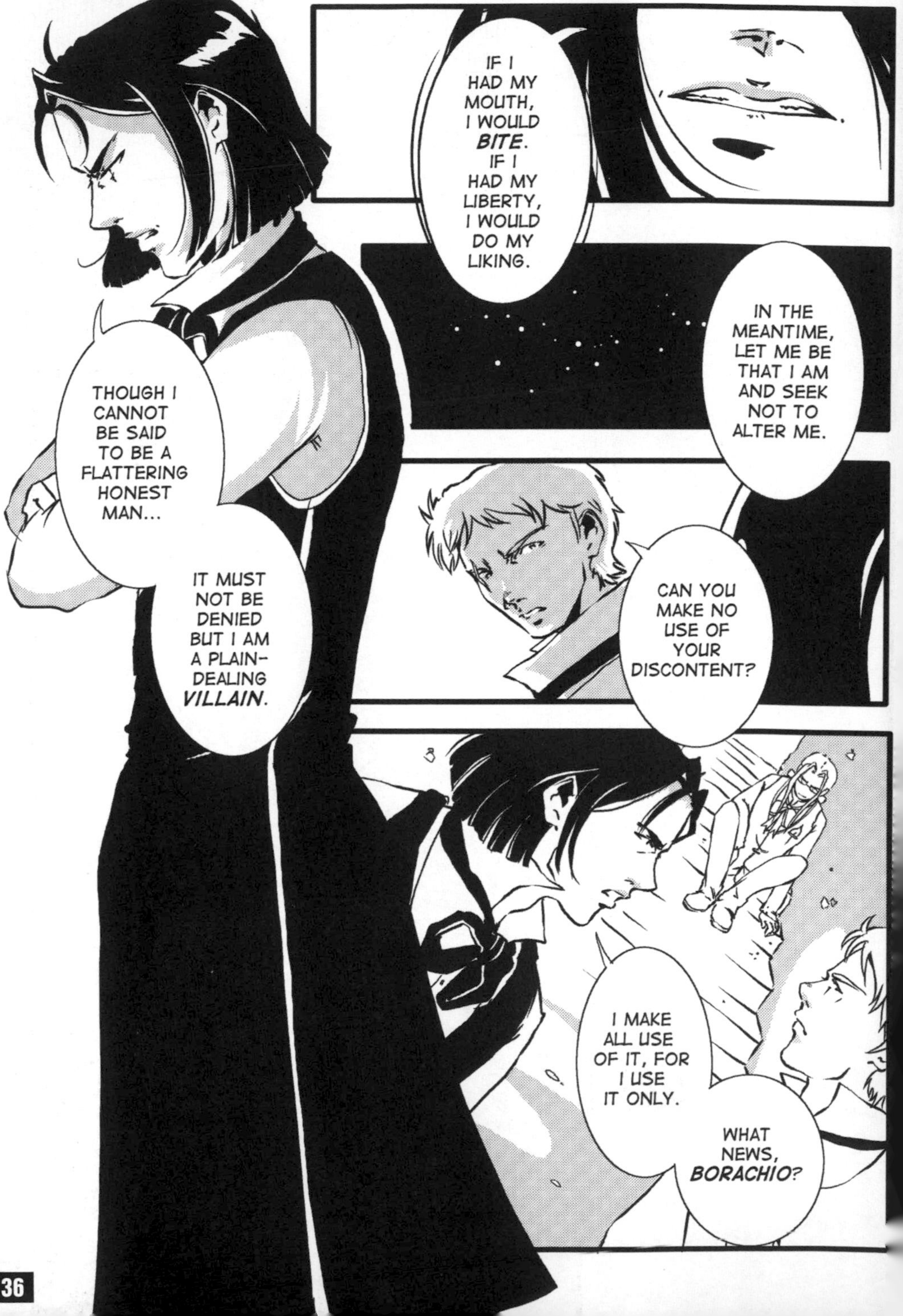

THOUGH I CANNOT BE SAID TO BE A FLATTERING HONEST MAN...
IT MUST NOT BE DENIED BUT I AM A PLAIN-DEALING ***VILLAIN***.
IF I HAD MY MOUTH, I WOULD ***BITE***. IF I HAD MY LIBERTY, I WOULD DO MY LIKING.
IN THE MEANTIME, LET ME BE THAT I AM AND SEEK NOT TO ALTER ME.
CAN YOU MAKE NO USE OF YOUR DISCONTENT?
I MAKE ALL USE OF IT, FOR I USE IT ONLY.
WHAT NEWS, ***BORACHIO***?

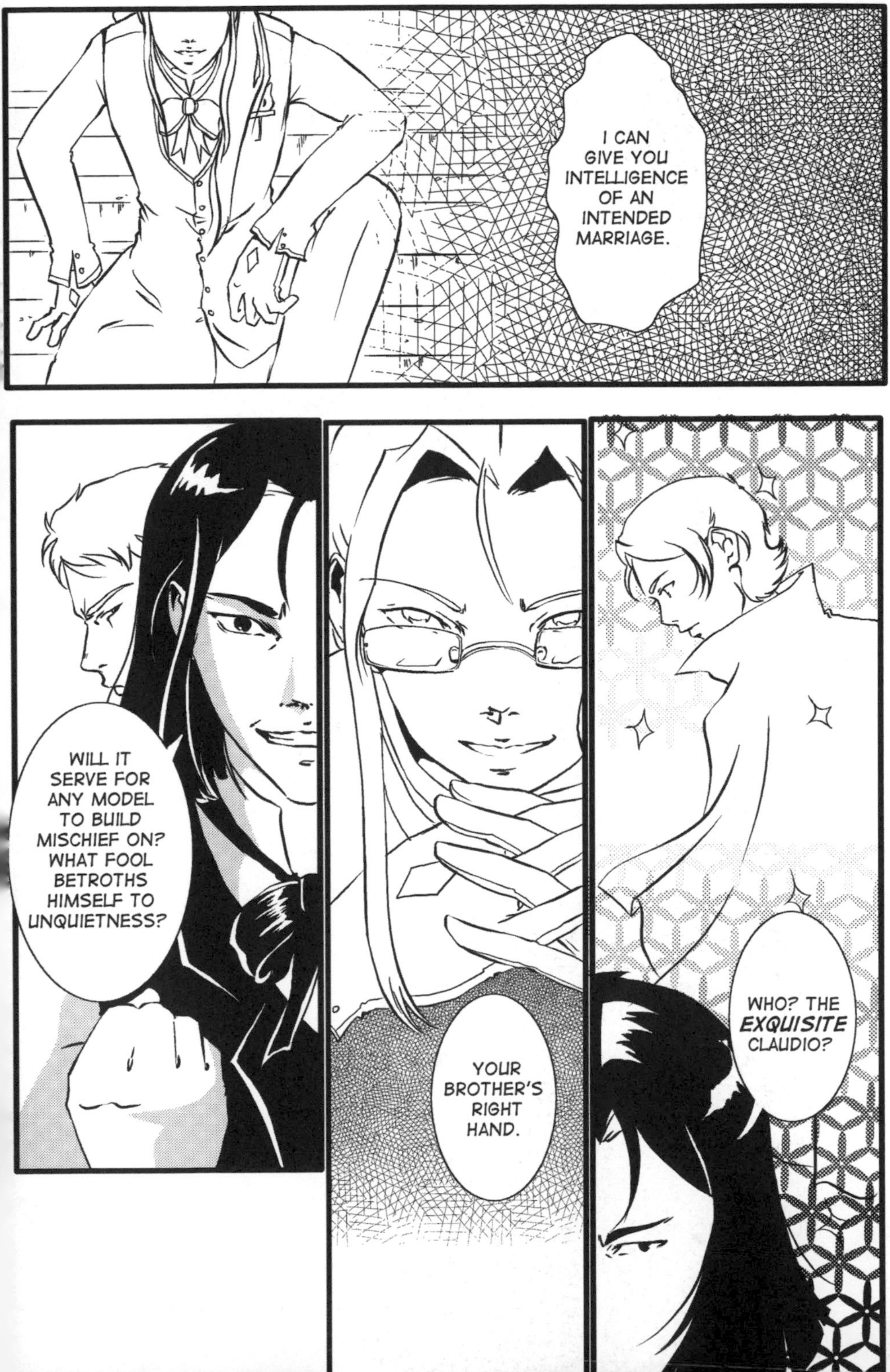
I CAN GIVE YOU INTELLIGENCE OF AN INTENDED MARRIAGE.
WILL IT SERVE FOR ANY MODEL TO BUILD MISCHIEF ON? WHAT FOOL BETROTHS HIMSELF TO UNQUIETNESS?
YOUR BROTHER'S RIGHT HAND.
WHO? THE *EXQUISITE* CLAUDIO?

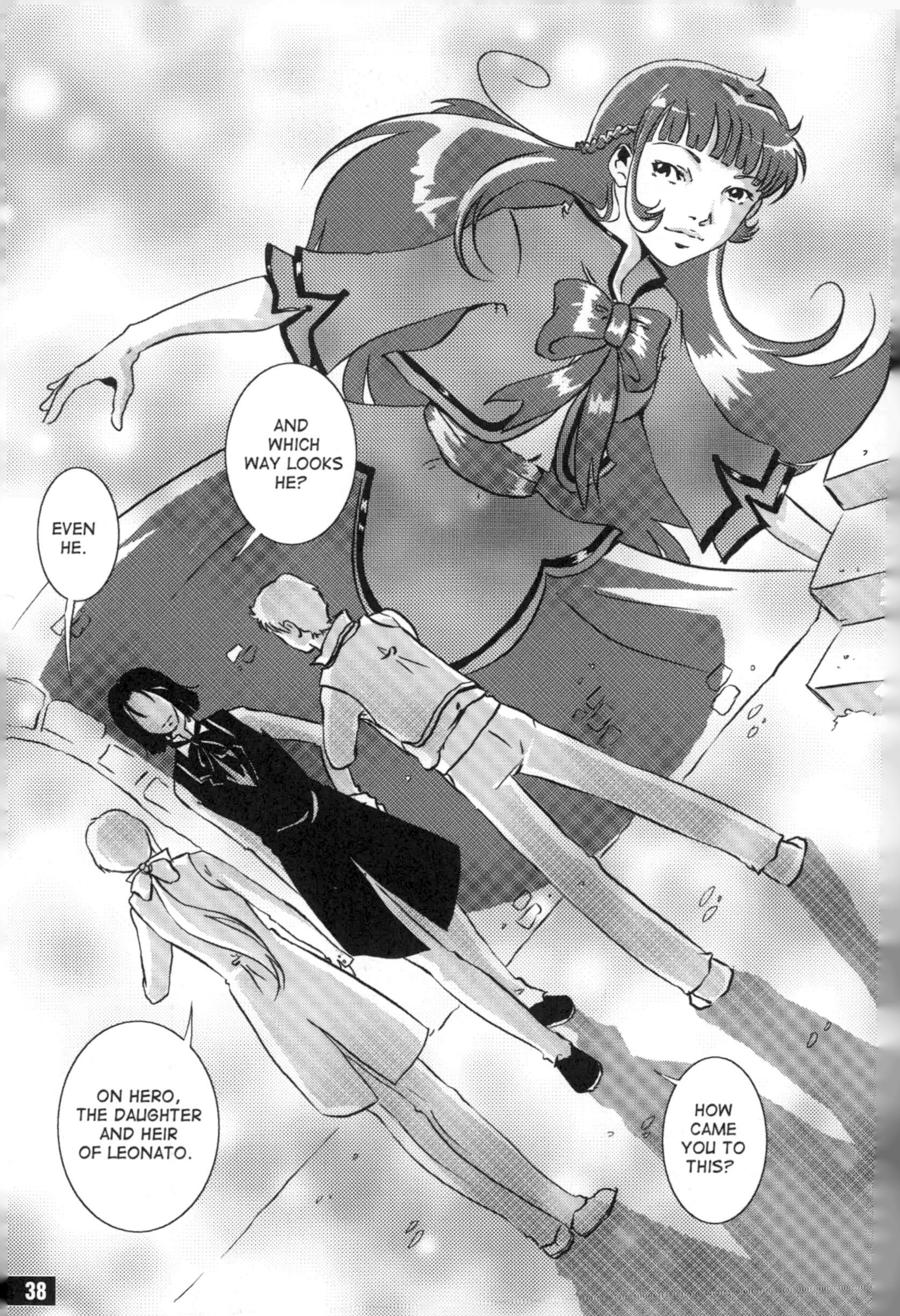
AND WHICH WAY LOOKS HE?
EVEN HE.
ON HERO, THE DAUGHTER AND HEIR OF LEONATO.
HOW CAME YOU TO THIS?

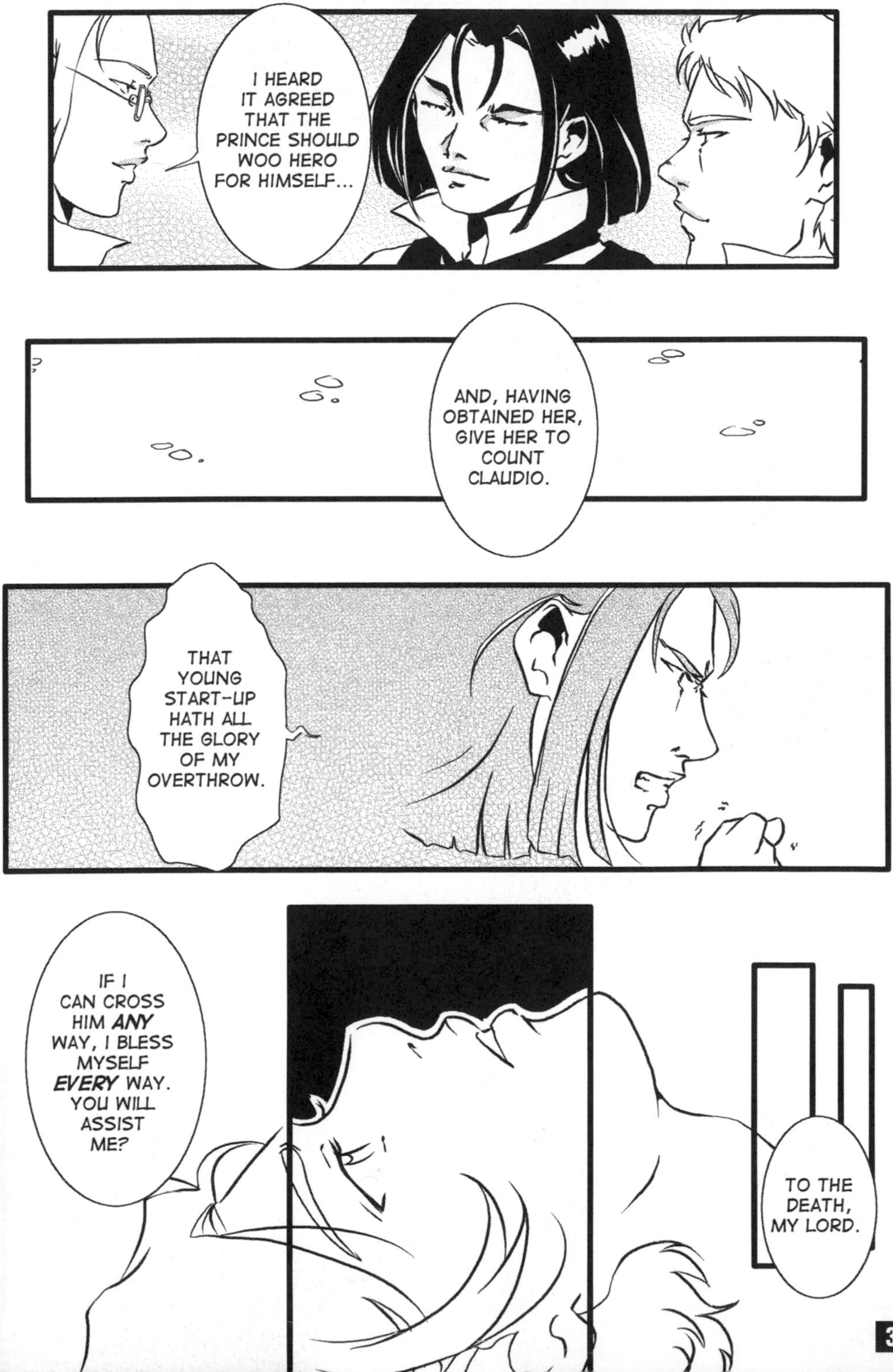
I HEARD IT AGREED THAT THE PRINCE SHOULD WOO HERO FOR HIMSELF...
AND, HAVING OBTAINED HER, GIVE HER TO COUNT CLAUDIO.
THAT YOUNG START-UP HATH ALL THE GLORY OF MY OVERTHROW.
IF I CAN CROSS HIM ANY WAY, I BLESS MYSELF EVERY WAY. YOU WILL ASSIST ME?
TO THE DEATH, MY LORD.

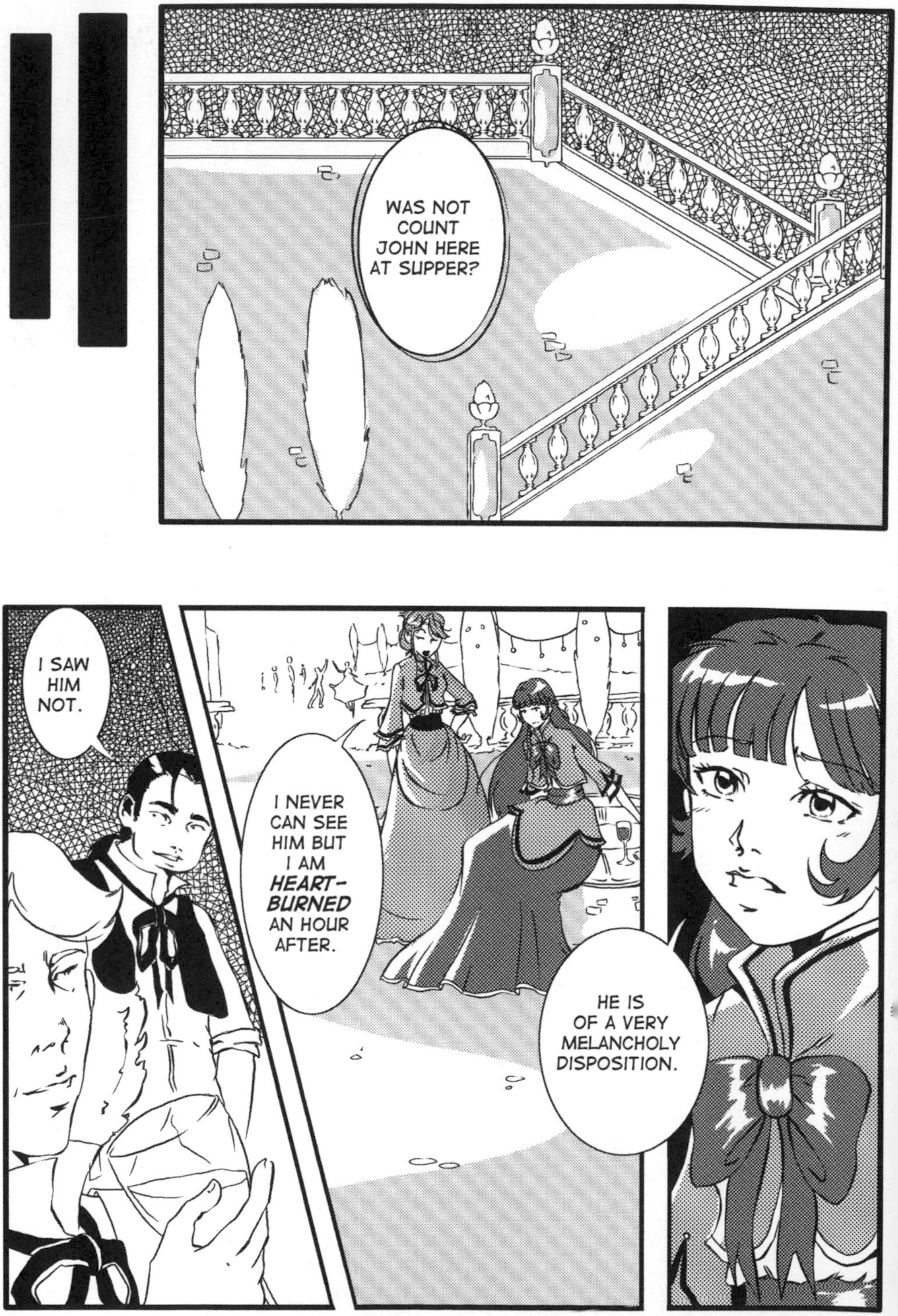
WAS NOT COUNT JOHN HERE AT SUPPER?
I SAW HIM NOT.
I NEVER CAN SEE HIM BUT I AM ***HEART-BURNED*** AN HOUR AFTER.
HE IS OF A VERY MELANCHOLY DISPOSITION.

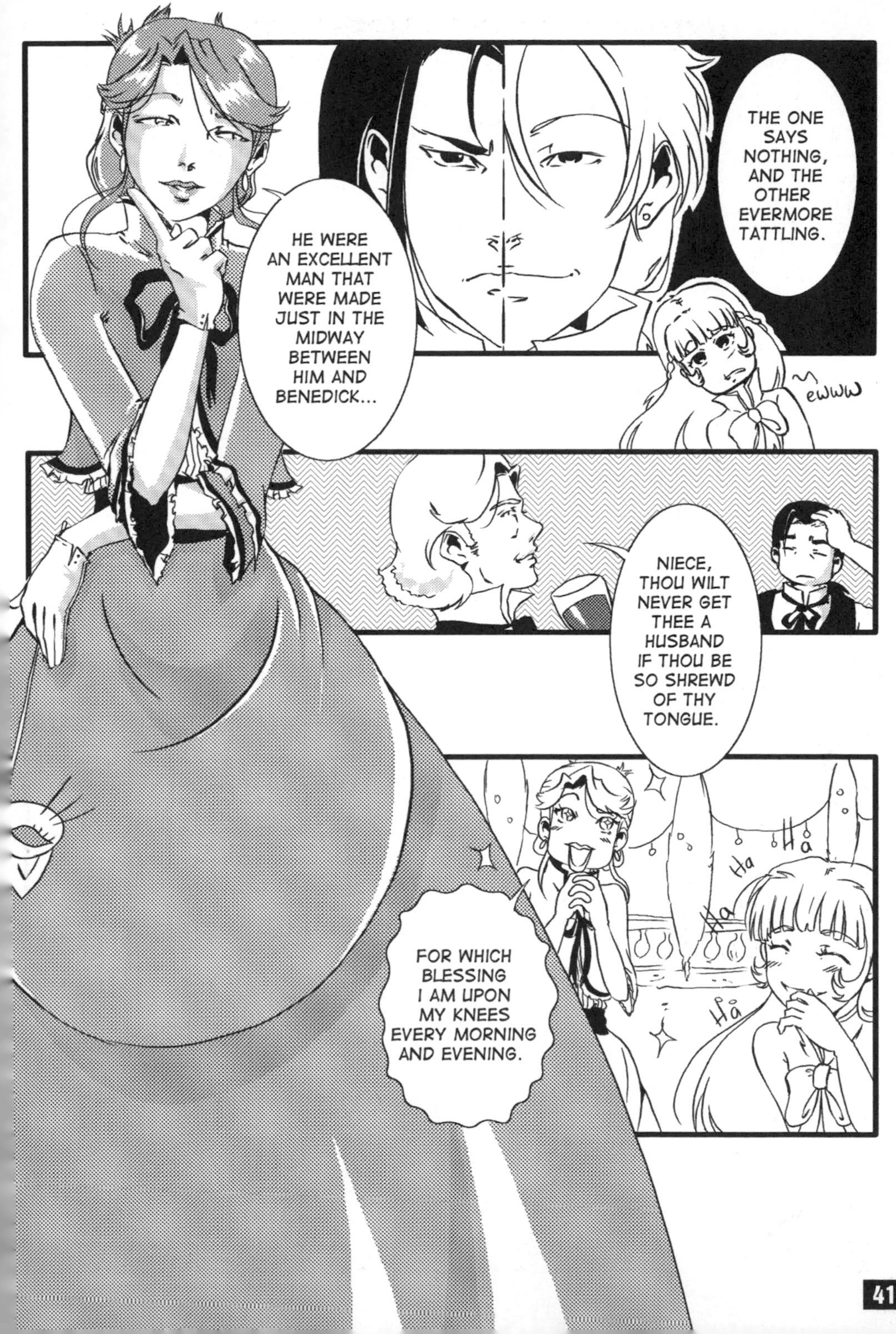
HE WERE AN EXCELLENT MAN THAT WERE MADE JUST IN THE MIDWAY BETWEEN HIM AND BENEDICK...
THE ONE SAYS NOTHING, AND THE OTHER EVERMORE TATTLING.
ewww
NIECE, THOU WILT NEVER GET THEE A HUSBAND IF THOU BE SO SHREWD OF THY TONGUE.
FOR WHICH BLESSING I AM UPON MY KNEES EVERY MORNING AND EVENING.
Ha Ha Ha Ha

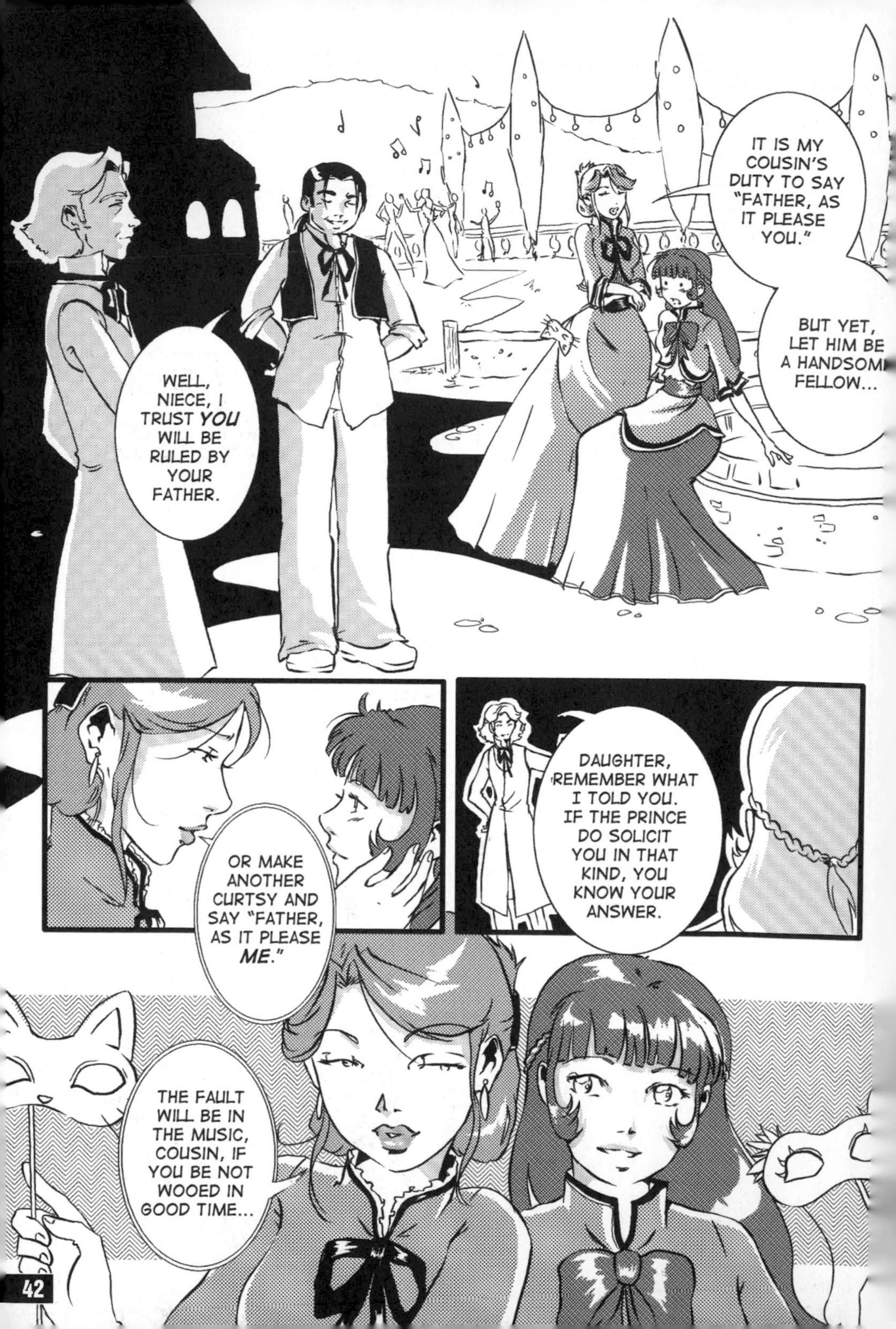
WELL, NIECE, I TRUST ***YOU*** WILL BE RULED BY YOUR FATHER.
IT IS MY COUSIN'S DUTY TO SAY "FATHER, AS IT PLEASE YOU."
BUT YET, LET HIM BE A HANDSOM FELLOW...
OR MAKE ANOTHER CURTSY AND SAY "FATHER, AS IT PLEASE ***ME***."
DAUGHTER, REMEMBER WHAT I TOLD YOU. IF THE PRINCE DO SOLICIT YOU IN THAT KIND, YOU KNOW YOUR ANSWER.
THE FAULT WILL BE IN THE MUSIC, COUSIN, IF YOU BE NOT WOOED IN GOOD TIME...

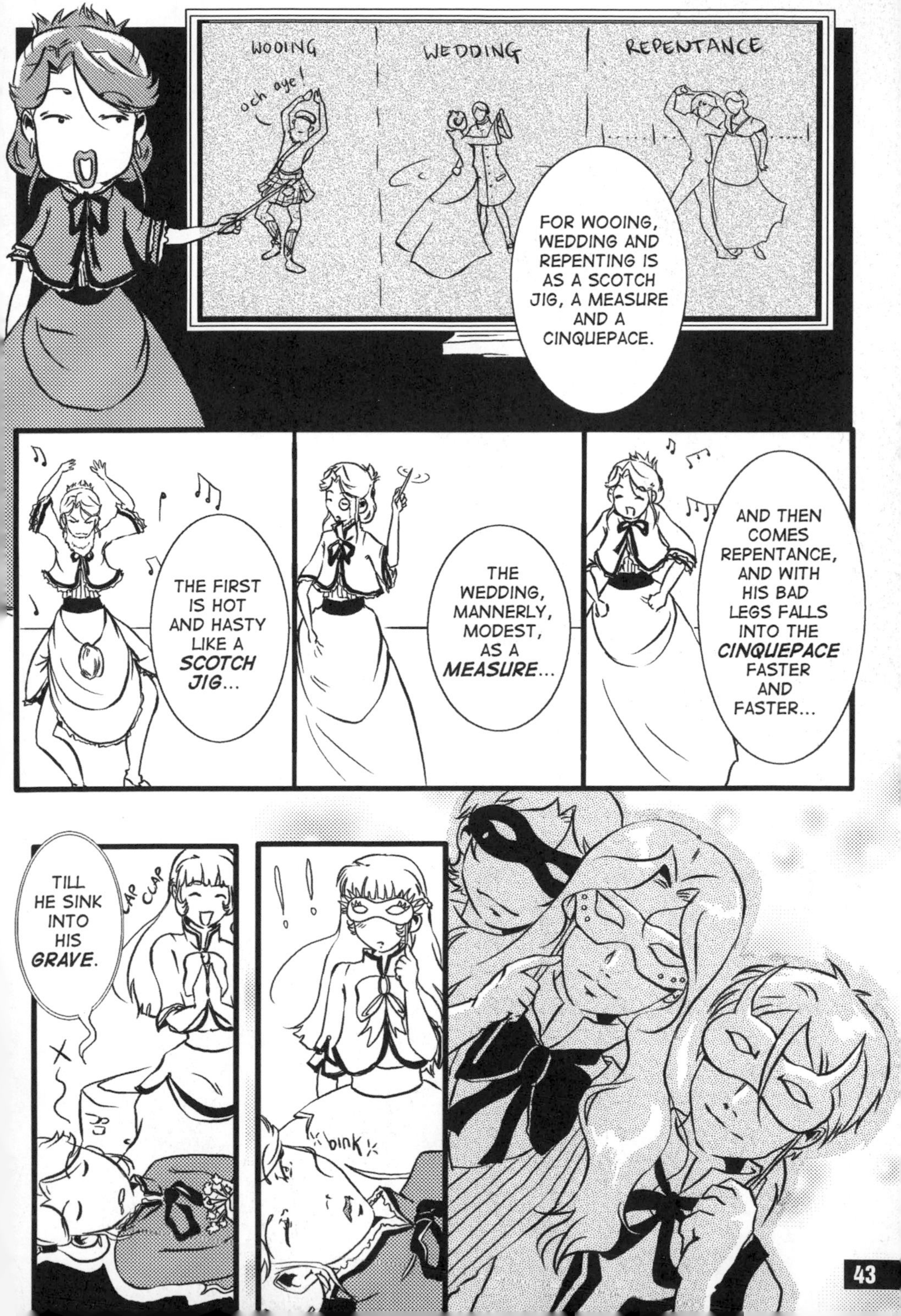
WOOING
och aye!
WEDDING
REPENTANCE
FOR WOOING, WEDDING AND REPENTING IS AS A SCOTCH JIG, A MEASURE AND A CINQUEPACE.
THE FIRST IS HOT AND HASTY LIKE A ***SCOTCH JIG***...
THE WEDDING, MANNERLY, MODEST, AS A ***MEASURE***...
AND THEN COMES REPENTANCE, AND WITH HIS BAD LEGS FALLS INTO THE ***CINQUEPACE*** FASTER AND FASTER...
TILL HE SINK INTO HIS ***GRAVE***.
CLAP CLAP
! !
bink

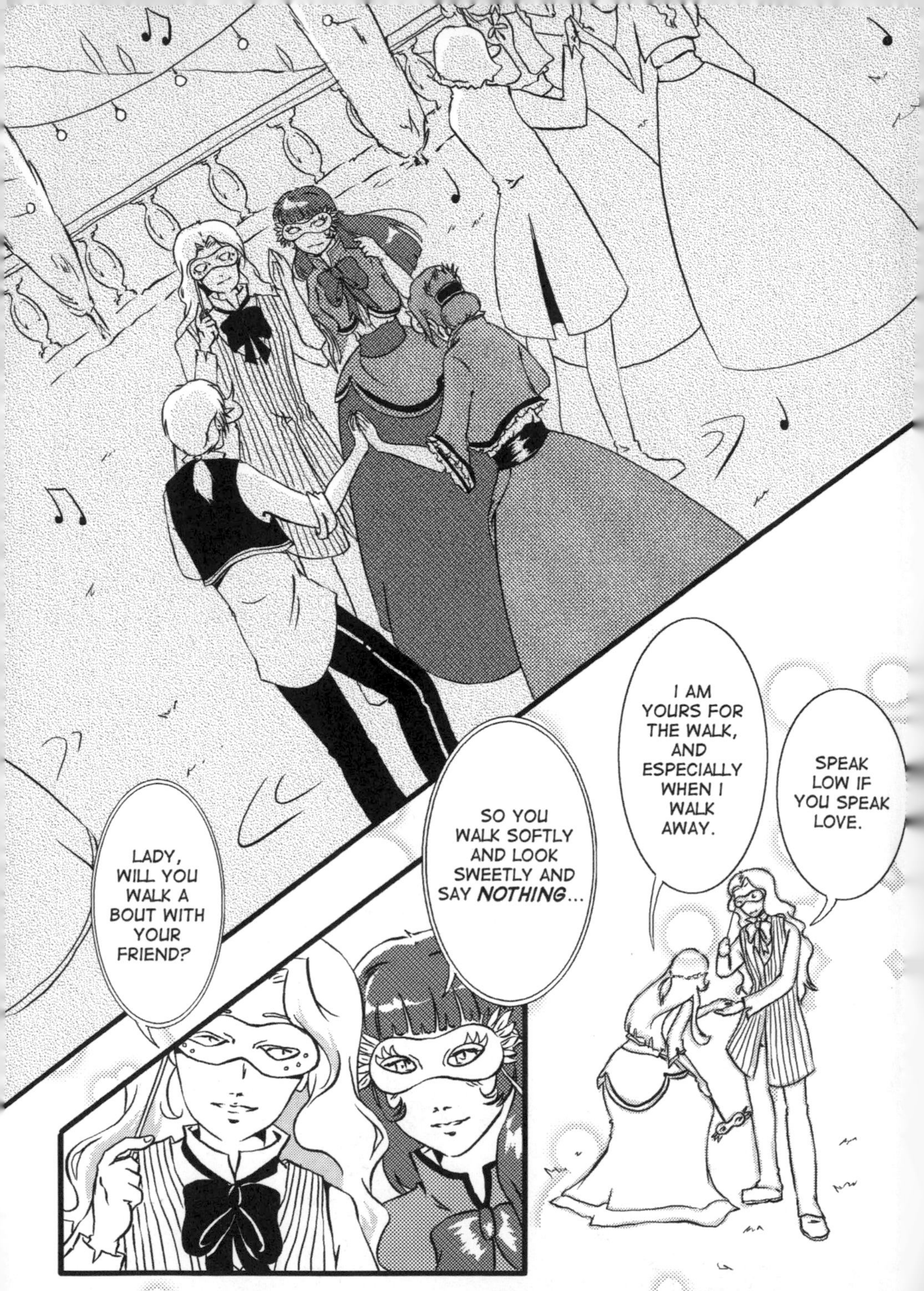
LADY, WILL YOU WALK A BOUT WITH YOUR FRIEND?
SO YOU WALK SOFTLY AND LOOK SWEETLY AND SAY ***NOTHING***...
I AM YOURS FOR THE WALK, AND ESPECIALLY WHEN I WALK AWAY.
SPEAK LOW IF YOU SPEAK LOVE.

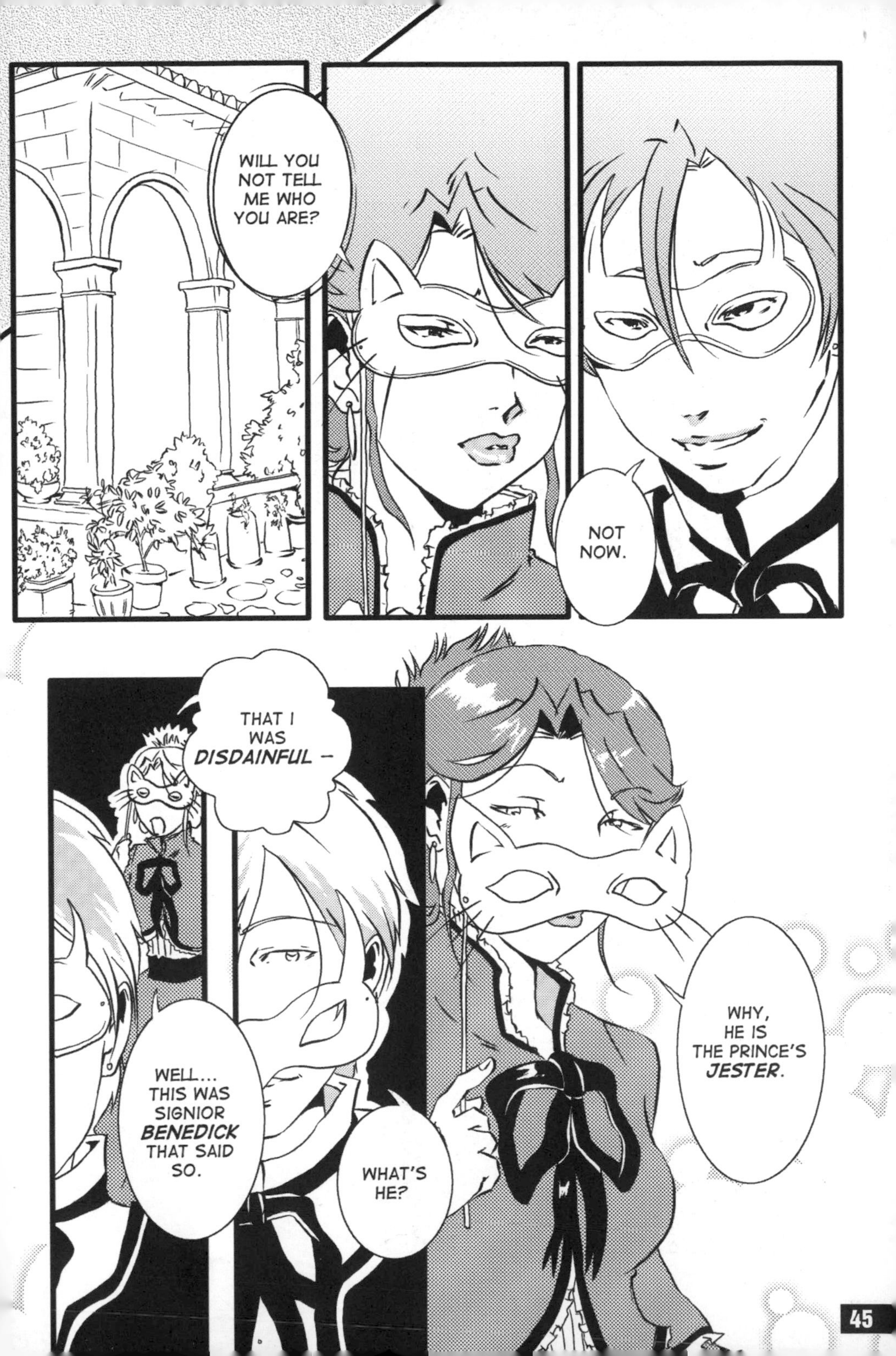
WILL YOU NOT TELL ME WHO YOU ARE?
NOT NOW.
THAT I WAS DISDAINFUL –
WELL... THIS WAS SIGNIOR BENEDICK THAT SAID SO.
WHAT'S HE?
WHY, HE IS THE PRINCE'S JESTER.

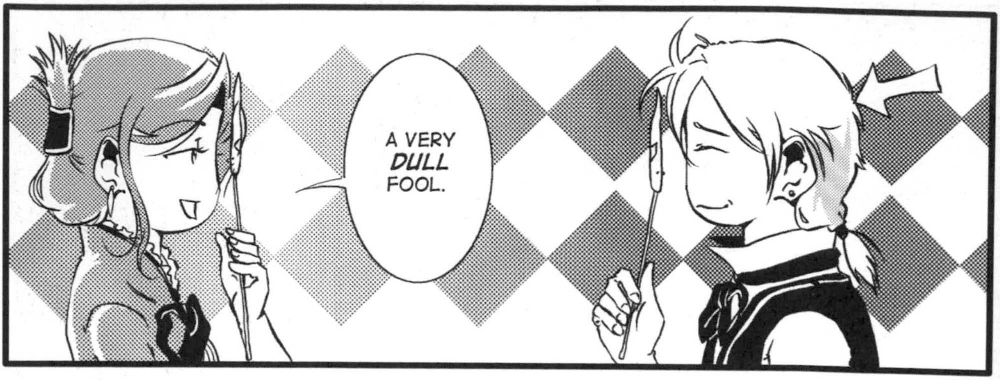
A VERY **DULL** FOOL.
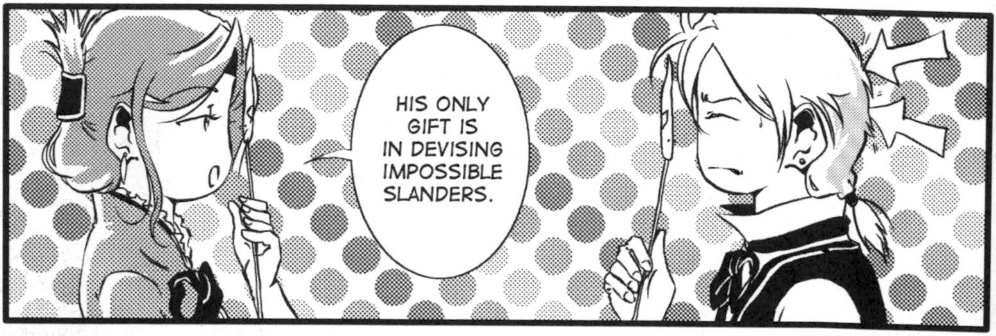
HIS ONLY GIFT IS IN DEVISING IMPOSSIBLE SLANDERS.
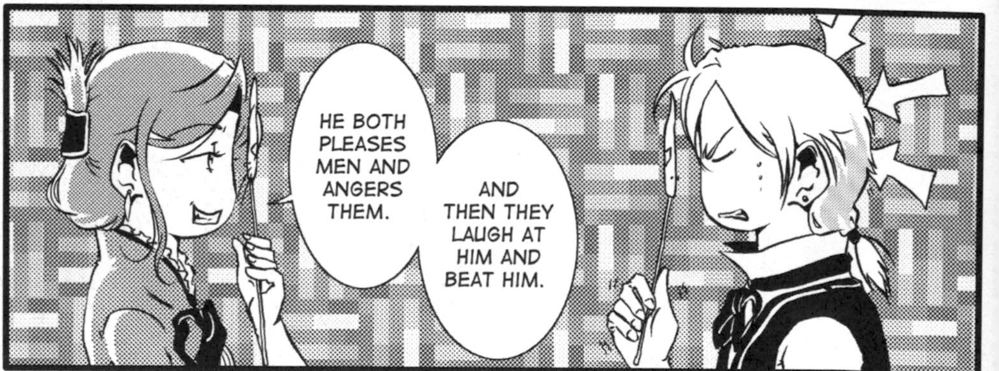
HE BOTH PLEASES MEN AND ANGERS THEM.
AND THEN THEY LAUGH AT HIM AND BEAT HIM.
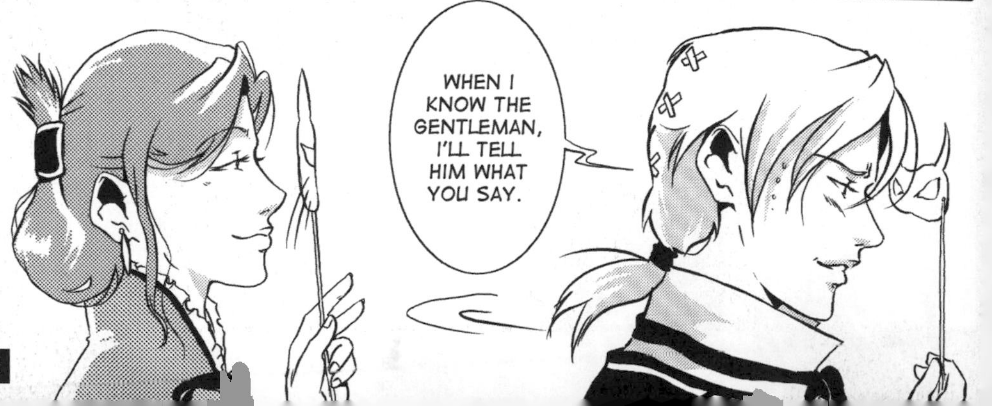
WHEN I KNOW THE GENTLEMAN, I'LL TELL HIM WHAT YOU SAY.

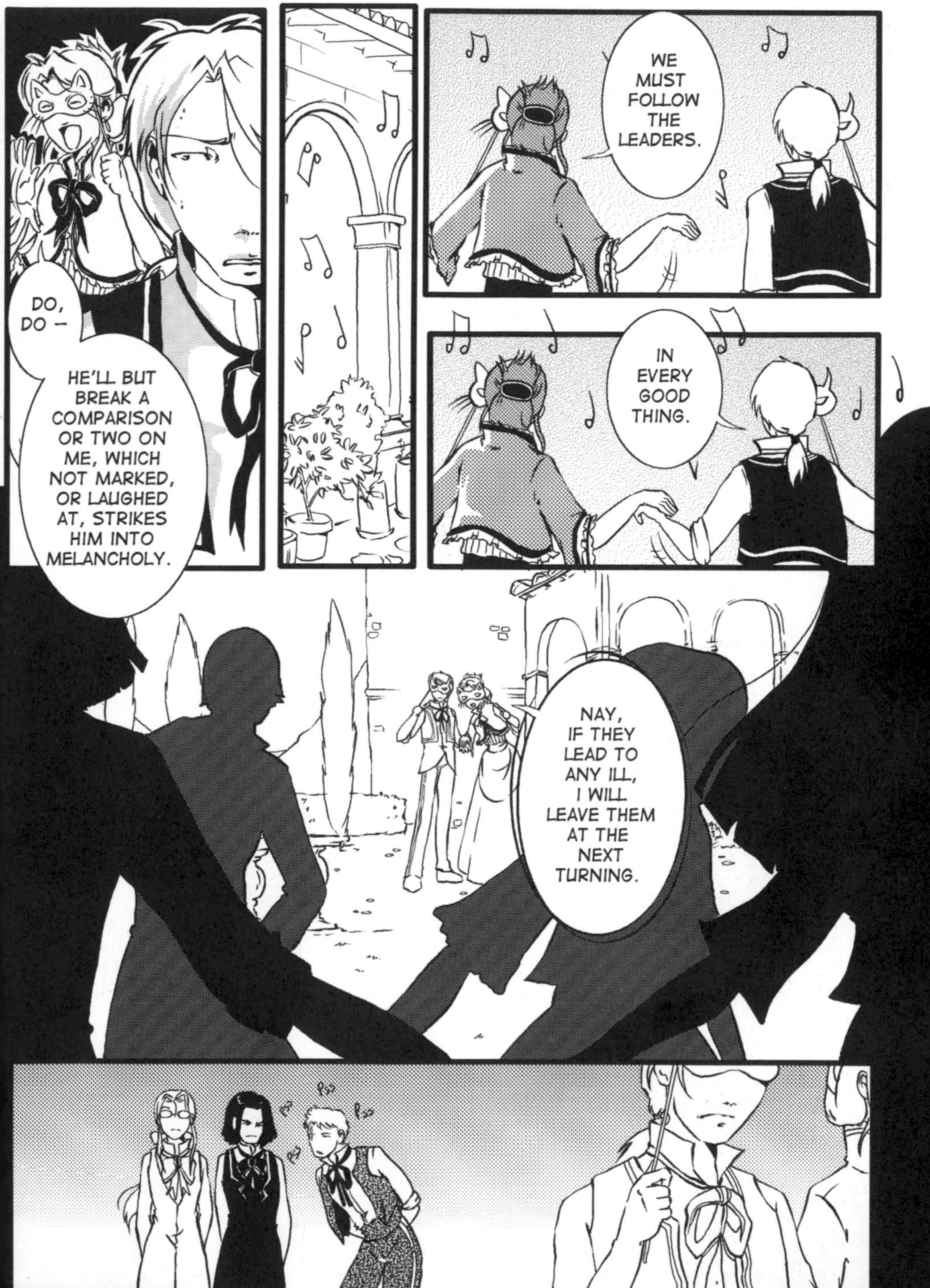
DO, DO —
HE'LL BUT BREAK A COMPARISON OR TWO ON ME, WHICH NOT MARKED, OR LAUGHED AT, STRIKES HIM INTO MELANCHOLY.
WE MUST FOLLOW THE LEADERS.
IN EVERY GOOD THING.
NAY, IF THEY LEAD TO ANY ILL, I WILL LEAVE THEM AT THE NEXT TURNING.

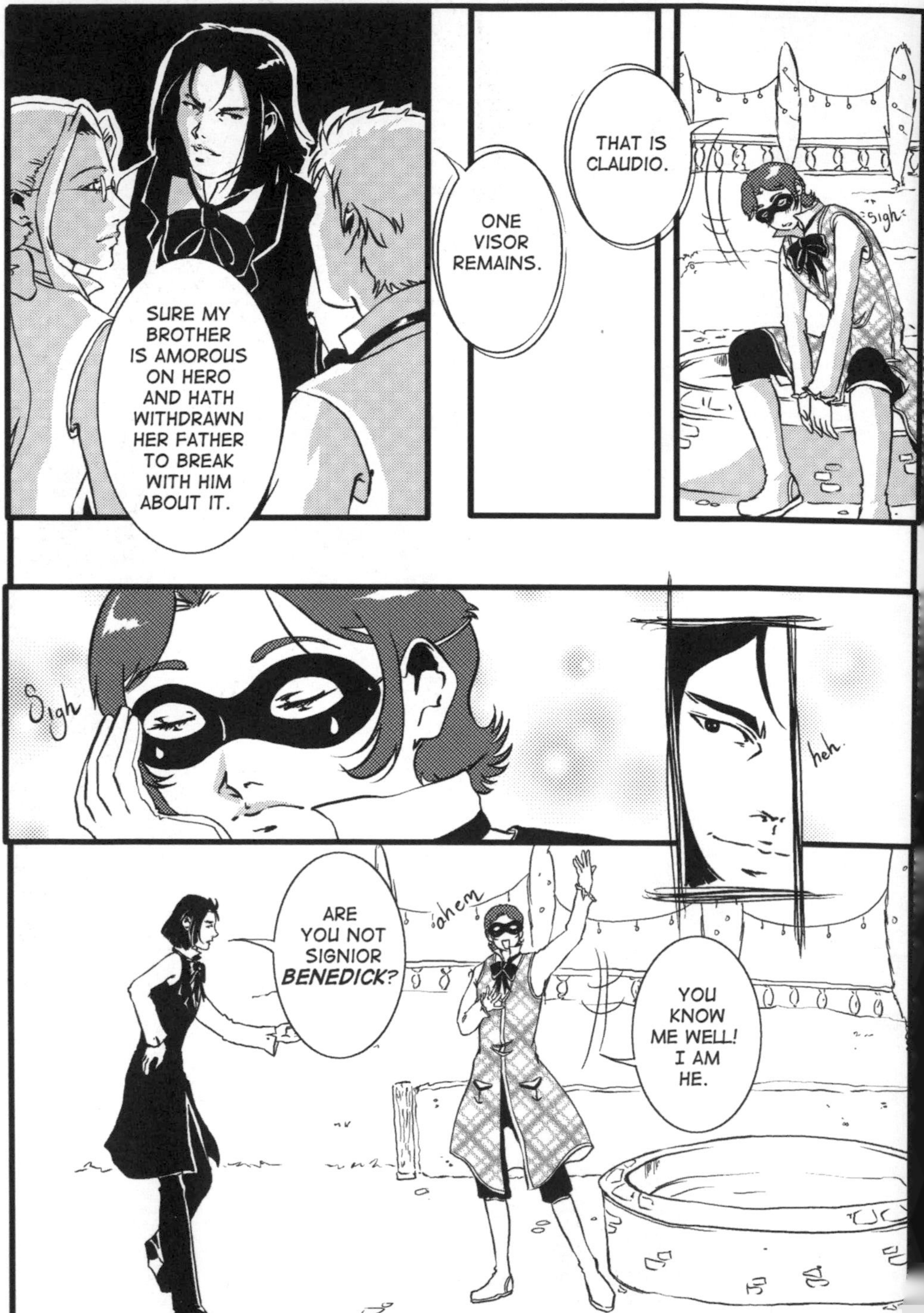
SURE MY BROTHER IS AMOROUS ON HERO AND HATH WITHDRAWN HER FATHER TO BREAK WITH HIM ABOUT IT.
THAT IS CLAUDIO.
ONE VISOR REMAINS.
sigh
Sigh
heh.
ahem
ARE YOU NOT SIGNIOR **BENEDICK**?
YOU KNOW ME WELL! I AM HE.

SIGNIOR, YOU ARE VERY NEAR MY BROTHER IN HIS *LOVE*.

HE IS ENAMOURED ON HERO.

I PRAY YOU, DISSUADE HIM FROM HER. SHE IS NO EQUAL FOR HIS BIRTH.

HOW KNOW YOU HE LOVES HER?

I HEARD HIM SWEAR HIS AFFECTION.

SO DID I TOO. AND HE SWORE HE WOULD MARRY HER TONIGHT.

...

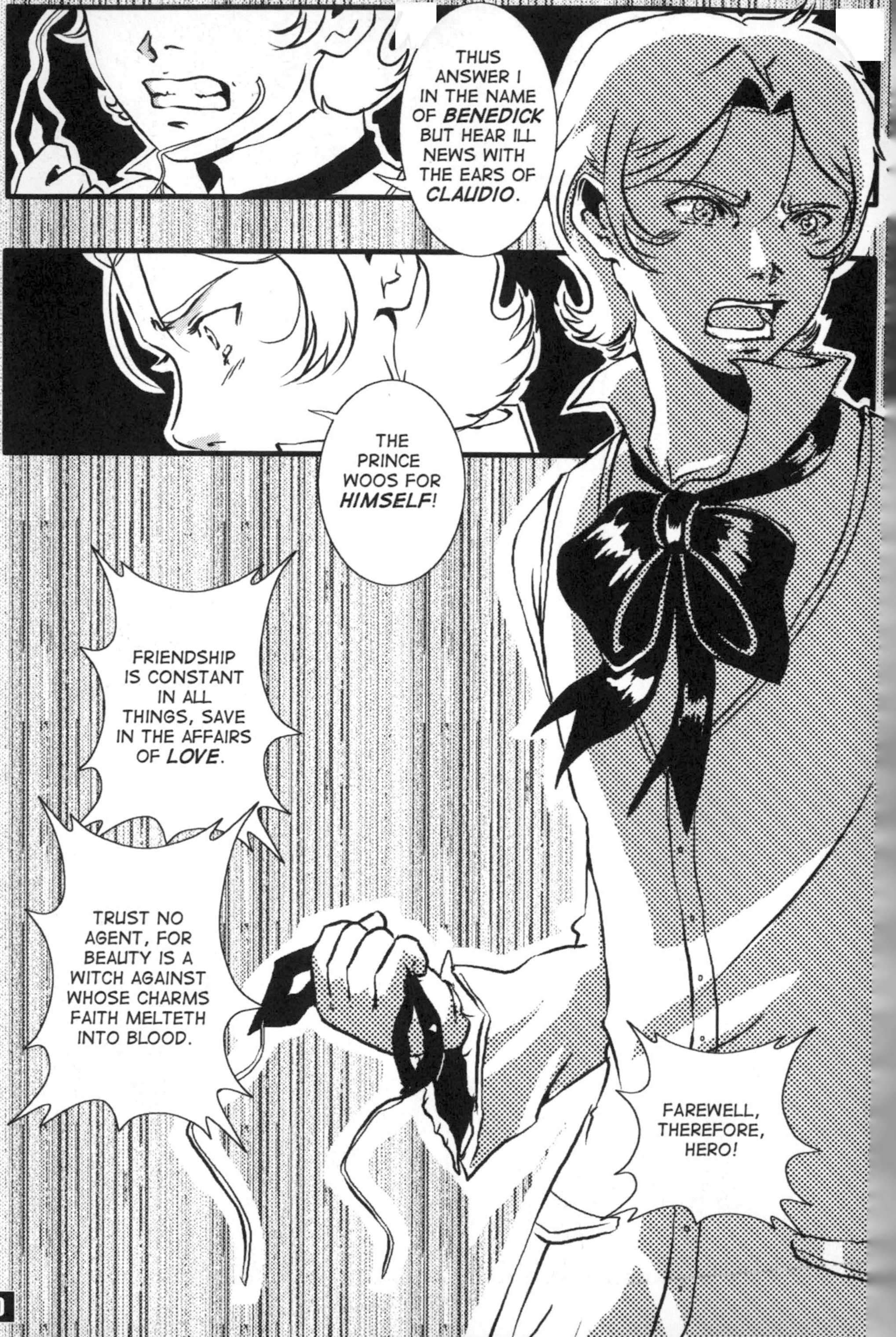
THUS ANSWER I IN THE NAME OF **BENEDICK** BUT HEAR ILL NEWS WITH THE EARS OF **CLAUDIO**.
THE PRINCE WOOS FOR **HIMSELF**!
FRIENDSHIP IS CONSTANT IN ALL THINGS, SAVE IN THE AFFAIRS OF **LOVE**.
TRUST NO AGENT, FOR BEAUTY IS A WITCH AGAINST WHOSE CHARMS FAITH MELTETH INTO BLOOD.
FAREWELL, THEREFORE, HERO!

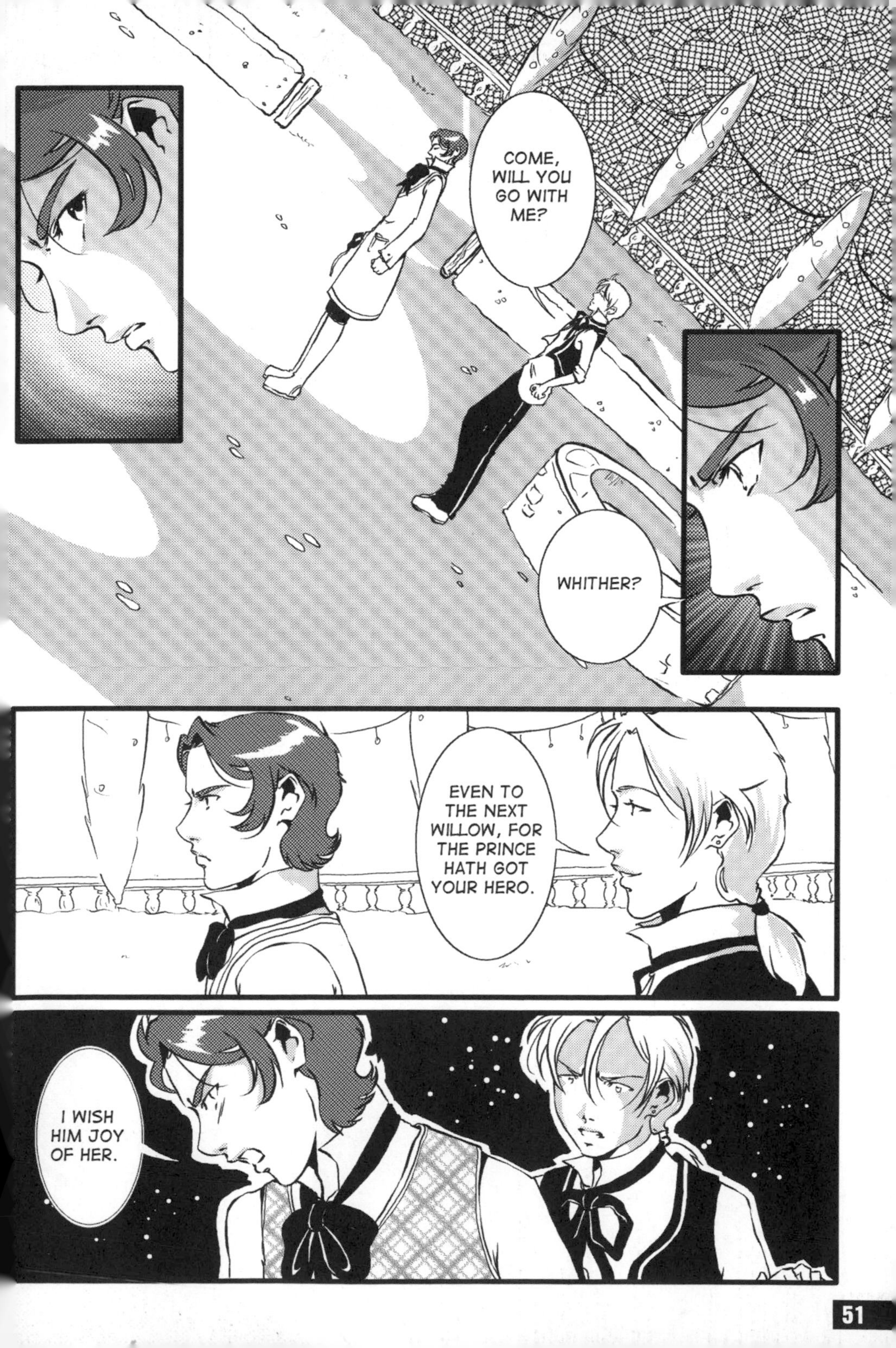
COME, WILL YOU GO WITH ME?
WHITHER?
EVEN TO THE NEXT WILLOW, FOR THE PRINCE HATH GOT YOUR HERO.
I WISH HIM JOY OF HER.

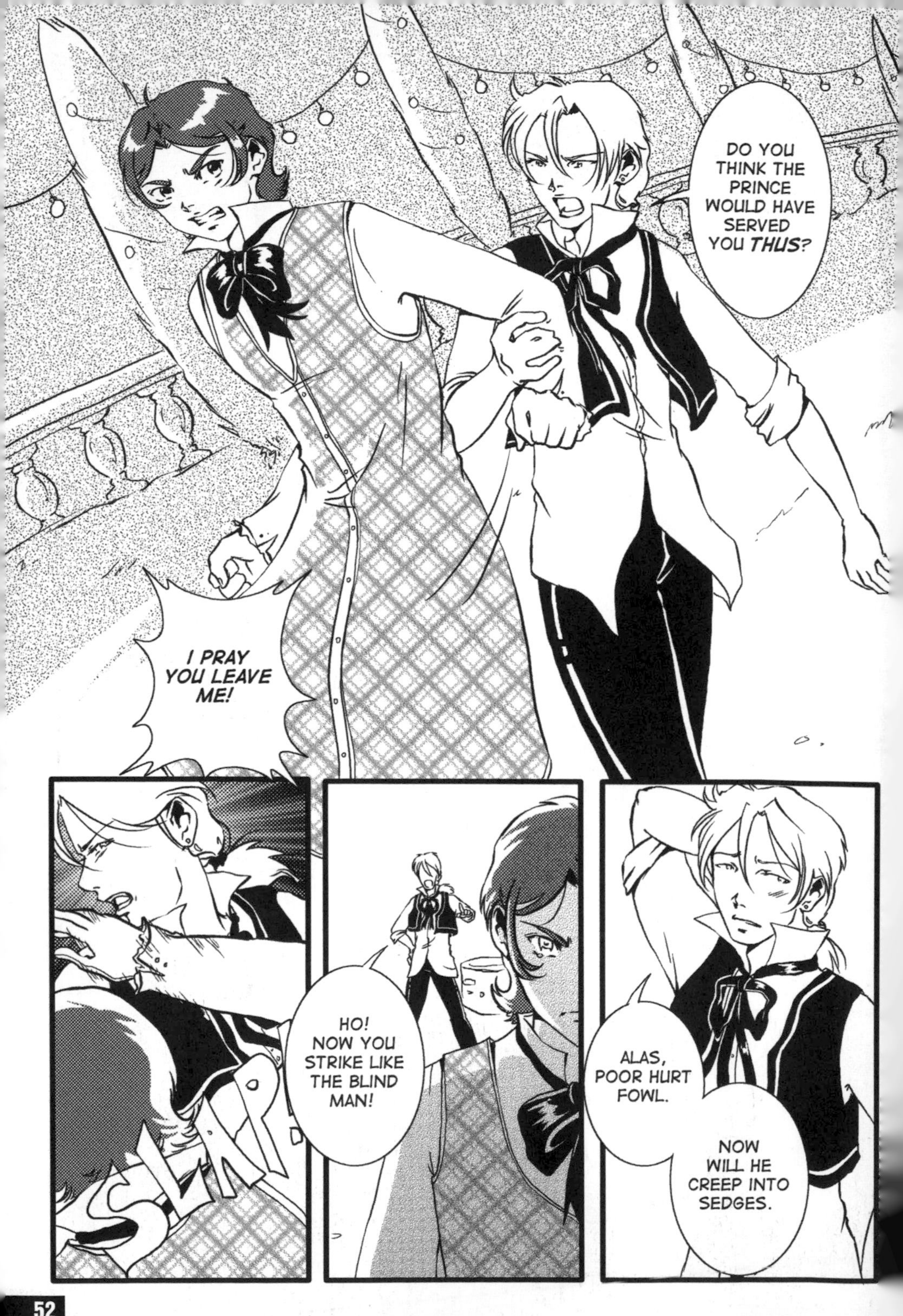
DO YOU THINK THE PRINCE WOULD HAVE SERVED YOU *THUS*?
I PRAY YOU LEAVE ME!
HO! NOW YOU STRIKE LIKE THE BLIND MAN!
ALAS, POOR HURT FOWL.
NOW WILL HE CREEP INTO SEDGES.

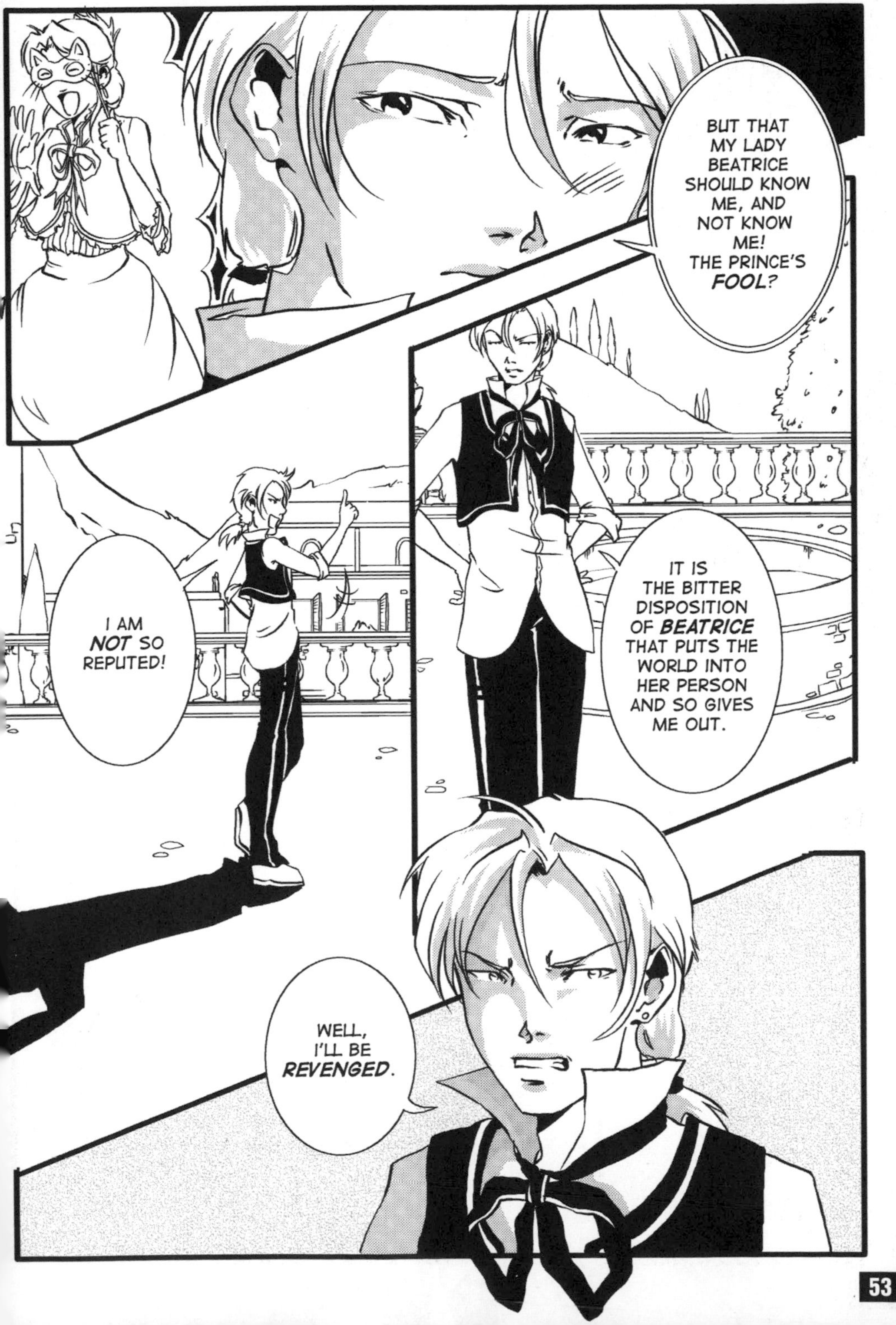
BUT THAT MY LADY BEATRICE SHOULD KNOW ME, AND NOT KNOW ME! THE PRINCE'S FOOL?
I AM NOT SO REPUTED!
IT IS THE BITTER DISPOSITION OF BEATRICE THAT PUTS THE WORLD INTO HER PERSON AND SO GIVES ME OUT.
WELL, I'LL BE REVENGED.

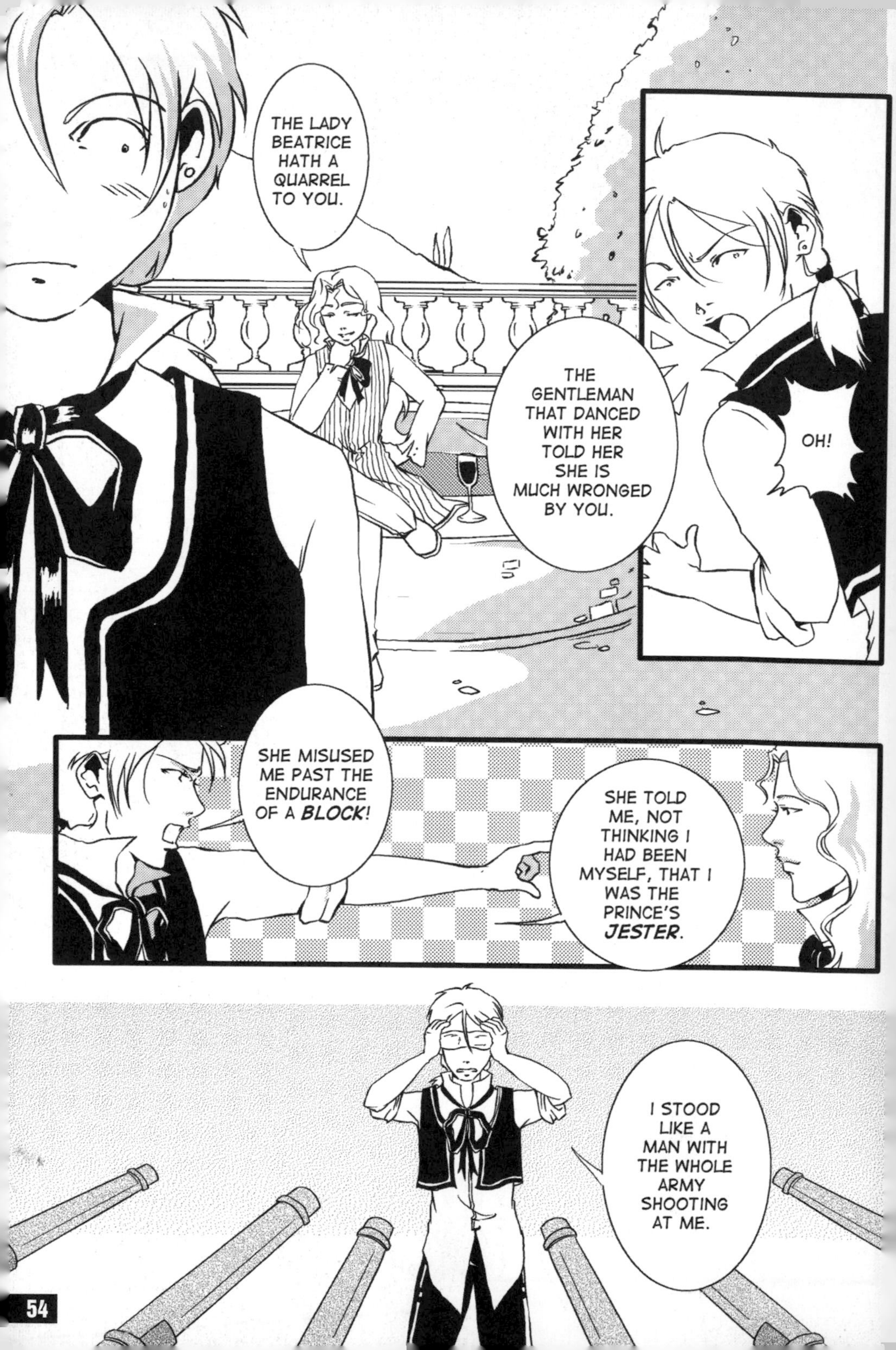
THE LADY BEATRICE HATH A QUARREL TO YOU.
THE GENTLEMAN THAT DANCED WITH HER TOLD HER SHE IS MUCH WRONGED BY YOU.
OH!
SHE MISUSED ME PAST THE ENDURANCE OF A ***BLOCK***!
SHE TOLD ME, NOT THINKING I HAD BEEN MYSELF, THAT I WAS THE PRINCE'S ***JESTER***.
I STOOD LIKE A MAN WITH THE WHOLE ARMY SHOOTING AT ME.

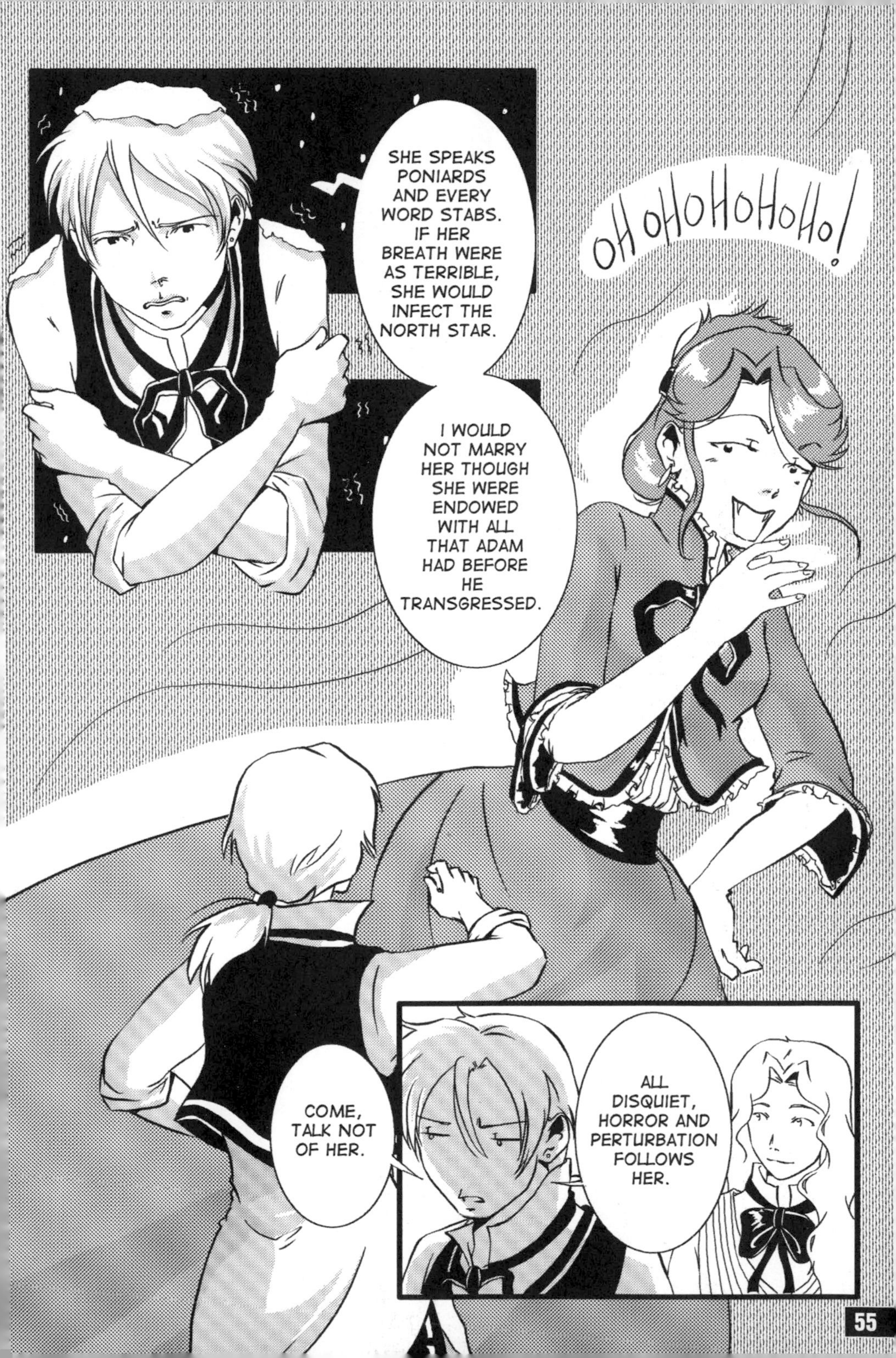
SHE SPEAKS PONIARDS AND EVERY WORD STABS. IF HER BREATH WERE AS TERRIBLE, SHE WOULD INFECT THE NORTH STAR.
I WOULD NOT MARRY HER THOUGH SHE WERE ENDOWED WITH ALL THAT ADAM HAD BEFORE HE TRANSGRESSED.
OH OHOHOHOHOHO!
COME, TALK NOT OF HER.
ALL DISQUIET, HORROR AND PERTURBATION FOLLOWS HER.

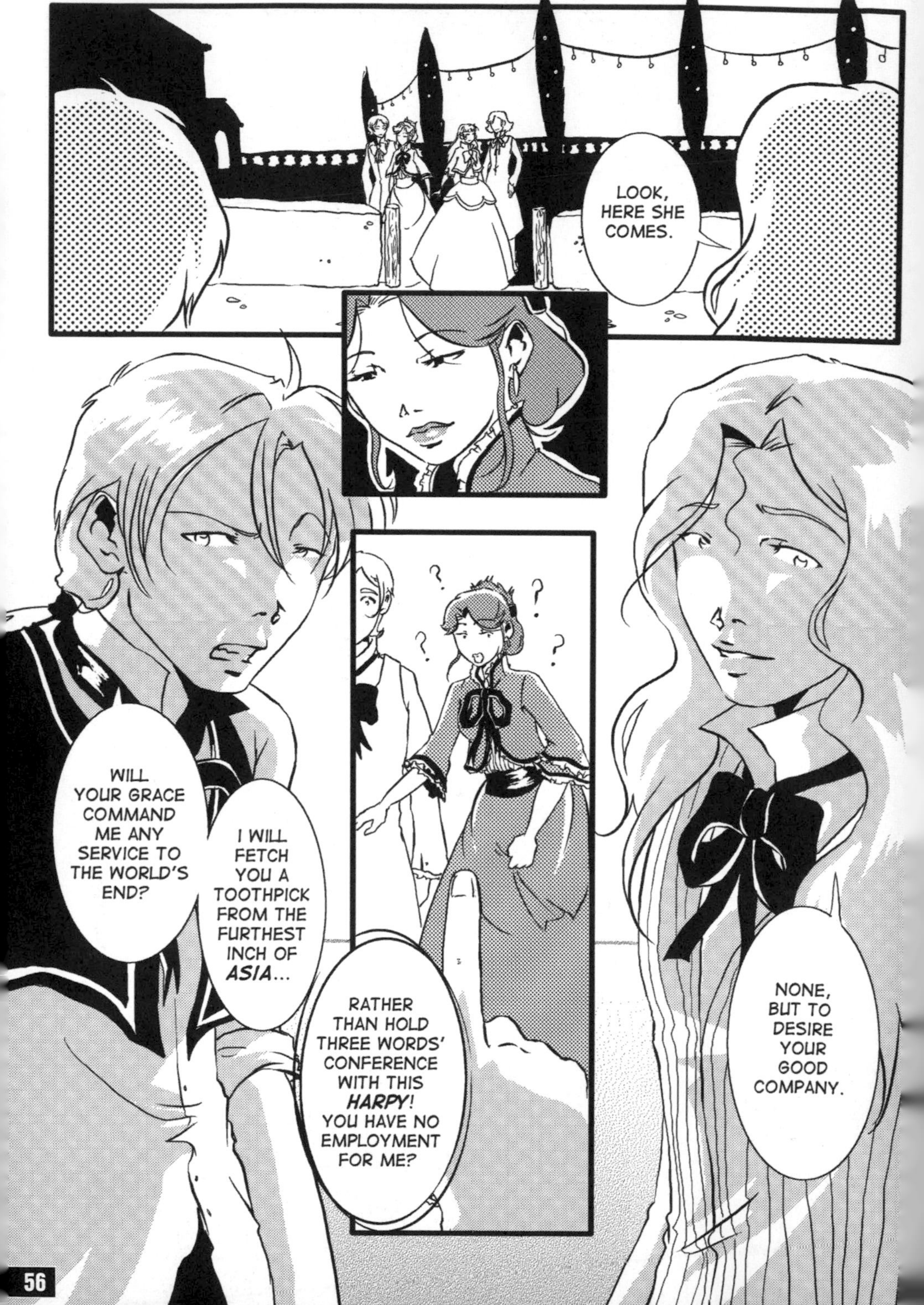
LOOK, HERE SHE COMES.
WILL YOUR GRACE COMMAND ME ANY SERVICE TO THE WORLD'S END?
I WILL FETCH YOU A TOOTHPICK FROM THE FURTHEST INCH OF *ASIA*...
RATHER THAN HOLD THREE WORDS' CONFERENCE WITH THIS *HARPY*! YOU HAVE NO EMPLOYMENT FOR ME?
NONE, BUT TO DESIRE YOUR GOOD COMPANY.

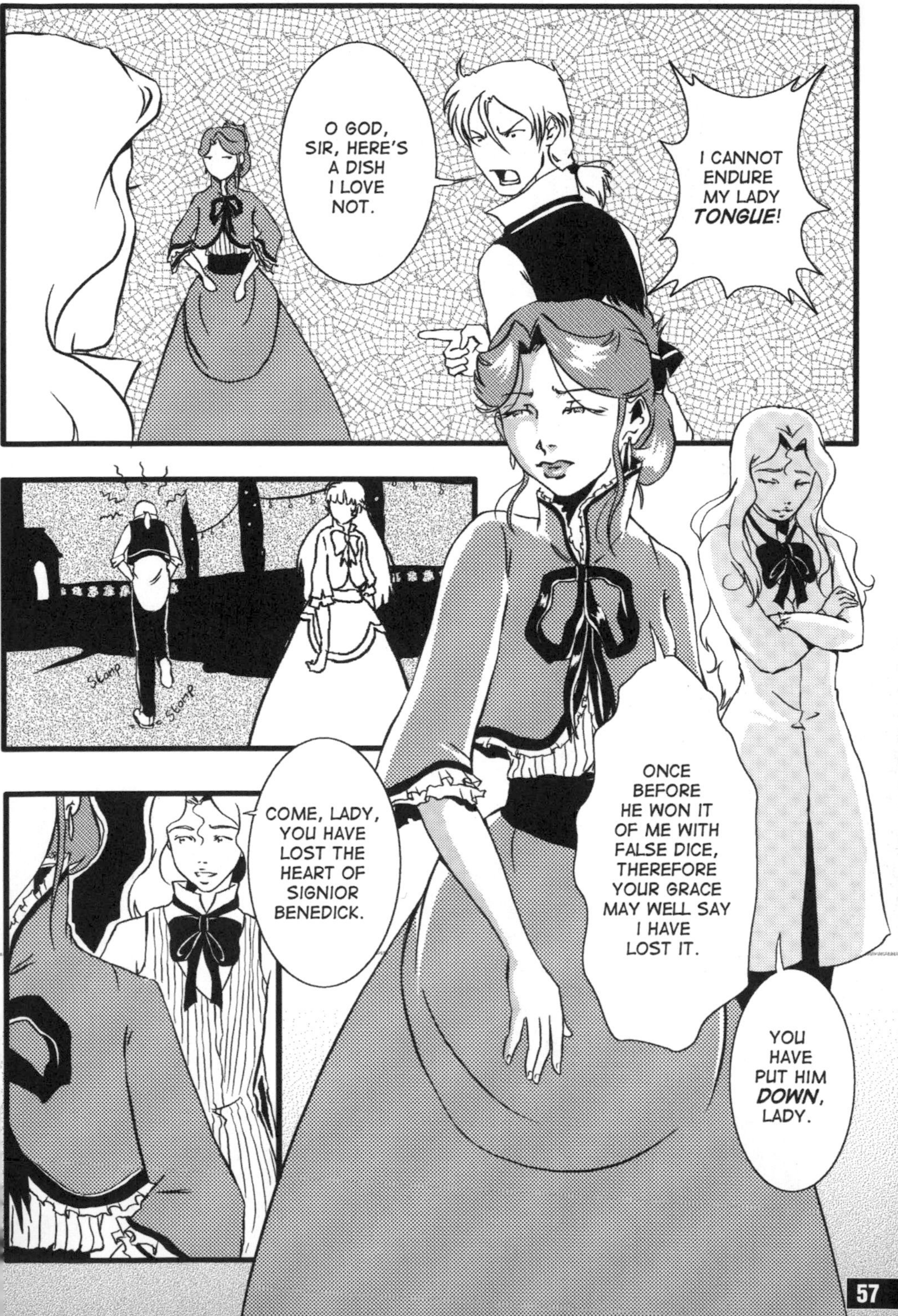
O GOD, SIR, HERE'S A DISH I LOVE NOT.
I CANNOT ENDURE MY LADY ***TONGUE***!
Stomp
Stomp
COME, LADY, YOU HAVE LOST THE HEART OF SIGNIOR BENEDICK.
ONCE BEFORE HE WON IT OF ME WITH FALSE DICE, THEREFORE YOUR GRACE MAY WELL SAY I HAVE LOST IT.
YOU HAVE PUT HIM ***DOWN***, LADY.

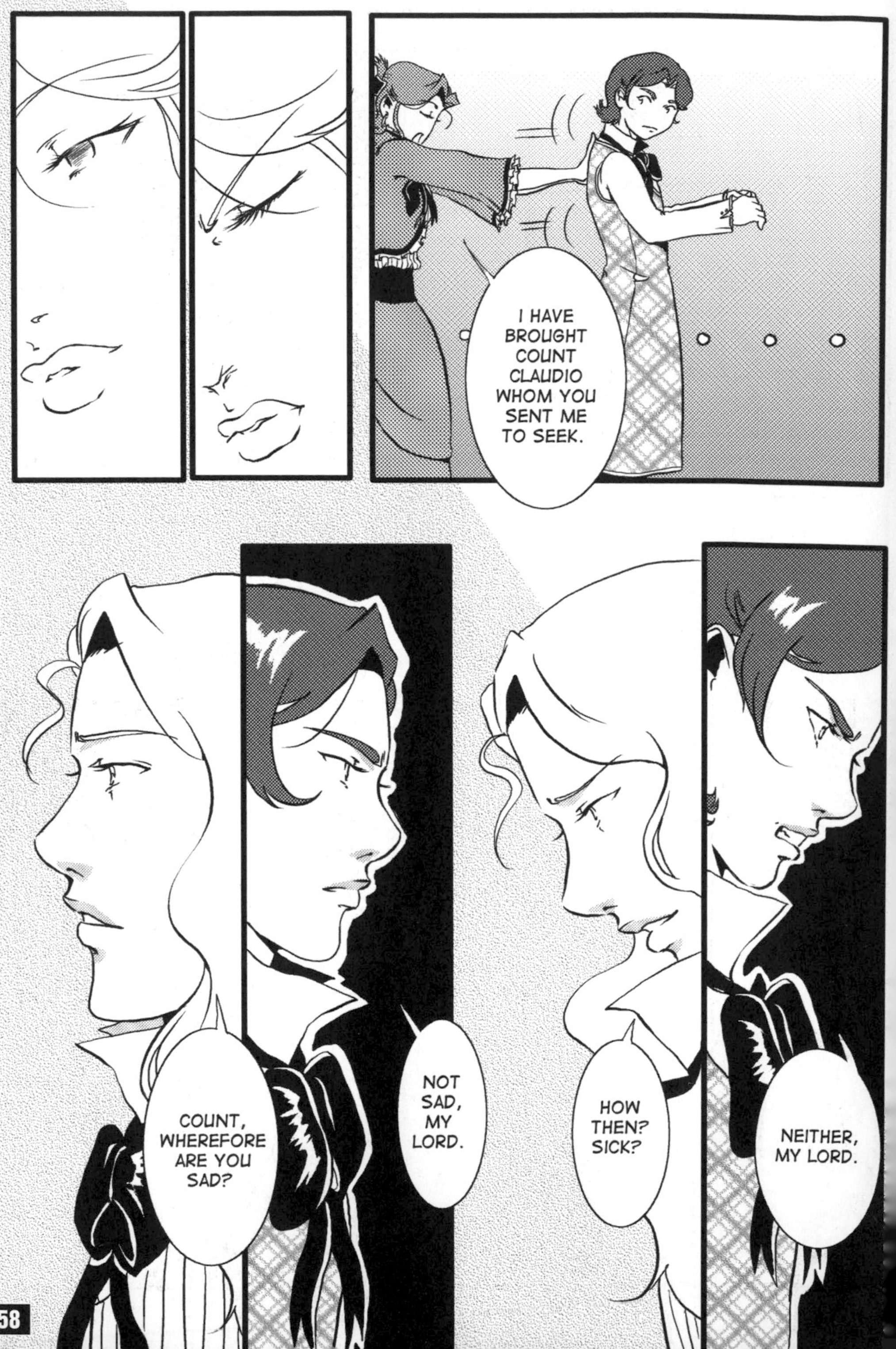

I HAVE BROUGHT COUNT CLAUDIO WHOM YOU SENT ME TO SEEK.
COUNT, WHEREFORE ARE YOU SAD?
NOT SAD, MY LORD.
HOW THEN? SICK?
NEITHER, MY LORD.

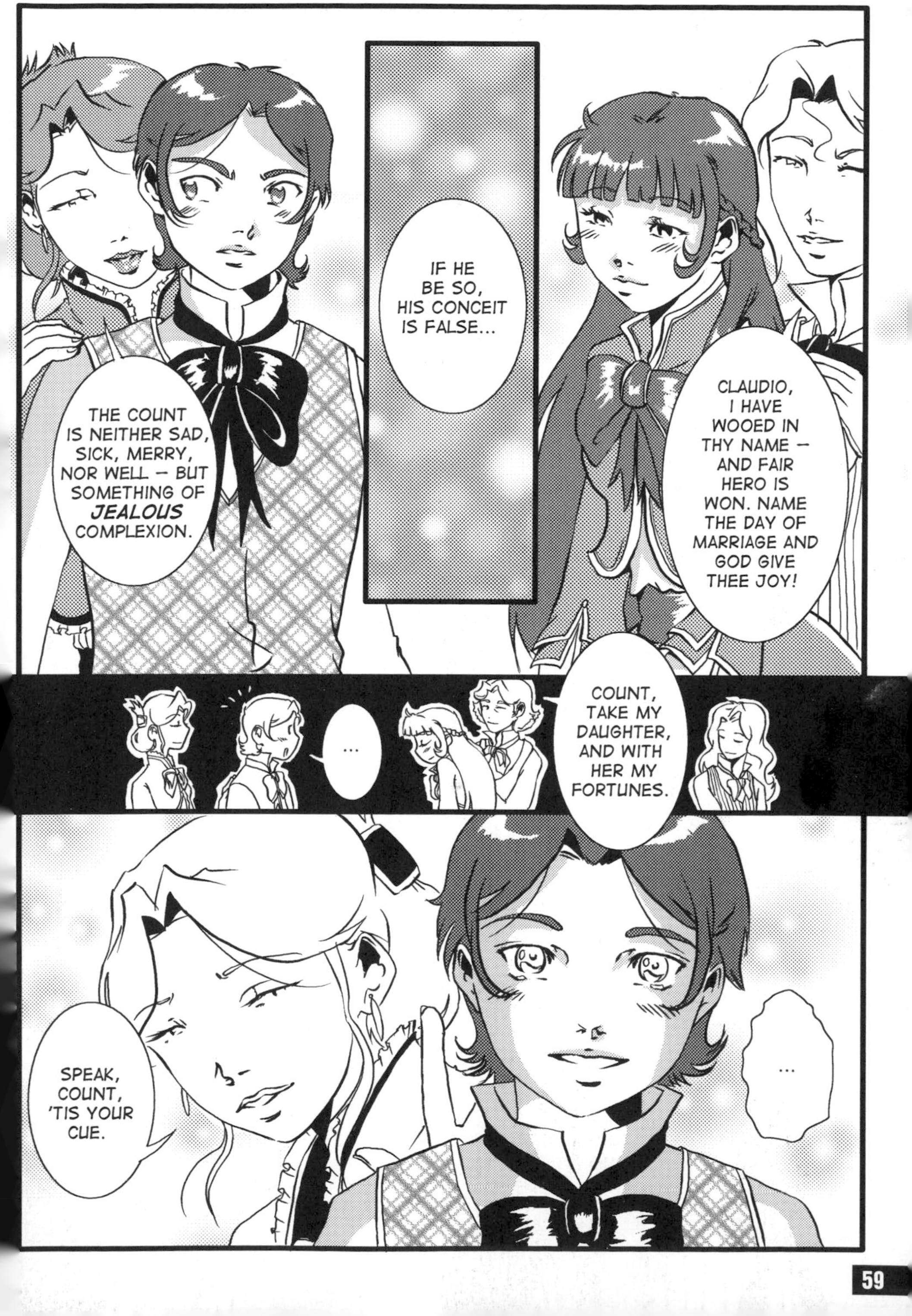
THE COUNT IS NEITHER SAD, SICK, MERRY, NOR WELL — BUT SOMETHING OF ***JEALOUS*** COMPLEXION.
IF HE BE SO, HIS CONCEIT IS FALSE...
CLAUDIO, I HAVE WOOED IN THY NAME — AND FAIR HERO IS WON. NAME THE DAY OF MARRIAGE AND GOD GIVE THEE JOY!
...
COUNT, TAKE MY DAUGHTER, AND WITH HER MY FORTUNES.
SPEAK, COUNT, 'TIS YOUR CUE.
...

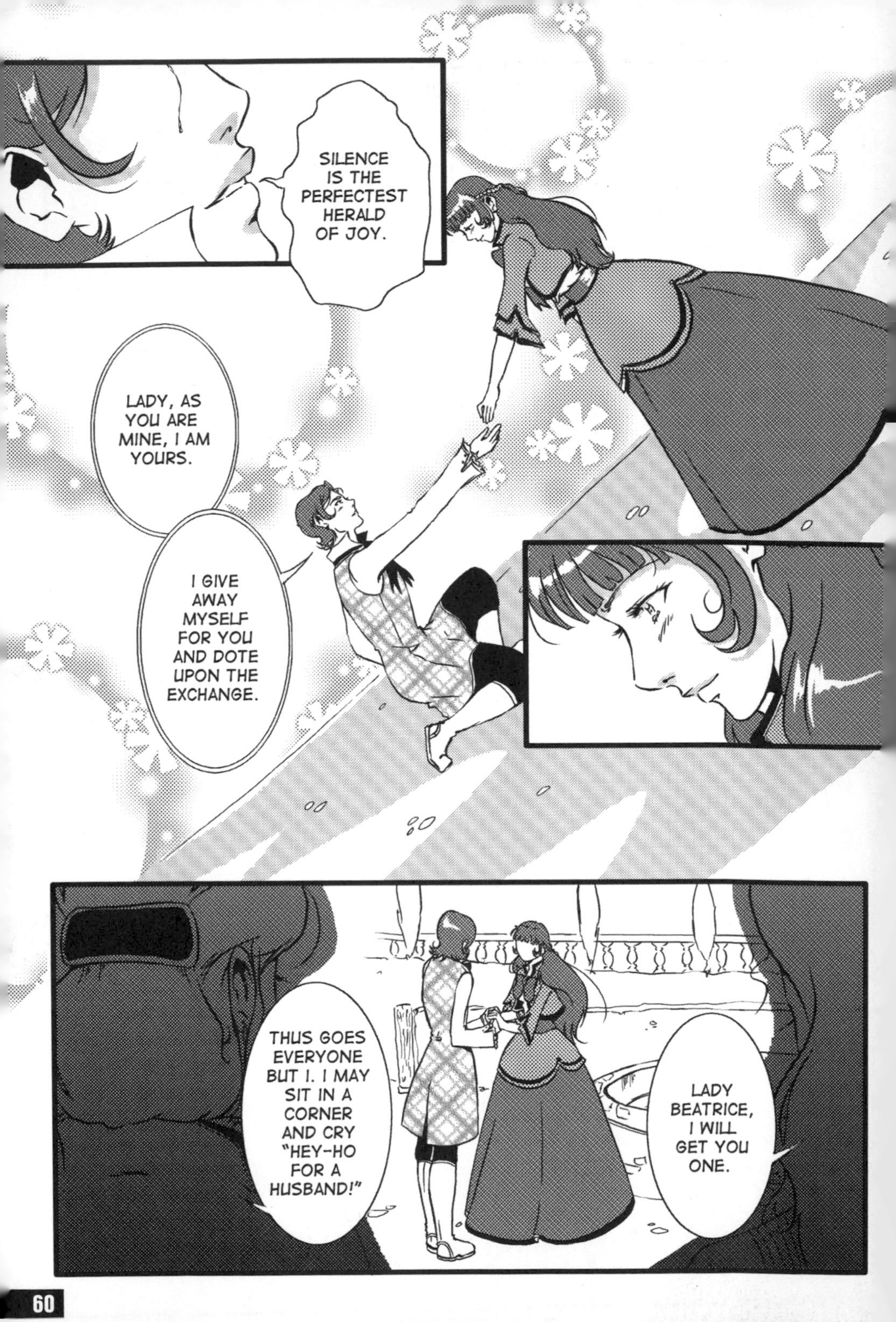
SILENCE IS THE PERFECTEST HERALD OF JOY.
LADY, AS YOU ARE MINE, I AM YOURS.
I GIVE AWAY MYSELF FOR YOU AND DOTE UPON THE EXCHANGE.
THUS GOES EVERYONE BUT I. I MAY SIT IN A CORNER AND CRY "HEY-HO FOR A HUSBAND!"
LADY BEATRICE, I WILL GET YOU ONE.

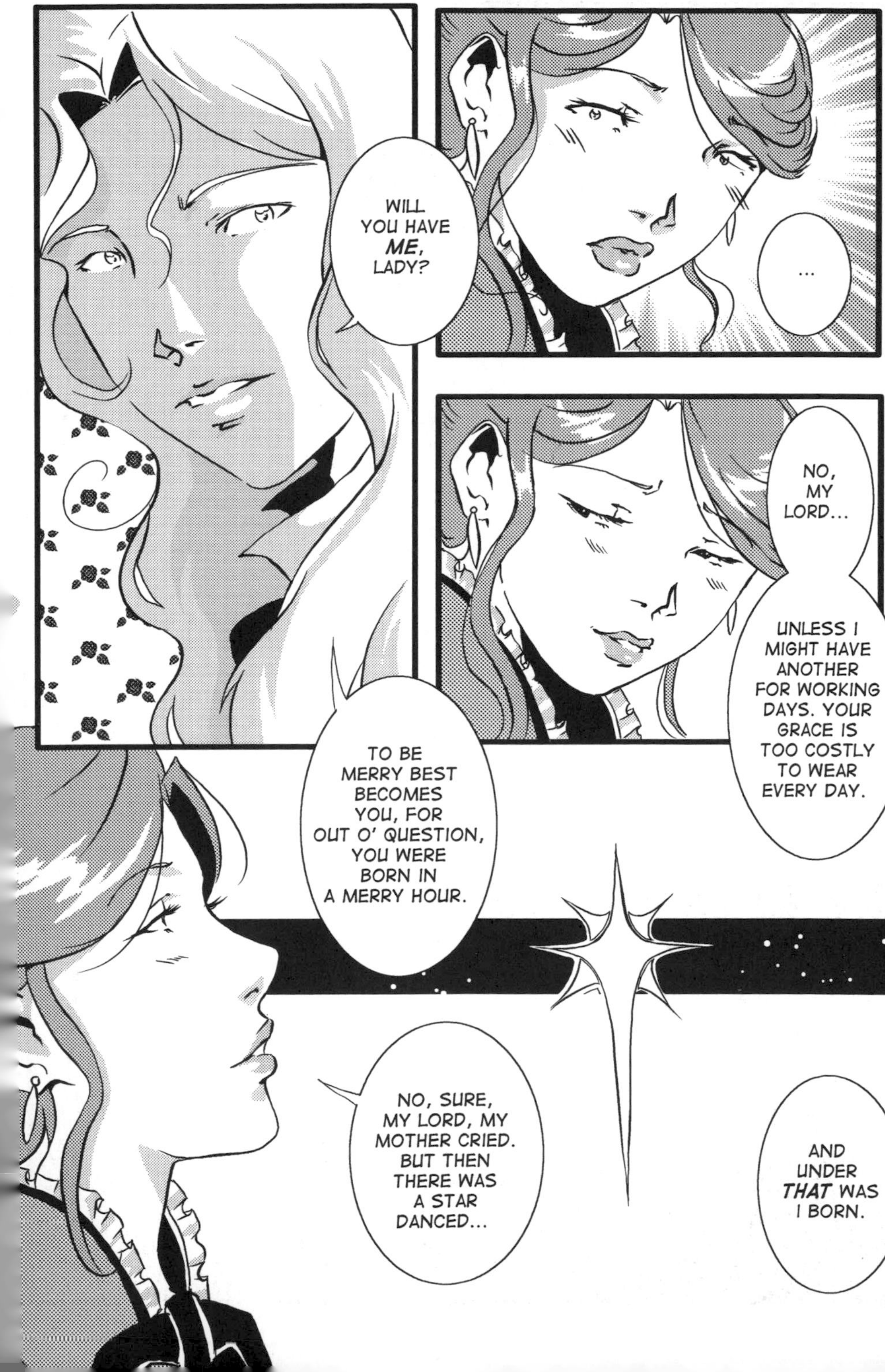
WILL YOU HAVE ME, LADY?
...
NO, MY LORD...
UNLESS I MIGHT HAVE ANOTHER FOR WORKING DAYS. YOUR GRACE IS TOO COSTLY TO WEAR EVERY DAY.
TO BE MERRY BEST BECOMES YOU, FOR OUT O' QUESTION, YOU WERE BORN IN A MERRY HOUR.
NO, SURE, MY LORD, MY MOTHER CRIED. BUT THEN THERE WAS A STAR DANCED...
AND UNDER THAT WAS I BORN.

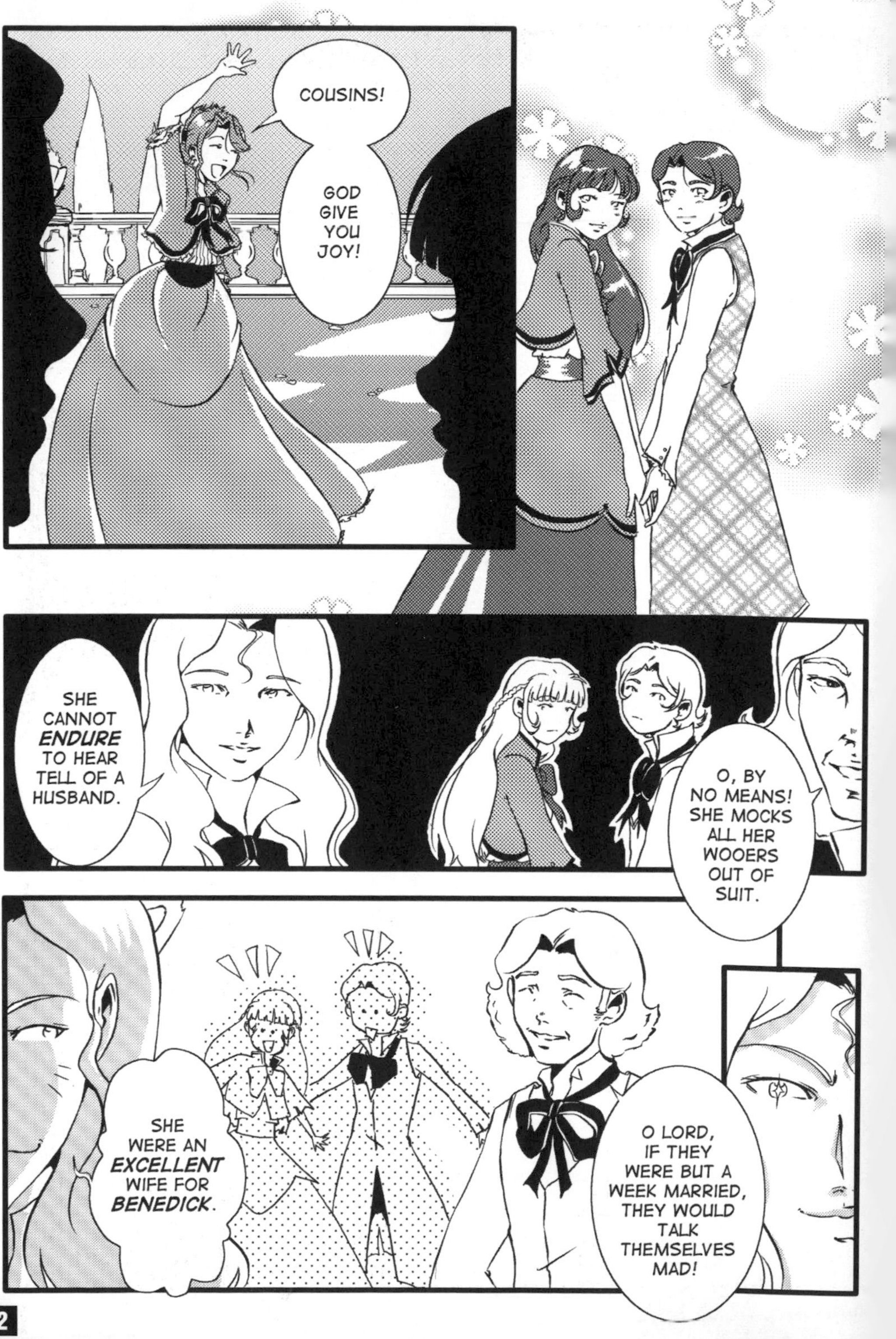
COUSINS!
GOD GIVE YOU JOY!
SHE CANNOT ENDURE TO HEAR TELL OF A HUSBAND.
O, BY NO MEANS! SHE MOCKS ALL HER WOOERS OUT OF SUIT.
SHE WERE AN EXCELLENT WIFE FOR BENEDICK.
O LORD, IF THEY WERE BUT A WEEK MARRIED, THEY WOULD TALK THEMSELVES MAD!

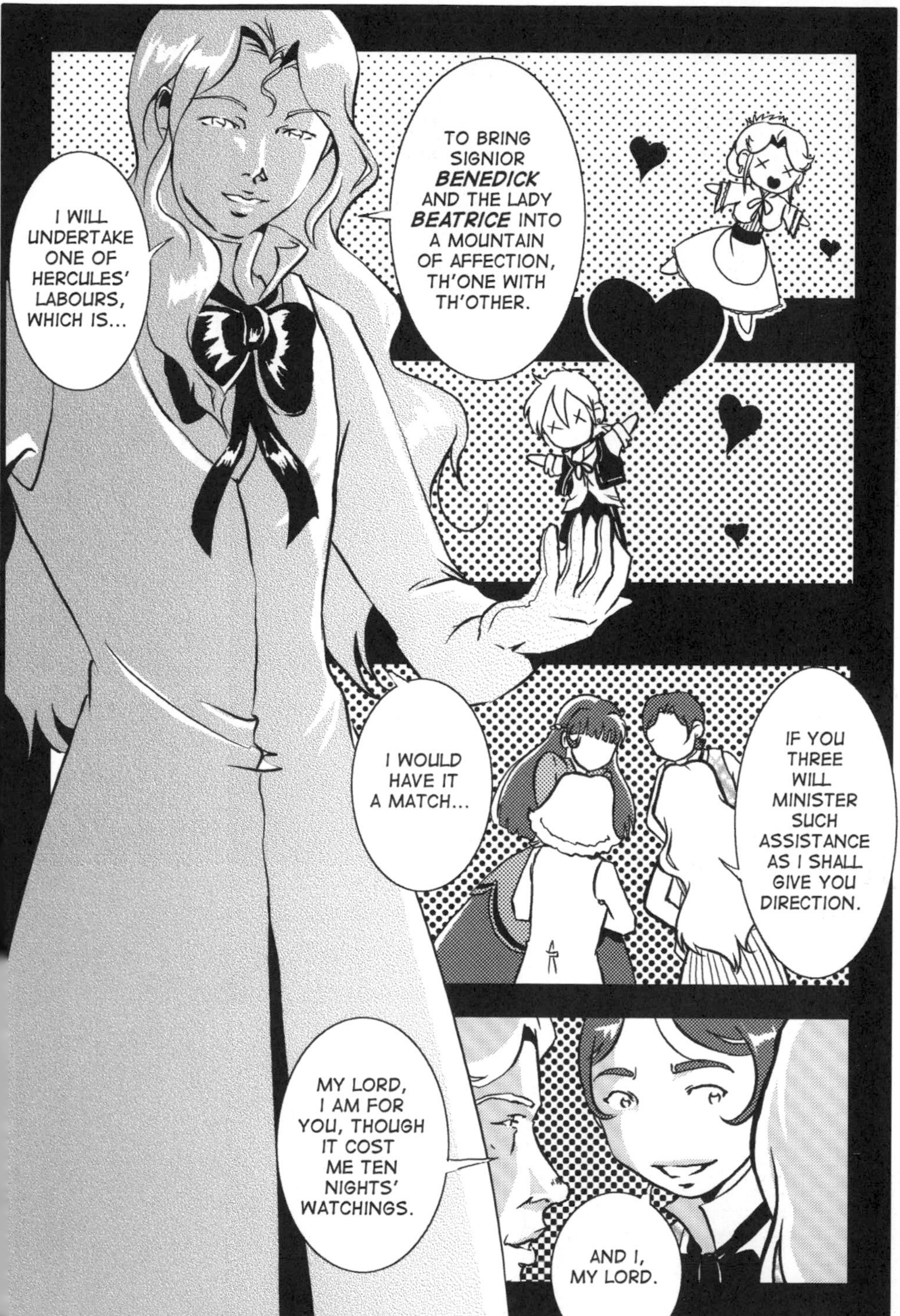
I WILL UNDERTAKE ONE OF HERCULES' LABOURS, WHICH IS...
TO BRING SIGNIOR **BENEDICK** AND THE LADY **BEATRICE** INTO A MOUNTAIN OF AFFECTION, TH'ONE WITH TH'OTHER.
I WOULD HAVE IT A MATCH...
IF YOU THREE WILL MINISTER SUCH ASSISTANCE AS I SHALL GIVE YOU DIRECTION.
MY LORD, I AM FOR YOU, THOUGH IT COST ME TEN NIGHTS' WATCHINGS.
AND I, MY LORD.

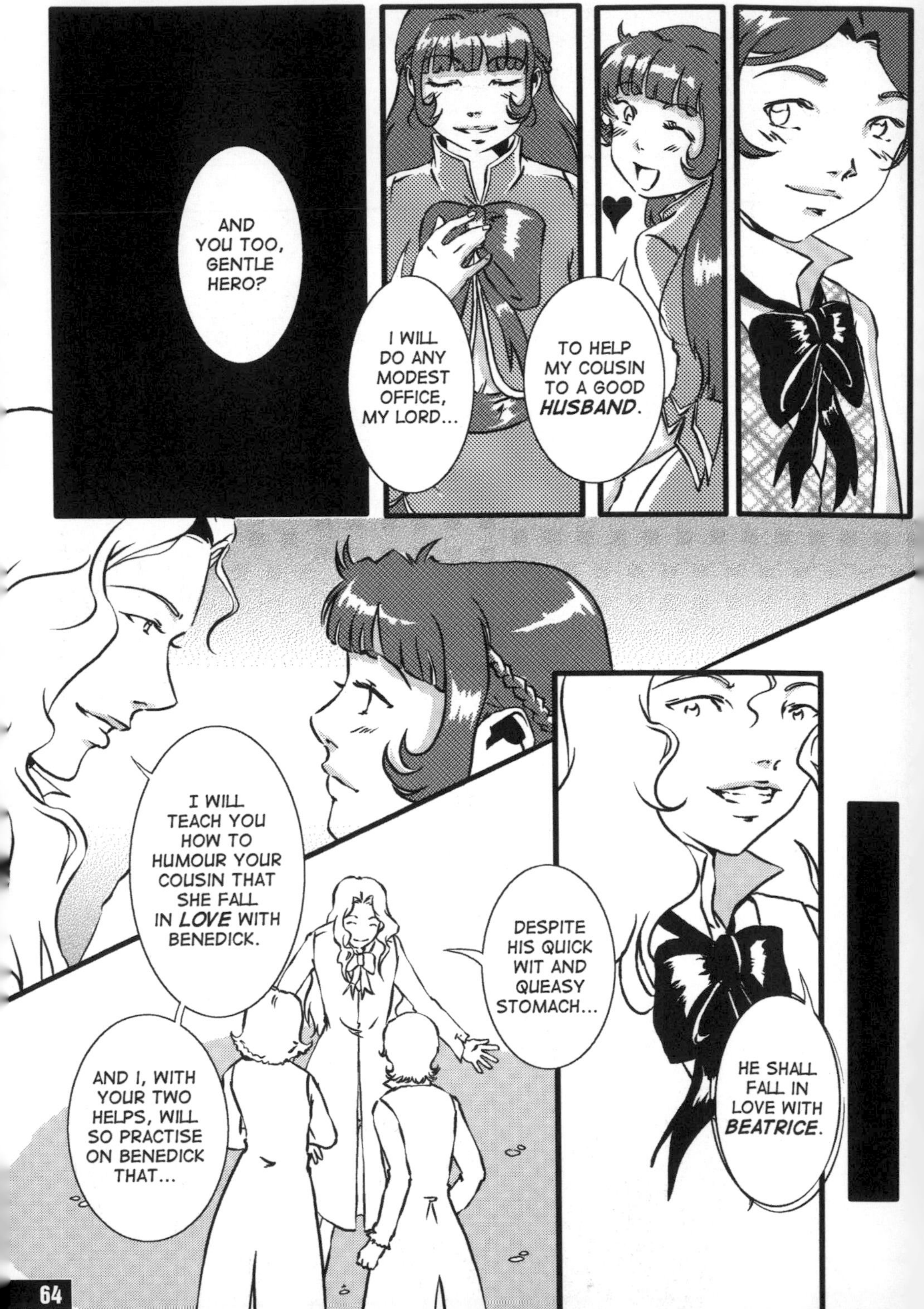
AND YOU TOO, GENTLE HERO?
I WILL DO ANY MODEST OFFICE, MY LORD...
TO HELP MY COUSIN TO A GOOD *HUSBAND*.
I WILL TEACH YOU HOW TO HUMOUR YOUR COUSIN THAT SHE FALL IN *LOVE* WITH BENEDICK.
AND I, WITH YOUR TWO HELPS, WILL SO PRACTISE ON BENEDICK THAT...
DESPITE HIS QUICK WIT AND QUEASY STOMACH...
HE SHALL FALL IN LOVE WITH *BEATRICE*.

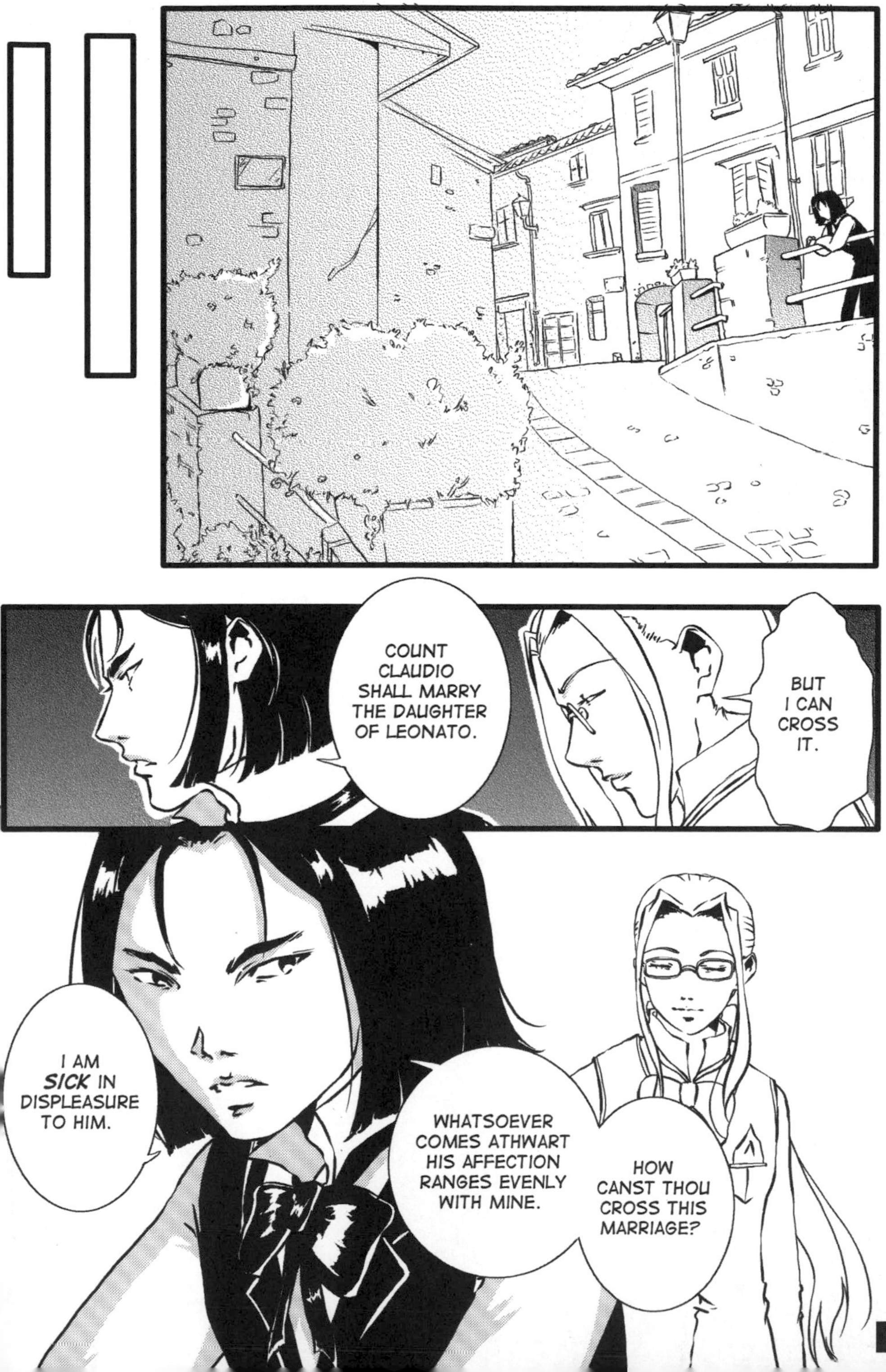
COUNT CLAUDIO SHALL MARRY THE DAUGHTER OF LEONATO.
BUT I CAN CROSS IT.
I AM *SICK* IN DISPLEASURE TO HIM.
WHATSOEVER COMES ATHWART HIS AFFECTION RANGES EVENLY WITH MINE.
HOW CANST THOU CROSS THIS MARRIAGE?

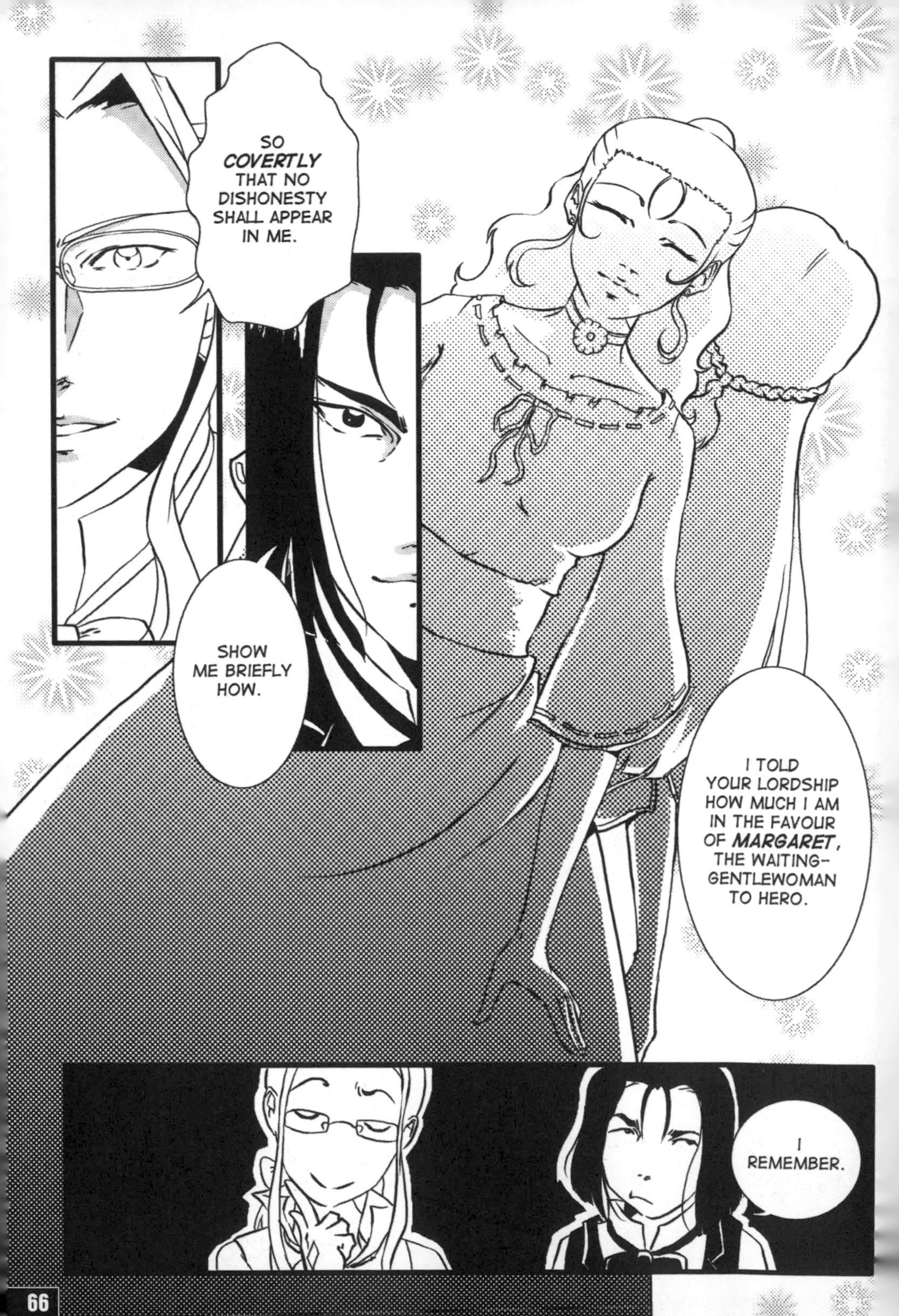
SO *COVERTLY* THAT NO DISHONESTY SHALL APPEAR IN ME.
SHOW ME BRIEFLY HOW.
I TOLD YOUR LORDSHIP HOW MUCH I AM IN THE FAVOUR OF *MARGARET*, THE WAITING-GENTLEWOMAN TO HERO.
I REMEMBER.

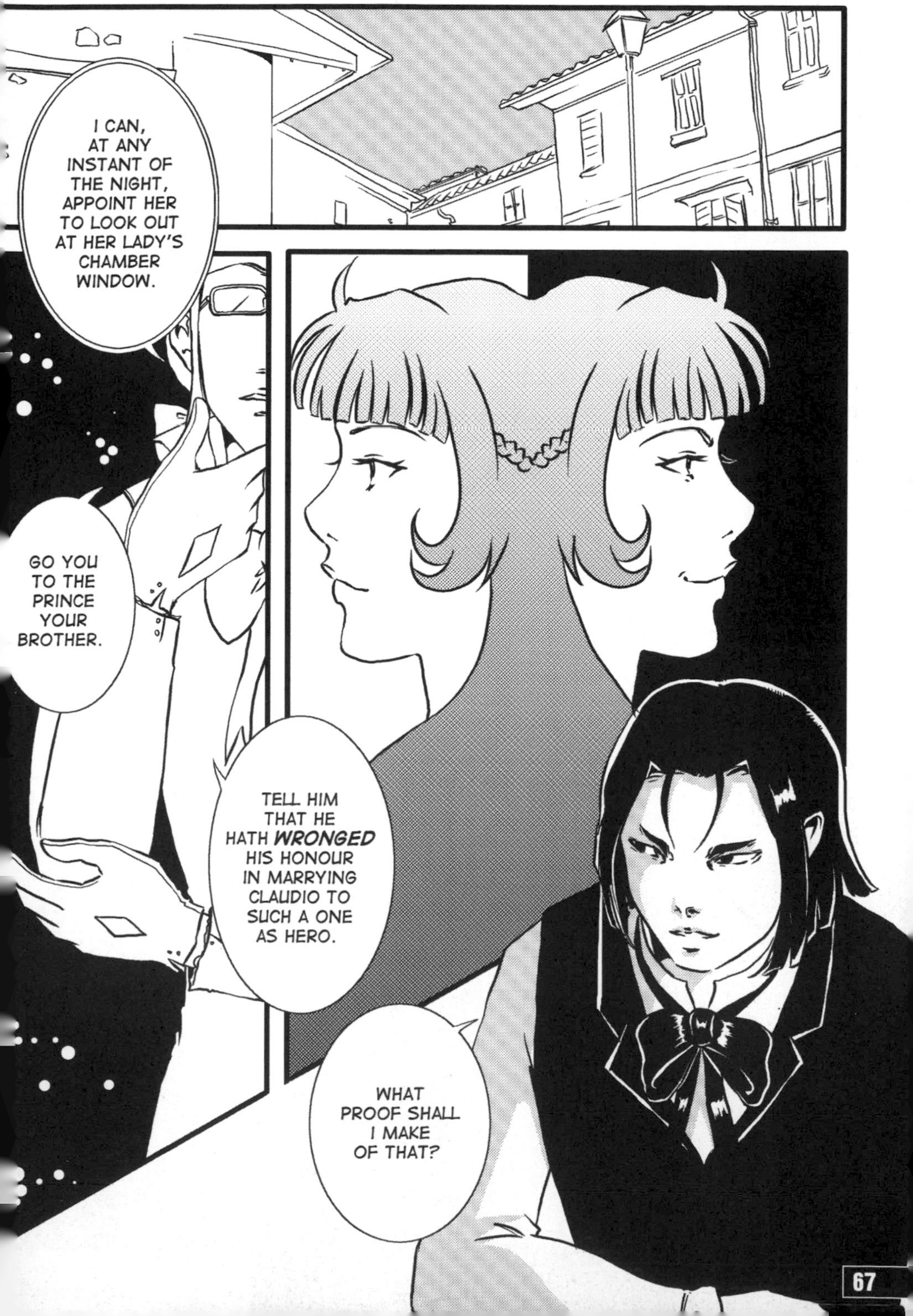
I CAN, AT ANY INSTANT OF THE NIGHT, APPOINT HER TO LOOK OUT AT HER LADY'S CHAMBER WINDOW.
GO YOU TO THE PRINCE YOUR BROTHER.
TELL HIM THAT HE HATH ***WRONGED*** HIS HONOUR IN MARRYING CLAUDIO TO SUCH A ONE AS HERO.
WHAT PROOF SHALL I MAKE OF THAT?

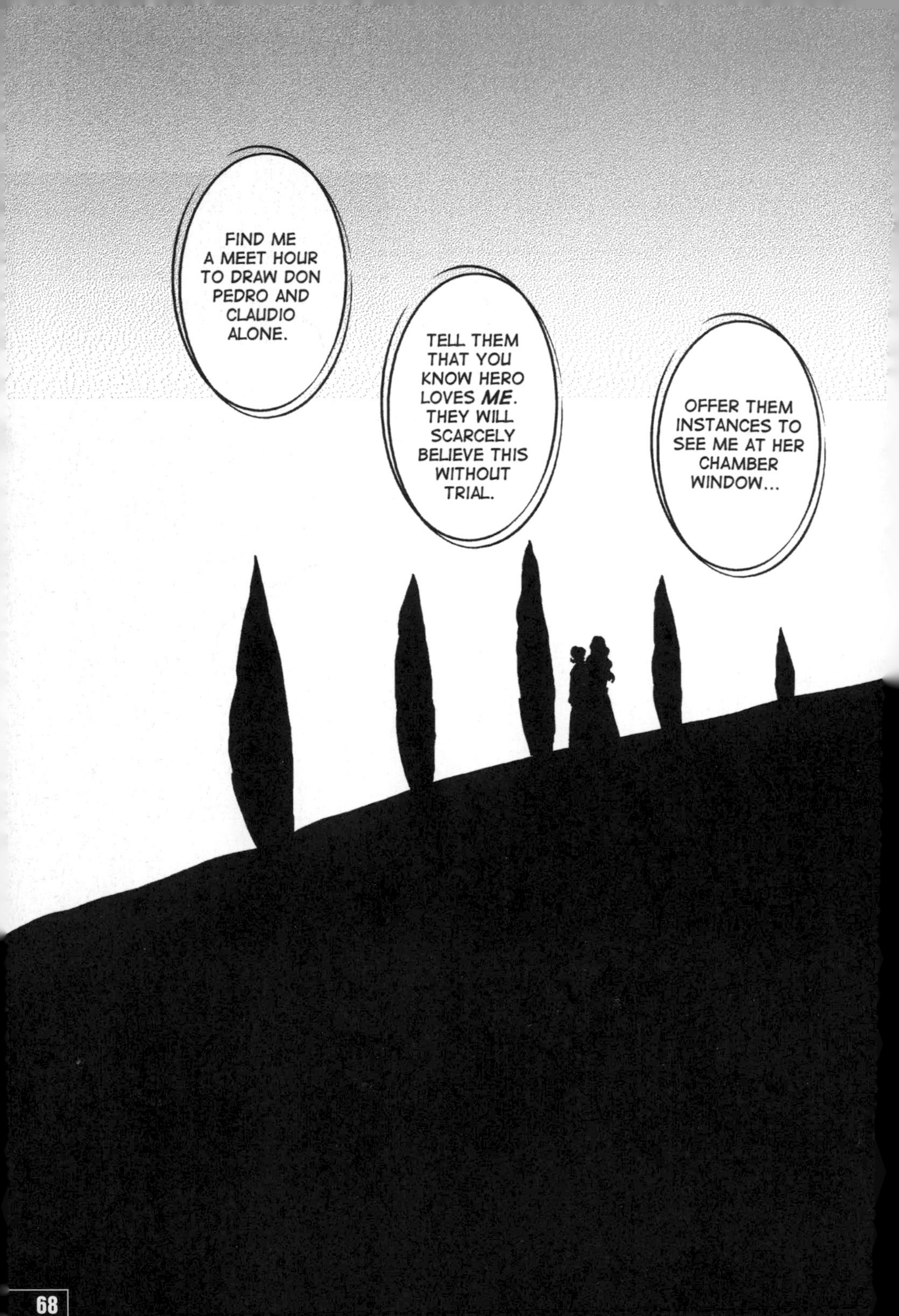
FIND ME A MEET HOUR TO DRAW DON PEDRO AND CLAUDIO ALONE.
TELL THEM THAT YOU KNOW HERO LOVES ME. THEY WILL SCARCELY BELIEVE THIS WITHOUT TRIAL.
OFFER THEM INSTANCES TO SEE ME AT HER CHAMBER WINDOW...

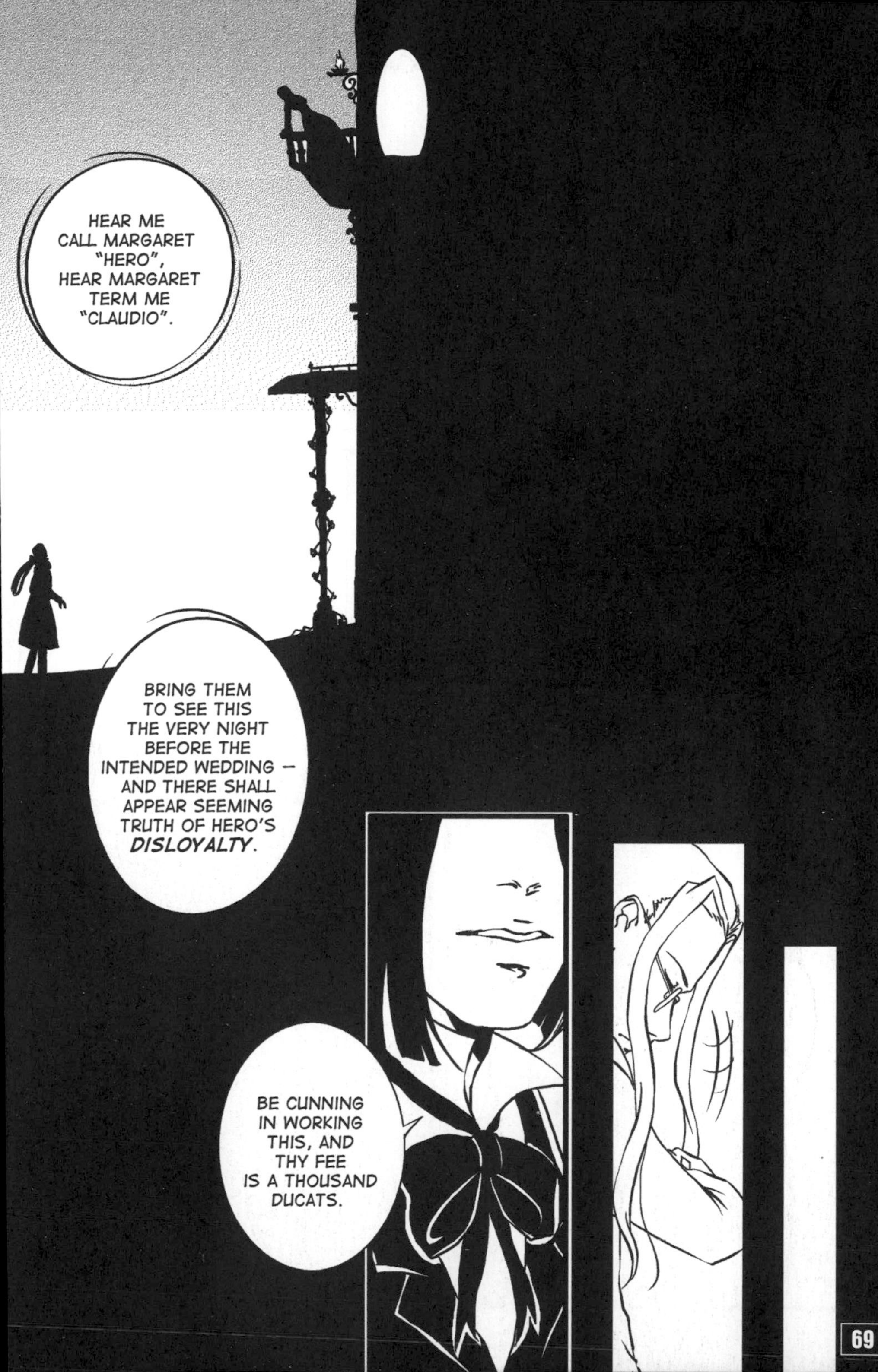
HEAR ME CALL MARGARET "HERO", HEAR MARGARET TERM ME "CLAUDIO".
BRING THEM TO SEE THIS THE VERY NIGHT BEFORE THE INTENDED WEDDING — AND THERE SHALL APPEAR SEEMING TRUTH OF HERO'S DISLOYALTY.
BE CUNNING IN WORKING THIS, AND THY FEE IS A THOUSAND DUCATS.

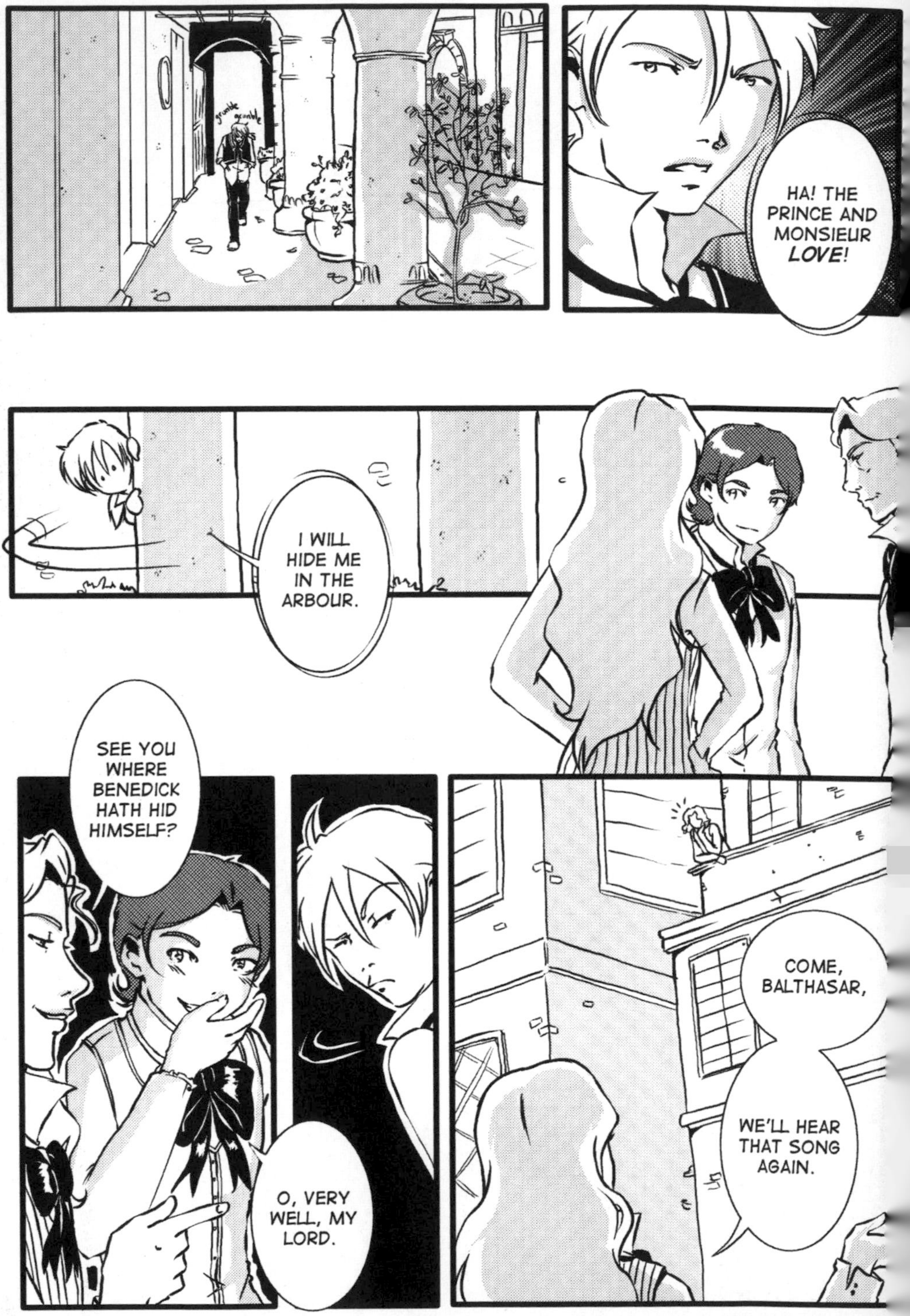
grumble grumble
HA! THE PRINCE AND MONSIEUR *LOVE*!
I WILL HIDE ME IN THE ARBOUR.
SEE YOU WHERE BENEDICK HATH HID HIMSELF?
O, VERY WELL, MY LORD.
COME, BALTHASAR,
WE'LL HEAR THAT SONG AGAIN.

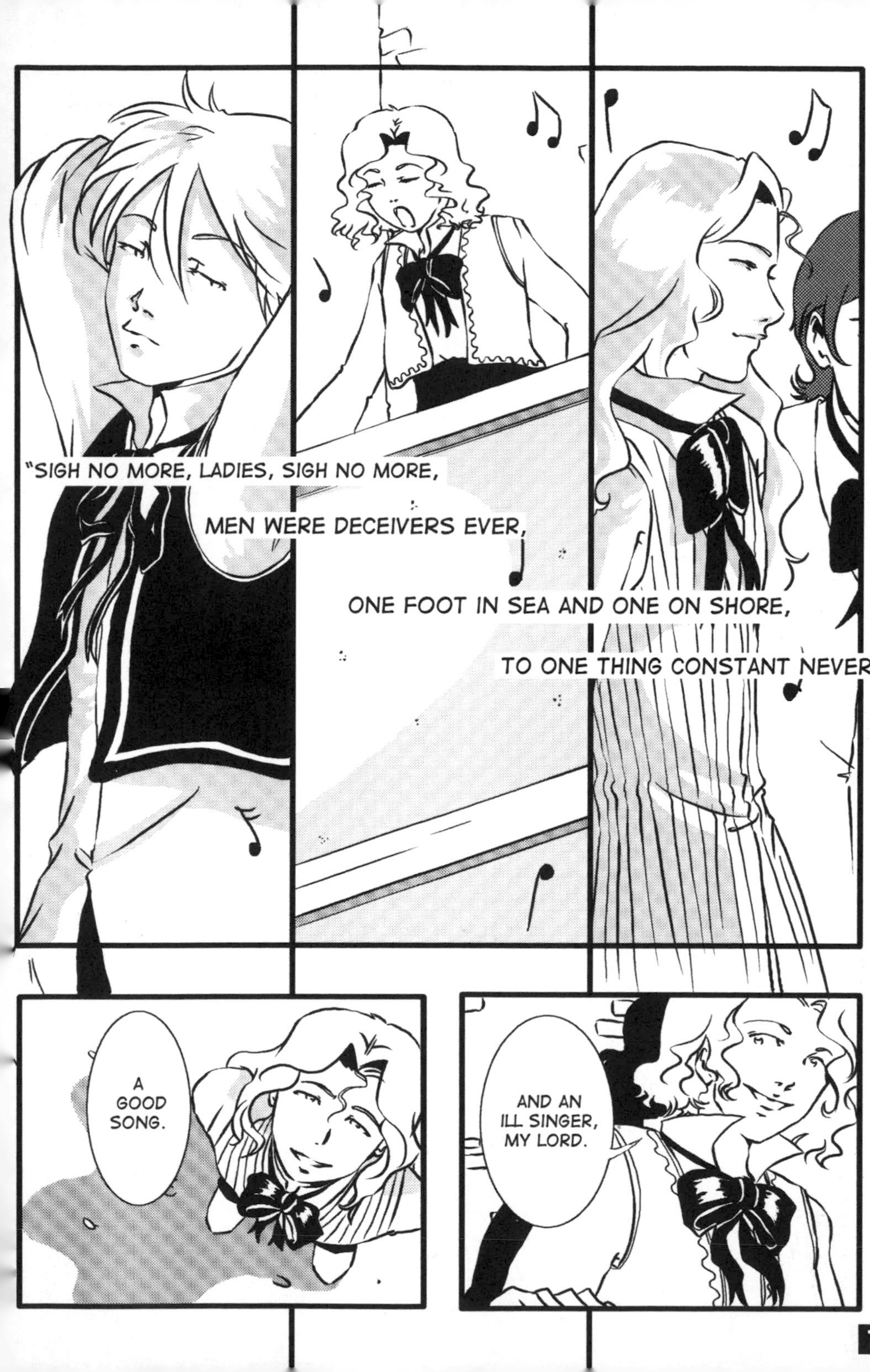
"SIGH NO MORE, LADIES, SIGH NO MORE,
MEN WERE DECEIVERS EVER,
ONE FOOT IN SEA AND ONE ON SHORE,
TO ONE THING CONSTANT NEVER."
A GOOD SONG.
AND AN ILL SINGER, MY LORD.

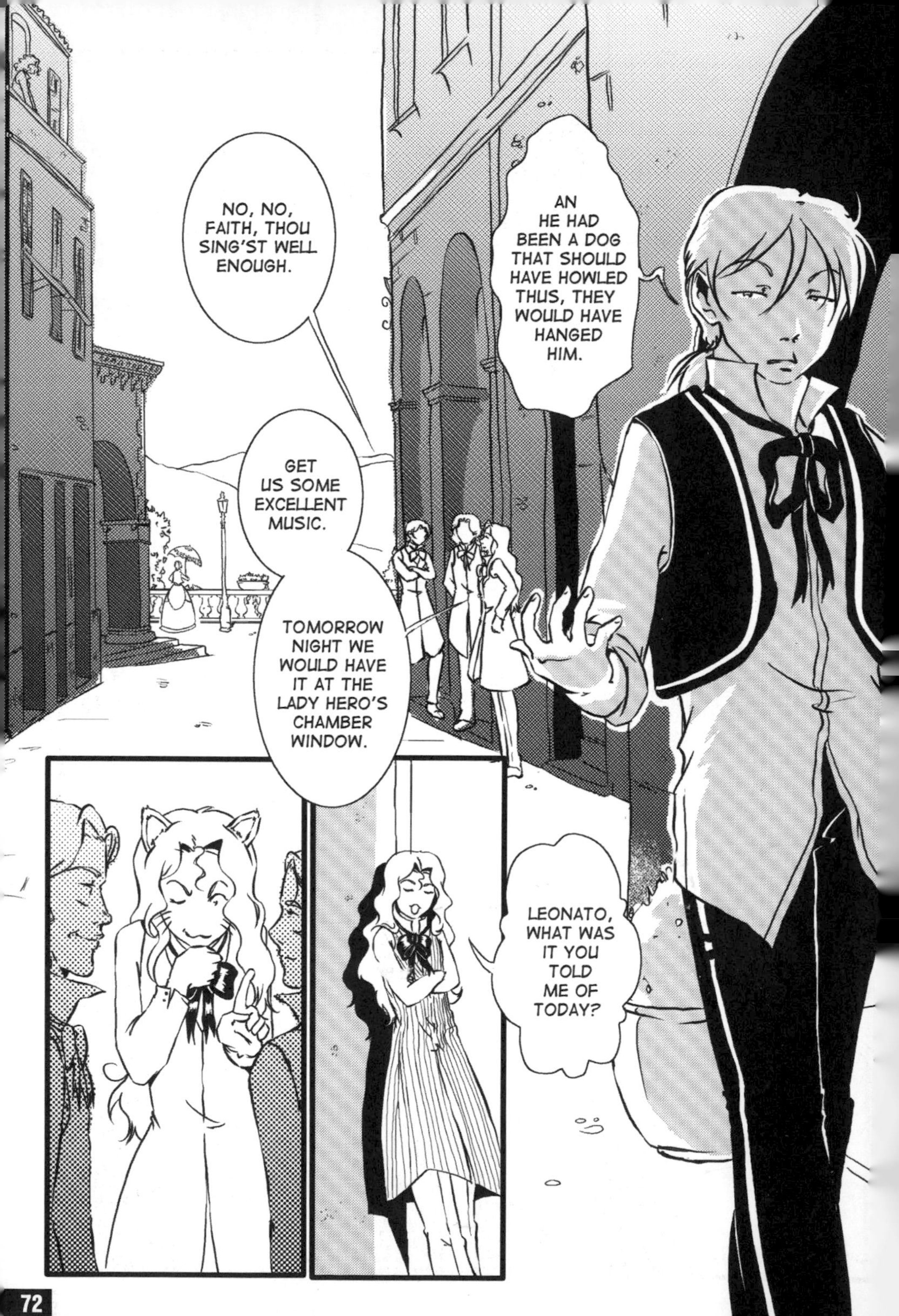
NO, NO, FAITH, THOU SING'ST WELL ENOUGH.
AN HE HAD BEEN A DOG THAT SHOULD HAVE HOWLED THUS, THEY WOULD HAVE HANGED HIM.
GET US SOME EXCELLENT MUSIC.
TOMORROW NIGHT WE WOULD HAVE IT AT THE LADY HERO'S CHAMBER WINDOW.
LEONATO, WHAT WAS IT YOU TOLD ME OF TODAY?

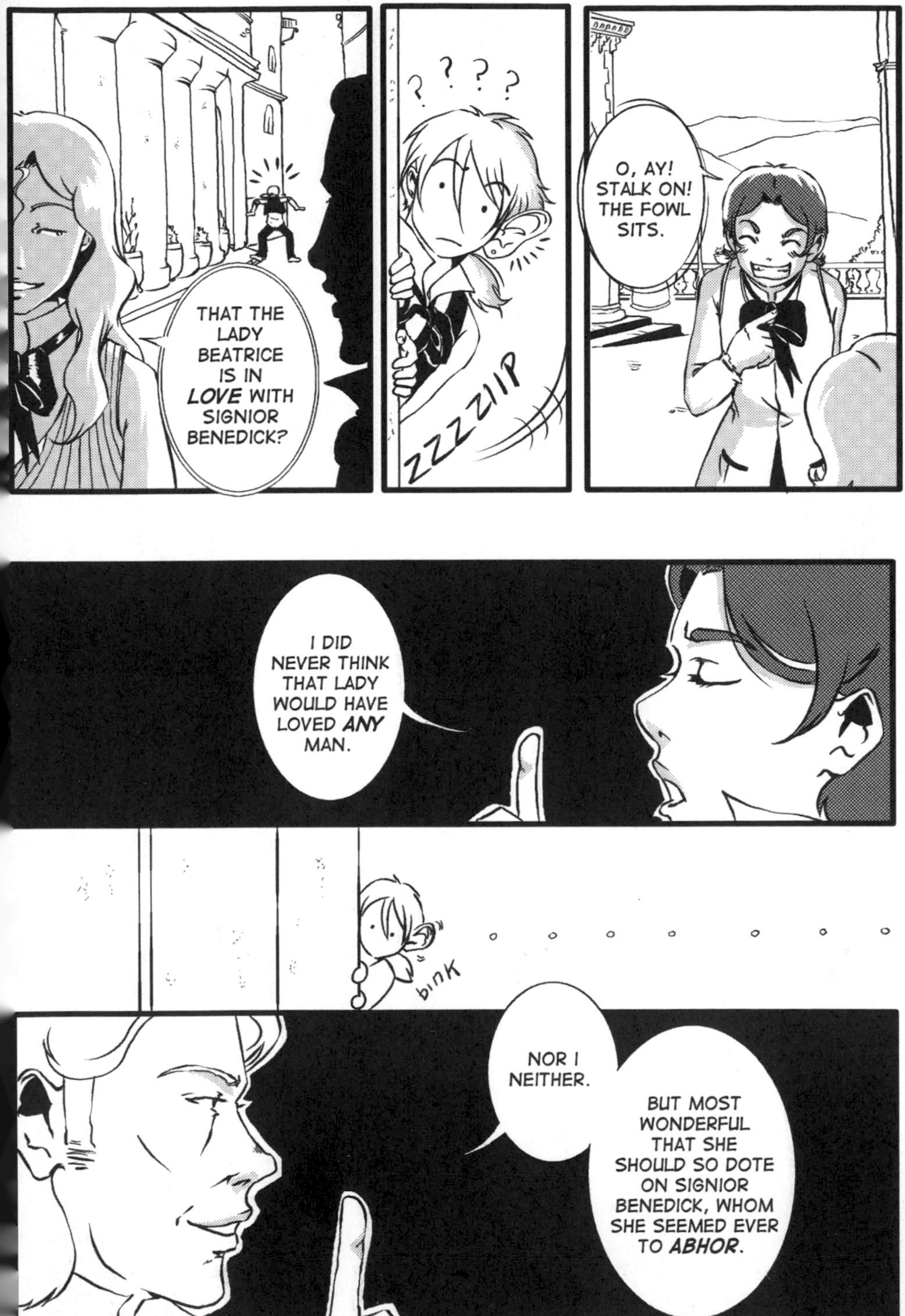
THAT THE LADY BEATRICE IS IN ***LOVE*** WITH SIGNIOR BENEDICK?
? ? ? ?
ZZZZZIIP
O, AY! STALK ON! THE FOWL SITS.
I DID NEVER THINK THAT LADY WOULD HAVE LOVED ***ANY*** MAN.
bink
NOR I NEITHER.
BUT MOST WONDERFUL THAT SHE SHOULD SO DOTE ON SIGNIOR BENEDICK, WHOM SHE SEEMED EVER TO ***ABHOR***.

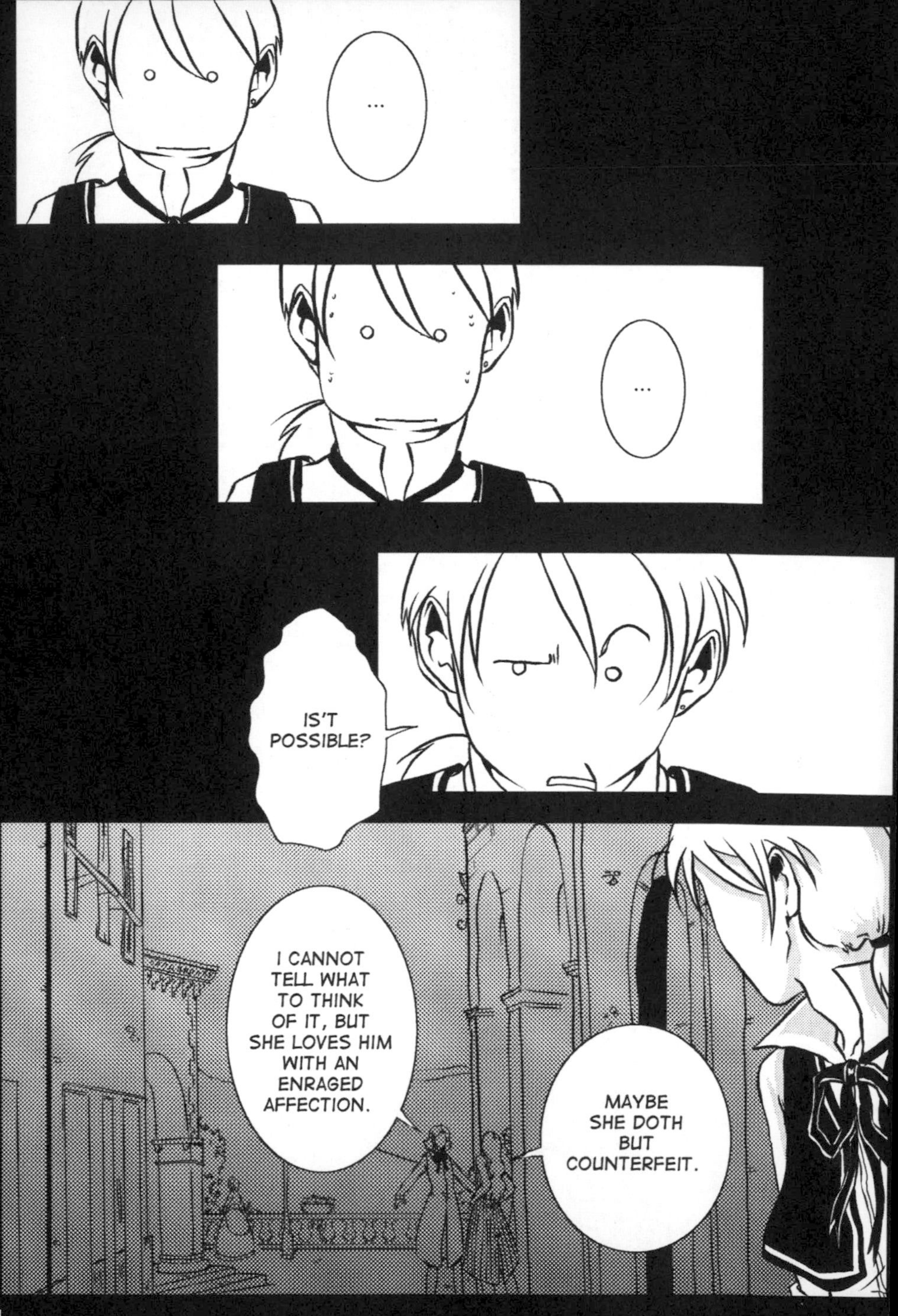
...
...
IS'T POSSIBLE?
I CANNOT TELL WHAT TO THINK OF IT, BUT SHE LOVES HIM WITH AN ENRAGED AFFECTION.
MAYBE SHE DOTH BUT COUNTERFEIT.

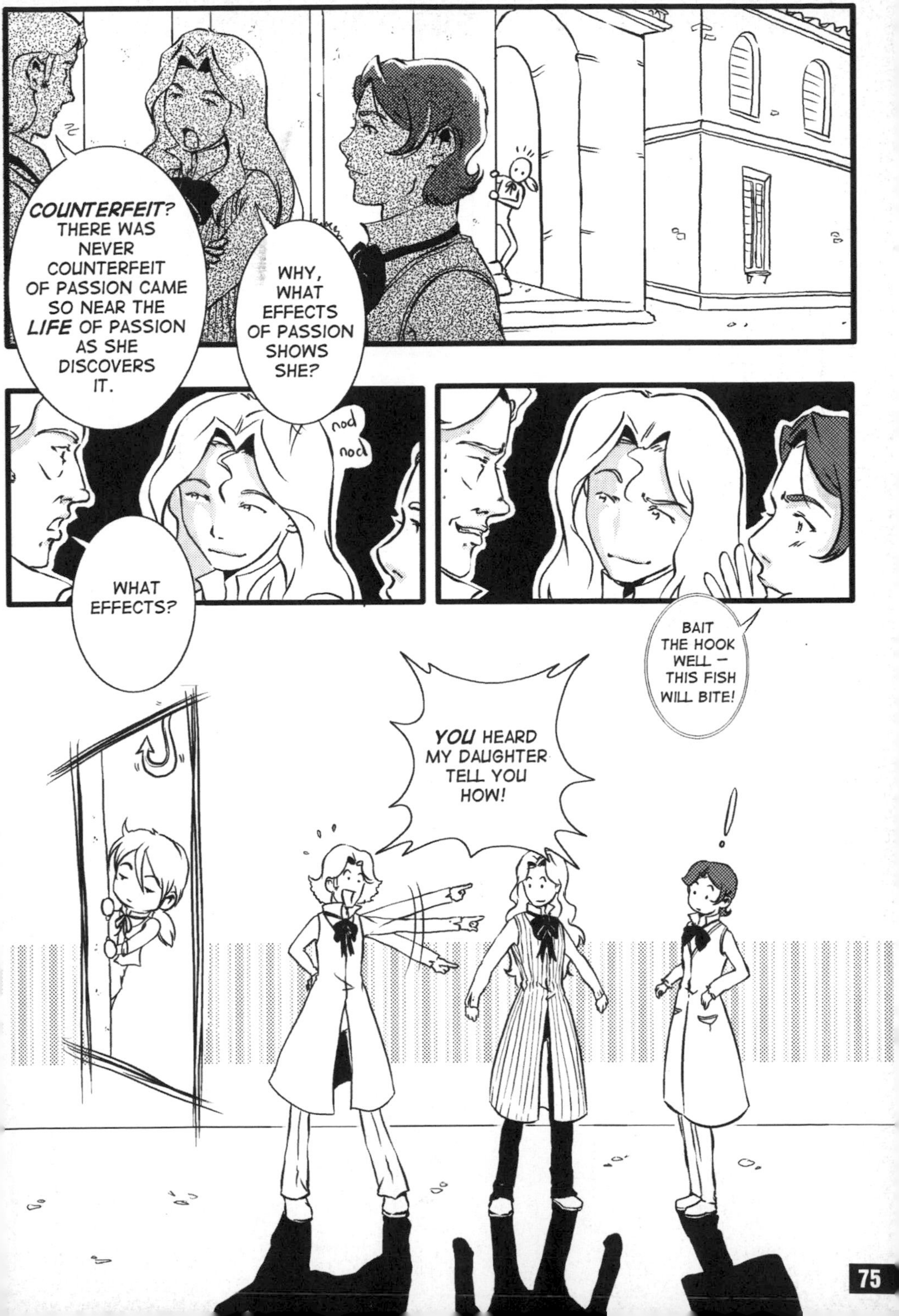
COUNTERFEIT? THERE WAS NEVER COUNTERFEIT OF PASSION CAME SO NEAR THE LIFE OF PASSION AS SHE DISCOVERS IT.
WHY, WHAT EFFECTS OF PASSION SHOWS SHE?
nod nod
WHAT EFFECTS?
BAIT THE HOOK WELL — THIS FISH WILL BITE!
YOU HEARD MY DAUGHTER TELL YOU HOW!
!

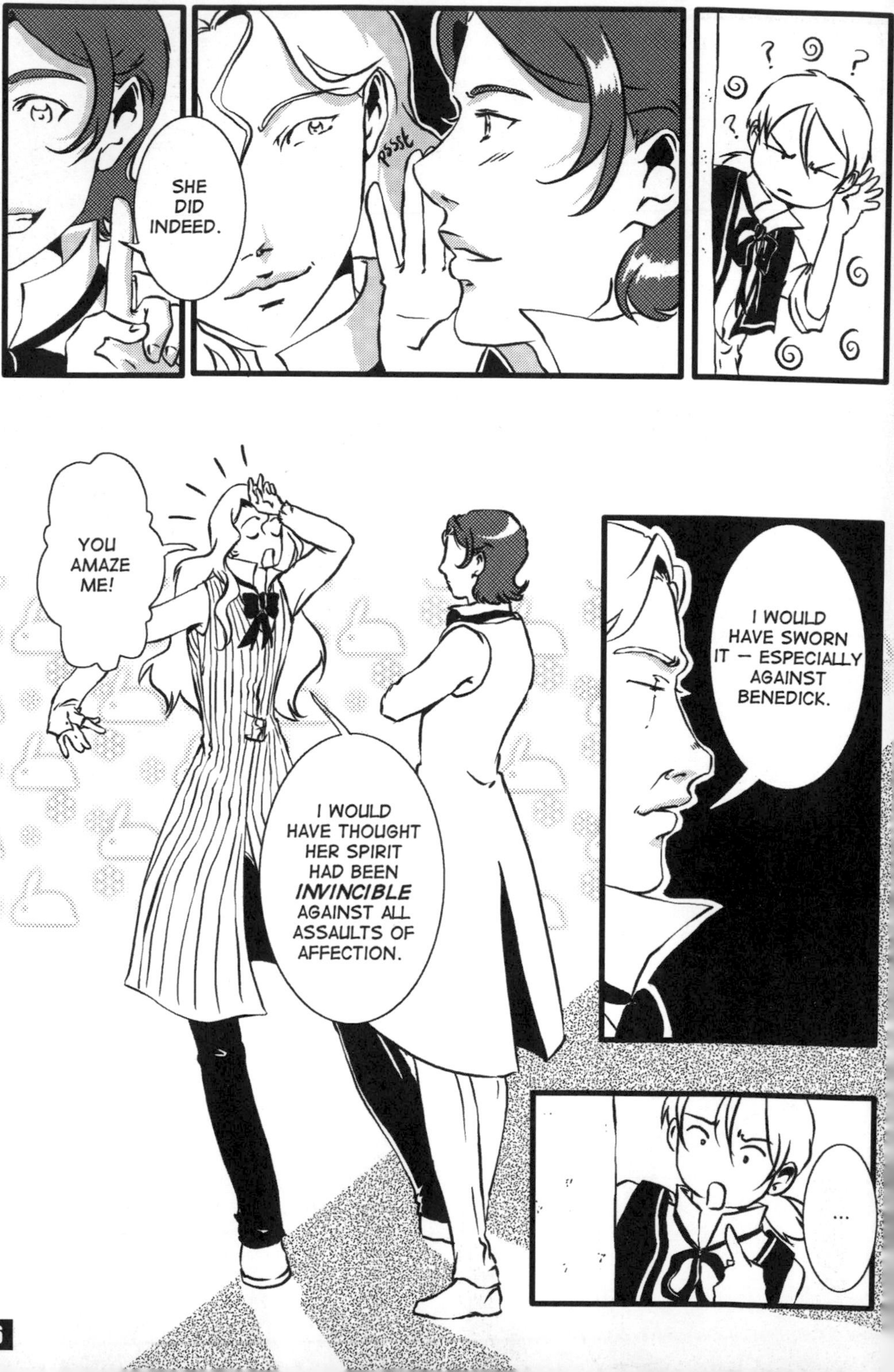
SHE DID INDEED.
pssst
YOU AMAZE ME!
I WOULD HAVE THOUGHT HER SPIRIT HAD BEEN *INVINCIBLE* AGAINST ALL ASSAULTS OF AFFECTION.
I WOULD HAVE SWORN IT — ESPECIALLY AGAINST BENEDICK.
...

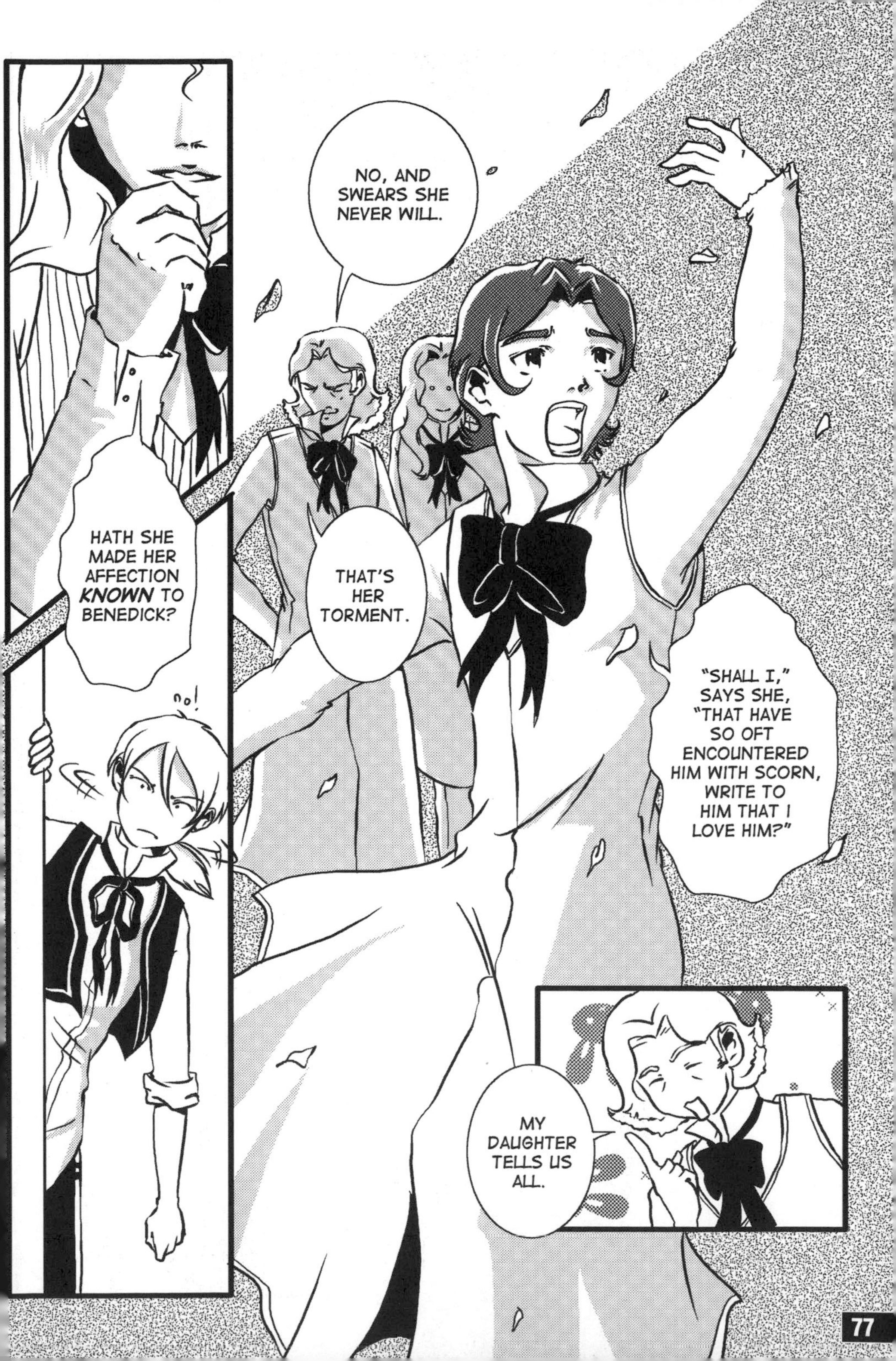
HATH SHE MADE HER AFFECTION *KNOWN* TO BENEDICK?
no!
NO, AND SWEARS SHE NEVER WILL.
THAT'S HER TORMENT.
"SHALL I," SAYS SHE, "THAT HAVE SO OFT ENCOUNTERED HIM WITH SCORN, WRITE TO HIM THAT I LOVE HIM?"
MY DAUGHTER TELLS US ALL.

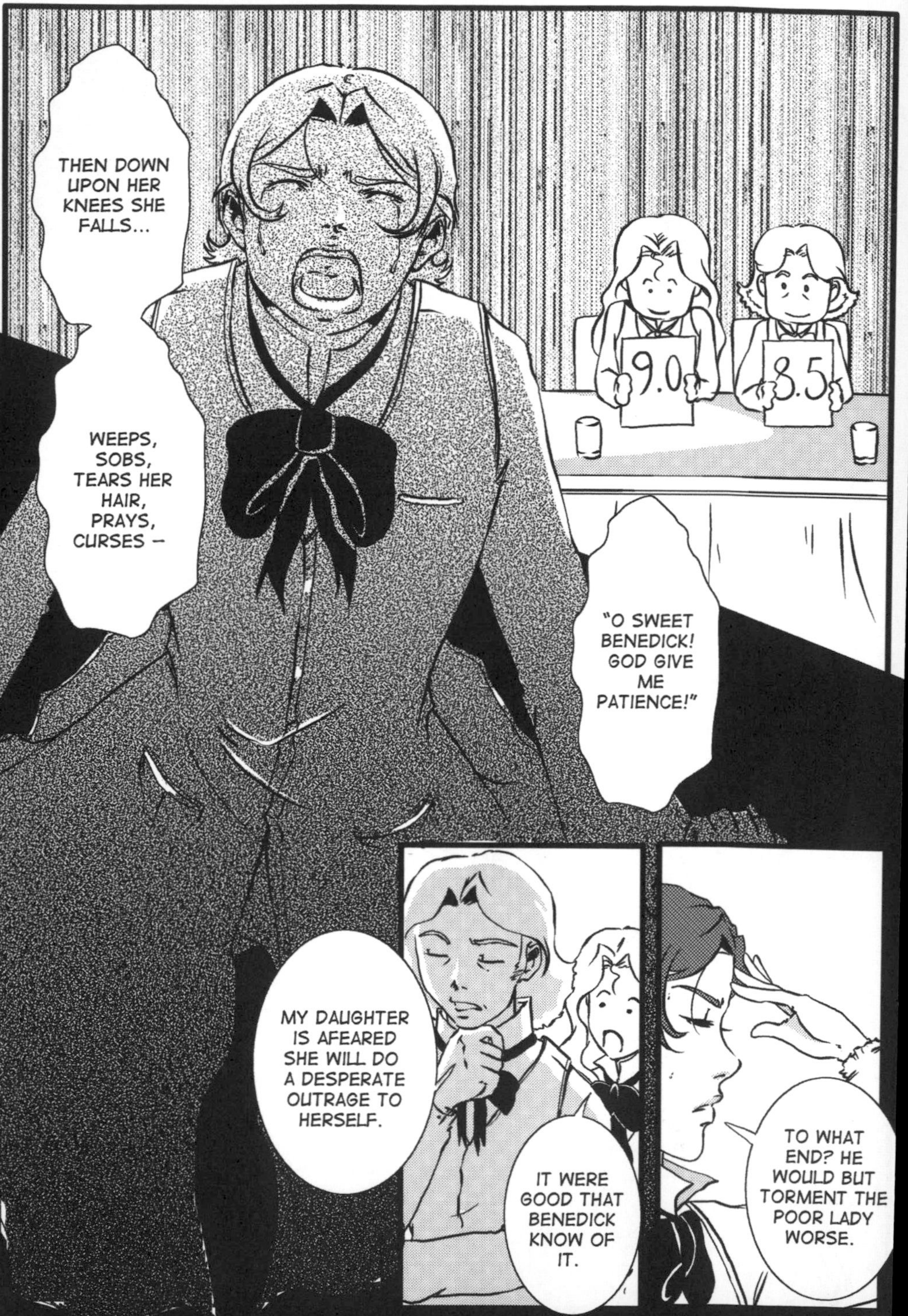
THEN DOWN UPON HER KNEES SHE FALLS...
WEEPS, SOBS, TEARS HER HAIR, PRAYS, CURSES –
9.0
8.5
"O SWEET BENEDICK! GOD GIVE ME PATIENCE!"
MY DAUGHTER IS AFEARED SHE WILL DO A DESPERATE OUTRAGE TO HERSELF.
IT WERE GOOD THAT BENEDICK KNOW OF IT.
TO WHAT END? HE WOULD BUT TORMENT THE POOR LADY WORSE.

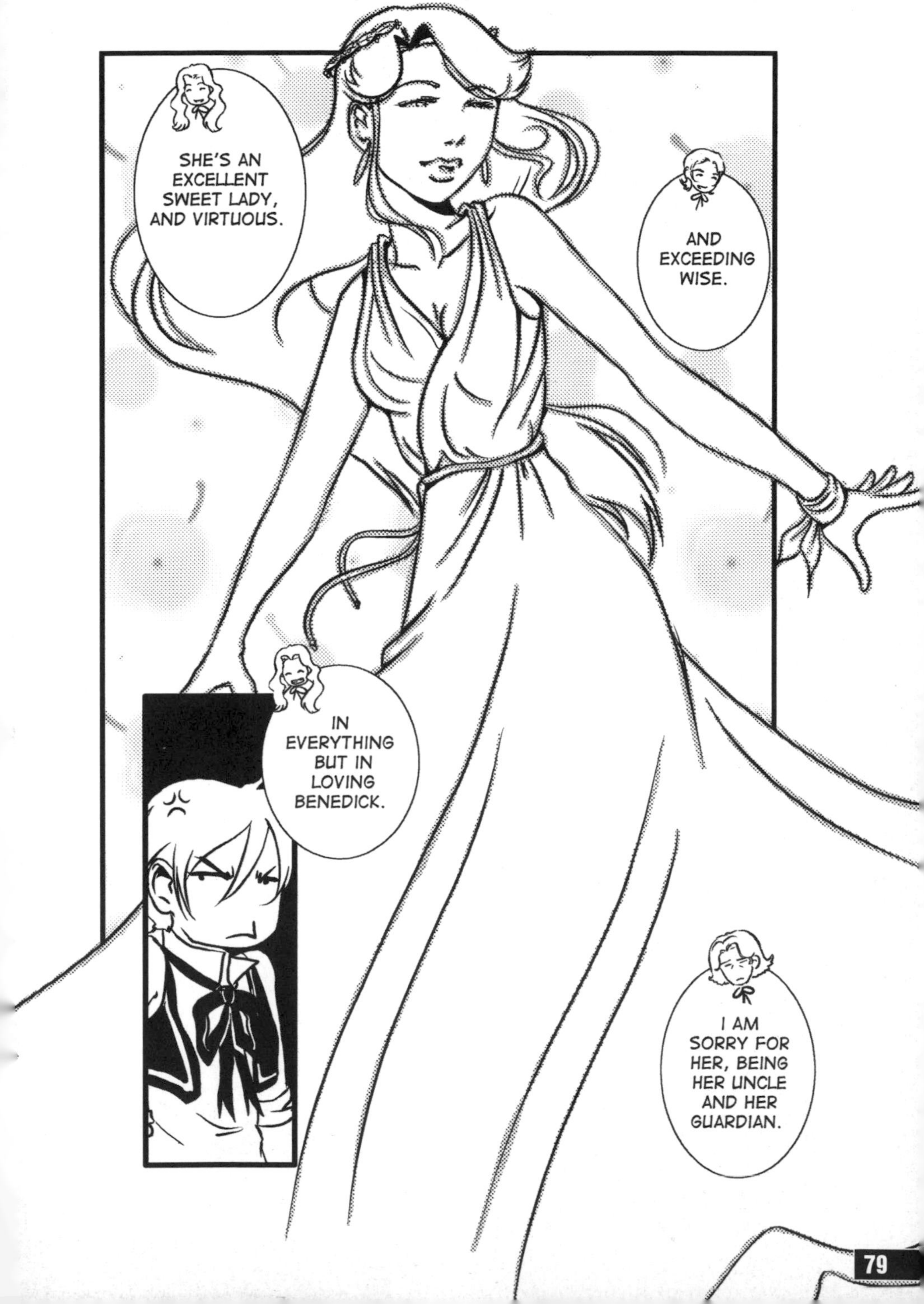
SHE'S AN EXCELLENT SWEET LADY, AND VIRTUOUS.
AND EXCEEDING WISE.
IN EVERYTHING BUT IN LOVING BENEDICK.
I AM SORRY FOR HER, BEING HER UNCLE AND HER GUARDIAN.

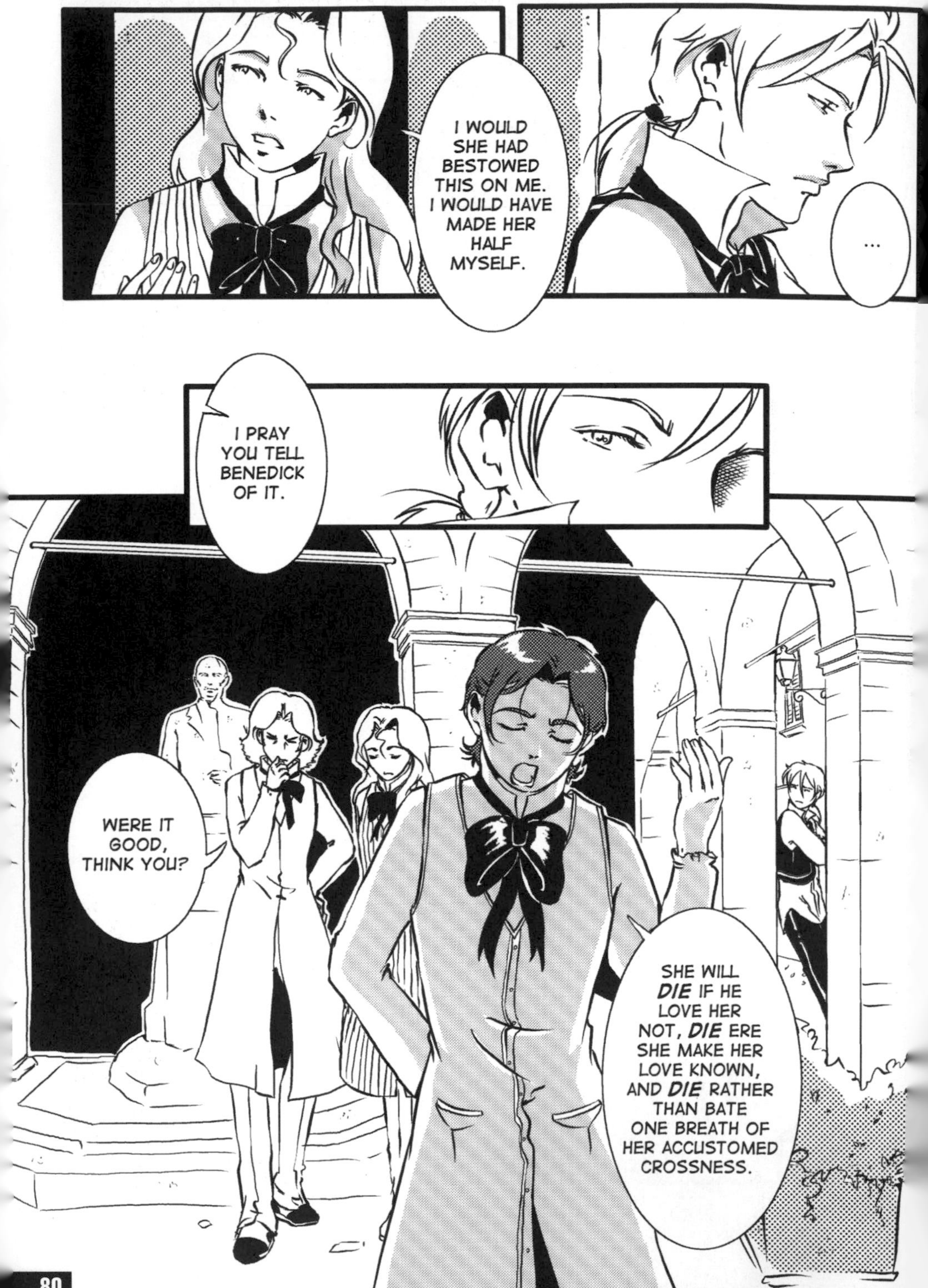
I WOULD SHE HAD BESTOWED THIS ON ME. I WOULD HAVE MADE HER HALF MYSELF.
...
I PRAY YOU TELL BENEDICK OF IT.
WERE IT GOOD, THINK YOU?
SHE WILL ***DIE*** IF HE LOVE HER NOT, ***DIE*** ERE SHE MAKE HER LOVE KNOWN, AND ***DIE*** RATHER THAN BATE ONE BREATH OF HER ACCUSTOMED CROSSNESS.

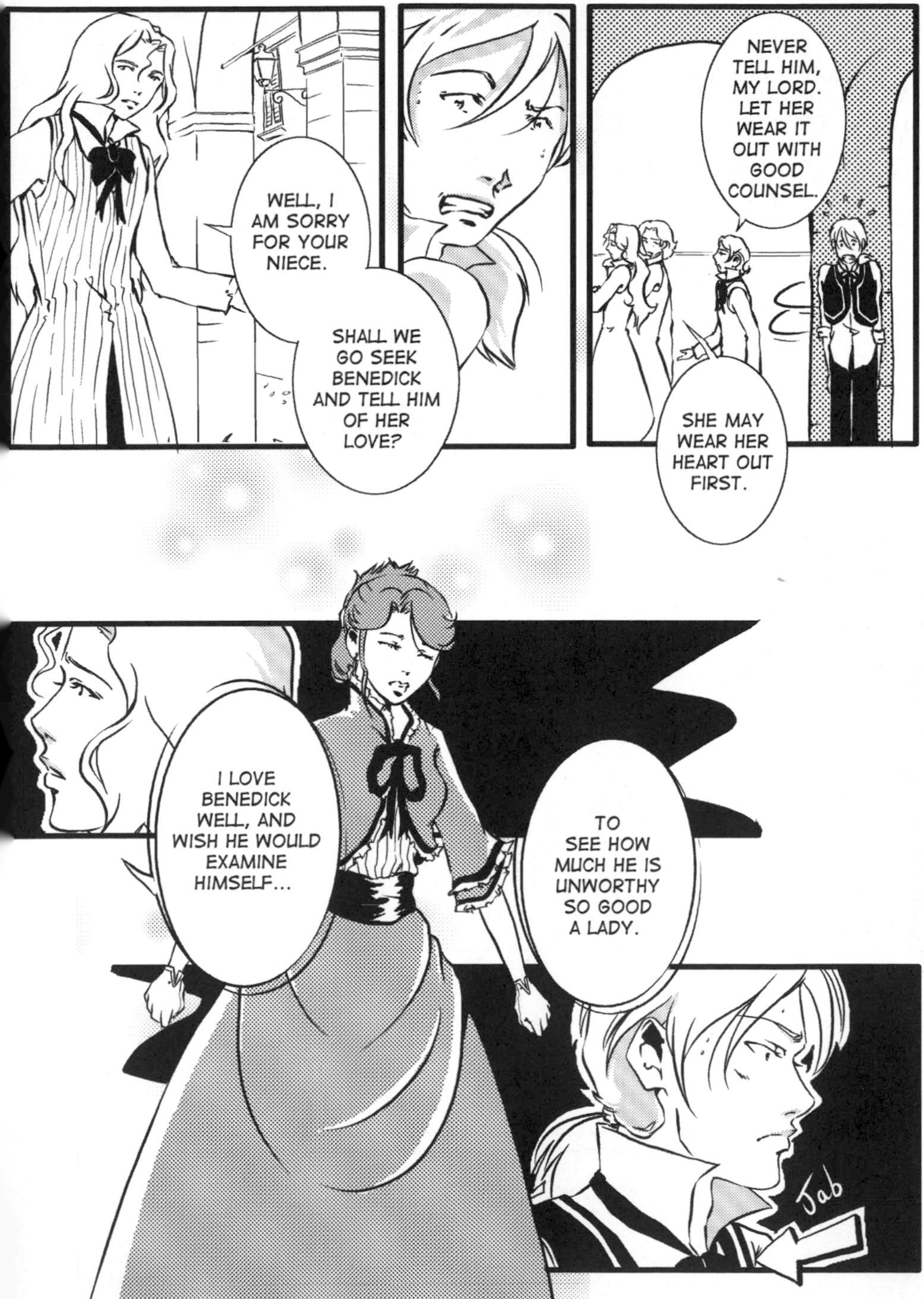
WELL, I AM SORRY FOR YOUR NIECE.
SHALL WE GO SEEK BENEDICK AND TELL HIM OF HER LOVE?
NEVER TELL HIM, MY LORD. LET HER WEAR IT OUT WITH GOOD COUNSEL.
SHE MAY WEAR HER HEART OUT FIRST.
I LOVE BENEDICK WELL, AND WISH HE WOULD EXAMINE HIMSELF...
TO SEE HOW MUCH HE IS UNWORTHY SO GOOD A LADY.
Jab

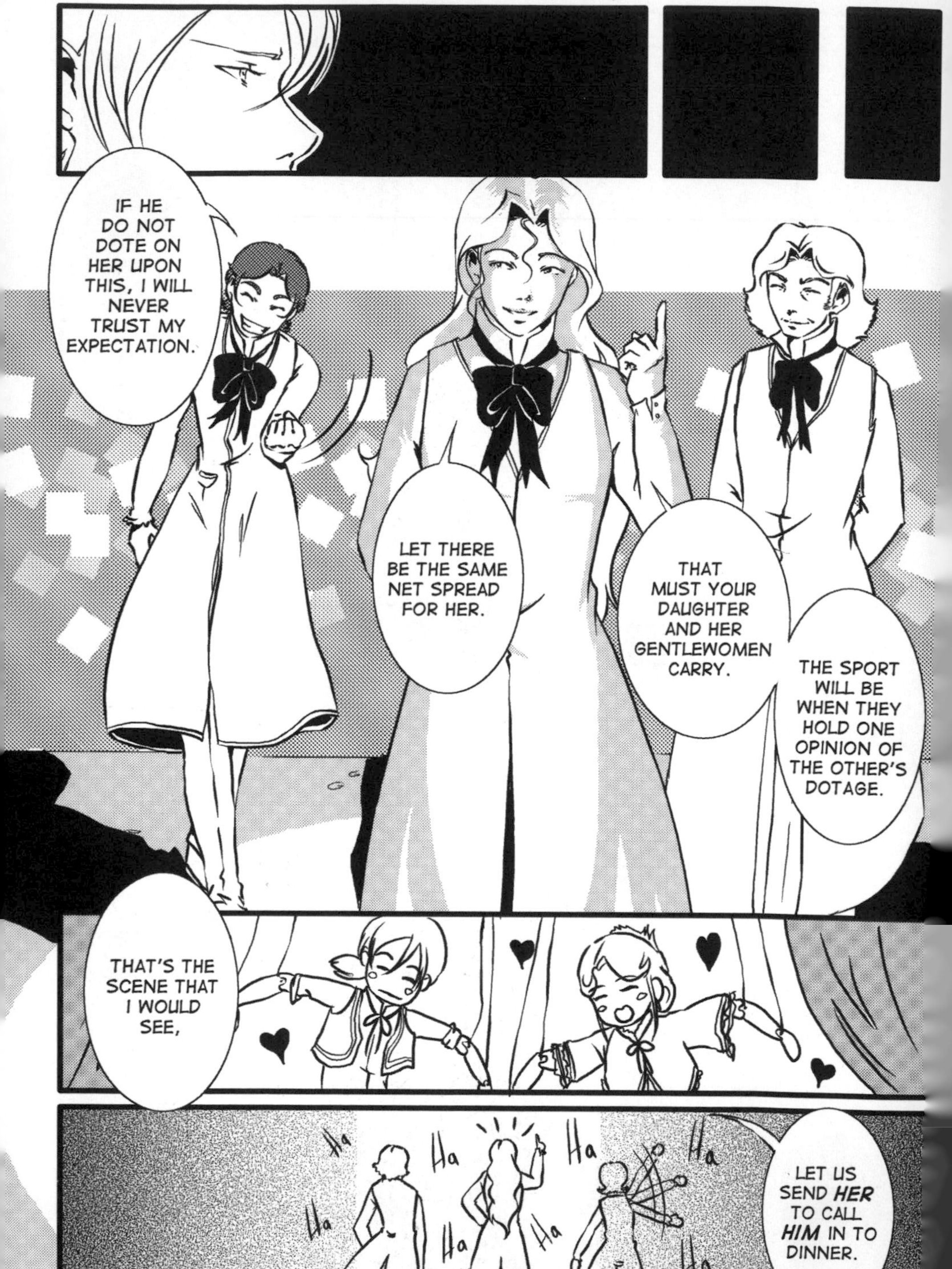

IF HE DO NOT DOTE ON HER UPON THIS, I WILL NEVER TRUST MY EXPECTATION.
LET THERE BE THE SAME NET SPREAD FOR HER.
THAT MUST YOUR DAUGHTER AND HER GENTLEWOMEN CARRY.
THE SPORT WILL BE WHEN THEY HOLD ONE OPINION OF THE OTHER'S DOTAGE.
THAT'S THE SCENE THAT I WOULD SEE,
Ha Ha Ha Ha Ha Ha Ha Ha
LET US SEND ***HER*** TO CALL ***HIM*** IN TO DINNER.

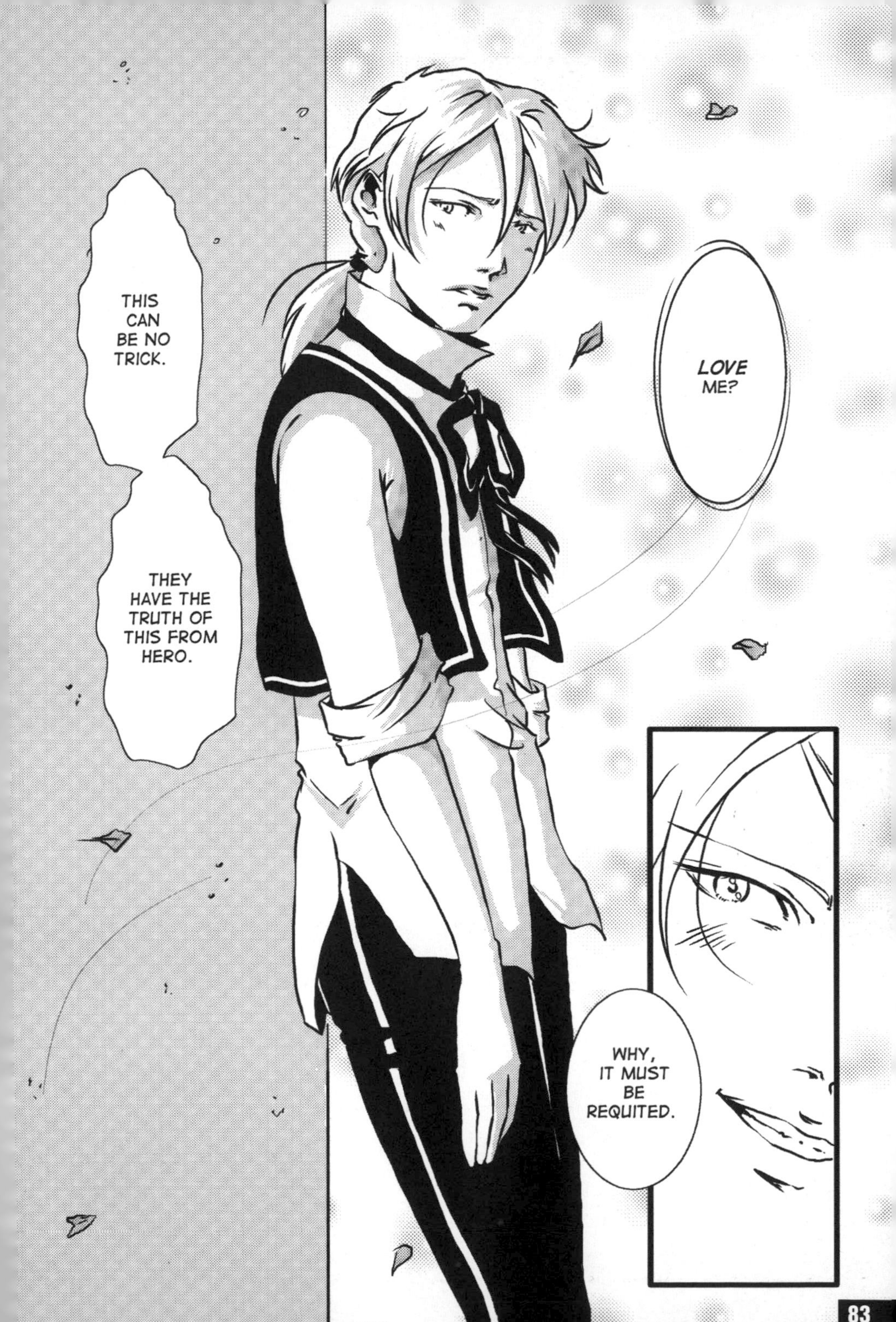
THIS CAN BE NO TRICK.
THEY HAVE THE TRUTH OF THIS FROM HERO.
*LOVE* ME?
WHY, IT MUST BE REQUITED.

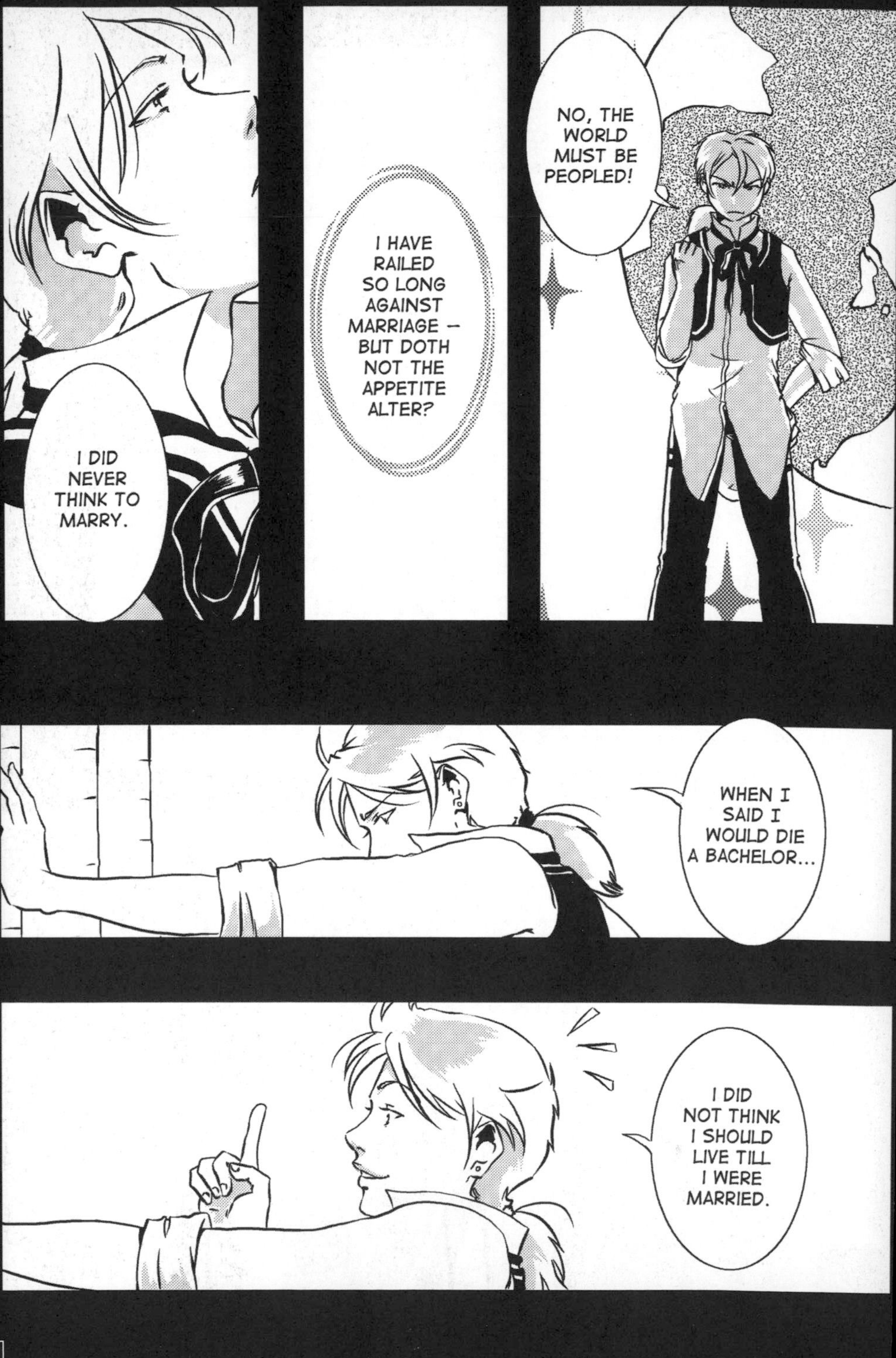
I DID NEVER THINK TO MARRY.
I HAVE RAILED SO LONG AGAINST MARRIAGE — BUT DOTH NOT THE APPETITE ALTER?
NO, THE WORLD MUST BE PEOPLED!
WHEN I SAID I WOULD DIE A BACHELOR...
I DID NOT THINK I SHOULD LIVE TILL I WERE MARRIED.

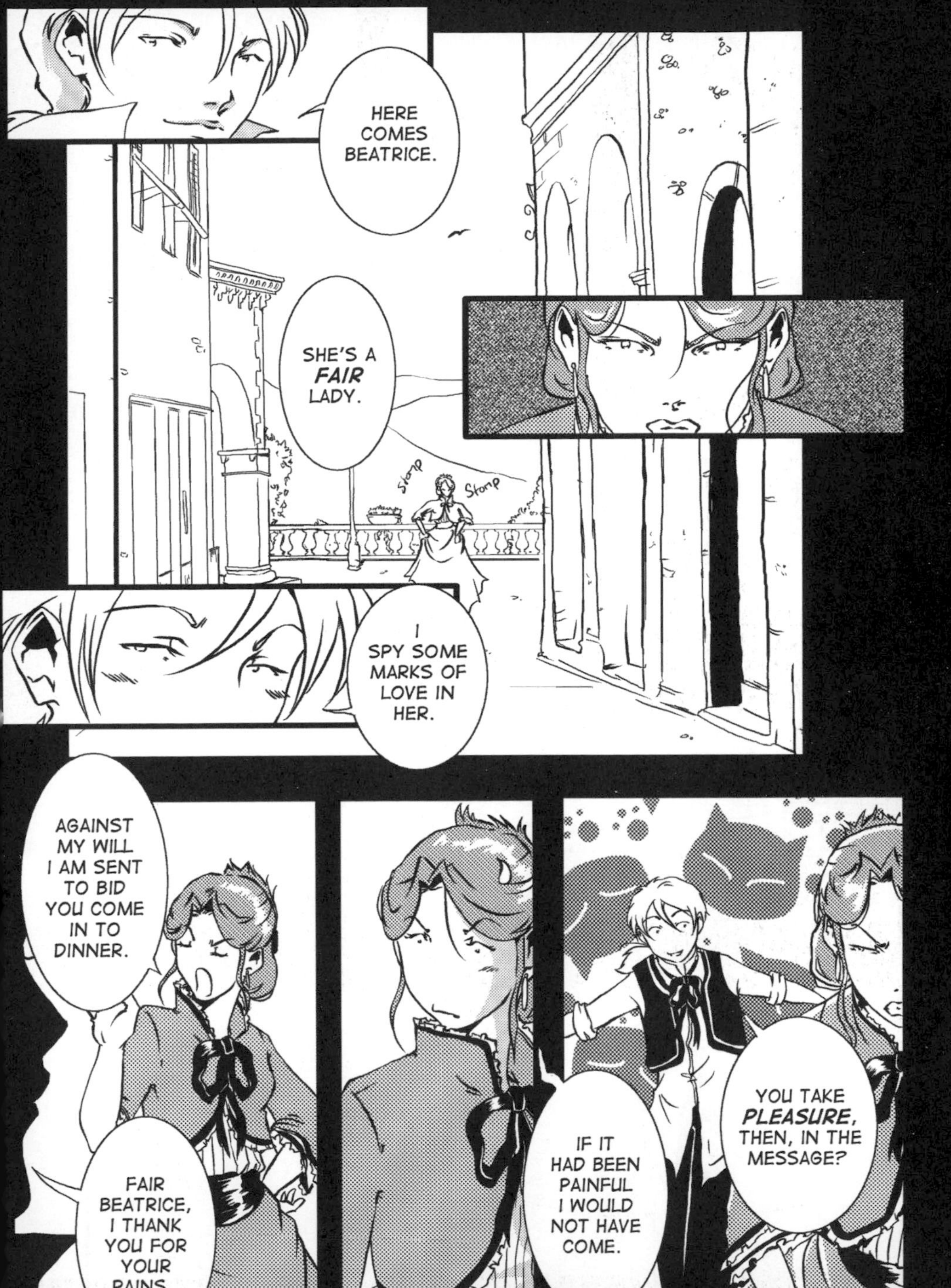

HERE COMES BEATRICE.
SHE'S A ***FAIR*** LADY.
Stomp
Stomp
I SPY SOME MARKS OF LOVE IN HER.
AGAINST MY WILL I AM SENT TO BID YOU COME IN TO DINNER.
FAIR BEATRICE, I THANK YOU FOR YOUR PAINS.
IF IT HAD BEEN PAINFUL I WOULD NOT HAVE COME.
YOU TAKE ***PLEASURE***, THEN, IN THE MESSAGE?

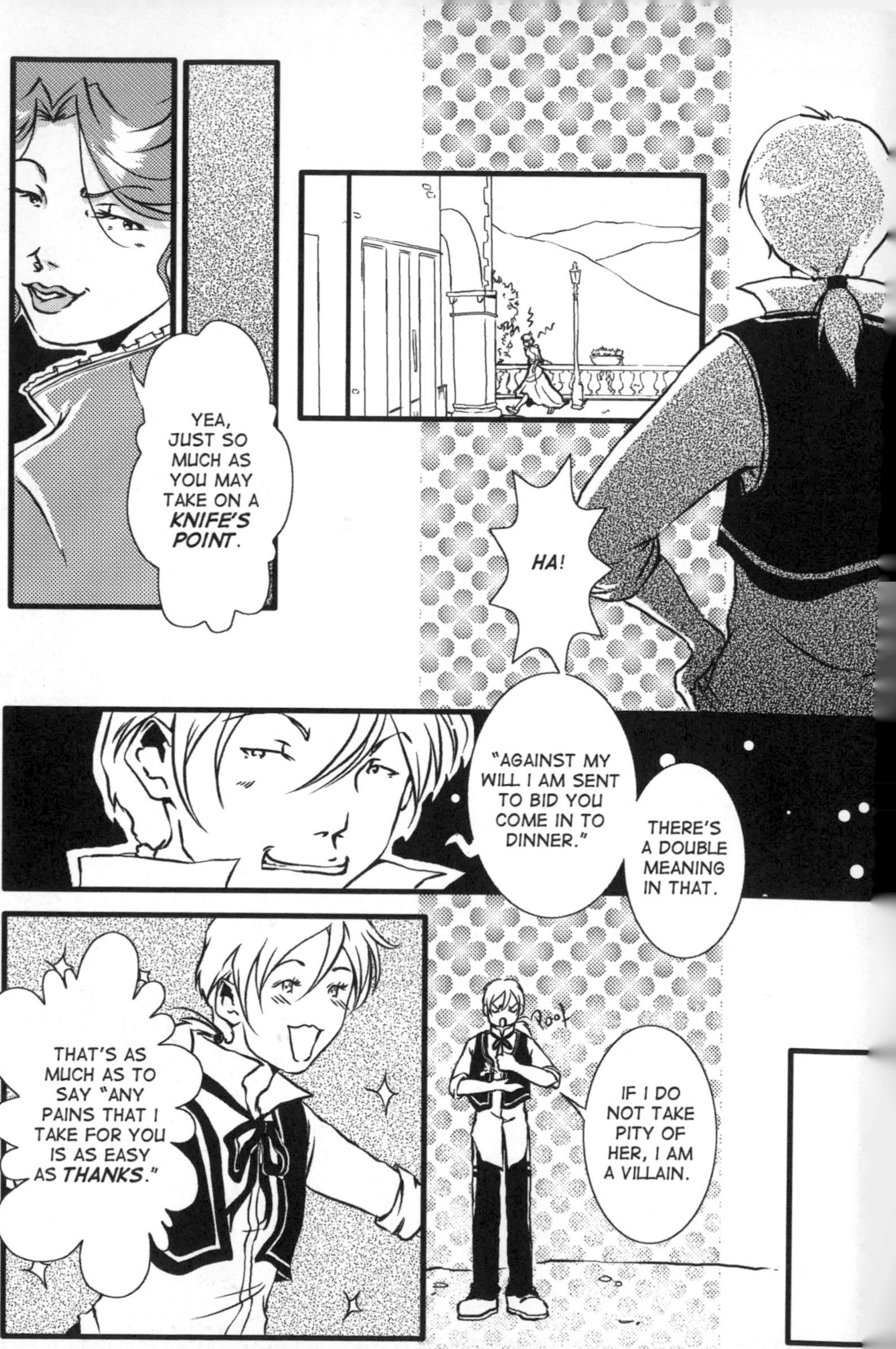
YEA, JUST SO MUCH AS YOU MAY TAKE ON A *KNIFE'S POINT*.
HA!
"AGAINST MY WILL I AM SENT TO BID YOU COME IN TO DINNER."
THERE'S A DOUBLE MEANING IN THAT.
THAT'S AS MUCH AS TO SAY "ANY PAINS THAT I TAKE FOR YOU IS AS EASY AS *THANKS*."
Poof
IF I DO NOT TAKE PITY OF HER, I AM A VILLAIN.

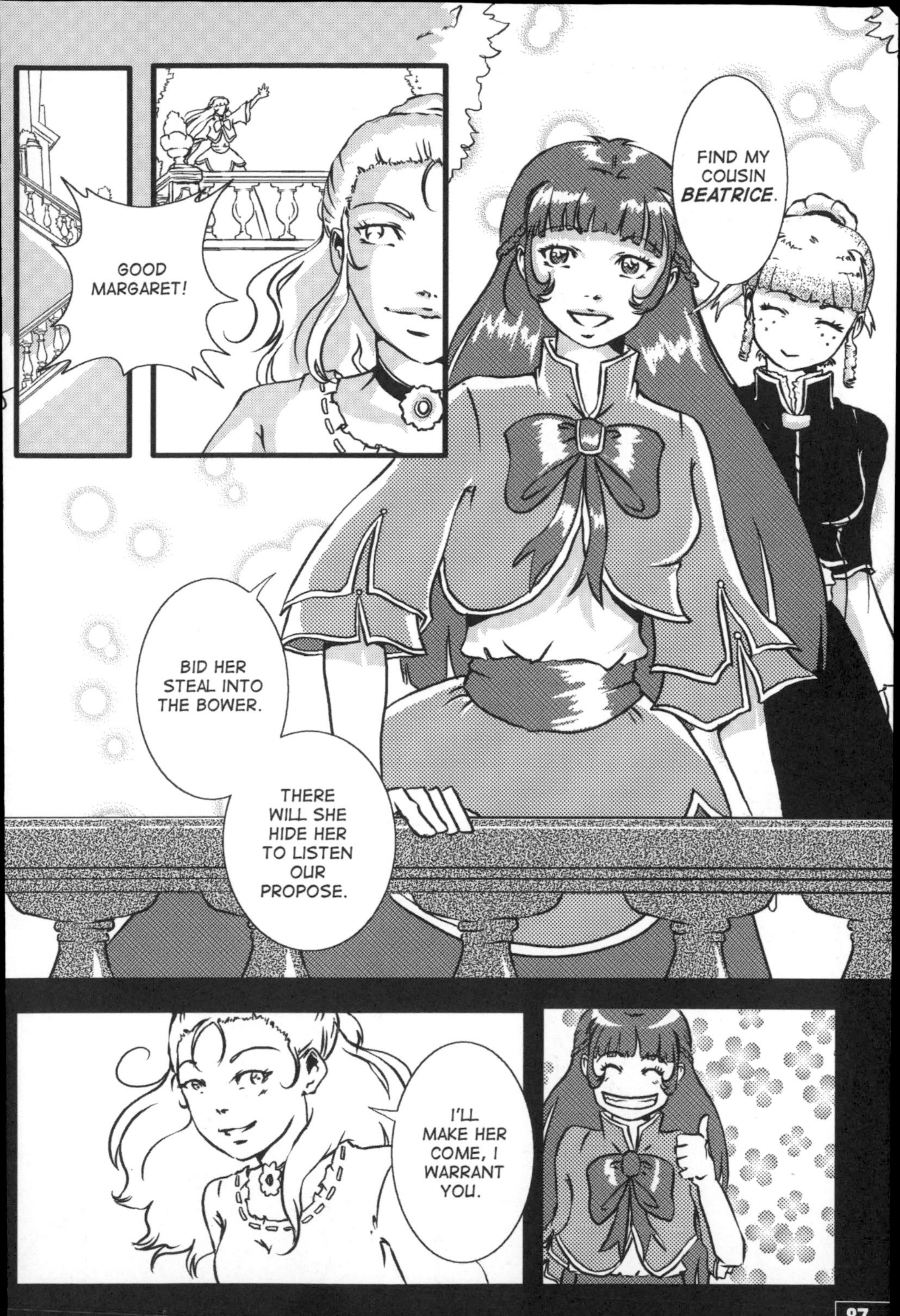
GOOD MARGARET!
FIND MY COUSIN BEATRICE.
BID HER STEAL INTO THE BOWER.
THERE WILL SHE HIDE HER TO LISTEN OUR PROPOSE.
I'LL MAKE HER COME, I WARRANT YOU.

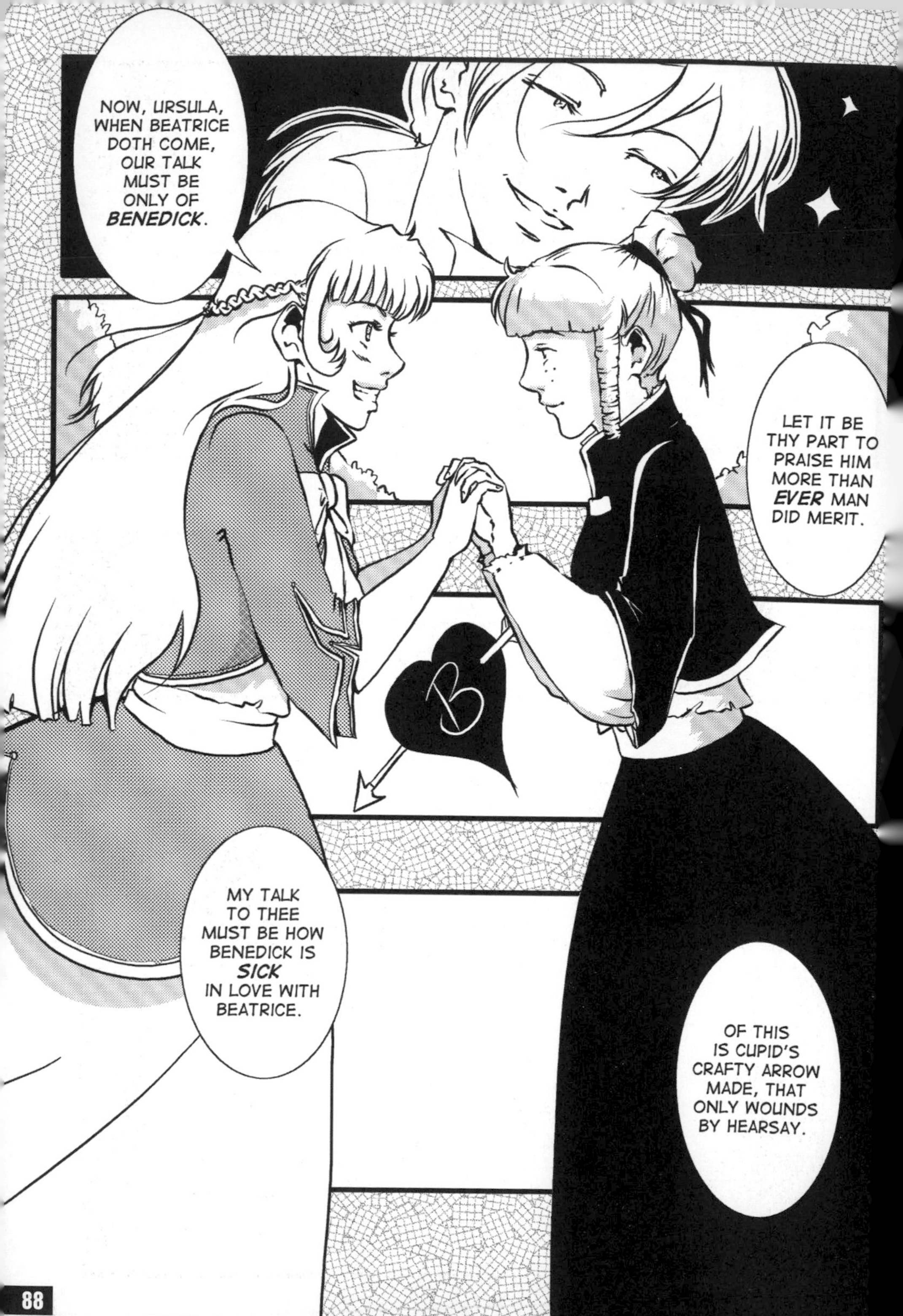

NOW, URSULA, WHEN BEATRICE DOTH COME, OUR TALK MUST BE ONLY OF **BENEDICK**.
LET IT BE THY PART TO PRAISE HIM MORE THAN **EVER** MAN DID MERIT.
MY TALK TO THEE MUST BE HOW BENEDICK IS **SICK** IN LOVE WITH BEATRICE.
OF THIS IS CUPID'S CRAFTY ARROW MADE, THAT ONLY WOUNDS BY HEARSAY.

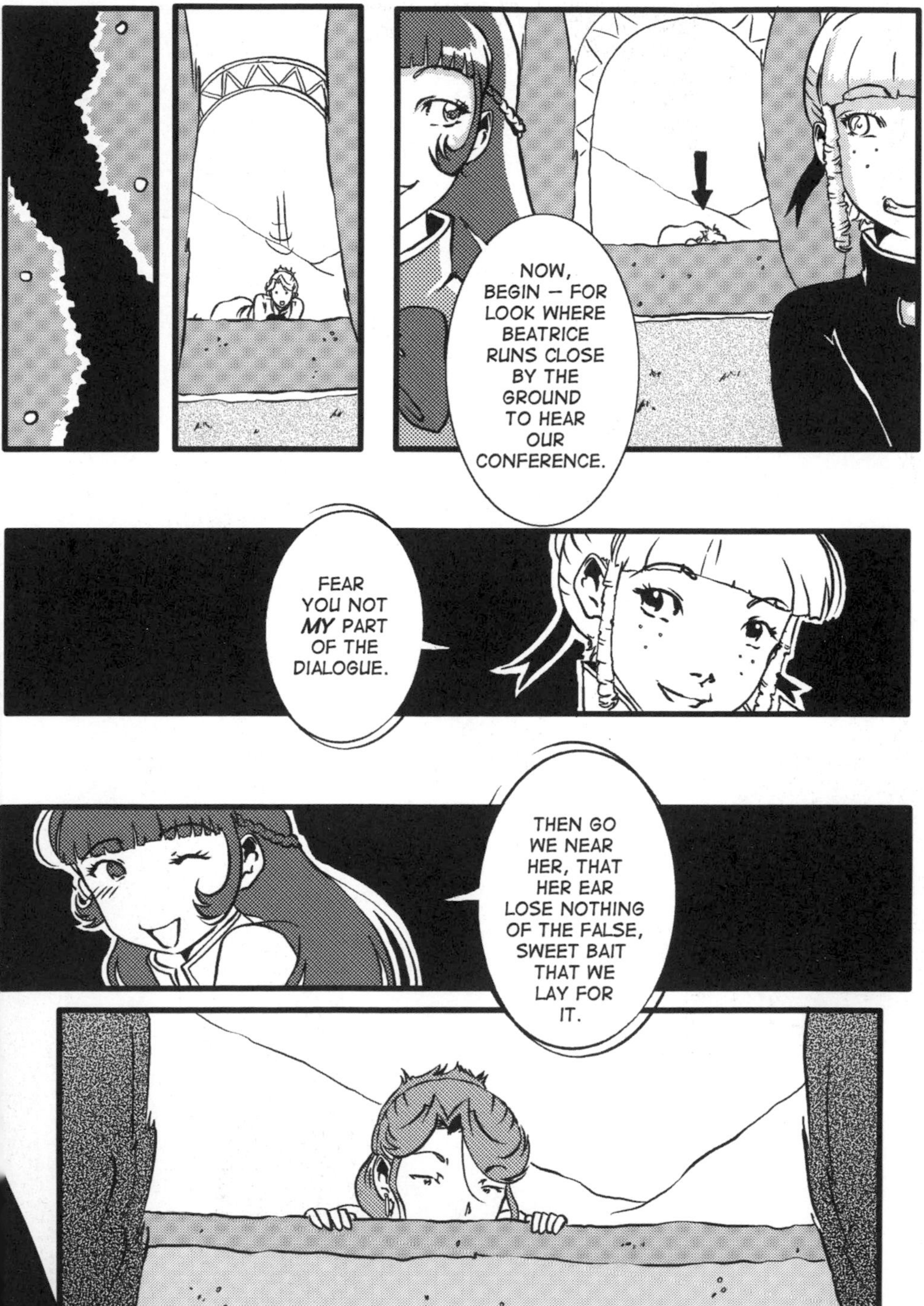
NOW, BEGIN — FOR LOOK WHERE BEATRICE RUNS CLOSE BY THE GROUND TO HEAR OUR CONFERENCE.
FEAR YOU NOT *MY* PART OF THE DIALOGUE.
THEN GO WE NEAR HER, THAT HER EAR LOSE NOTHING OF THE FALSE, SWEET BAIT THAT WE LAY FOR IT.

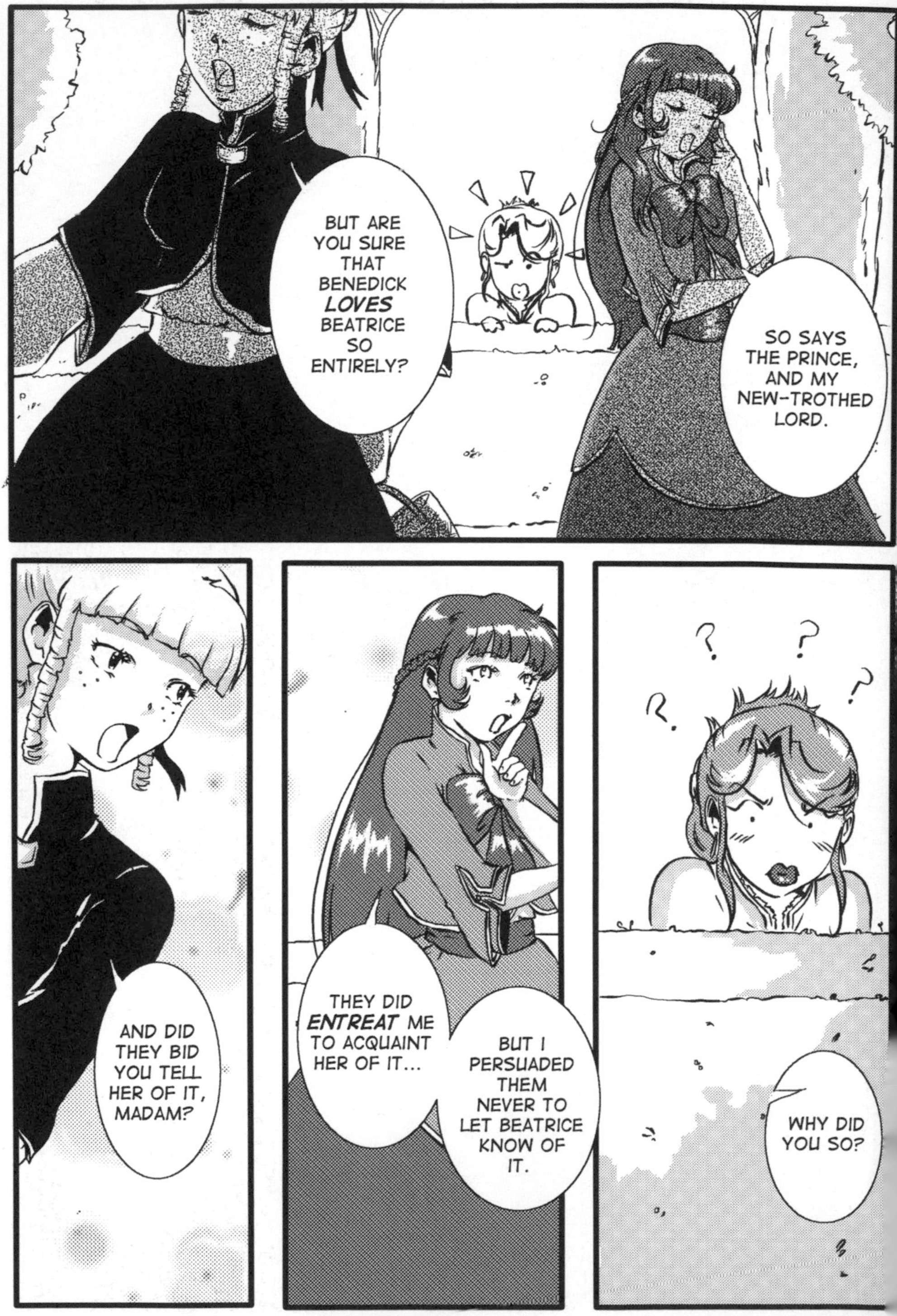
BUT ARE YOU SURE THAT BENEDICK LOVES BEATRICE SO ENTIRELY?
SO SAYS THE PRINCE, AND MY NEW-TROTHED LORD.
AND DID THEY BID YOU TELL HER OF IT, MADAM?
THEY DID ENTREAT ME TO ACQUAINT HER OF IT...
BUT I PERSUADED THEM NEVER TO LET BEATRICE KNOW OF IT.
WHY DID YOU SO?

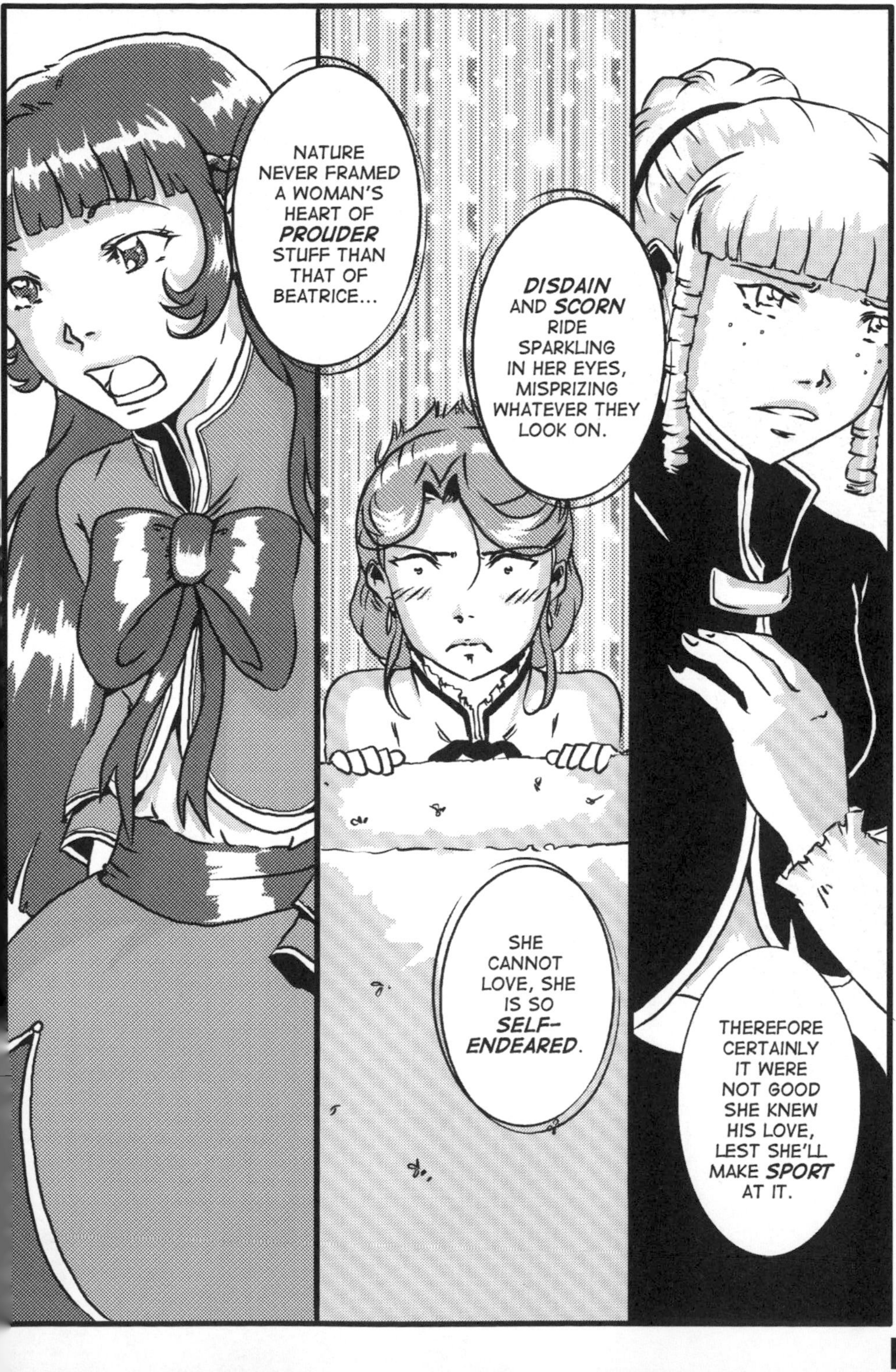
NATURE NEVER FRAMED A WOMAN'S HEART OF PROUDER STUFF THAN THAT OF BEATRICE...
DISDAIN AND SCORN RIDE SPARKLING IN HER EYES, MISPRIZING WHATEVER THEY LOOK ON.
SHE CANNOT LOVE, SHE IS SO SELF-ENDEARED.
THEREFORE CERTAINLY IT WERE NOT GOOD SHE KNEW HIS LOVE, LEST SHE'LL MAKE SPORT AT IT.

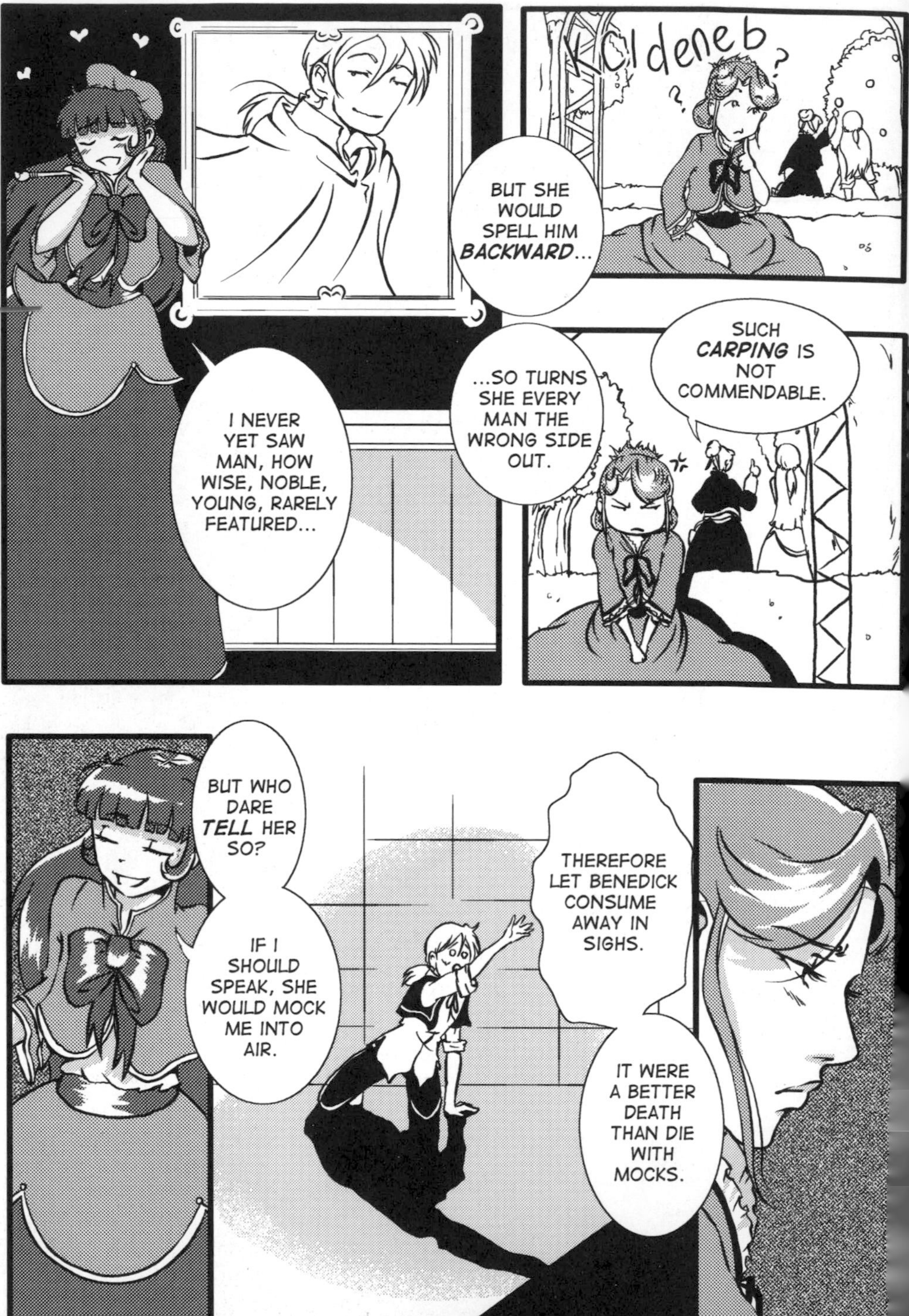
I NEVER YET SAW MAN, HOW WISE, NOBLE, YOUNG, RARELY FEATURED...
BUT SHE WOULD SPELL HIM **BACKWARD**...
Kcideneb
? ?
...SO TURNS SHE EVERY MAN THE WRONG SIDE OUT.
SUCH **CARPING** IS NOT COMMENDABLE.
BUT WHO DARE **TELL** HER SO?
IF I SHOULD SPEAK, SHE WOULD MOCK ME INTO AIR.
THEREFORE LET BENEDICK CONSUME AWAY IN SIGHS.
IT WERE A BETTER DEATH THAN DIE WITH MOCKS.

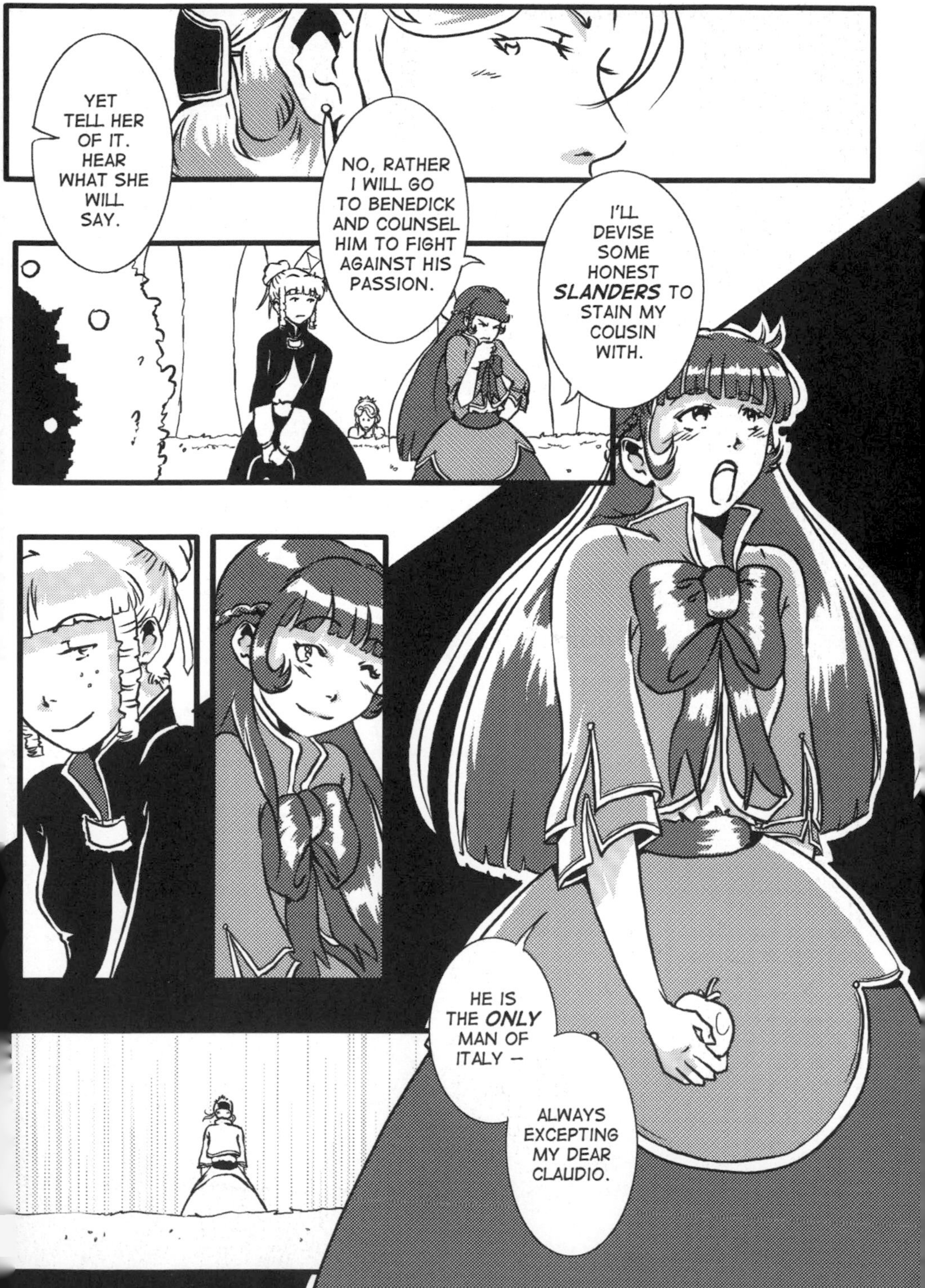
YET TELL HER OF IT. HEAR WHAT SHE WILL SAY.
NO, RATHER I WILL GO TO BENEDICK AND COUNSEL HIM TO FIGHT AGAINST HIS PASSION.
I'LL DEVISE SOME HONEST ***SLANDERS*** TO STAIN MY COUSIN WITH.
HE IS THE ***ONLY*** MAN OF ITALY —
ALWAYS EXCEPTING MY DEAR CLAUDIO.

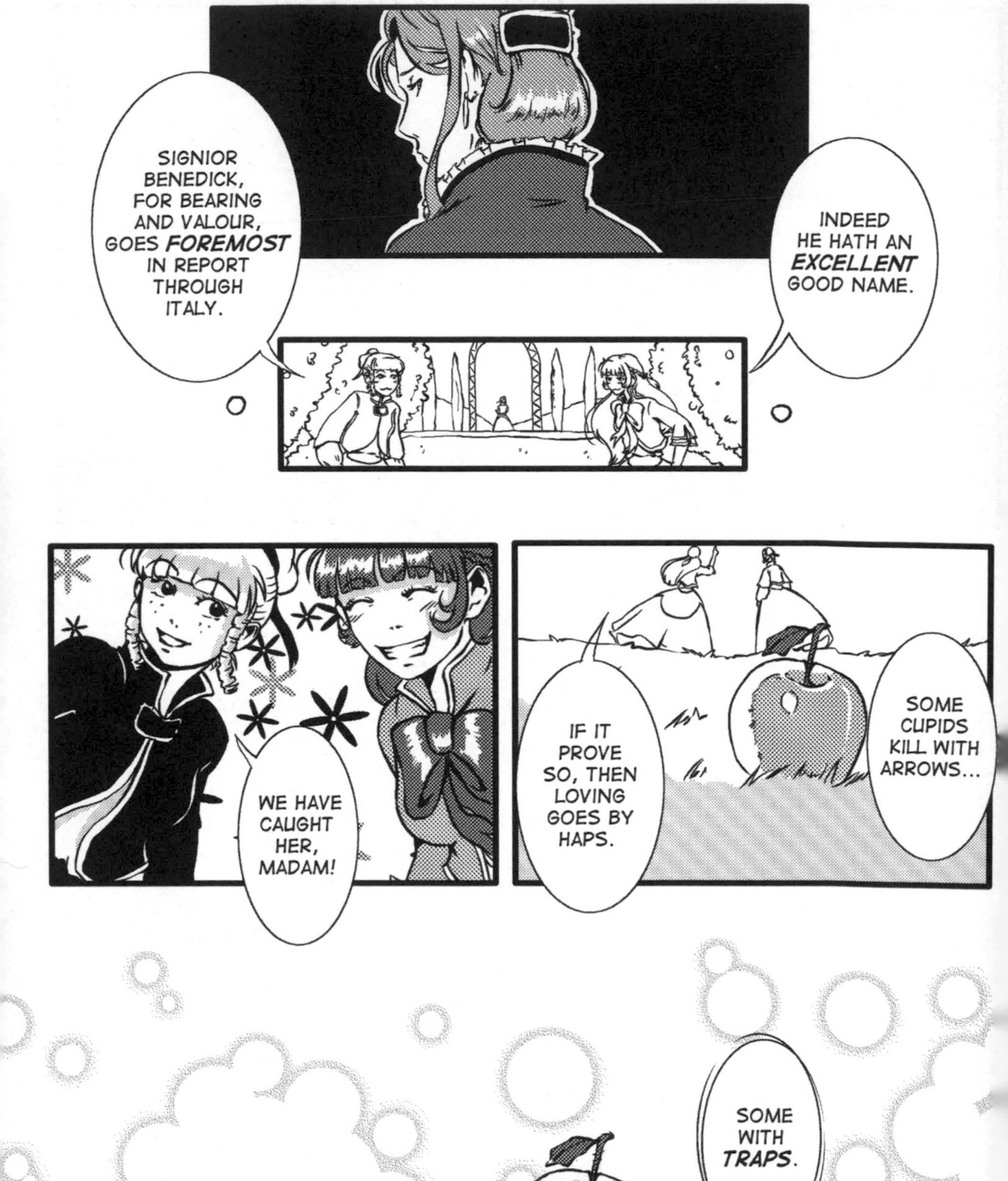
SIGNIOR BENEDICK, FOR BEARING AND VALOUR, GOES *FOREMOST* IN REPORT THROUGH ITALY.
INDEED HE HATH AN *EXCELLENT* GOOD NAME.
WE HAVE CAUGHT HER, MADAM!
IF IT PROVE SO, THEN LOVING GOES BY HAPS.
SOME CUPIDS KILL WITH ARROWS...
SOME WITH *TRAPS*.

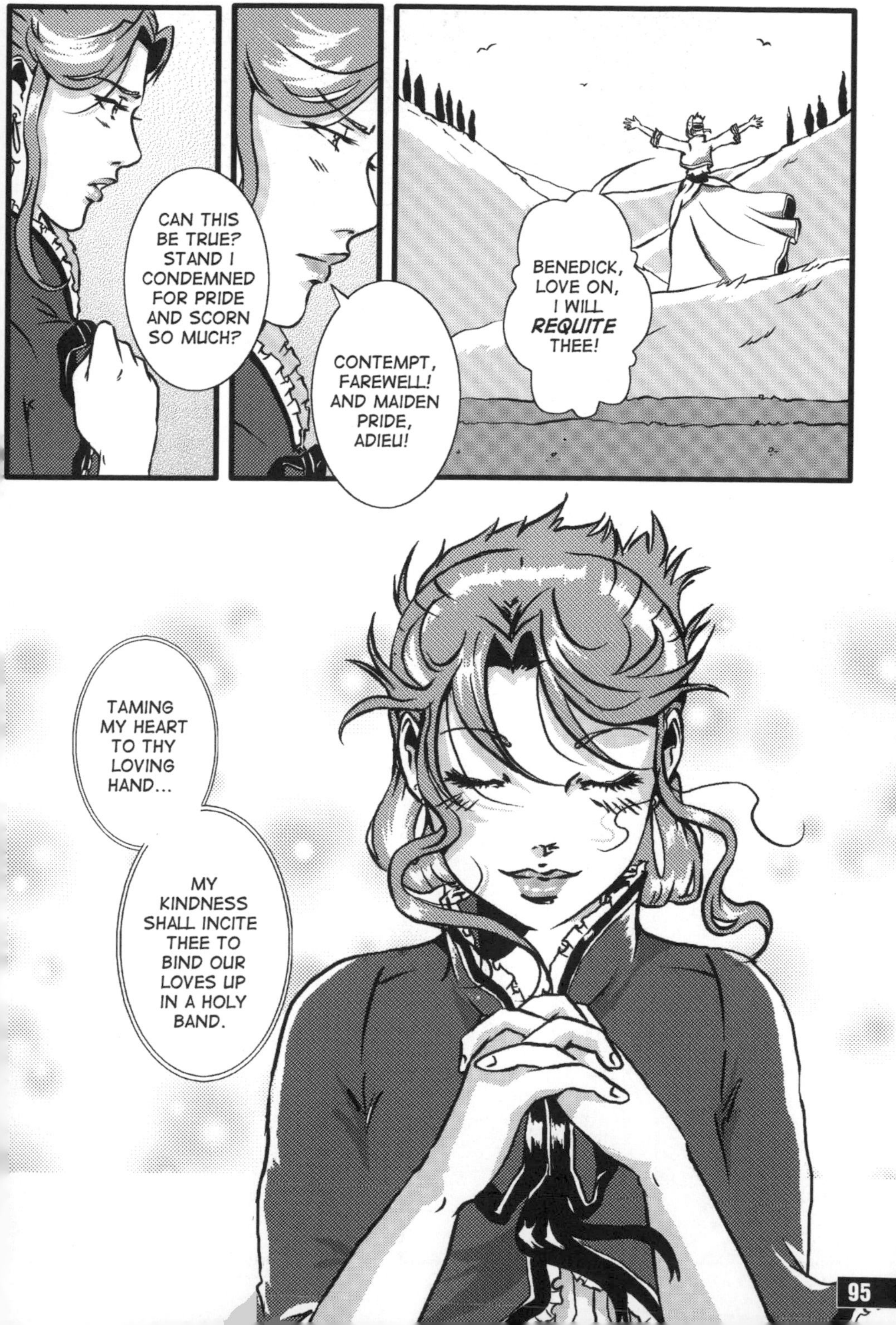
CAN THIS BE TRUE? STAND I CONDEMNED FOR PRIDE AND SCORN SO MUCH?
CONTEMPT, FAREWELL! AND MAIDEN PRIDE, ADIEU!
BENEDICK, LOVE ON, I WILL *REQUITE* THEE!
TAMING MY HEART TO THY LOVING HAND...
MY KINDNESS SHALL INCITE THEE TO BIND OUR LOVES UP IN A HOLY BAND.

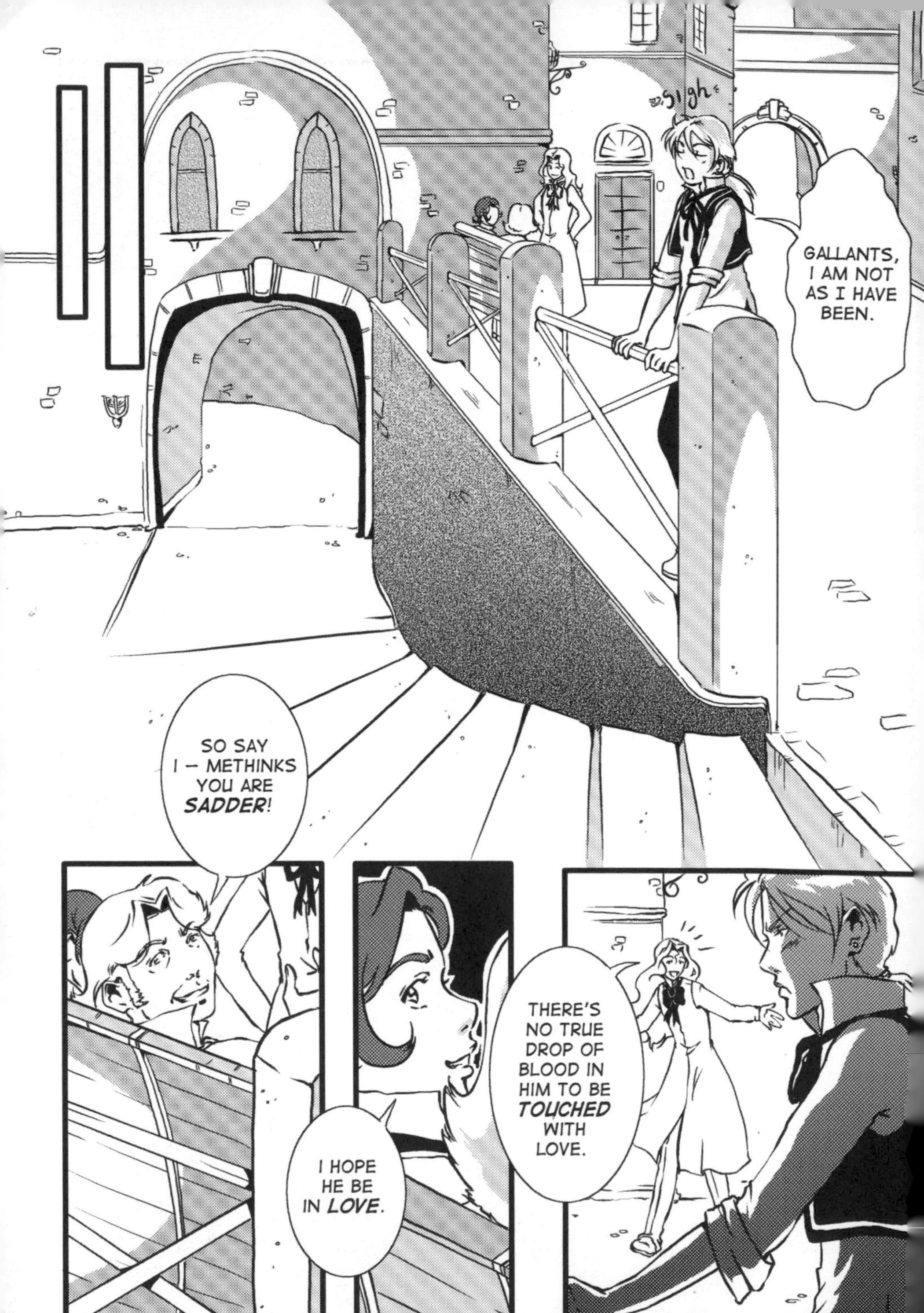
Sigh
GALLANTS, I AM NOT AS I HAVE BEEN.
SO SAY I — METHINKS YOU ARE **SADDER**!
I HOPE HE BE IN **LOVE**.
THERE'S NO TRUE DROP OF BLOOD IN HIM TO BE **TOUCHED** WITH LOVE.

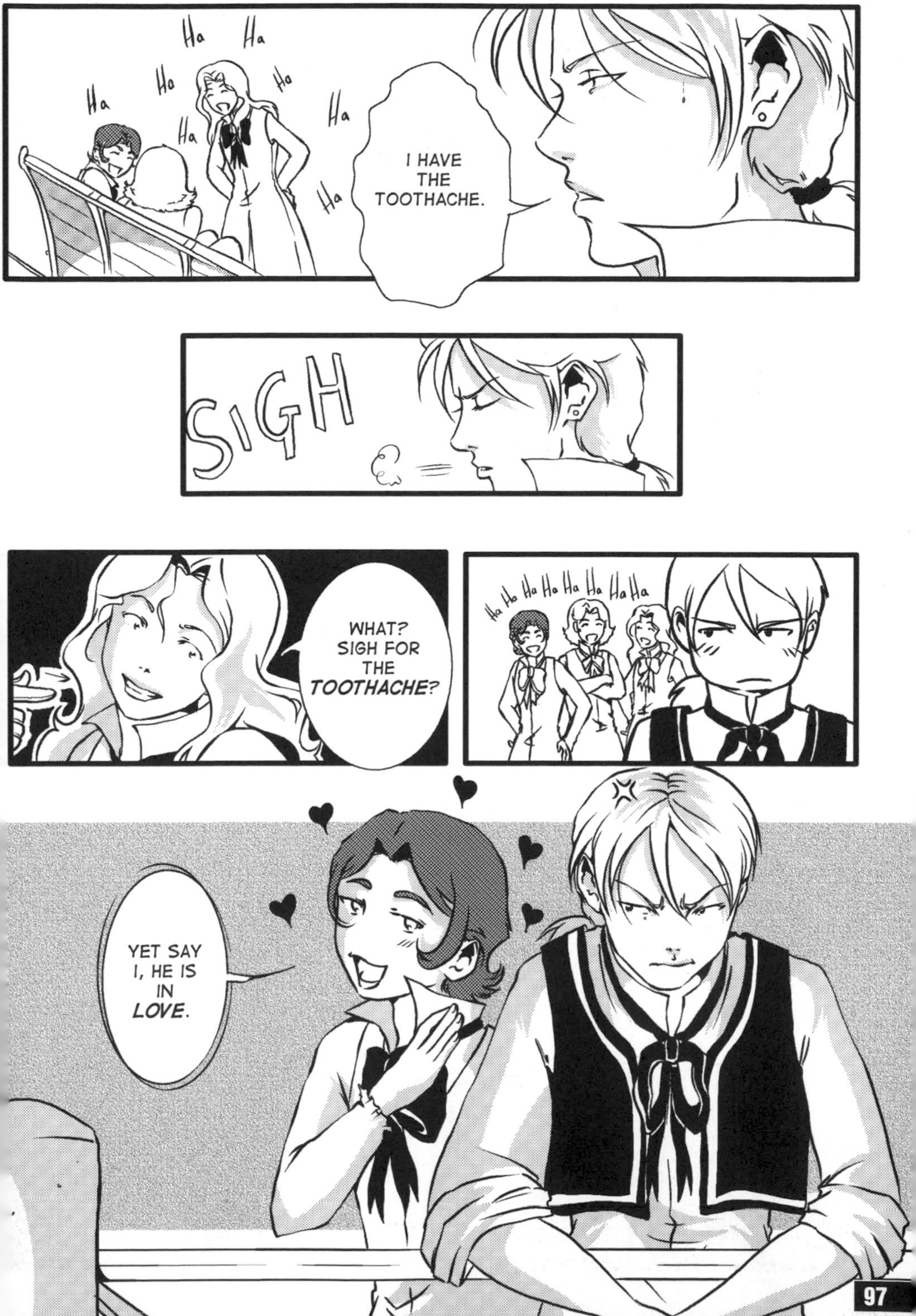
Ha Ha
Ha Ha Ha Ha Ha Ha Ha
I HAVE THE TOOTHACHE.
SIGH
WHAT? SIGH FOR THE *TOOTHACHE*?
Ha Ha Ha Ha Ha Ha Ha Ha
YET SAY I, HE IS IN *LOVE*.

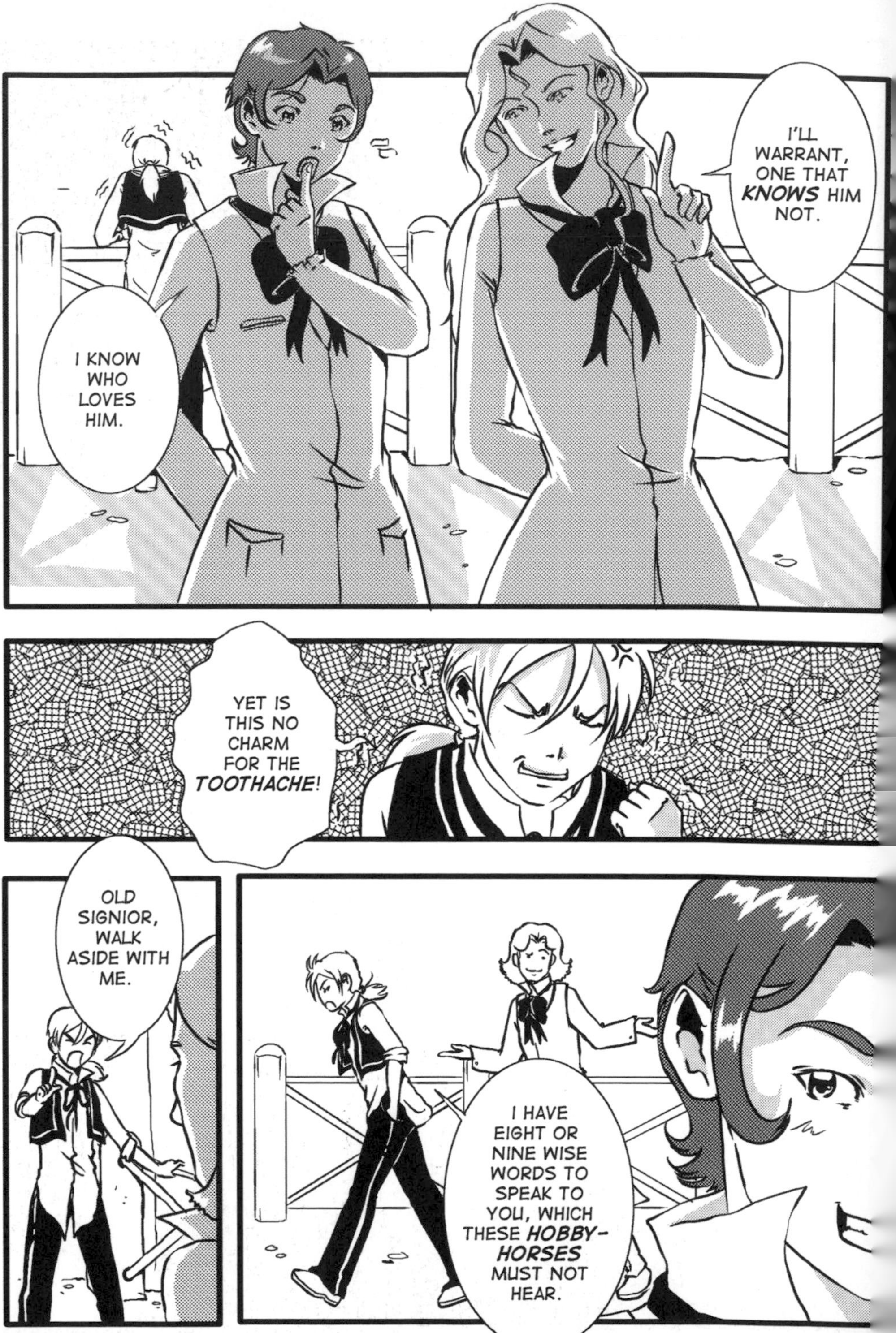

I KNOW WHO LOVES HIM.
I'LL WARRANT, ONE THAT ***KNOWS*** HIM NOT.
YET IS THIS NO CHARM FOR THE ***TOOTHACHE***!
OLD SIGNIOR, WALK ASIDE WITH ME.
I HAVE EIGHT OR NINE WISE WORDS TO SPEAK TO YOU, WHICH THESE ***HOBBY-HORSES*** MUST NOT HEAR.

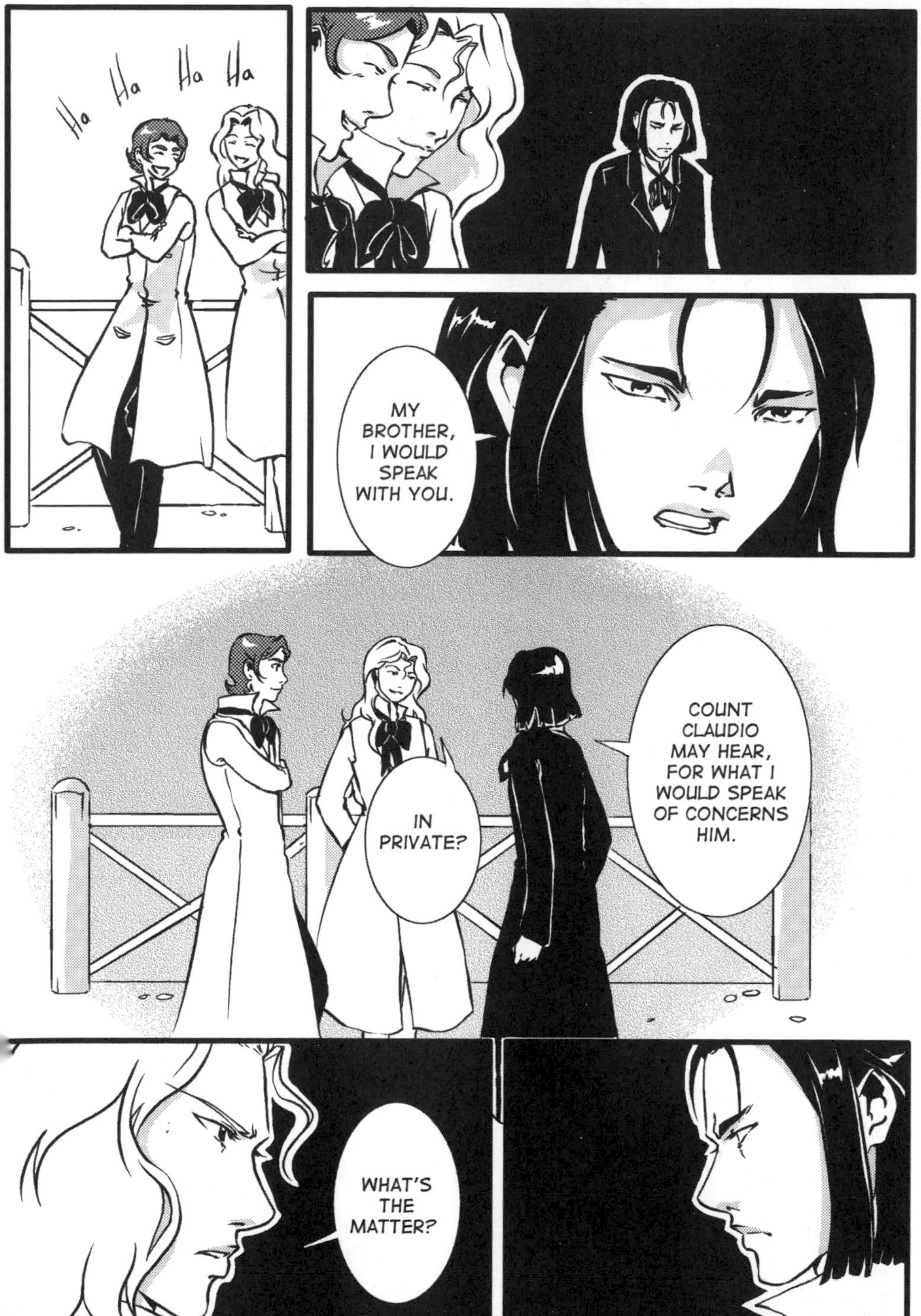
Ha Ha Ha Ha
MY BROTHER, I WOULD SPEAK WITH YOU.
IN PRIVATE?
COUNT CLAUDIO MAY HEAR, FOR WHAT I WOULD SPEAK OF CONCERNS HIM.
WHAT'S THE MATTER?

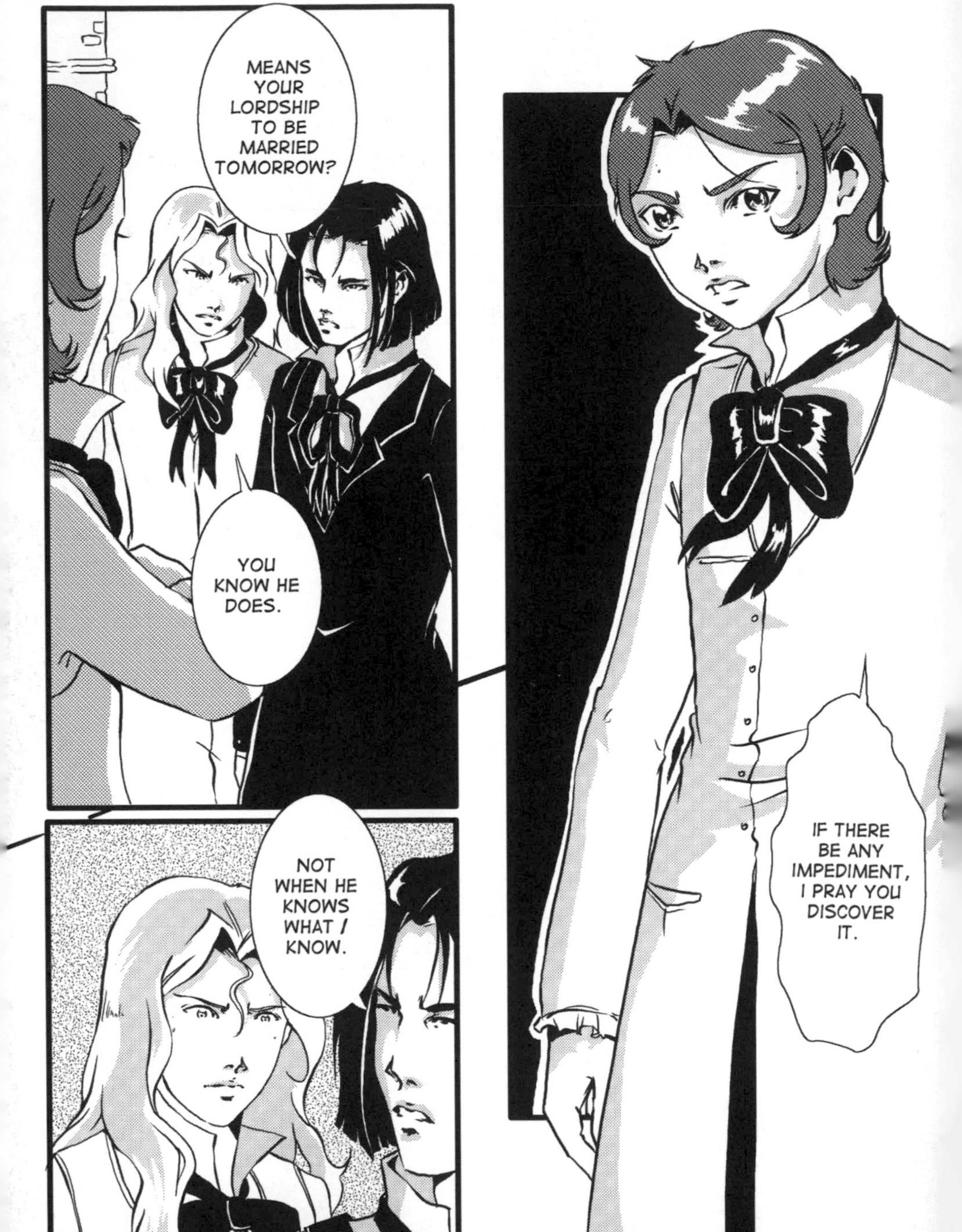
MEANS YOUR LORDSHIP TO BE MARRIED TOMORROW?
YOU KNOW HE DOES.
NOT WHEN HE KNOWS WHAT I KNOW.
IF THERE BE ANY IMPEDIMENT, I PRAY YOU DISCOVER IT.

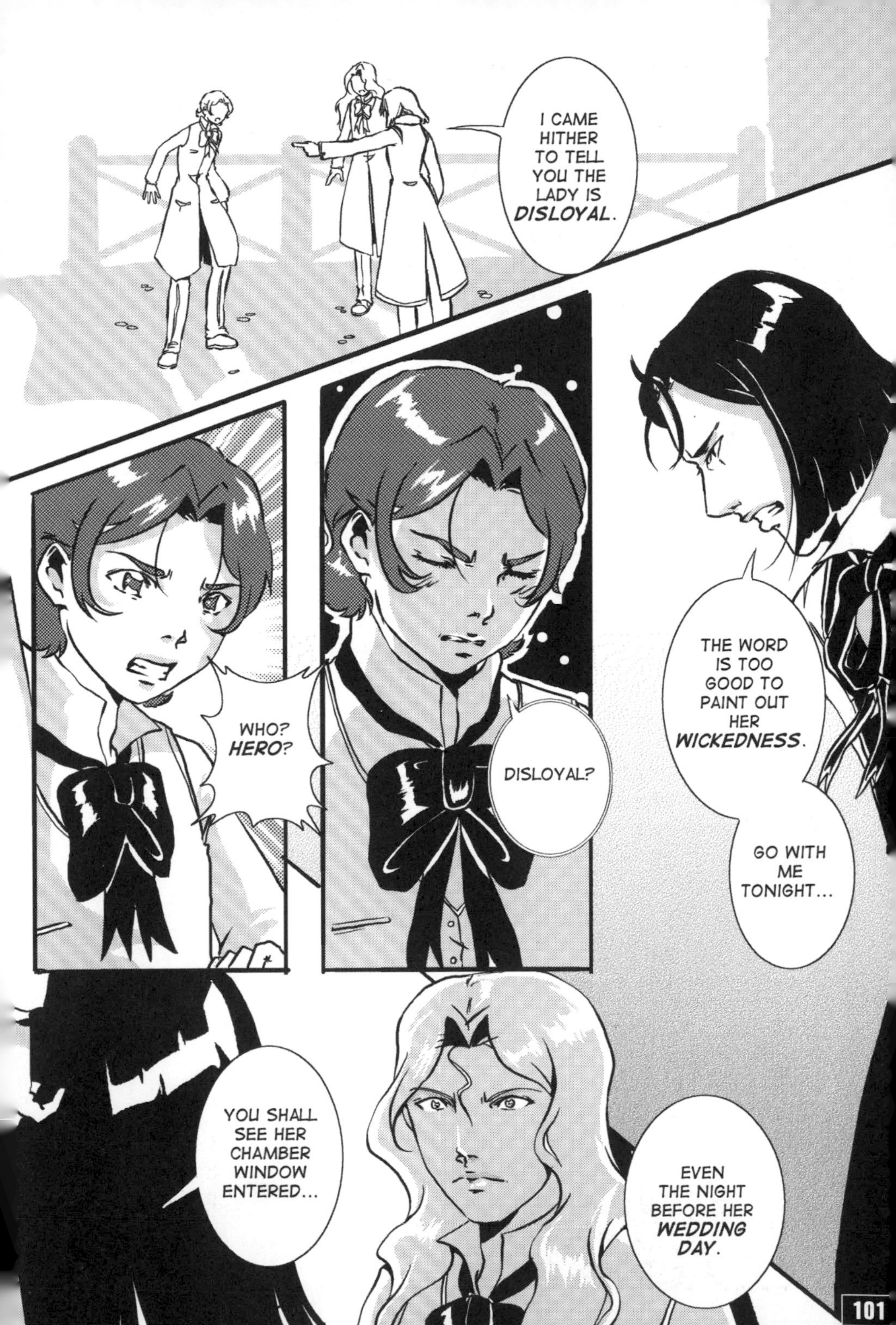
I CAME HITHER TO TELL YOU THE LADY IS DISLOYAL.
WHO? HERO?
DISLOYAL?
THE WORD IS TOO GOOD TO PAINT OUT HER WICKEDNESS.
GO WITH ME TONIGHT...
YOU SHALL SEE HER CHAMBER WINDOW ENTERED...
EVEN THE NIGHT BEFORE HER WEDDING DAY.

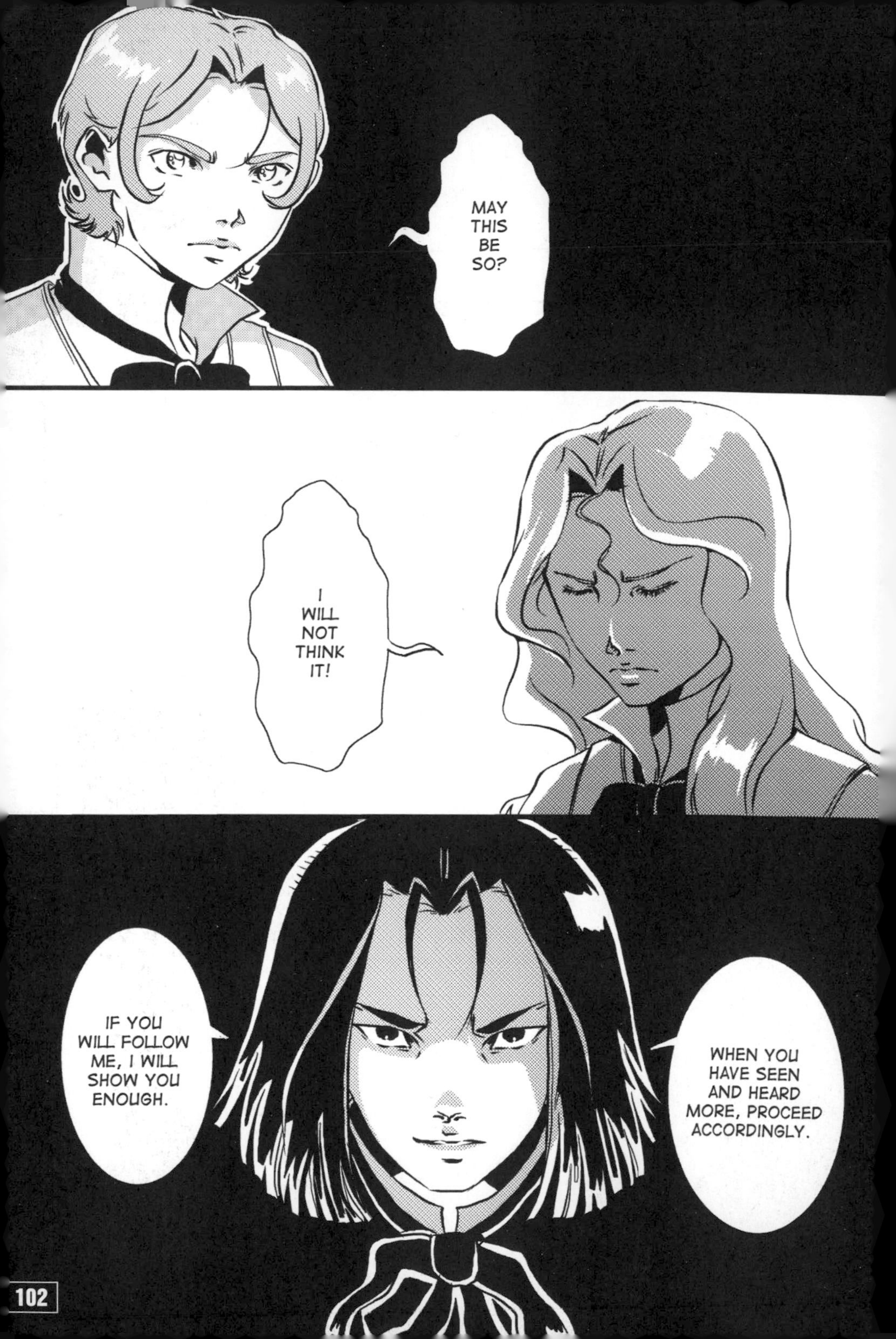
MAY THIS BE SO?
I WILL NOT THINK IT!
IF YOU WILL FOLLOW ME, I WILL SHOW YOU ENOUGH.
WHEN YOU HAVE SEEN AND HEARD MORE, PROCEED ACCORDINGLY.

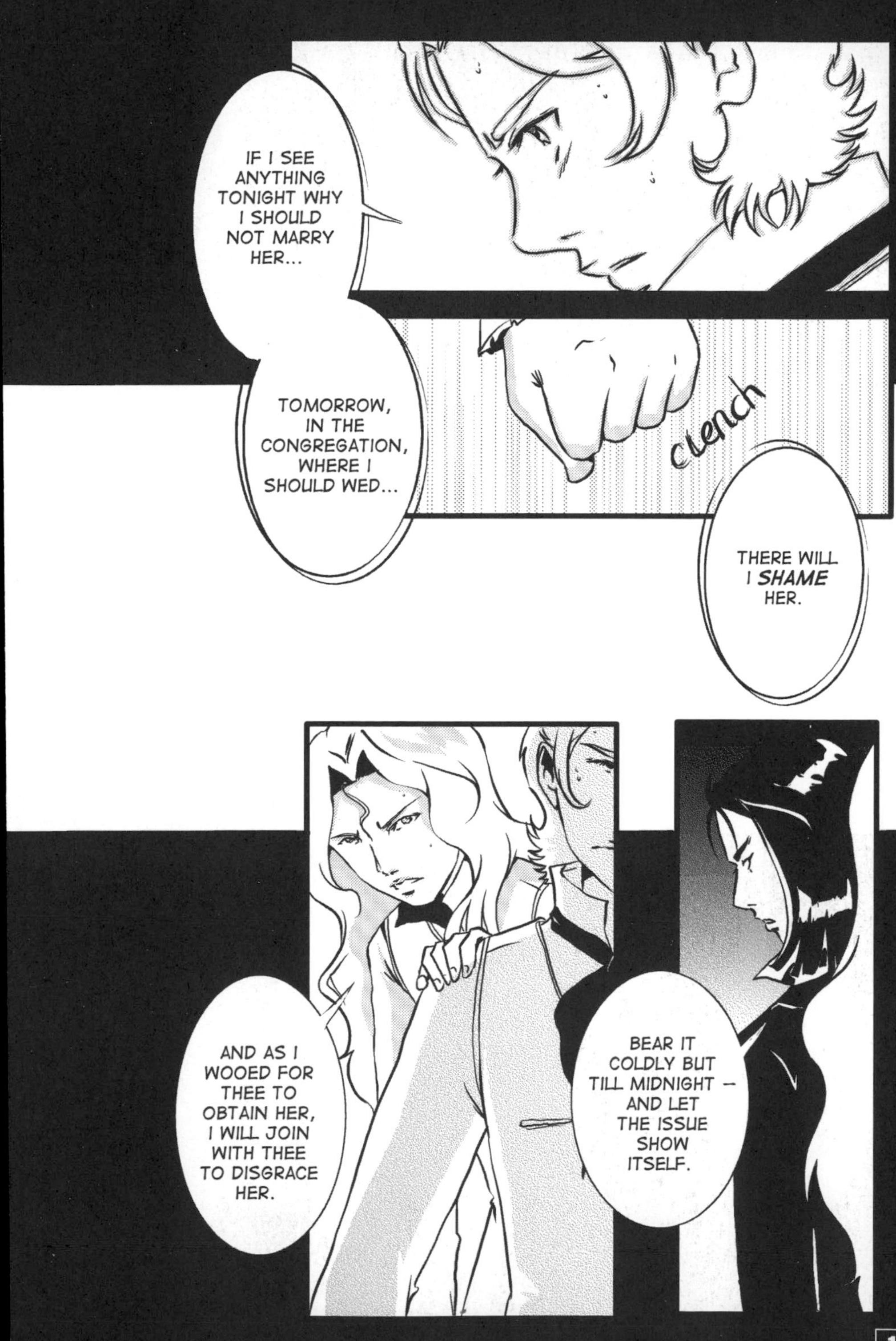
IF I SEE ANYTHING TONIGHT WHY I SHOULD NOT MARRY HER...
TOMORROW, IN THE CONGREGATION, WHERE I SHOULD WED...
clench
THERE WILL I *SHAME* HER.
AND AS I WOOED FOR THEE TO OBTAIN HER, I WILL JOIN WITH THEE TO DISGRACE HER.
BEAR IT COLDLY BUT TILL MIDNIGHT -- AND LET THE ISSUE SHOW ITSELF.

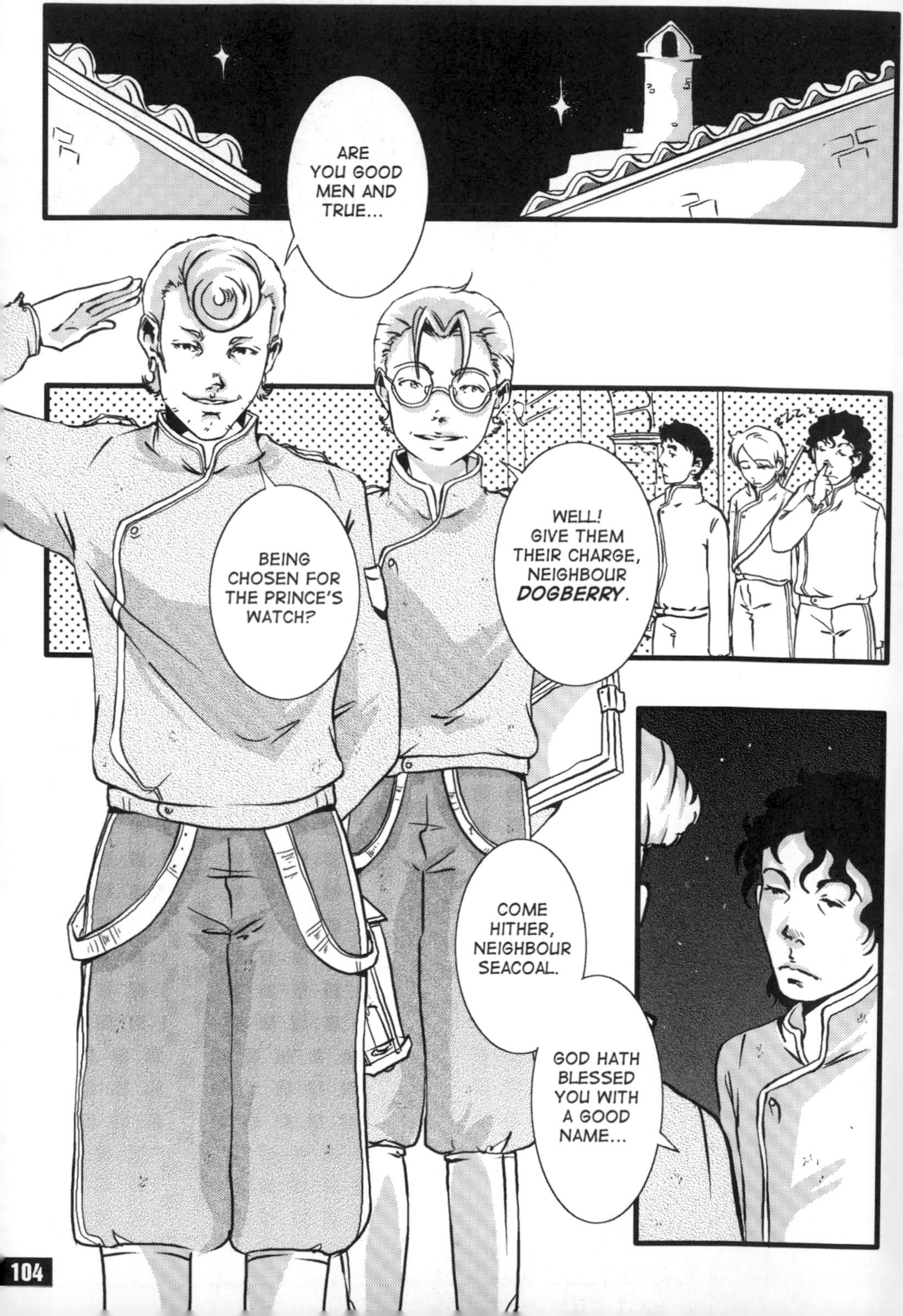
ARE YOU GOOD MEN AND TRUE...
BEING CHOSEN FOR THE PRINCE'S WATCH?
WELL! GIVE THEM THEIR CHARGE, NEIGHBOUR **DOGBERRY**.
COME HITHER, NEIGHBOUR SEACOAL.
GOD HATH BLESSED YOU WITH A GOOD NAME...

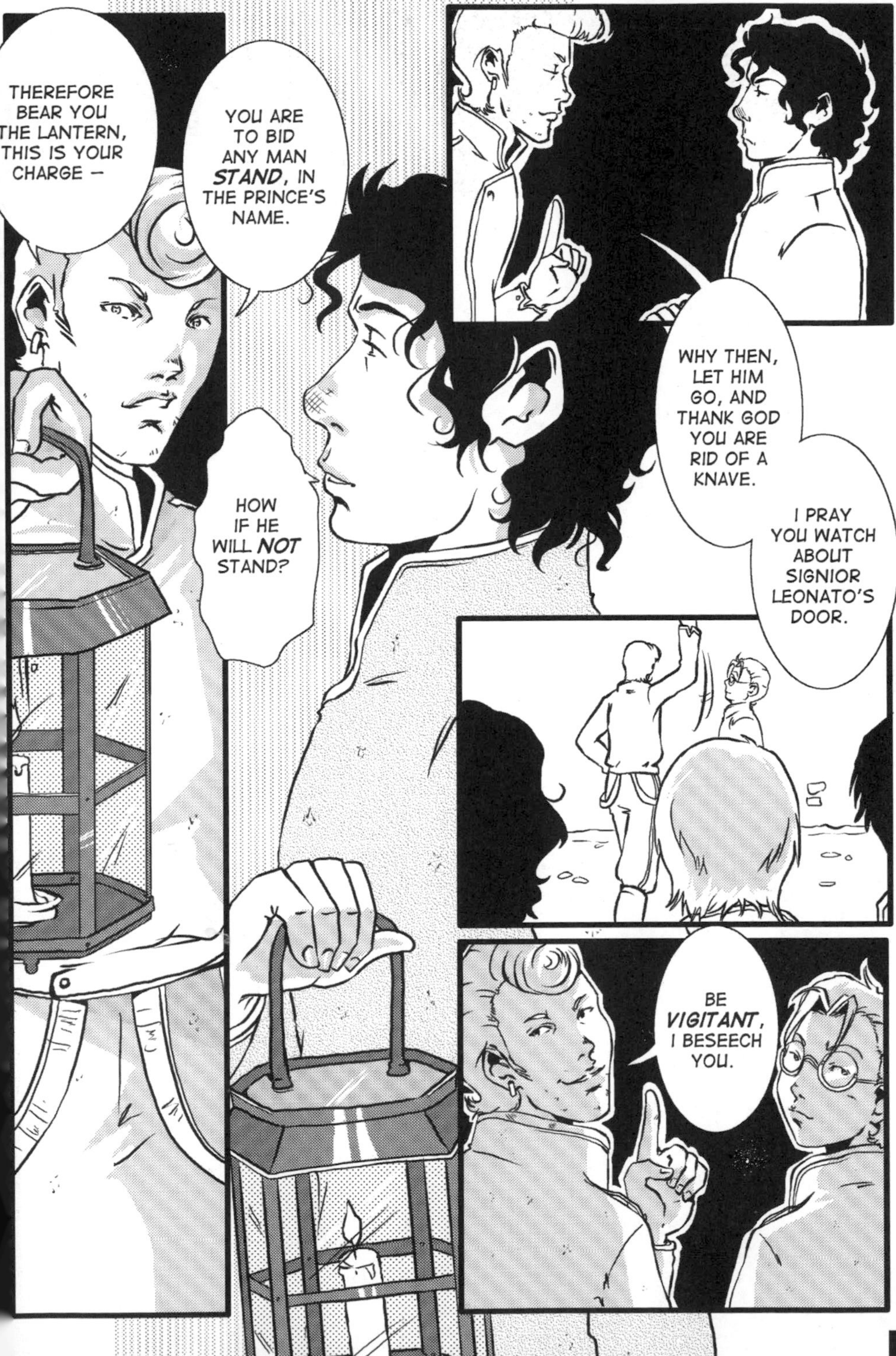
THEREFORE BEAR YOU THE LANTERN, THIS IS YOUR CHARGE –
YOU ARE TO BID ANY MAN *STAND*, IN THE PRINCE'S NAME.
HOW IF HE WILL *NOT* STAND?
WHY THEN, LET HIM GO, AND THANK GOD YOU ARE RID OF A KNAVE.
I PRAY YOU WATCH ABOUT SIGNIOR LEONATO'S DOOR.
BE *VIGITANT*, I BESEECH YOU.

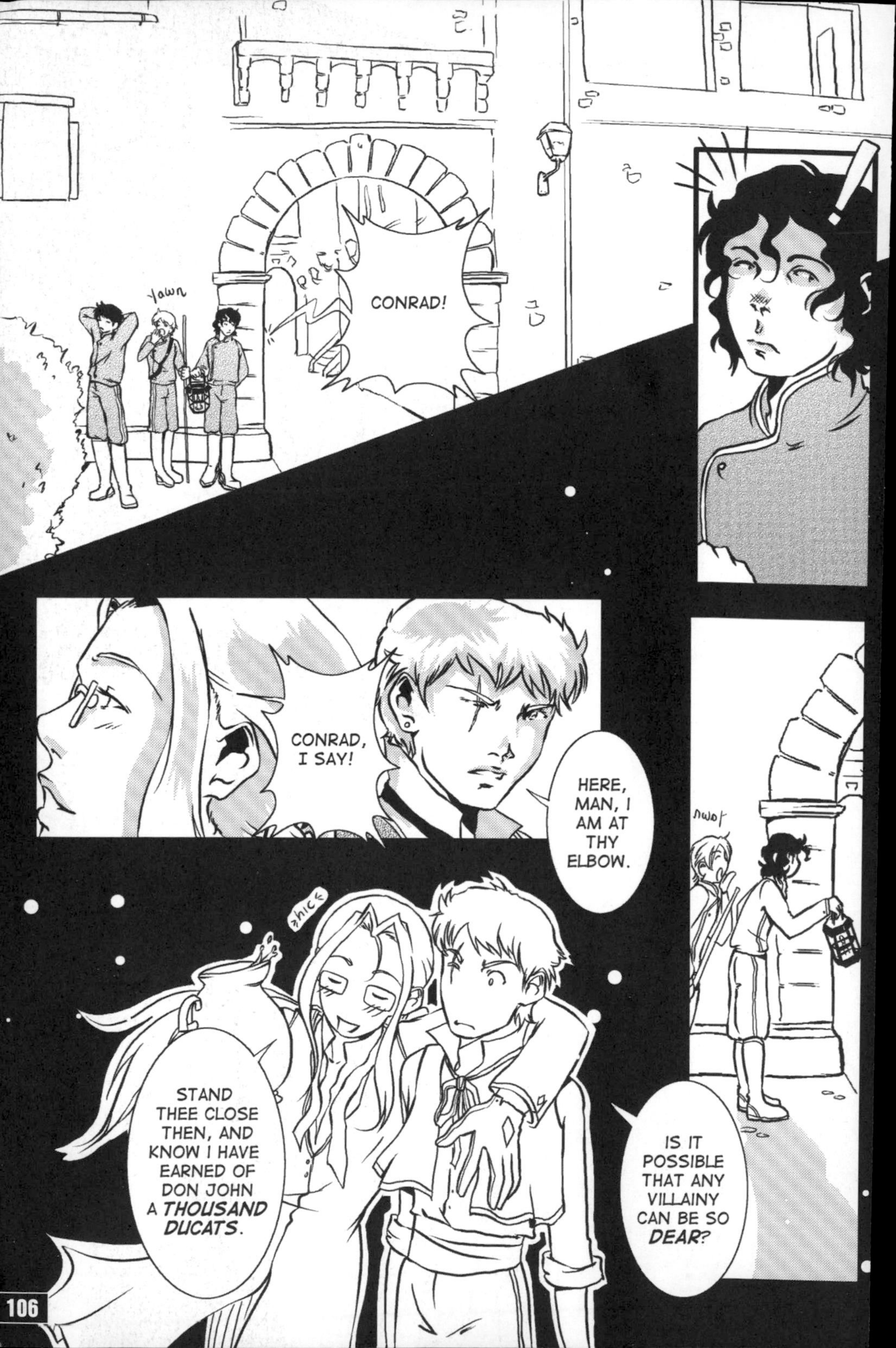

yawn
CONRAD!
CONRAD, I SAY!
HERE, MAN, I AM AT THY ELBOW.
hick
STAND THEE CLOSE THEN, AND KNOW I HAVE EARNED OF DON JOHN A **THOUSAND DUCATS**.
IS IT POSSIBLE THAT ANY VILLAINY CAN BE SO **DEAR**?

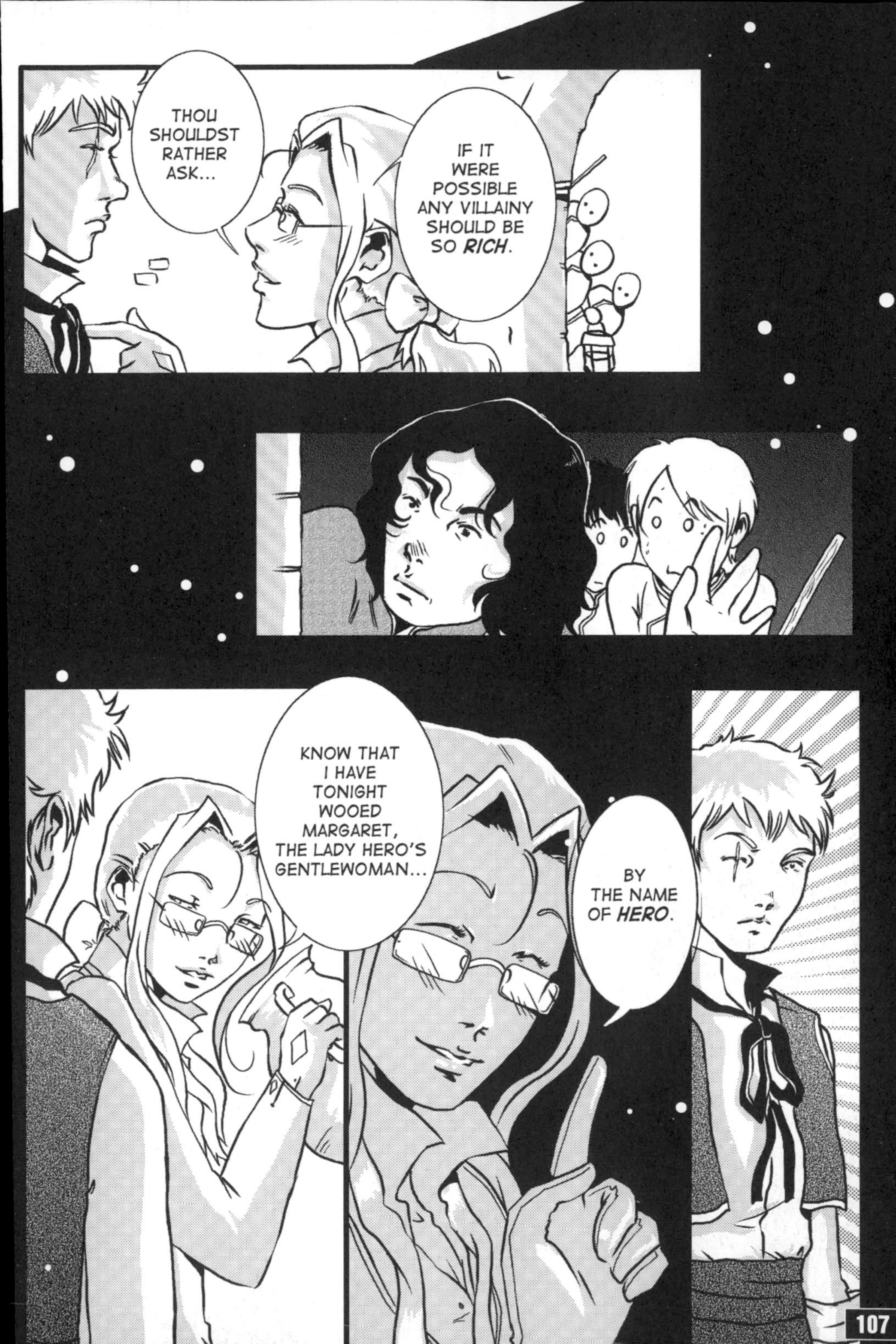
THOU SHOULDST RATHER ASK...
IF IT WERE POSSIBLE ANY VILLAINY SHOULD BE SO *RICH*.
KNOW THAT I HAVE TONIGHT WOOED MARGARET, THE LADY HERO'S GENTLEWOMAN...
BY THE NAME OF *HERO*.

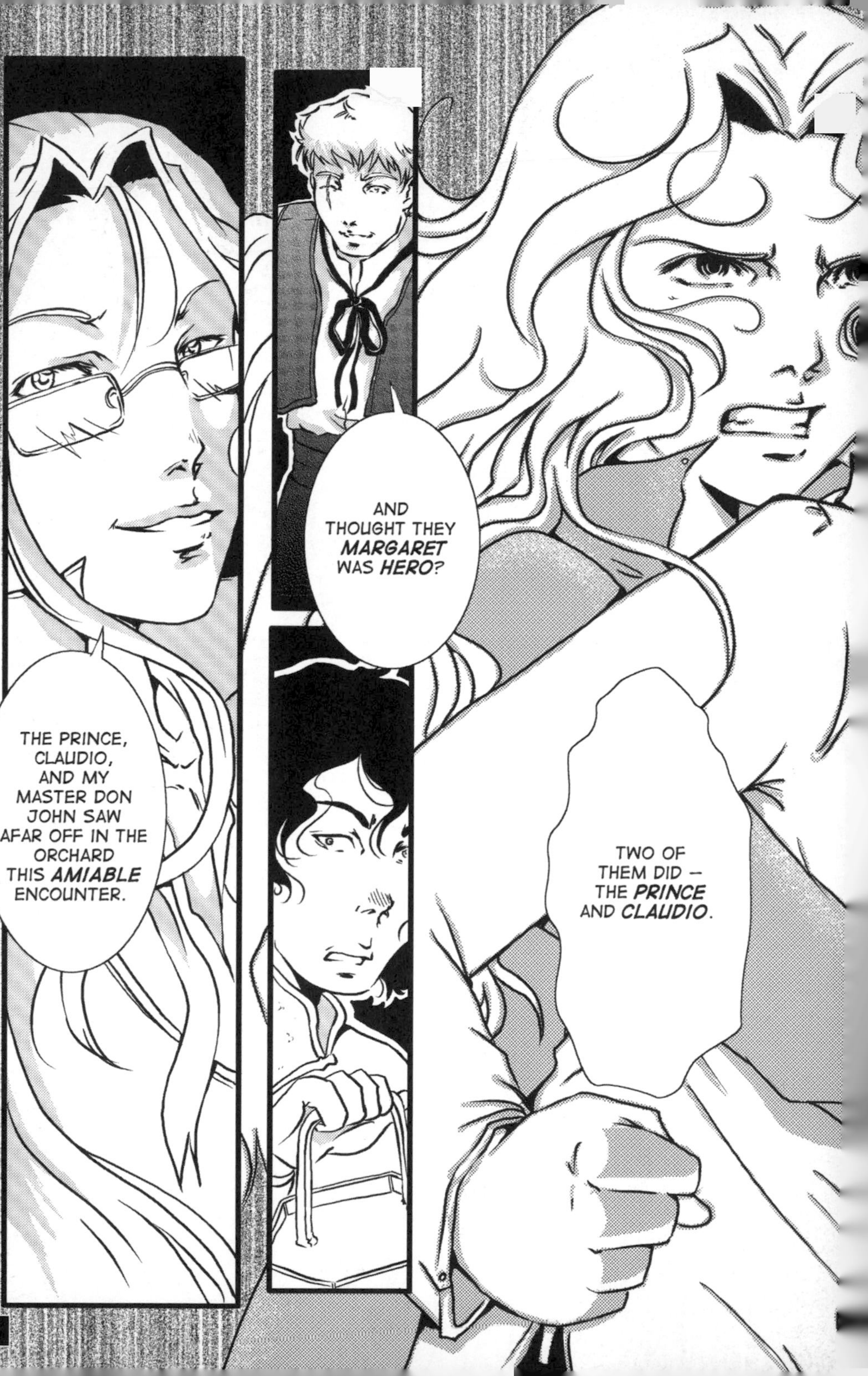
THE PRINCE, CLAUDIO, AND MY MASTER DON JOHN SAW AFAR OFF IN THE ORCHARD THIS *AMIABLE* ENCOUNTER.
AND THOUGHT THEY *MARGARET* WAS *HERO*?
TWO OF THEM DID – THE *PRINCE* AND *CLAUDIO*.

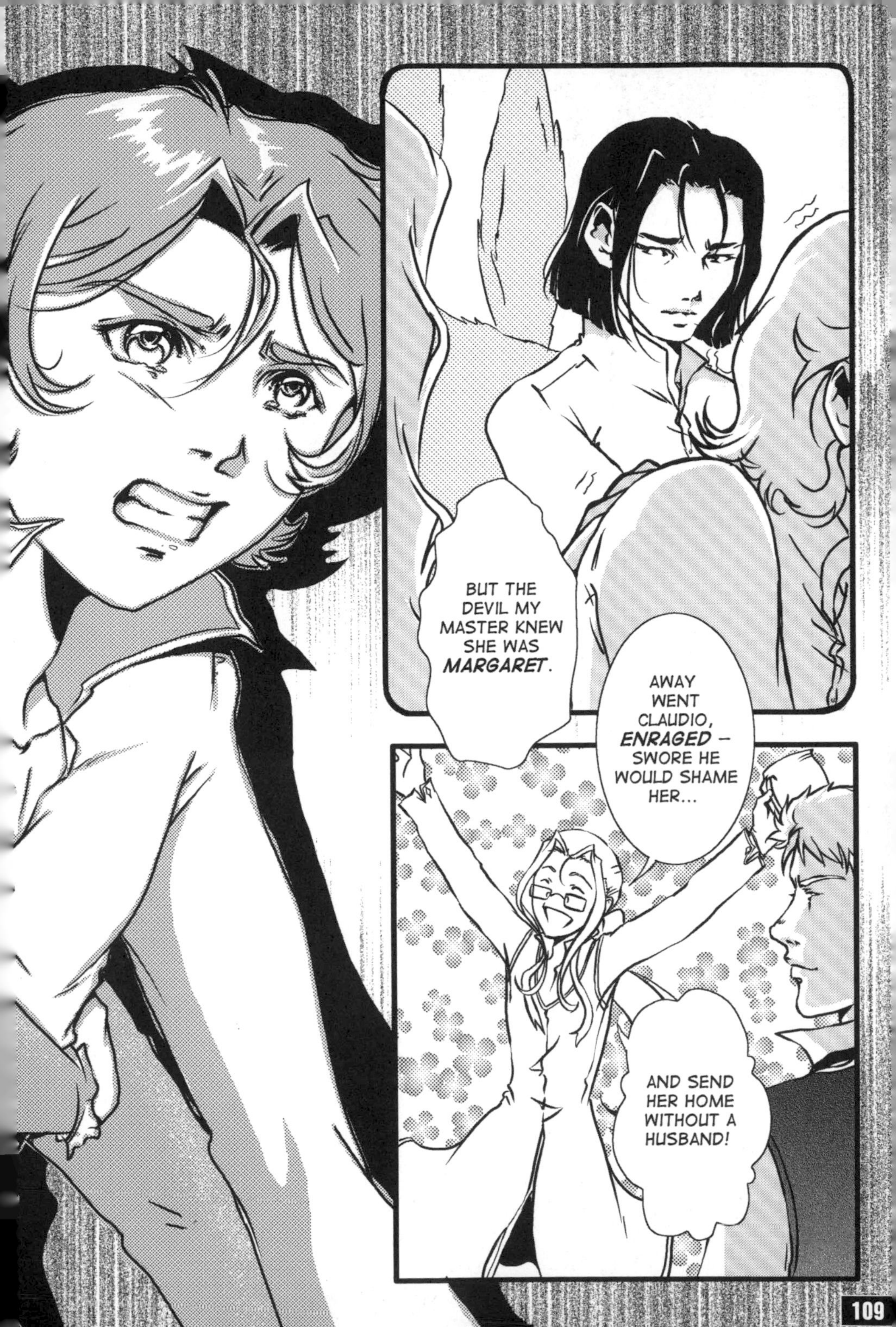
BUT THE DEVIL MY MASTER KNEW SHE WAS **MARGARET**.
AWAY WENT CLAUDIO, **ENRAGED** – SWORE HE WOULD SHAME HER...
AND SEND HER HOME WITHOUT A HUSBAND!

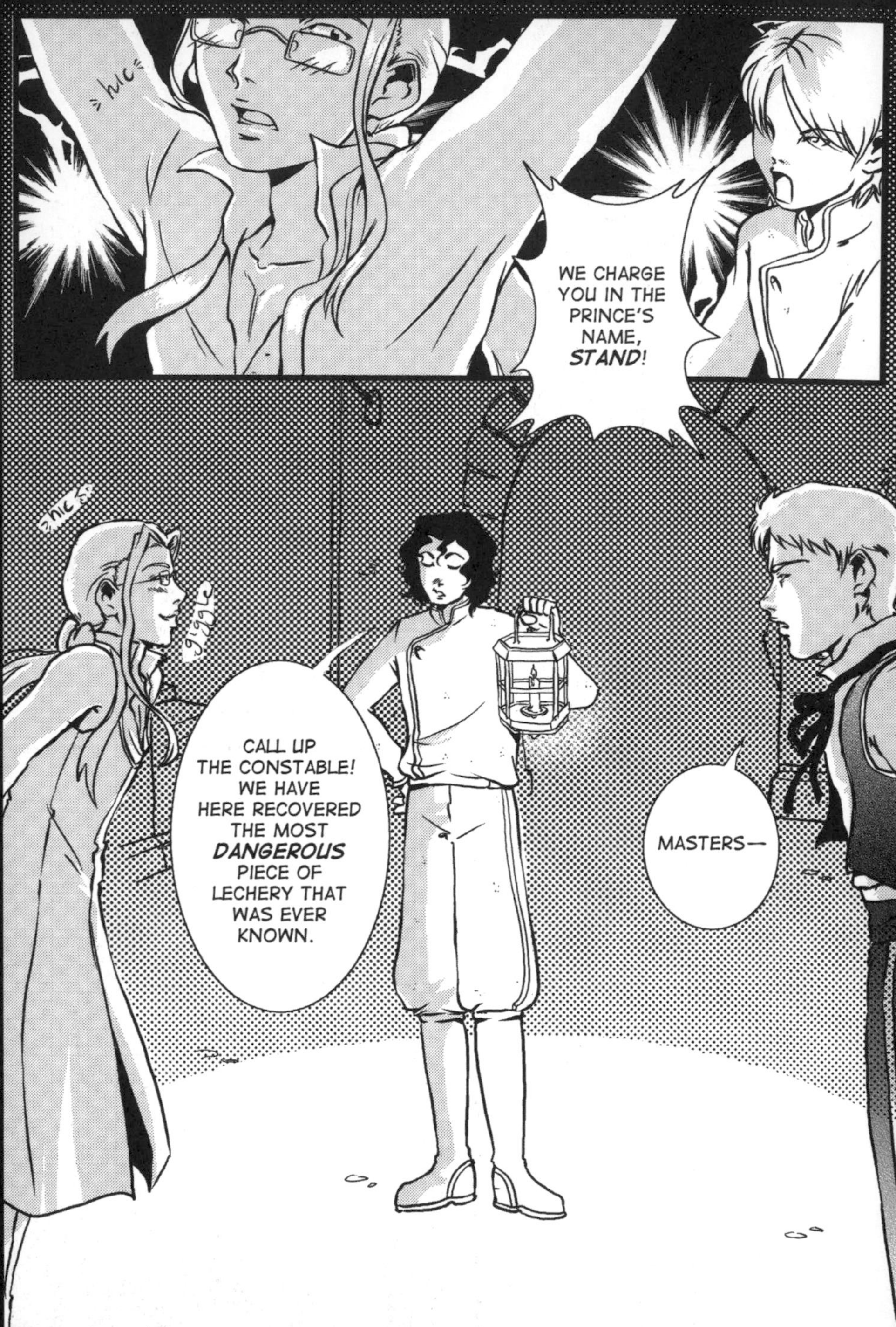
hic
WE CHARGE YOU IN THE PRINCE'S NAME, **STAND**!
hic
giggle
CALL UP THE CONSTABLE! WE HAVE HERE RECOVERED THE MOST **DANGEROUS** PIECE OF LECHERY THAT WAS EVER KNOWN.
MASTERS—

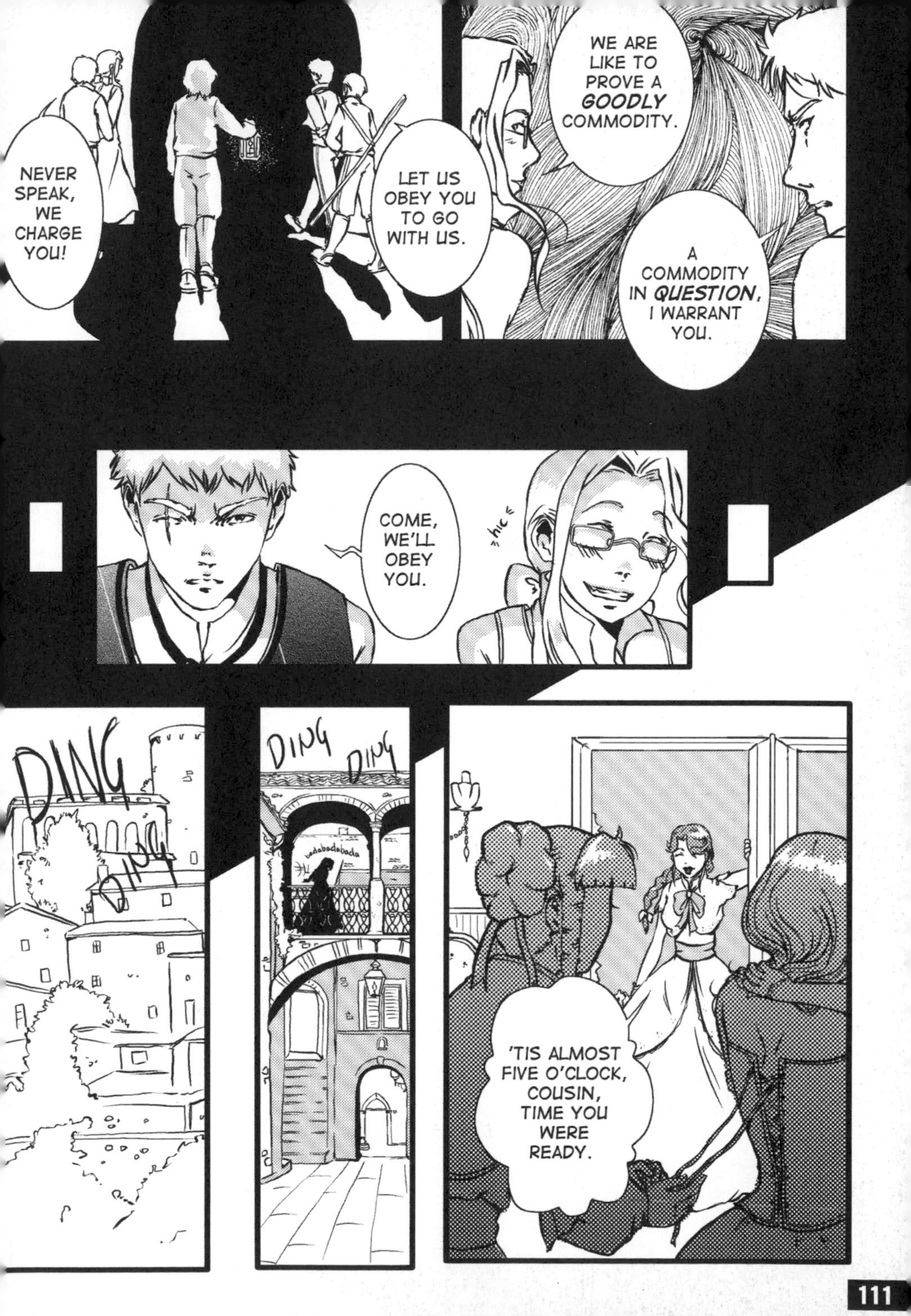
NEVER SPEAK, WE CHARGE YOU!
LET US OBEY YOU TO GO WITH US.
WE ARE LIKE TO PROVE A *GOODLY* COMMODITY.
A COMMODITY IN *QUESTION*, I WARRANT YOU.
COME, WE'LL OBEY YOU.
hic
DING
DING
DING
DING
badabadabada
'TIS ALMOST FIVE O'CLOCK, COUSIN, TIME YOU WERE READY.

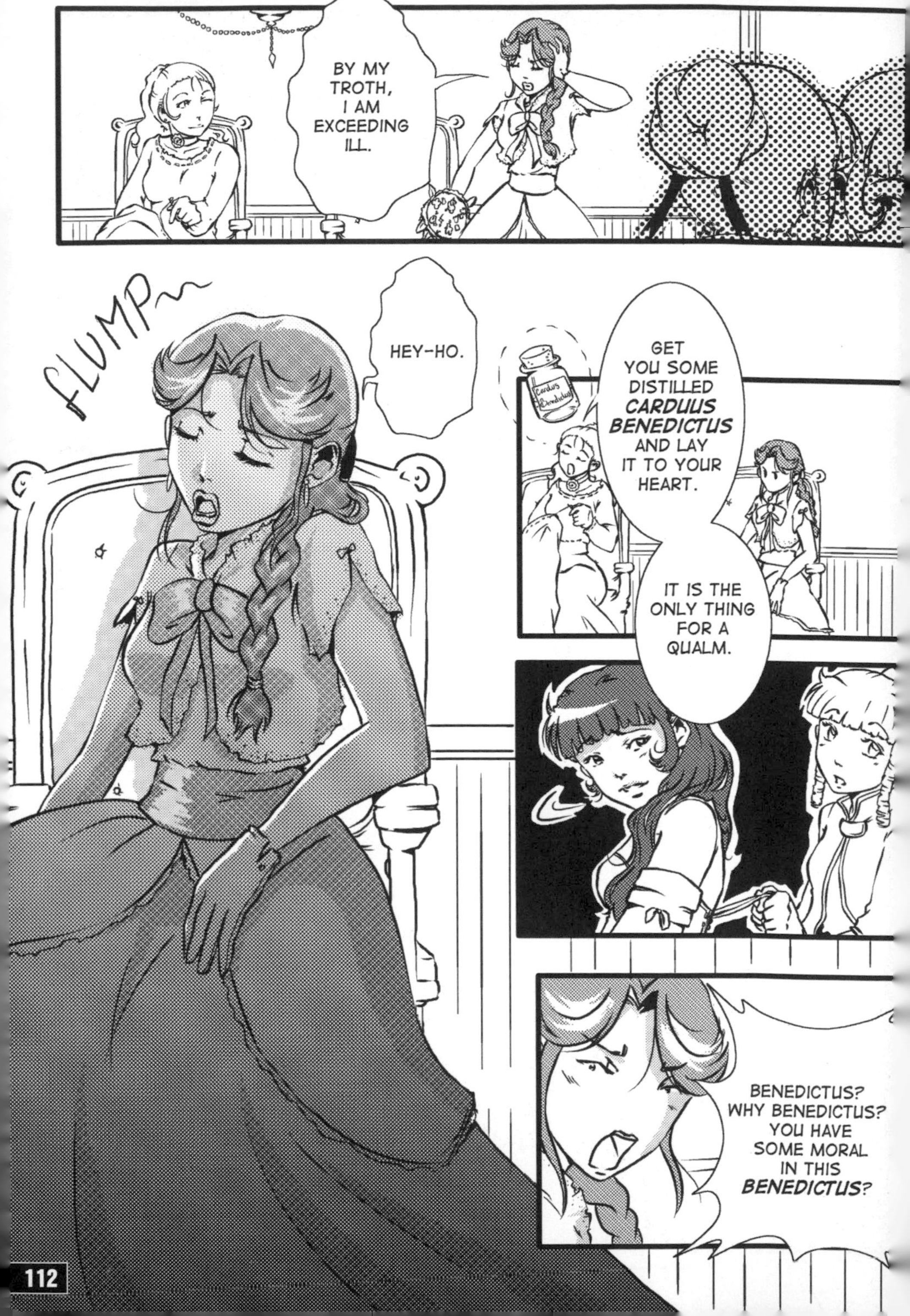
BY MY TROTH, I AM EXCEEDING ILL.
FLUMP~~
HEY-HO.
GET YOU SOME DISTILLED ***CARDUUS BENEDICTUS*** AND LAY IT TO YOUR HEART.
Cardus Benedictus
IT IS THE ONLY THING FOR A QUALM.
BENEDICTUS? WHY BENEDICTUS? YOU HAVE SOME MORAL IN THIS ***BENEDICTUS***?

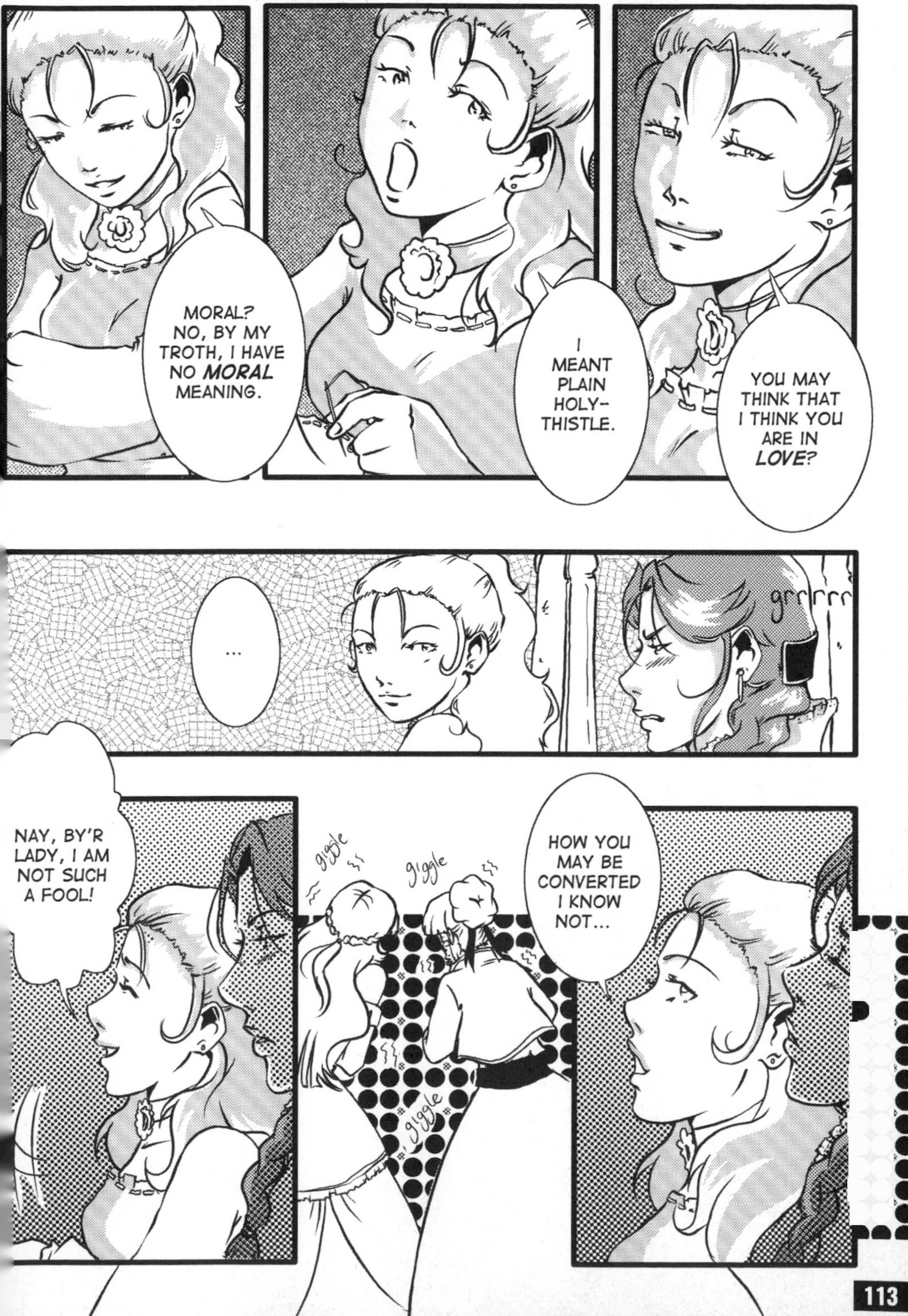
MORAL? NO, BY MY TROTH, I HAVE NO **MORAL** MEANING.
I MEANT PLAIN HOLY-THISTLE.
YOU MAY THINK THAT I THINK YOU ARE IN **LOVE**?
...
grrrrr
NAY, BY'R LADY, I AM NOT SUCH A FOOL!
giggle
giggle
giggle
HOW YOU MAY BE CONVERTED I KNOW NOT...

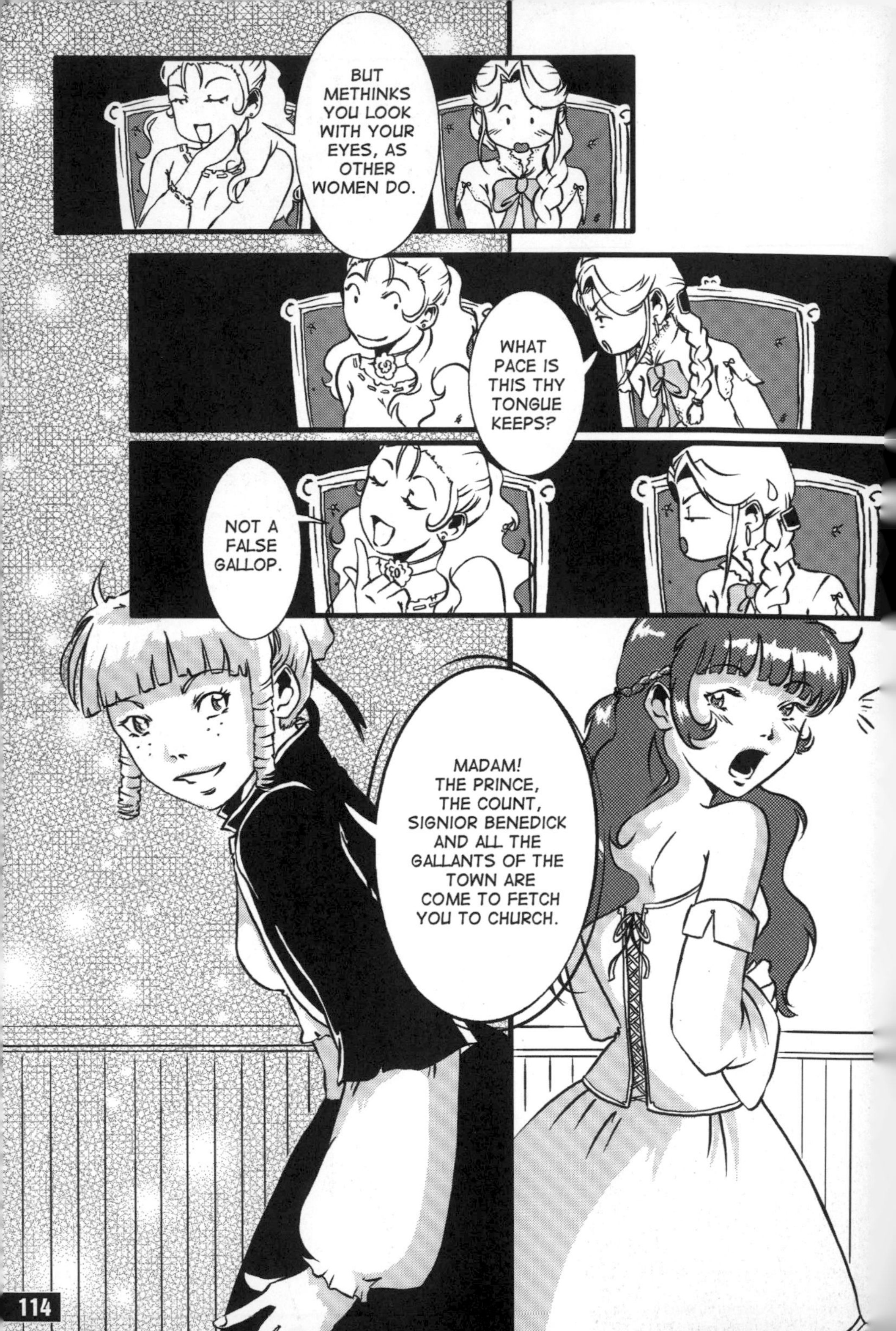

BUT METHINKS YOU LOOK WITH YOUR EYES, AS OTHER WOMEN DO.
WHAT PACE IS THIS THY TONGUE KEEPS?
NOT A FALSE GALLOP.
MADAM! THE PRINCE, THE COUNT, SIGNIOR BENEDICK AND ALL THE GALLANTS OF THE TOWN ARE COME TO FETCH YOU TO CHURCH.

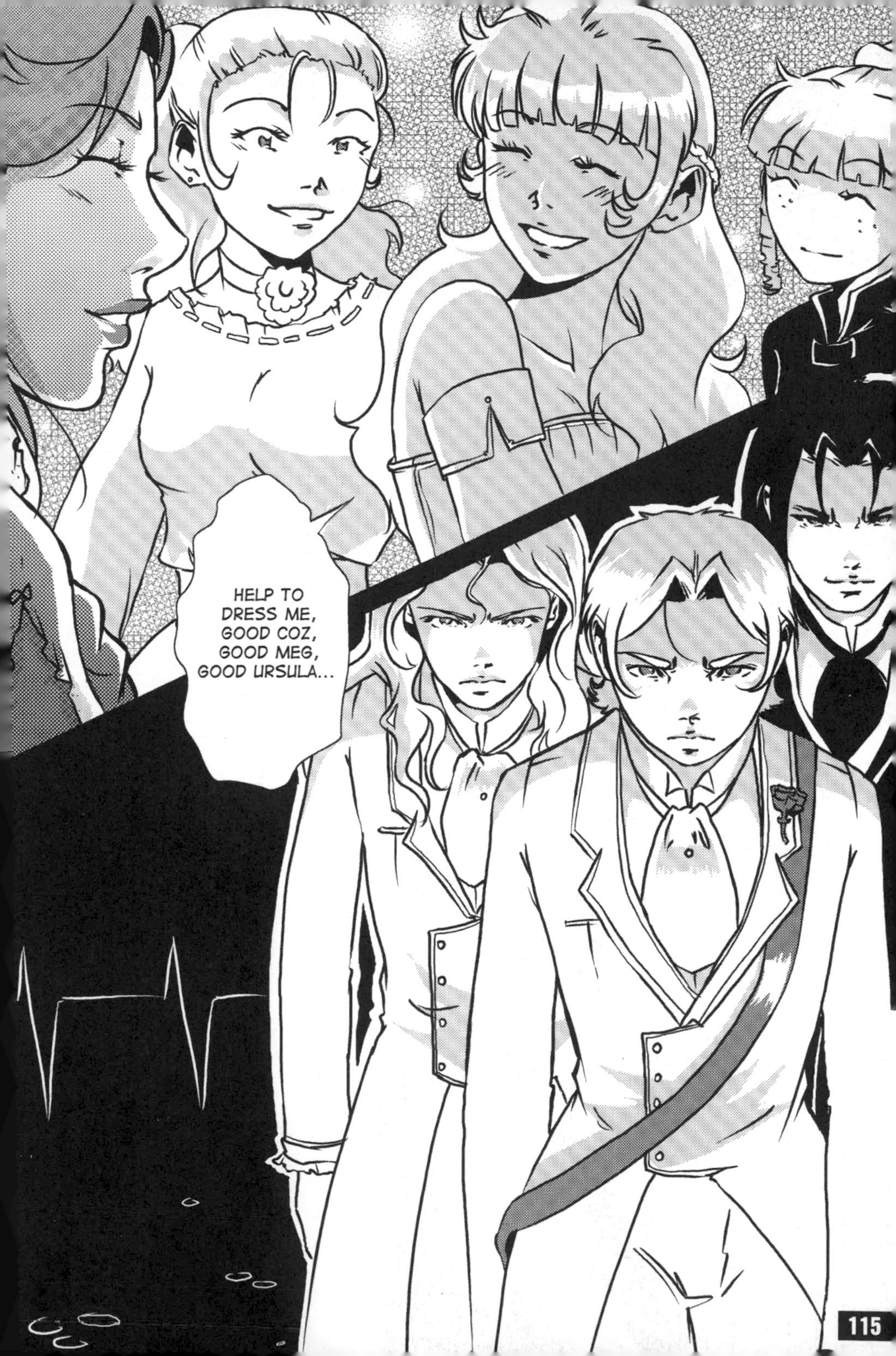
HELP TO DRESS ME, GOOD COZ, GOOD MEG, GOOD URSULA...

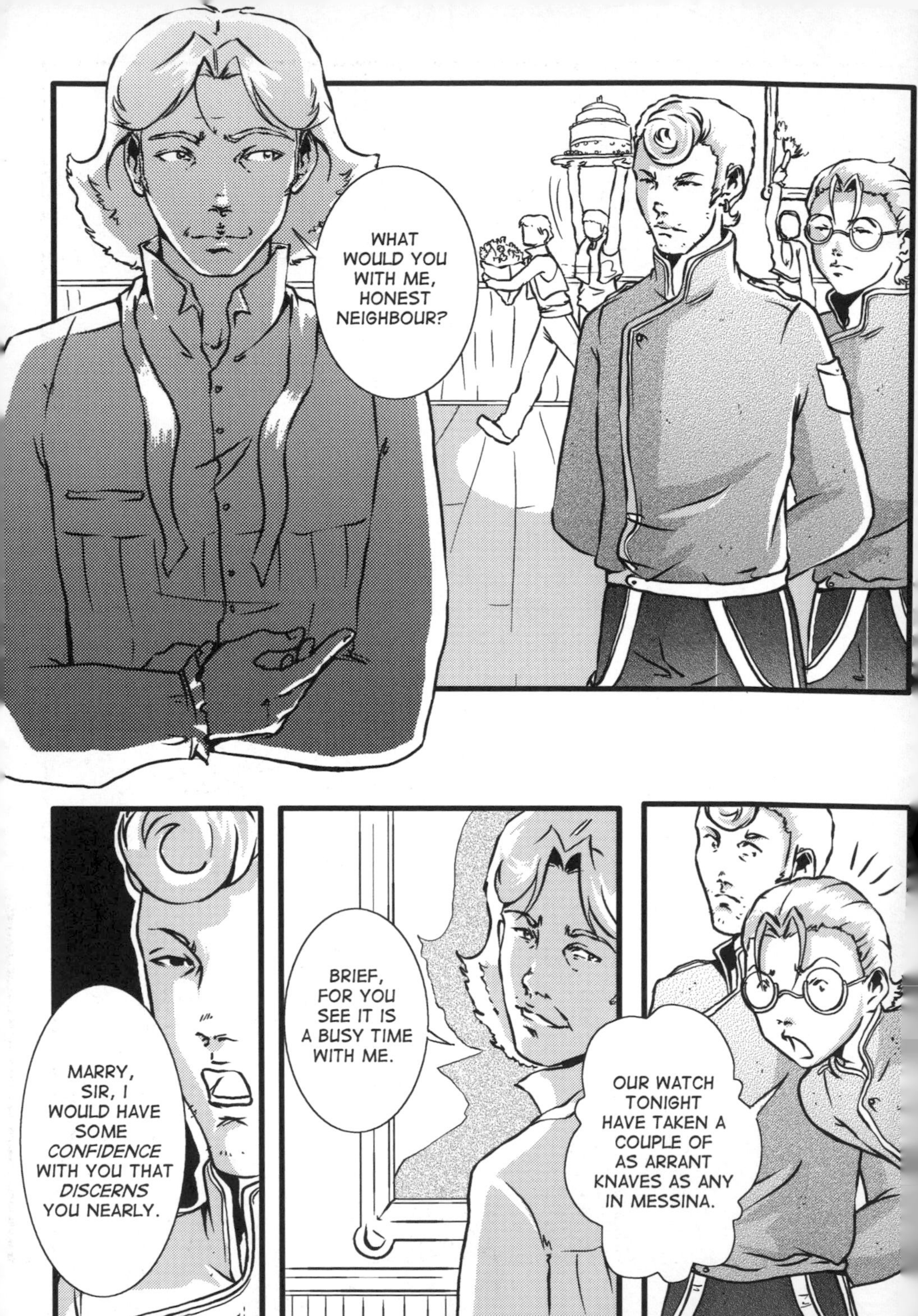
WHAT WOULD YOU WITH ME, HONEST NEIGHBOUR?
MARRY, SIR, I WOULD HAVE SOME *CONFIDENCE* WITH YOU THAT *DISCERNS* YOU NEARLY.
BRIEF, FOR YOU SEE IT IS A BUSY TIME WITH ME.
OUR WATCH TONIGHT HAVE TAKEN A COUPLE OF AS ARRANT KNAVES AS ANY IN MESSINA.

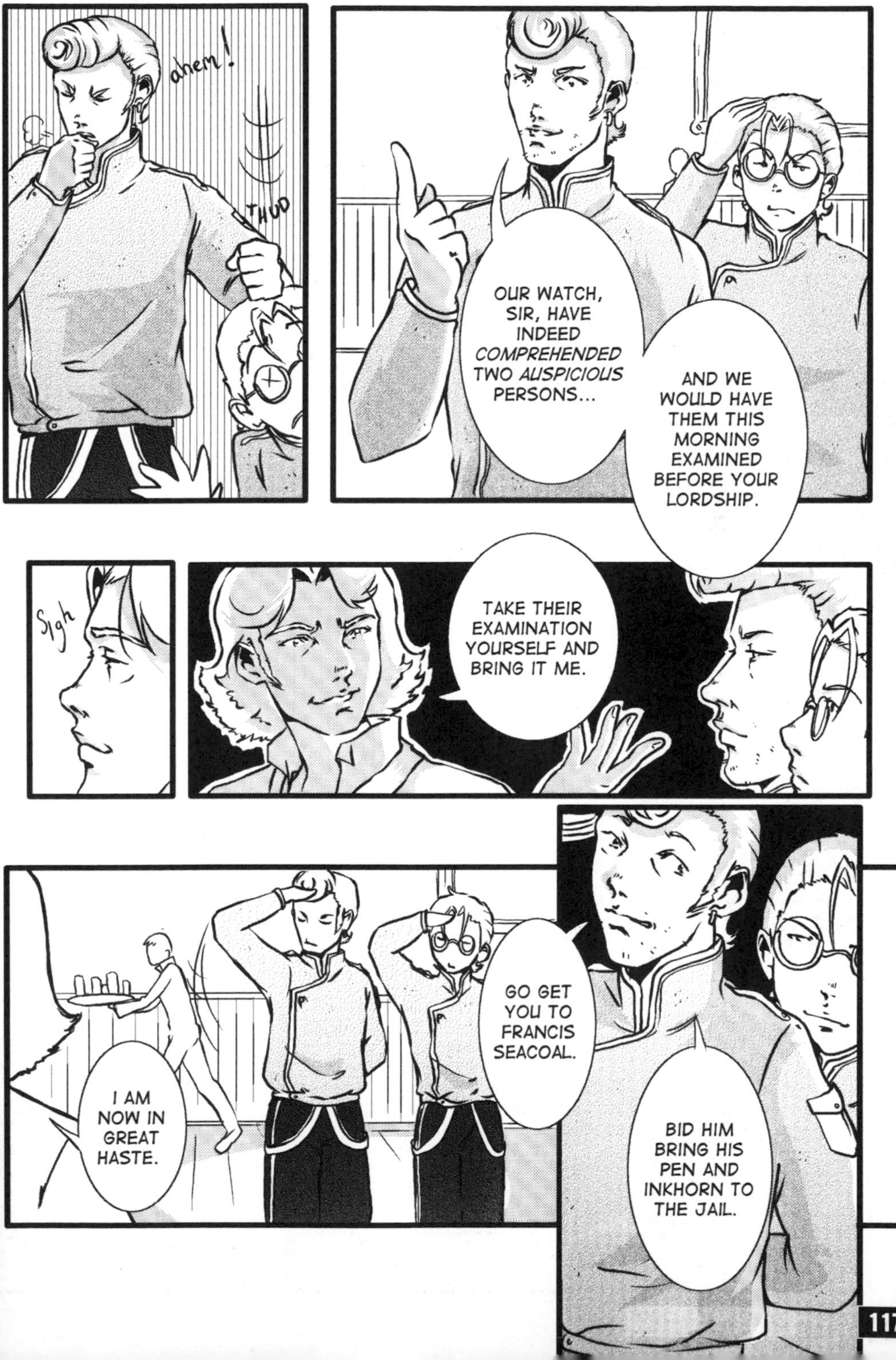
ahem!
THUD
OUR WATCH, SIR, HAVE INDEED *COMPREHENDED* TWO *AUSPICIOUS* PERSONS...
AND WE WOULD HAVE THEM THIS MORNING EXAMINED BEFORE YOUR LORDSHIP.
Sigh
TAKE THEIR EXAMINATION YOURSELF AND BRING IT ME.
I AM NOW IN GREAT HASTE.
GO GET YOU TO FRANCIS SEACOAL.
BID HIM BRING HIS PEN AND INKHORN TO THE JAIL.

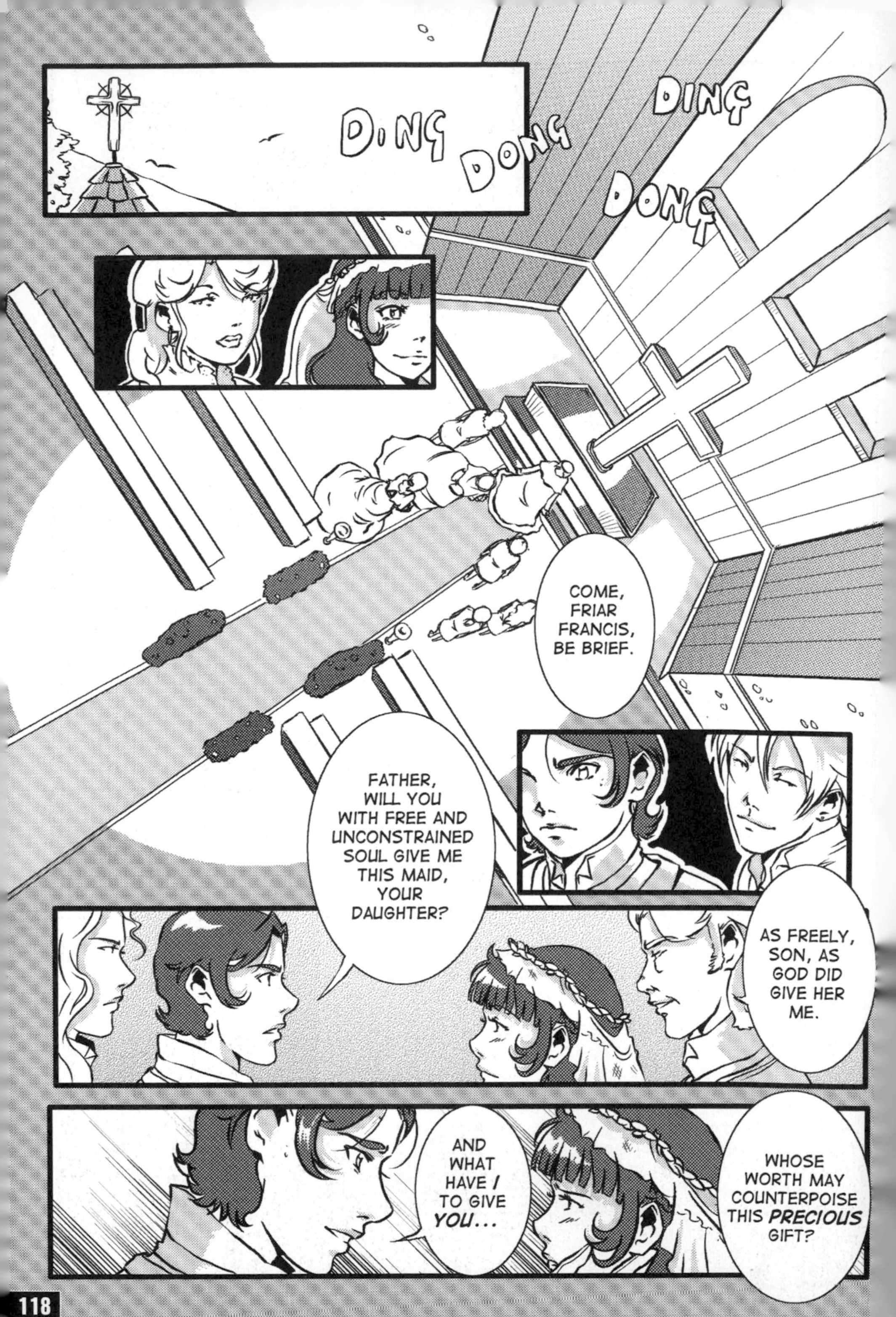
DING
DONG
DING
DONG
COME, FRIAR FRANCIS, BE BRIEF.
FATHER, WILL YOU WITH FREE AND UNCONSTRAINED SOUL GIVE ME THIS MAID, YOUR DAUGHTER?
AS FREELY, SON, AS GOD DID GIVE HER ME.
AND WHAT HAVE *I* TO GIVE ***YOU***...
WHOSE WORTH MAY COUNTERPOISE THIS ***PRECIOUS*** GIFT?

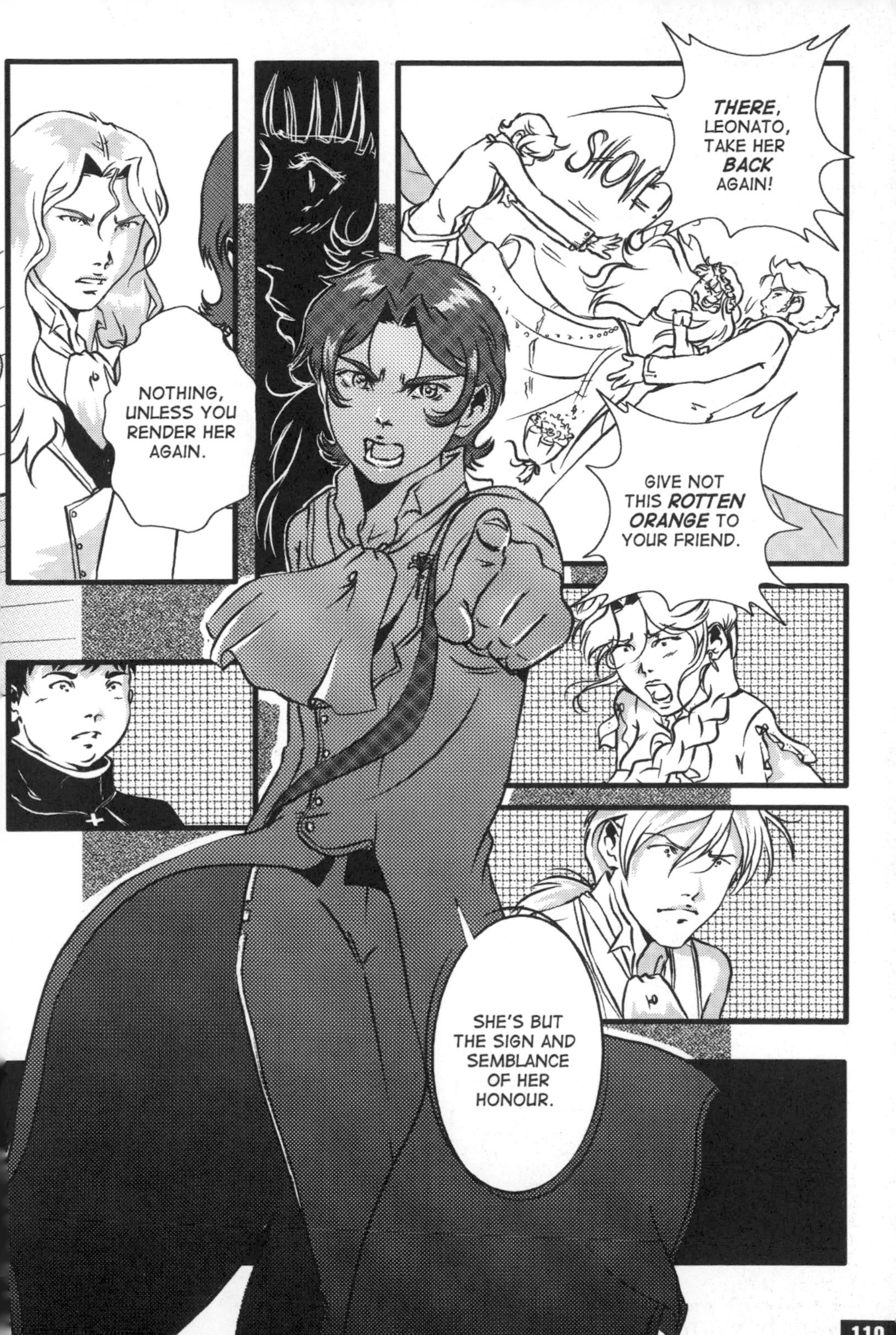
NOTHING, UNLESS YOU RENDER HER AGAIN.
SHOVE
***THERE***, LEONATO, TAKE HER ***BACK*** AGAIN!
GIVE NOT THIS ***ROTTEN ORANGE*** TO YOUR FRIEND.
SHE'S BUT THE SIGN AND SEMBLANCE OF HER HONOUR.

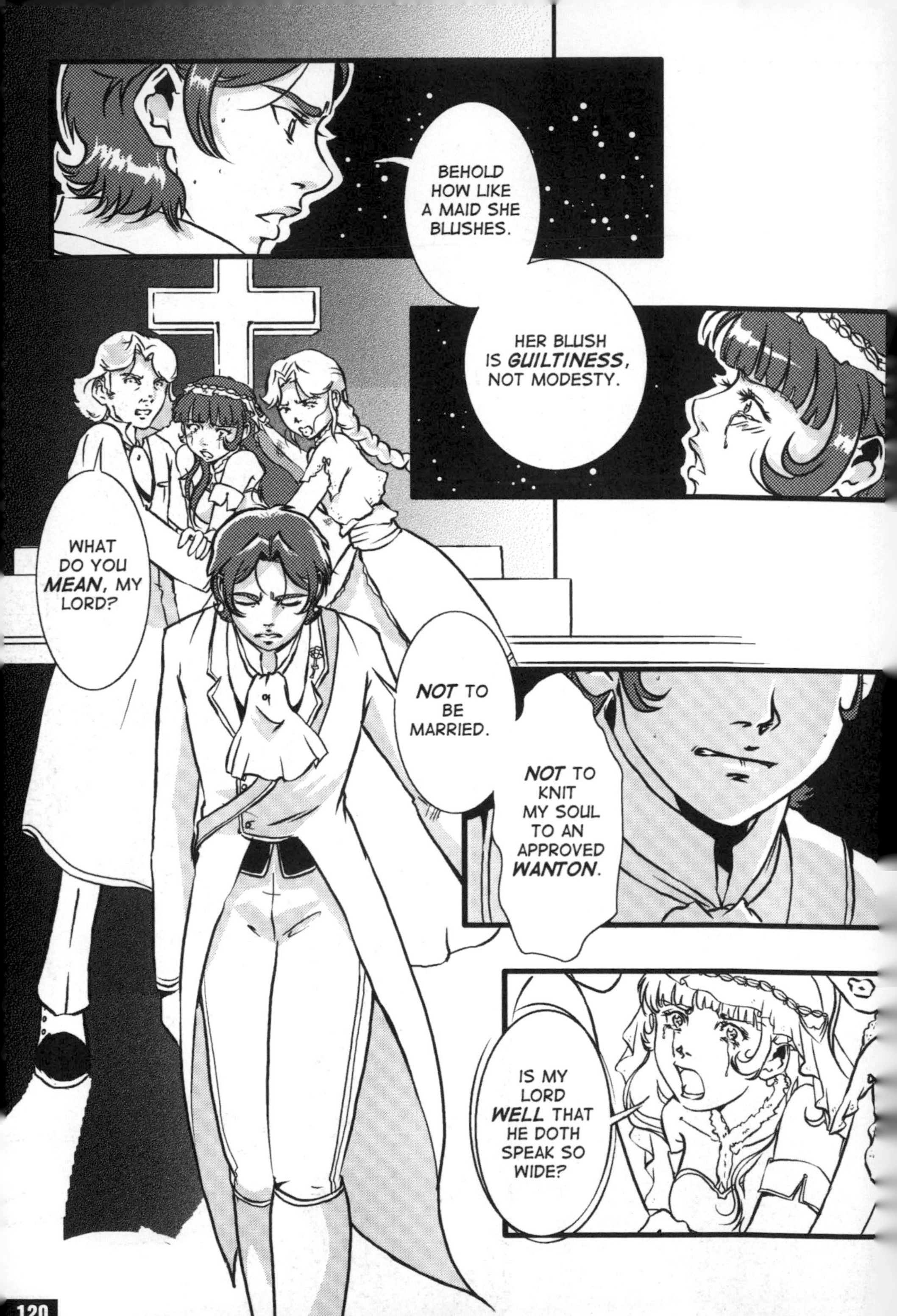

BEHOLD HOW LIKE A MAID SHE BLUSHES.
HER BLUSH IS ***GUILTINESS***, NOT MODESTY.
WHAT DO YOU ***MEAN***, MY LORD?
***NOT*** TO BE MARRIED.
***NOT*** TO KNIT MY SOUL TO AN APPROVED ***WANTON***.
IS MY LORD ***WELL*** THAT HE DOTH SPEAK SO WIDE?

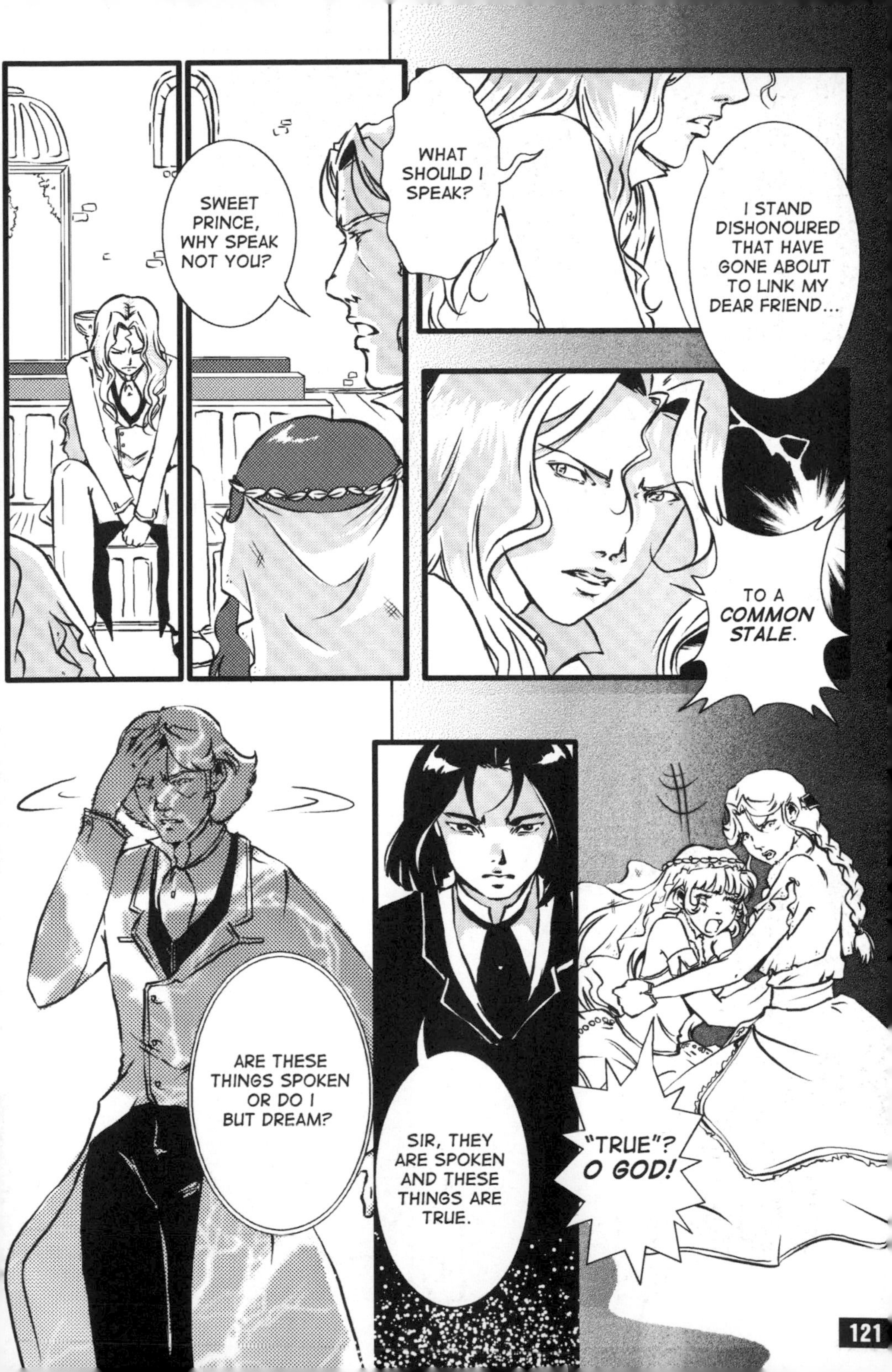
SWEET PRINCE, WHY SPEAK NOT YOU?
WHAT SHOULD I SPEAK?
I STAND DISHONOURED THAT HAVE GONE ABOUT TO LINK MY DEAR FRIEND...
TO A *COMMON STALE*.
ARE THESE THINGS SPOKEN OR DO I BUT DREAM?
SIR, THEY ARE SPOKEN AND THESE THINGS ARE TRUE.
"TRUE"? O GOD!

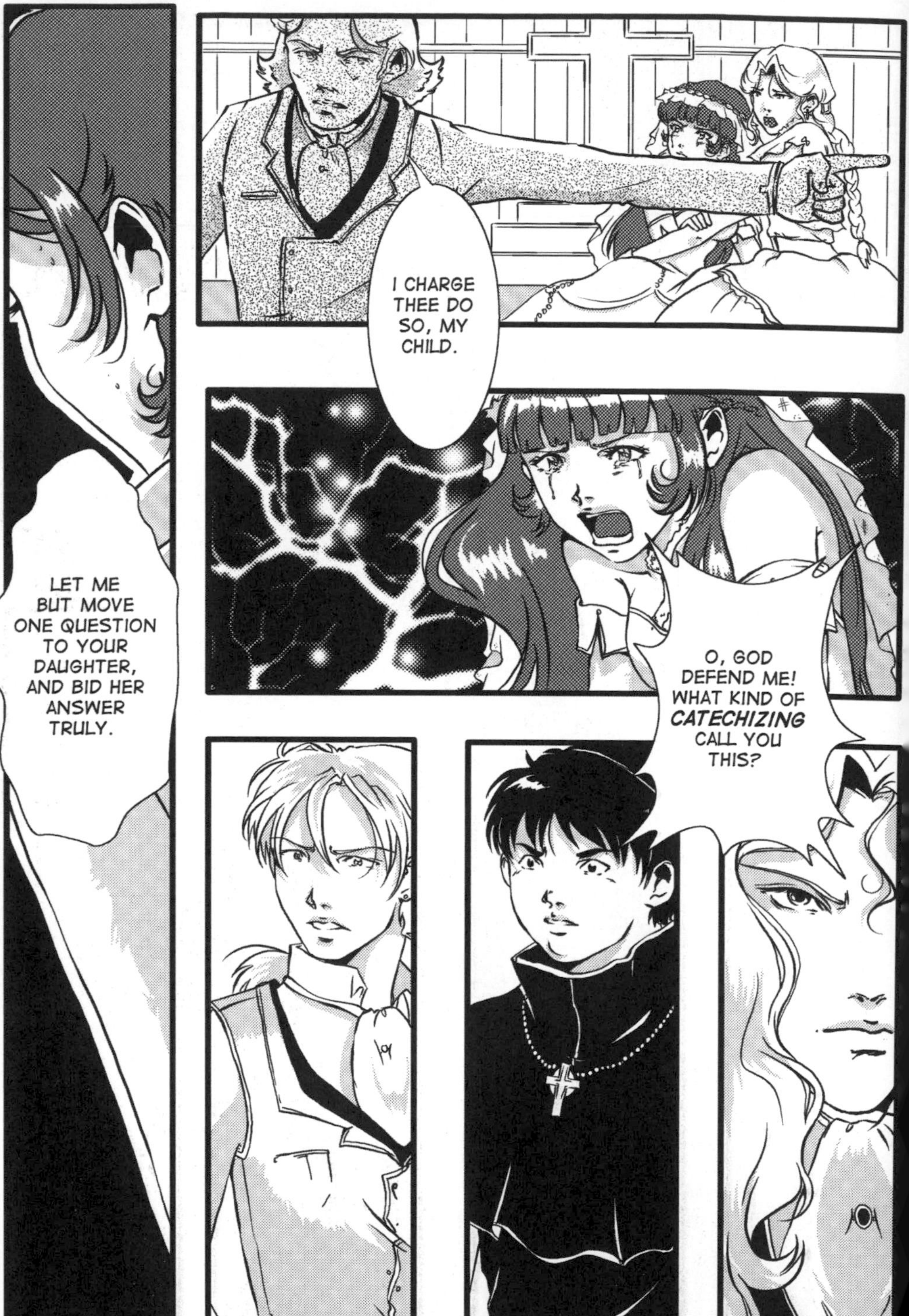
LET ME BUT MOVE ONE QUESTION TO YOUR DAUGHTER, AND BID HER ANSWER TRULY.
I CHARGE THEE DO SO, MY CHILD.
O, GOD DEFEND ME! WHAT KIND OF *CATECHIZING* CALL YOU THIS?

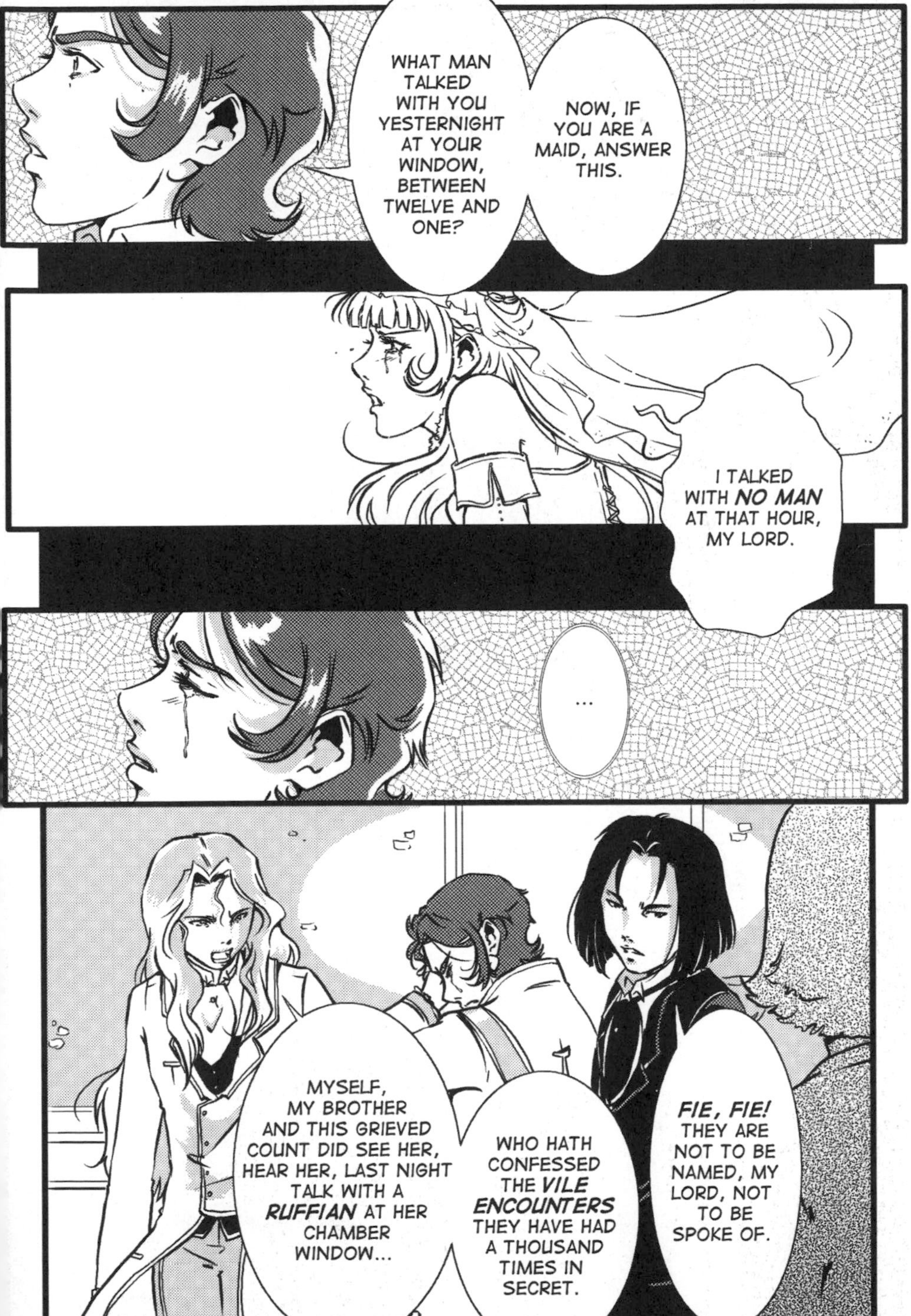
WHAT MAN TALKED WITH YOU YESTERNIGHT AT YOUR WINDOW, BETWEEN TWELVE AND ONE?
NOW, IF YOU ARE A MAID, ANSWER THIS.
I TALKED WITH **NO MAN** AT THAT HOUR, MY LORD.
...
MYSELF, MY BROTHER AND THIS GRIEVED COUNT DID SEE HER, HEAR HER, LAST NIGHT TALK WITH A **RUFFIAN** AT HER CHAMBER WINDOW...
WHO HATH CONFESSED THE **VILE ENCOUNTERS** THEY HAVE HAD A THOUSAND TIMES IN SECRET.
**FIE, FIE!** THEY ARE NOT TO BE NAMED, MY LORD, NOT TO BE SPOKE OF.

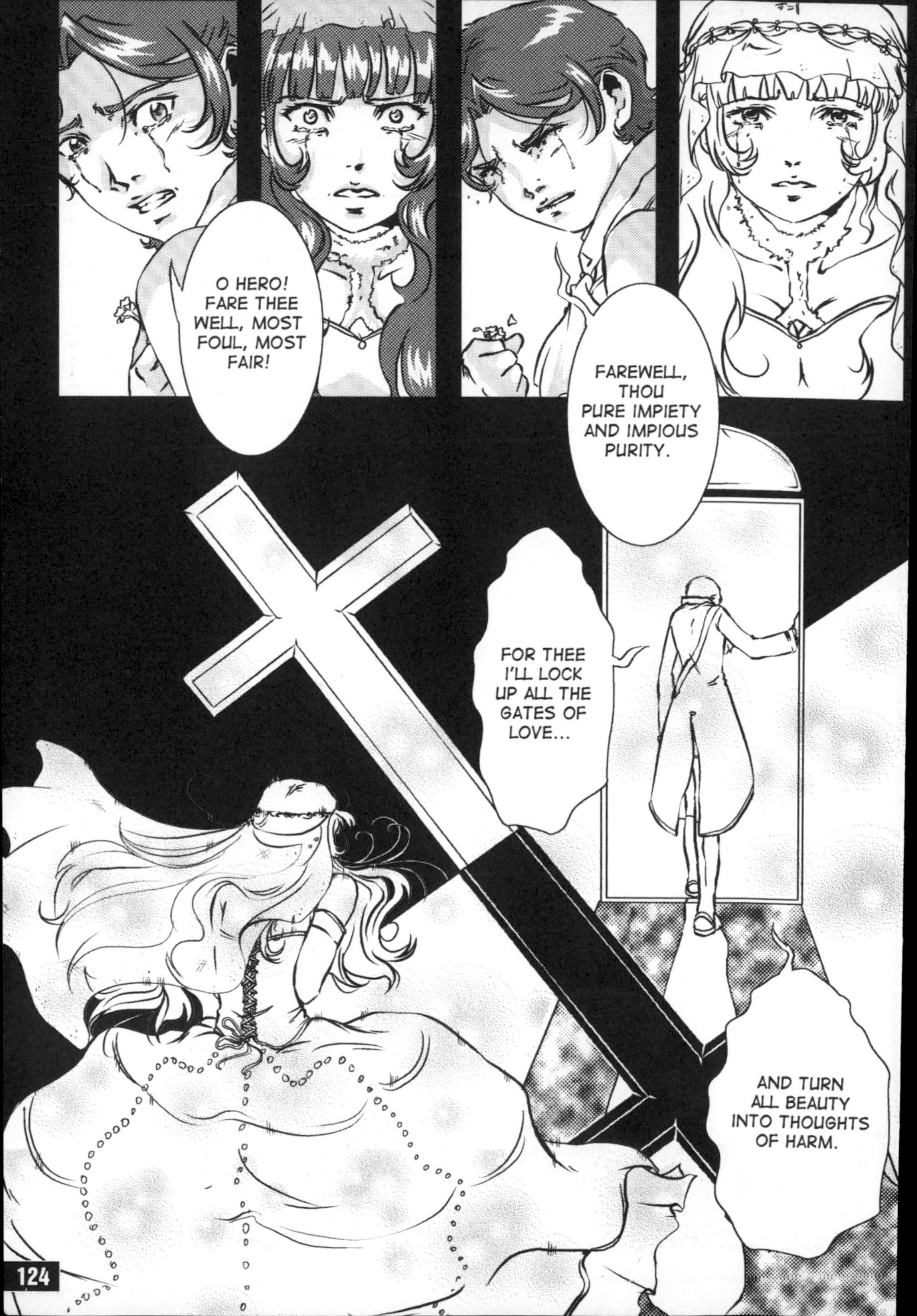
O HERO! FARE THEE WELL, MOST FOUL, MOST FAIR!
FAREWELL, THOU PURE IMPIETY AND IMPIOUS PURITY.
FOR THEE I'LL LOCK UP ALL THE GATES OF LOVE...
AND TURN ALL BEAUTY INTO THOUGHTS OF HARM.

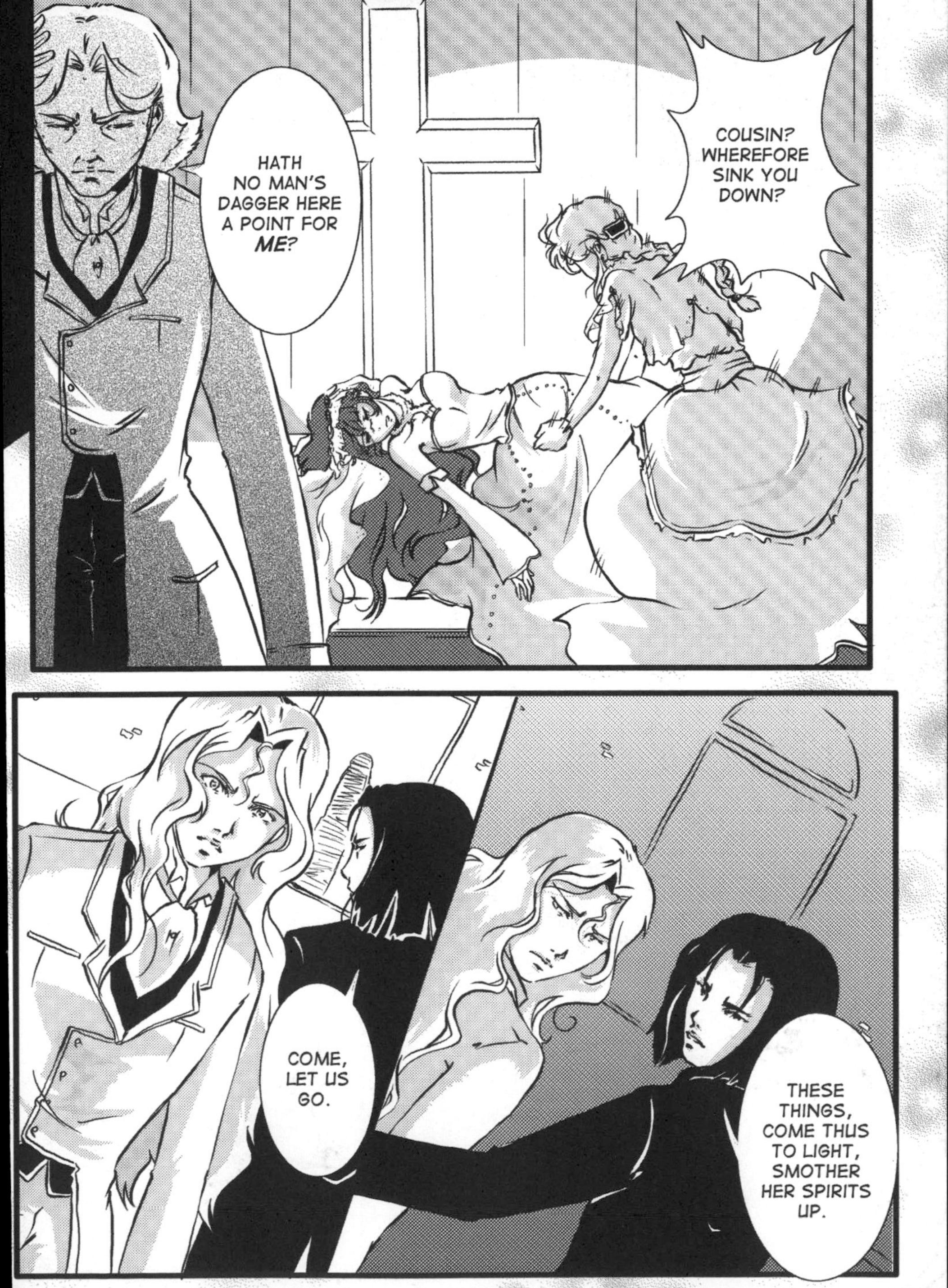
HATH NO MAN'S DAGGER HERE A POINT FOR *ME*?
COUSIN? WHEREFORE SINK YOU DOWN?
COME, LET US GO.
THESE THINGS, COME THUS TO LIGHT, SMOTHER HER SPIRITS UP.

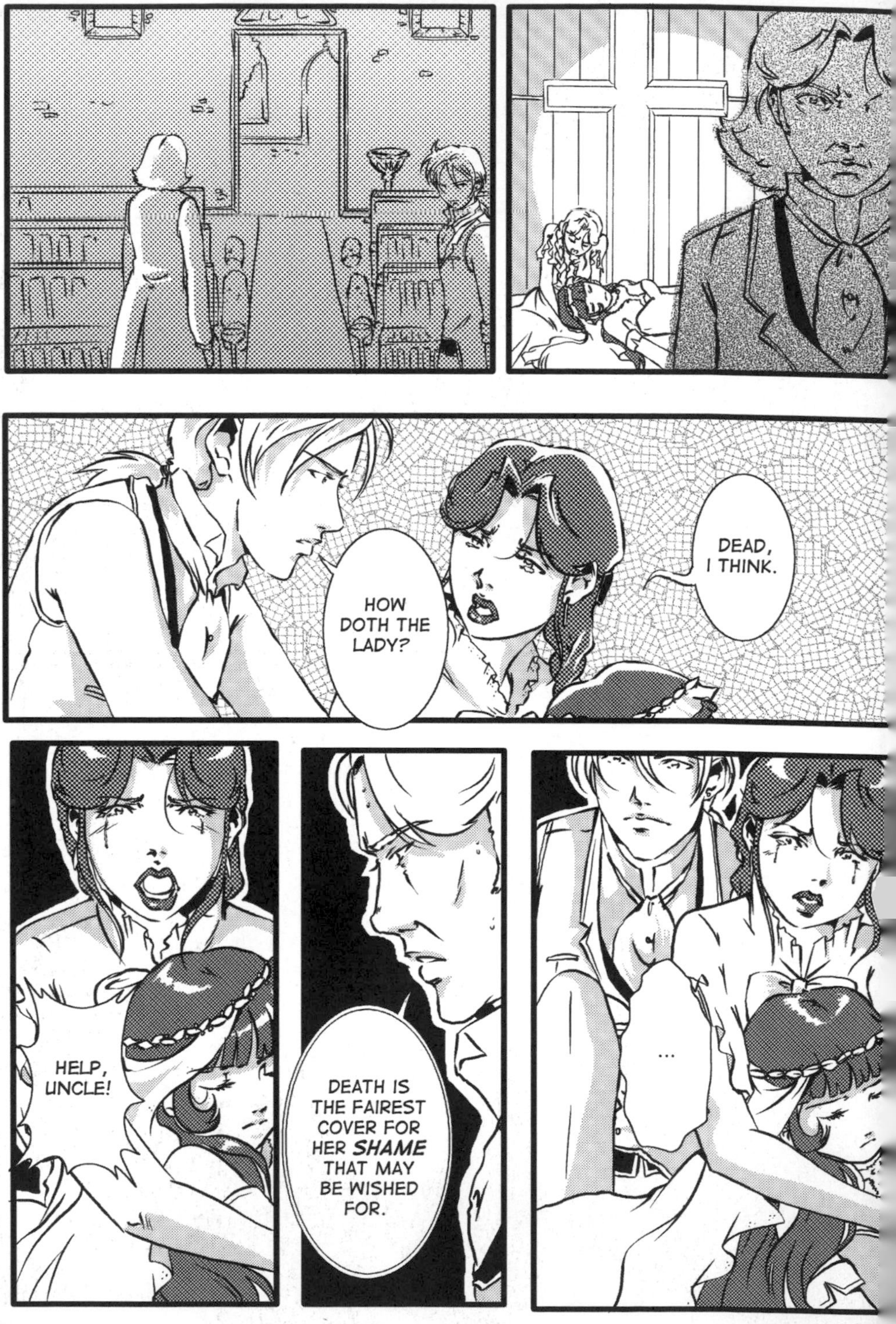
HOW DOTH THE LADY?
DEAD, I THINK.
HELP, UNCLE!
DEATH IS THE FAIREST COVER FOR HER SHAME THAT MAY BE WISHED FOR.
...

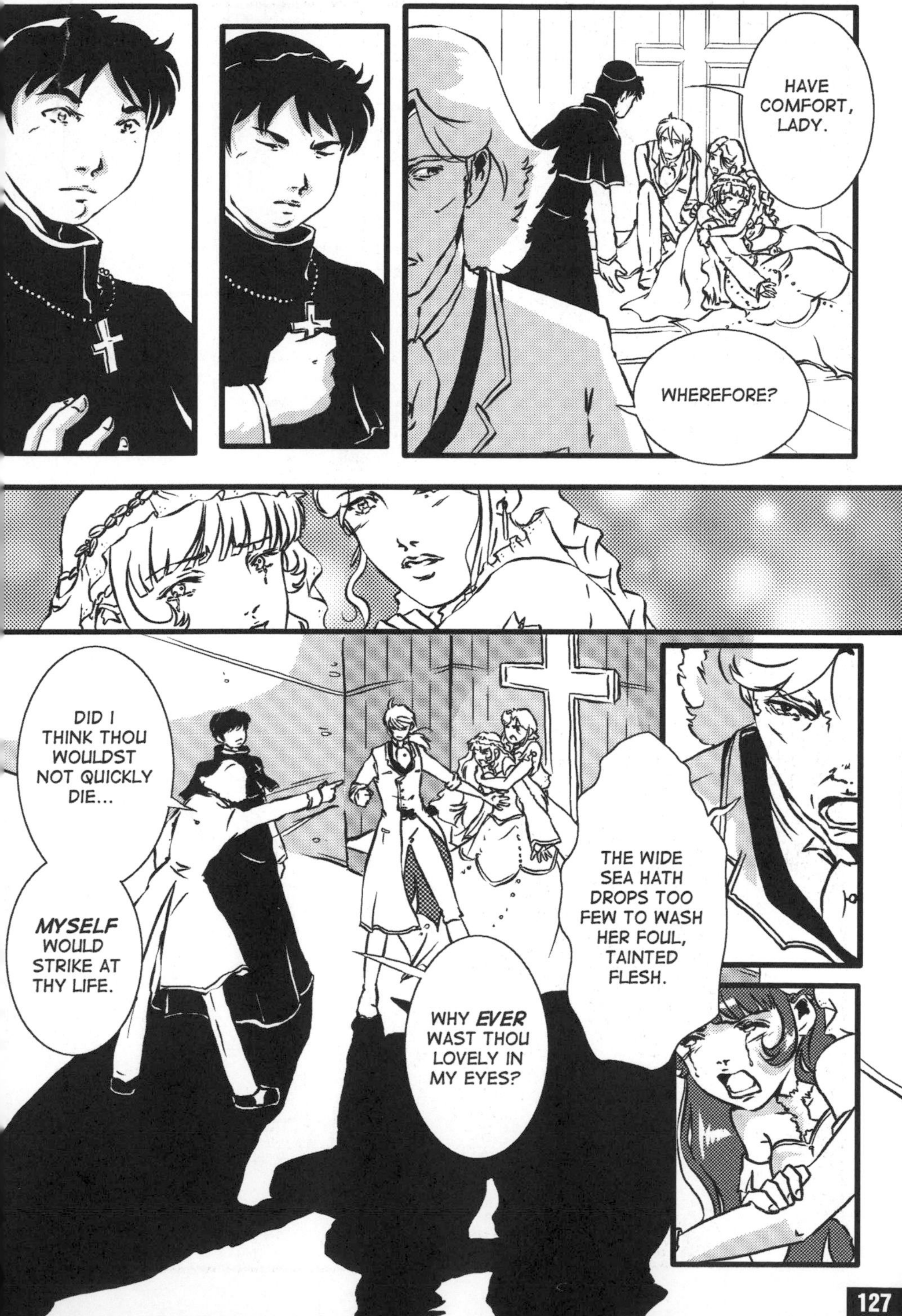
HAVE COMFORT, LADY.
WHEREFORE?
DID I THINK THOU WOULDST NOT QUICKLY DIE...
*MYSELF* WOULD STRIKE AT THY LIFE.
WHY *EVER* WAST THOU LOVELY IN MY EYES?
THE WIDE SEA HATH DROPS TOO FEW TO WASH HER FOUL, TAINTED FLESH.

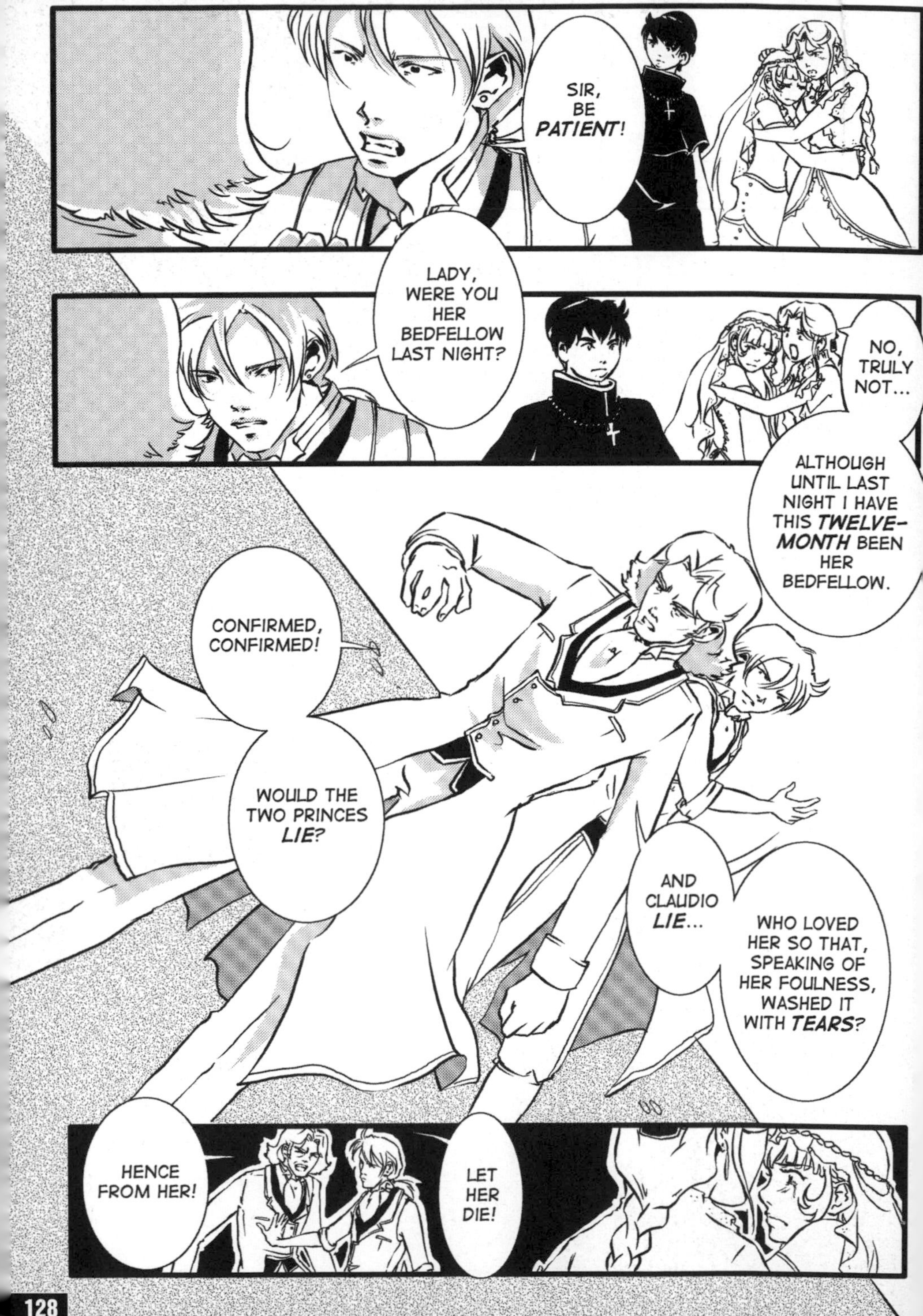
SIR, BE *PATIENT*!
LADY, WERE YOU HER BEDFELLOW LAST NIGHT?
NO, TRULY NOT...
ALTHOUGH UNTIL LAST NIGHT I HAVE THIS *TWELVE-MONTH* BEEN HER BEDFELLOW.
CONFIRMED, CONFIRMED!
WOULD THE TWO PRINCES *LIE*?
AND CLAUDIO *LIE*...
WHO LOVED HER SO THAT, SPEAKING OF HER FOULNESS, WASHED IT WITH *TEARS*?
HENCE FROM HER!
LET HER DIE!

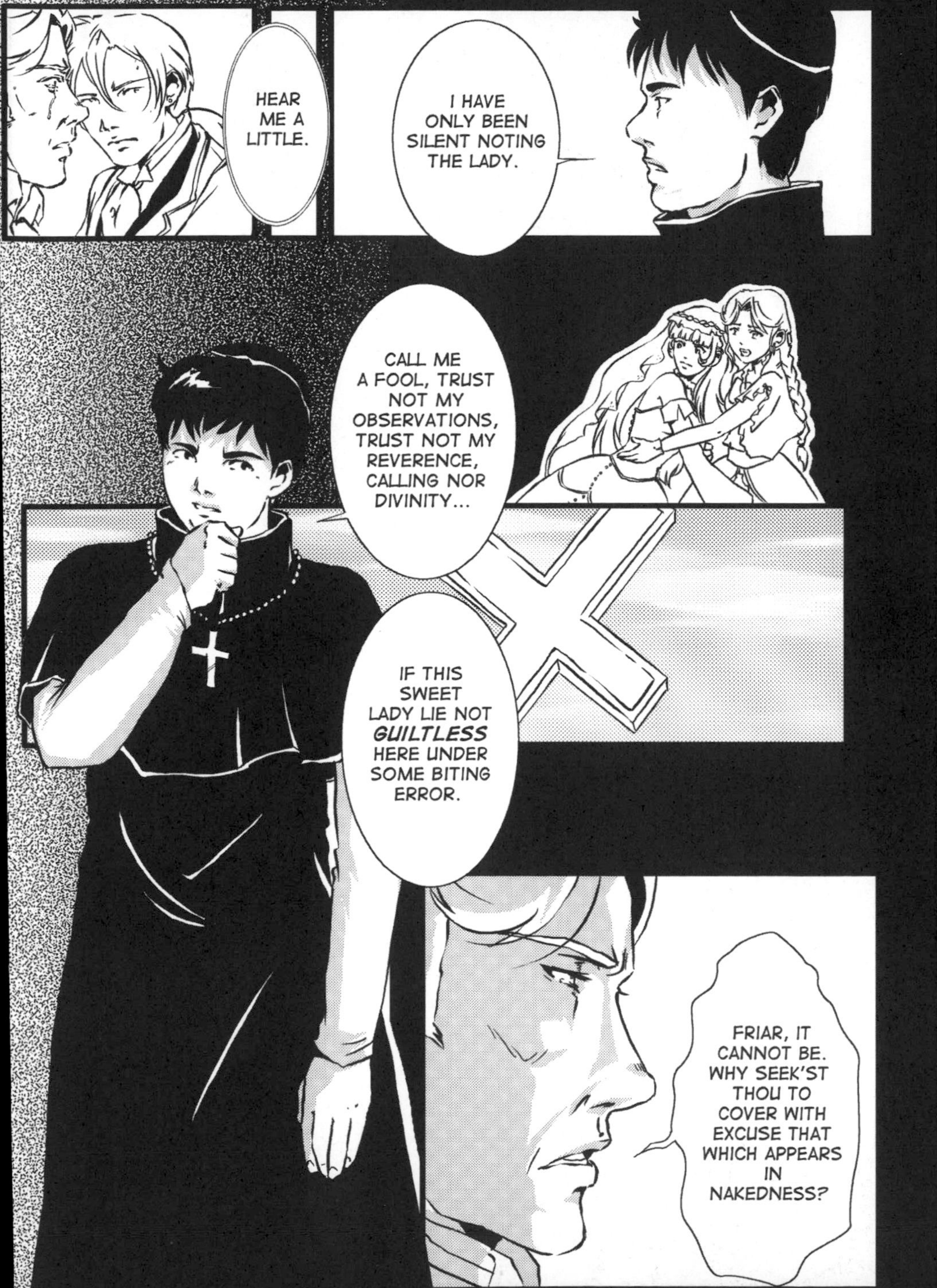
HEAR ME A LITTLE.
I HAVE ONLY BEEN SILENT NOTING THE LADY.
CALL ME A FOOL, TRUST NOT MY OBSERVATIONS, TRUST NOT MY REVERENCE, CALLING NOR DIVINITY...
IF THIS SWEET LADY LIE NOT ***GUILTLESS*** HERE UNDER SOME BITING ERROR.
FRIAR, IT CANNOT BE. WHY SEEK'ST THOU TO COVER WITH EXCUSE THAT WHICH APPEARS IN NAKEDNESS?

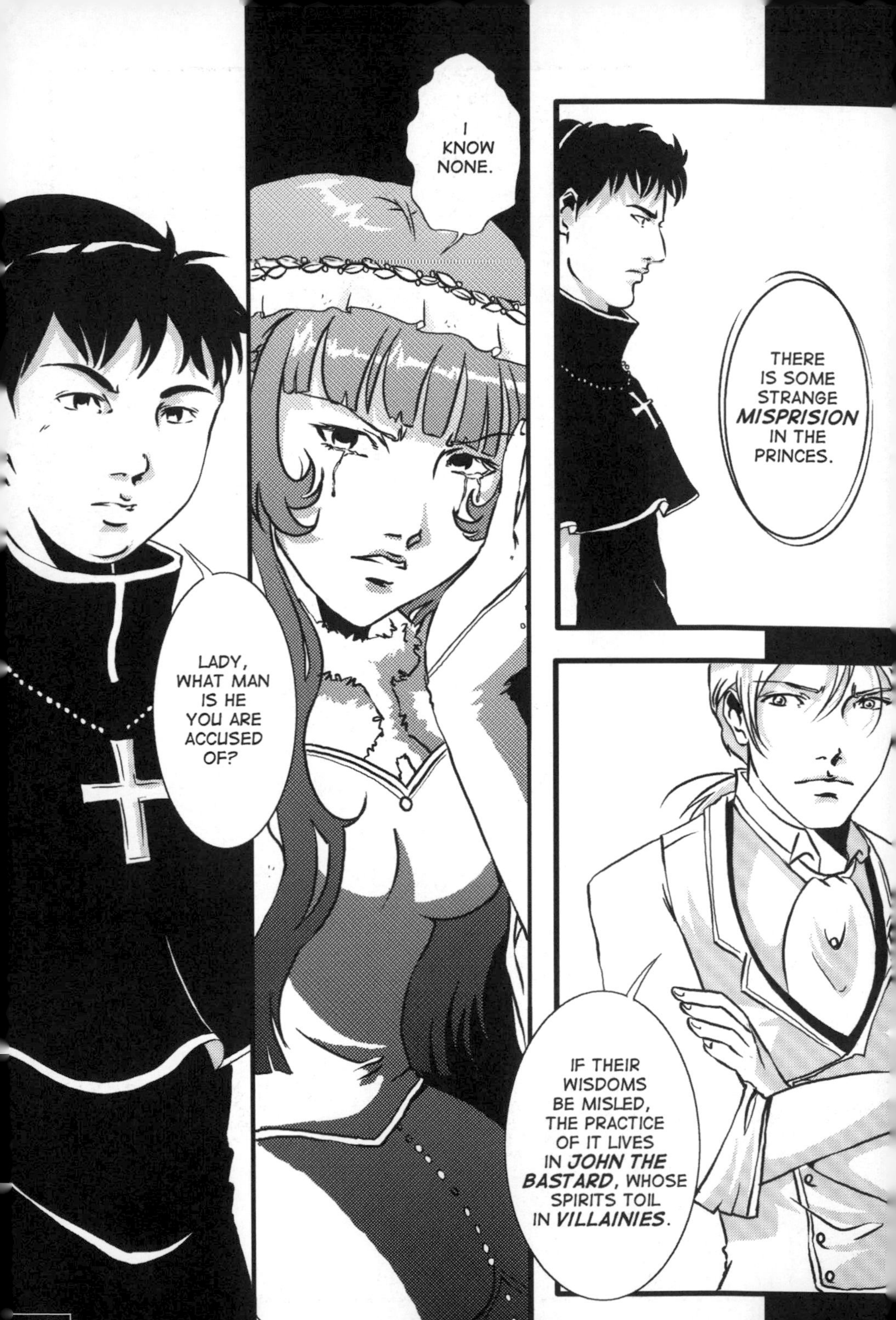
LADY, WHAT MAN IS HE YOU ARE ACCUSED OF?
I KNOW NONE.
THERE IS SOME STRANGE **MISPRISION** IN THE PRINCES.
IF THEIR WISDOMS BE MISLED, THE PRACTICE OF IT LIVES IN **JOHN THE BASTARD**, WHOSE SPIRITS TOIL IN **VILLAINIES**.

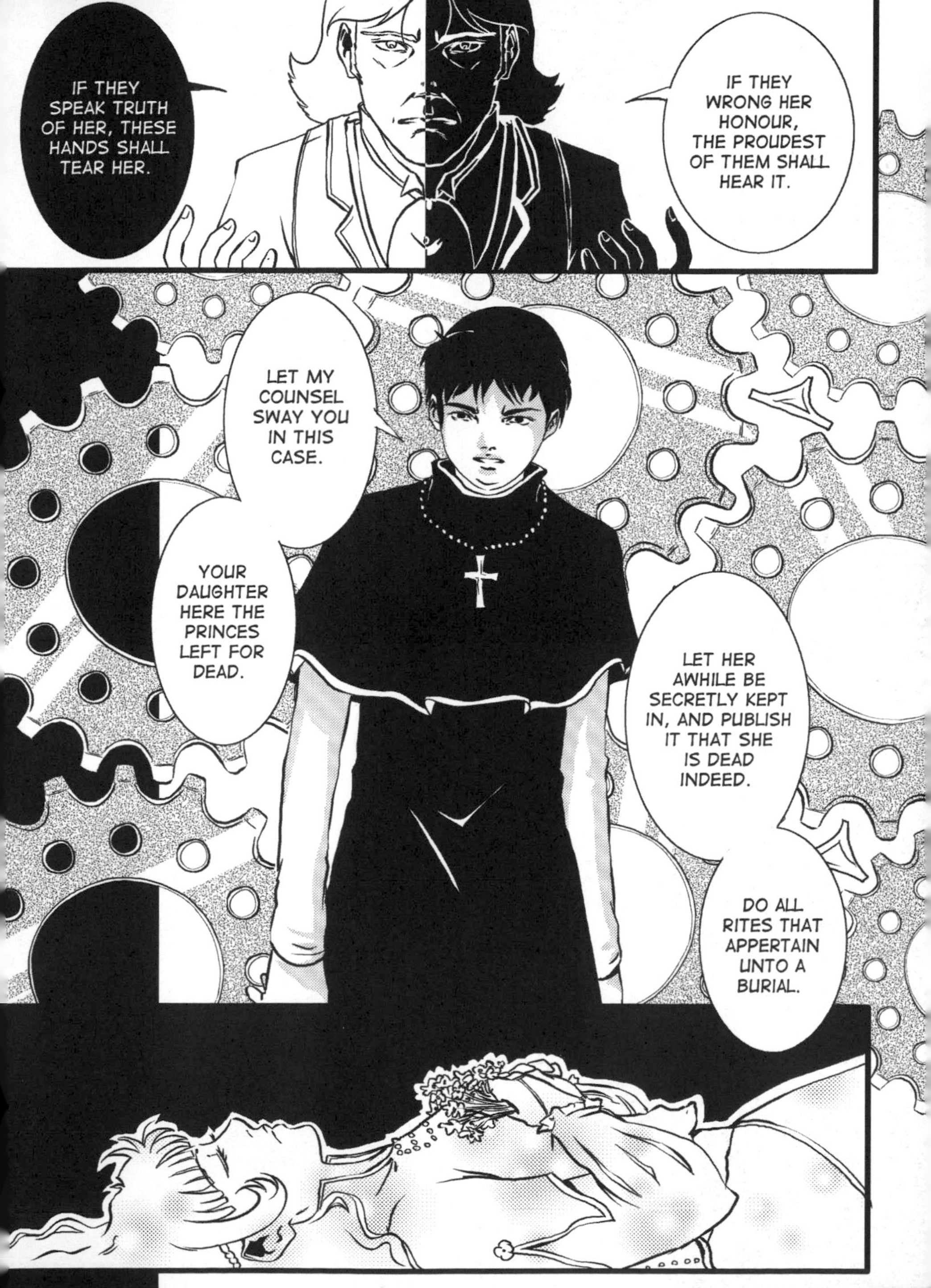
IF THEY SPEAK TRUTH OF HER, THESE HANDS SHALL TEAR HER.
IF THEY WRONG HER HONOUR, THE PROUDEST OF THEM SHALL HEAR IT.
LET MY COUNSEL SWAY YOU IN THIS CASE.
YOUR DAUGHTER HERE THE PRINCES LEFT FOR DEAD.
LET HER AWHILE BE SECRETLY KEPT IN, AND PUBLISH IT THAT SHE IS DEAD INDEED.
DO ALL RITES THAT APPERTAIN UNTO A BURIAL.

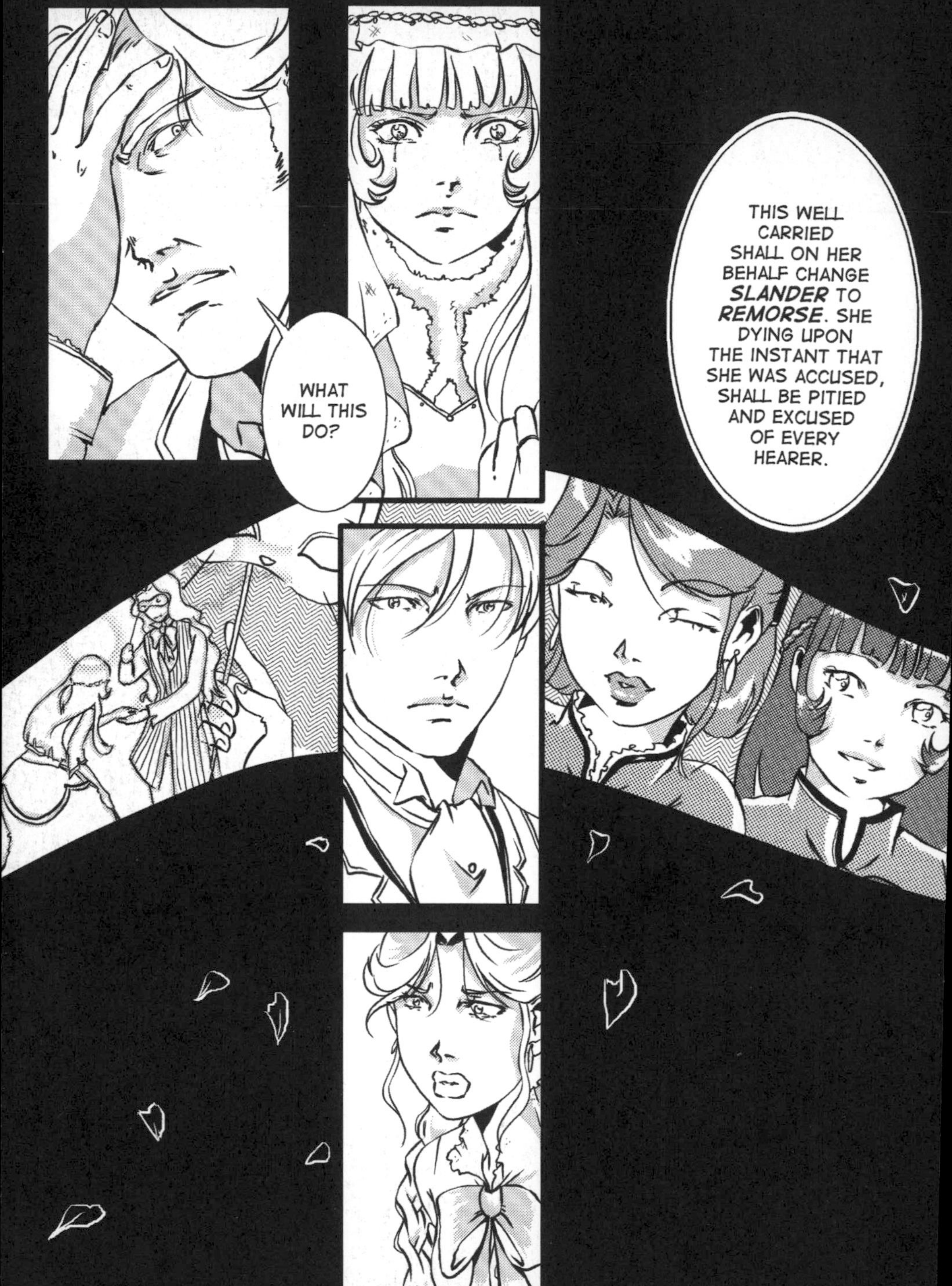
WHAT WILL THIS DO?
THIS WELL CARRIED SHALL ON HER BEHALF CHANGE **SLANDER** TO **REMORSE**. SHE DYING UPON THE INSTANT THAT SHE WAS ACCUSED, SHALL BE PITIED AND EXCUSED OF EVERY HEARER.

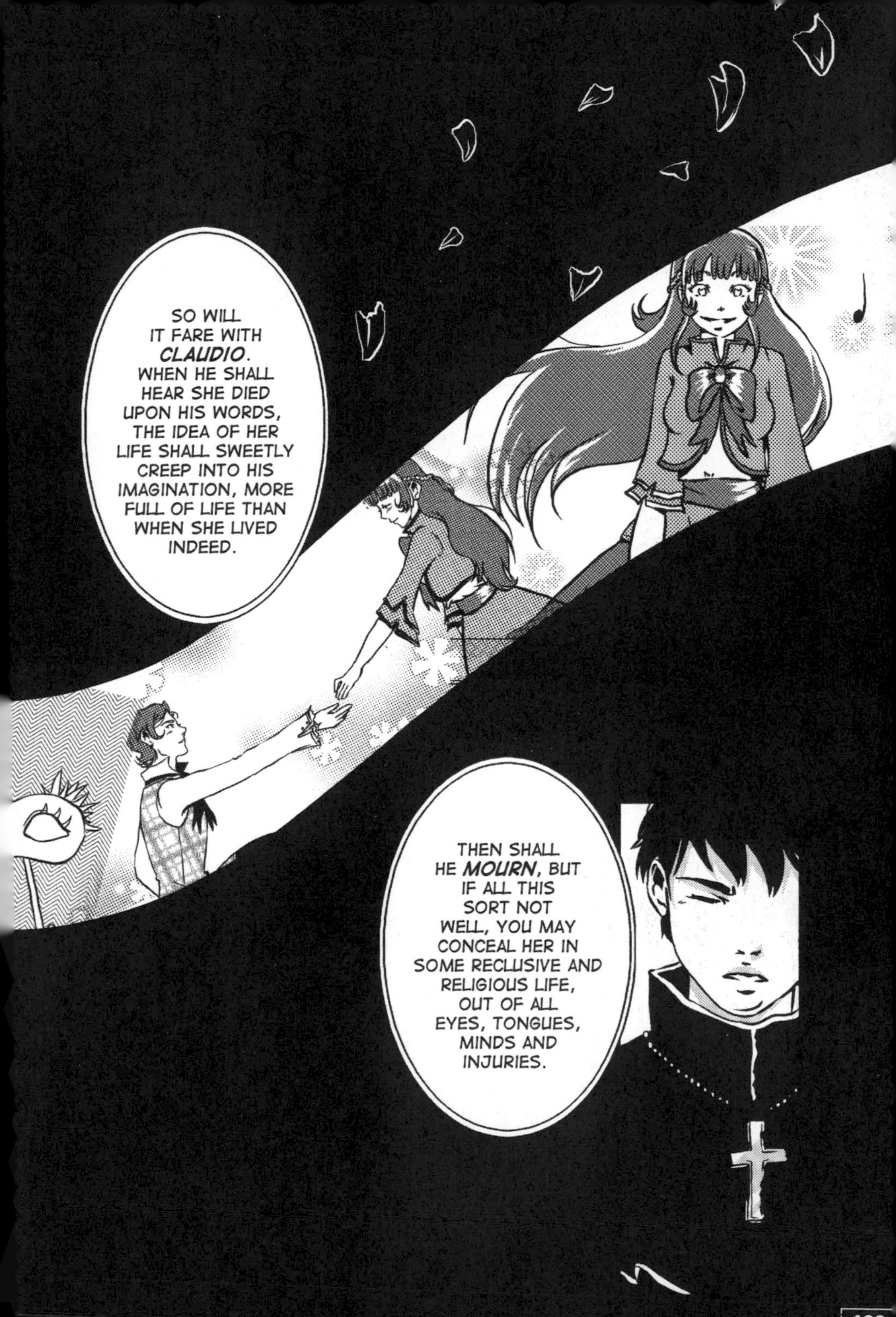
SO WILL IT FARE WITH CLAUDIO. WHEN HE SHALL HEAR SHE DIED UPON HIS WORDS, THE IDEA OF HER LIFE SHALL SWEETLY CREEP INTO HIS IMAGINATION, MORE FULL OF LIFE THAN WHEN SHE LIVED INDEED.
THEN SHALL HE MOURN, BUT IF ALL THIS SORT NOT WELL, YOU MAY CONCEAL HER IN SOME RECLUSIVE AND RELIGIOUS LIFE, OUT OF ALL EYES, TONGUES, MINDS AND INJURIES.

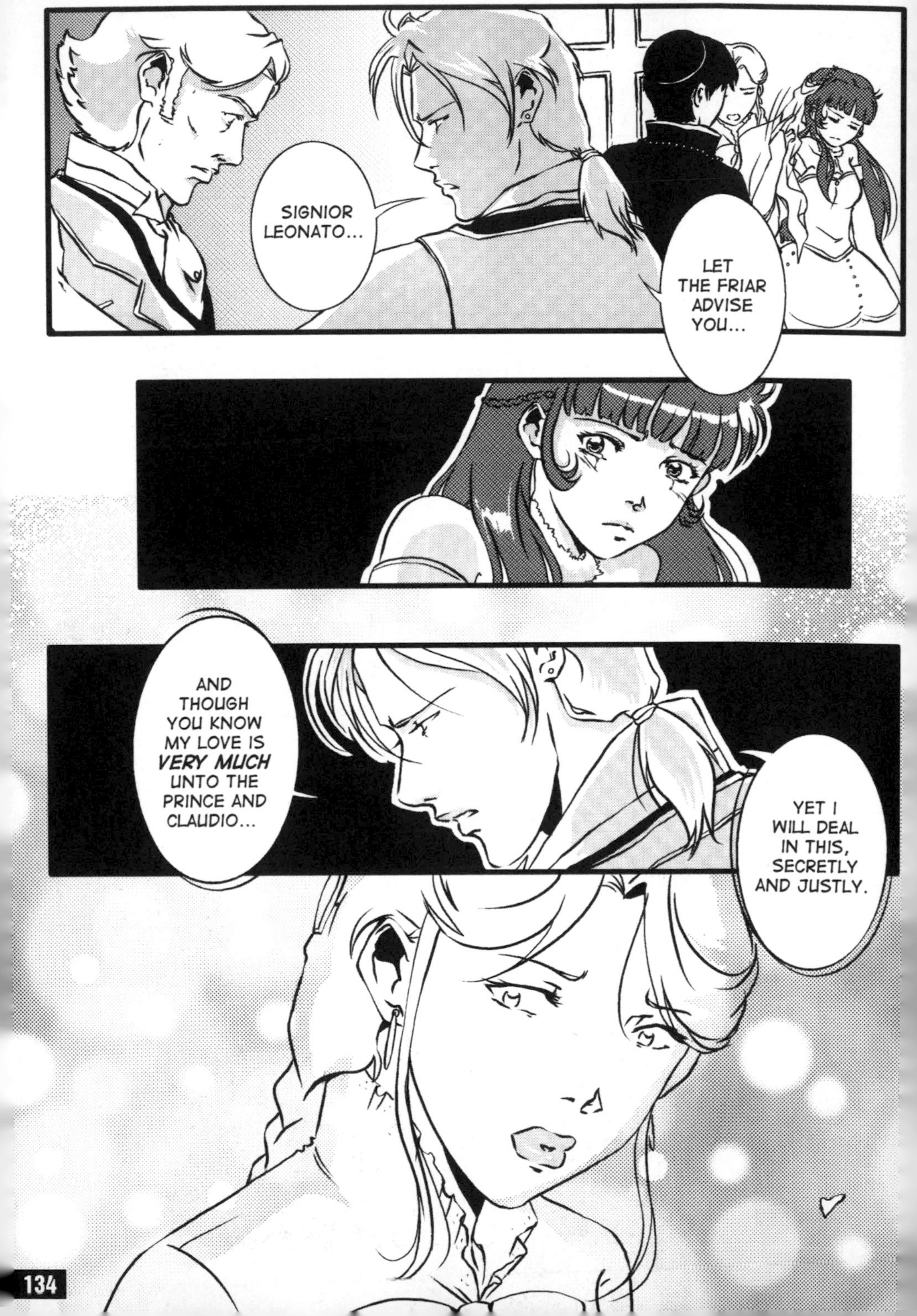
SIGNIOR LEONATO...
LET THE FRIAR ADVISE YOU...
AND THOUGH YOU KNOW MY LOVE IS ***VERY MUCH*** UNTO THE PRINCE AND CLAUDIO...
YET I WILL DEAL IN THIS, SECRETLY AND JUSTLY.

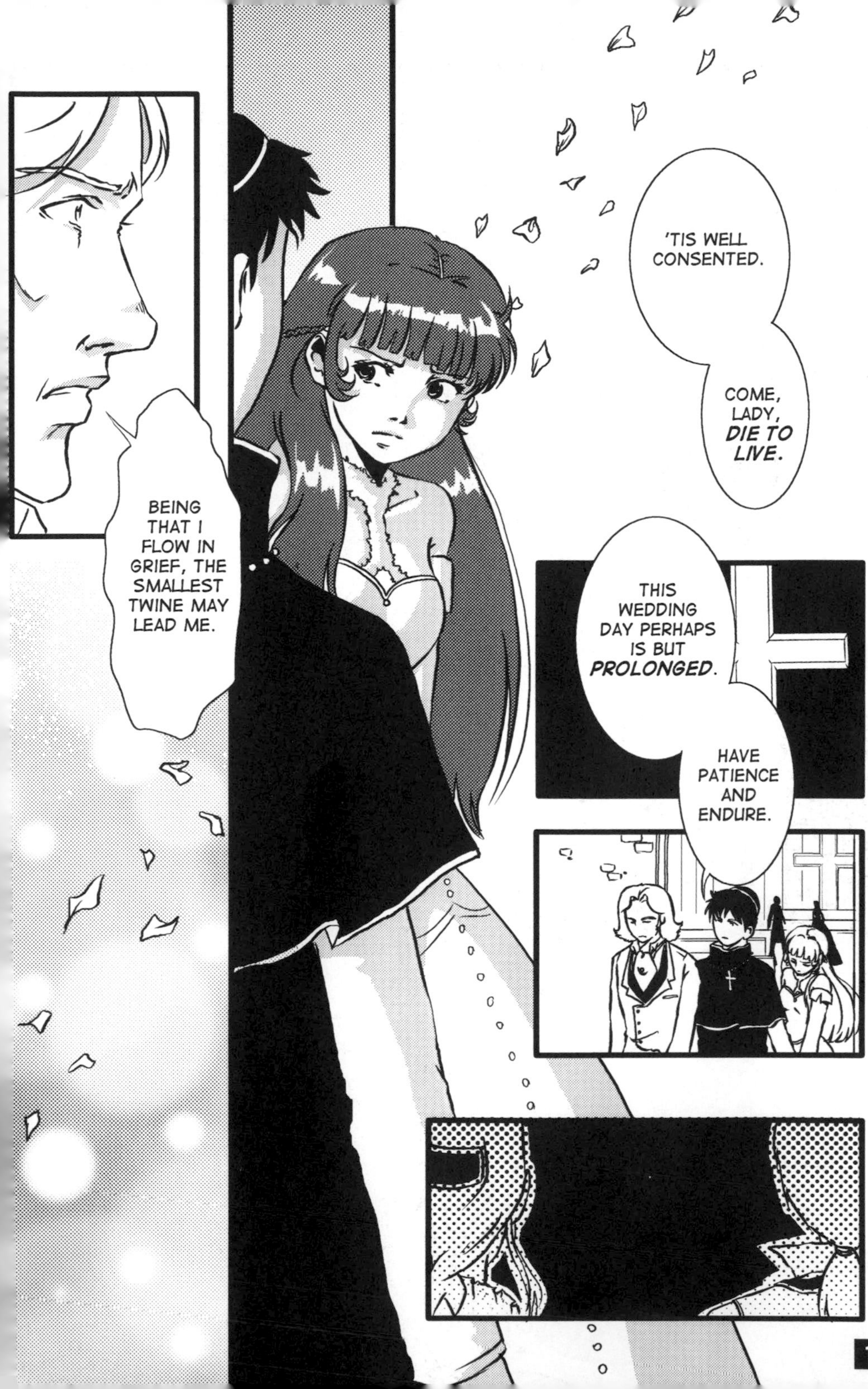
BEING THAT I FLOW IN GRIEF, THE SMALLEST TWINE MAY LEAD ME.
'TIS WELL CONSENTED.
COME, LADY, **DIE TO LIVE**.
THIS WEDDING DAY PERHAPS IS BUT **PROLONGED**.
HAVE PATIENCE AND ENDURE.

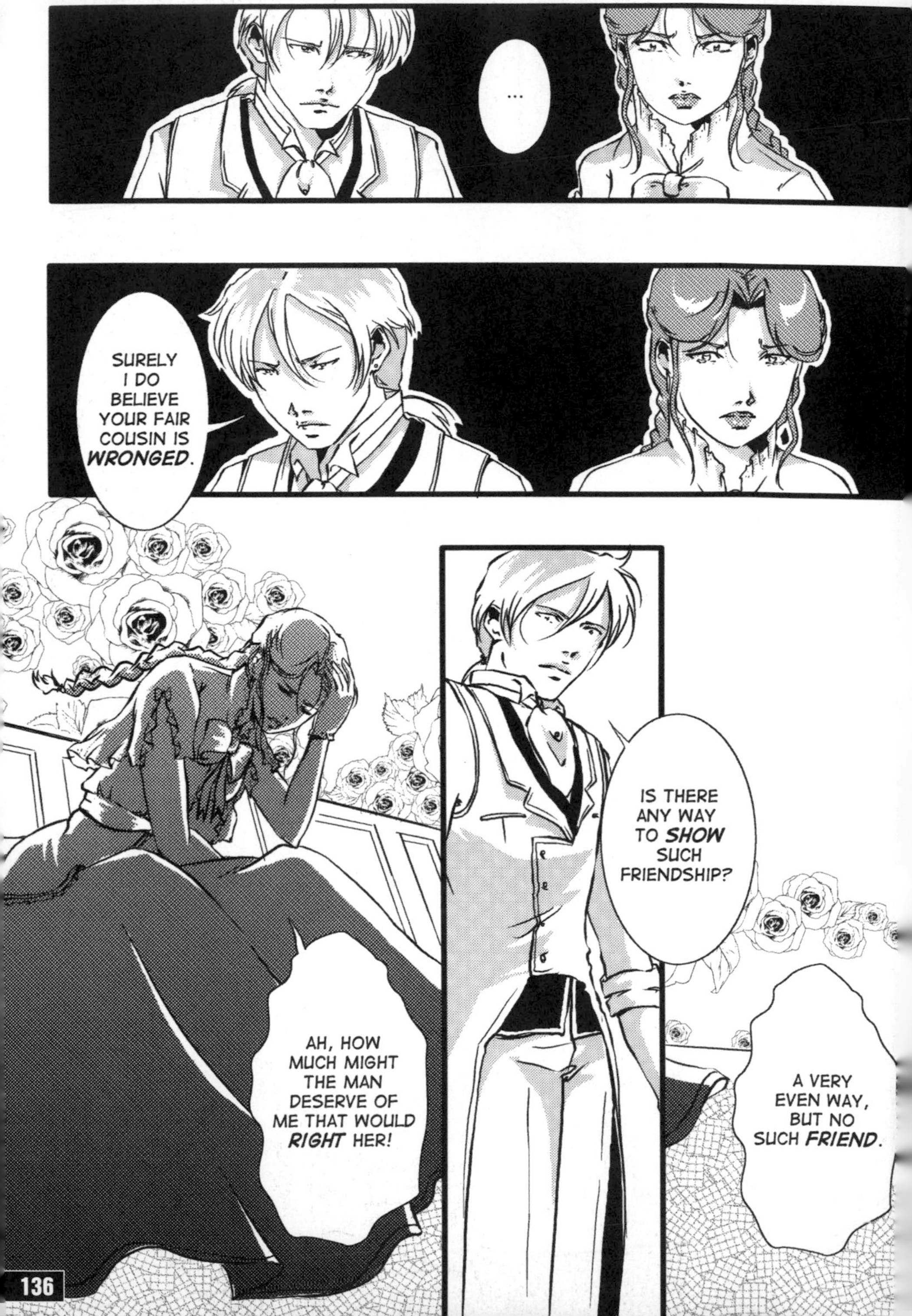
...
SURELY I DO BELIEVE YOUR FAIR COUSIN IS WRONGED.
AH, HOW MUCH MIGHT THE MAN DESERVE OF ME THAT WOULD RIGHT HER!
IS THERE ANY WAY TO SHOW SUCH FRIENDSHIP?
A VERY EVEN WAY, BUT NO SUCH FRIEND.

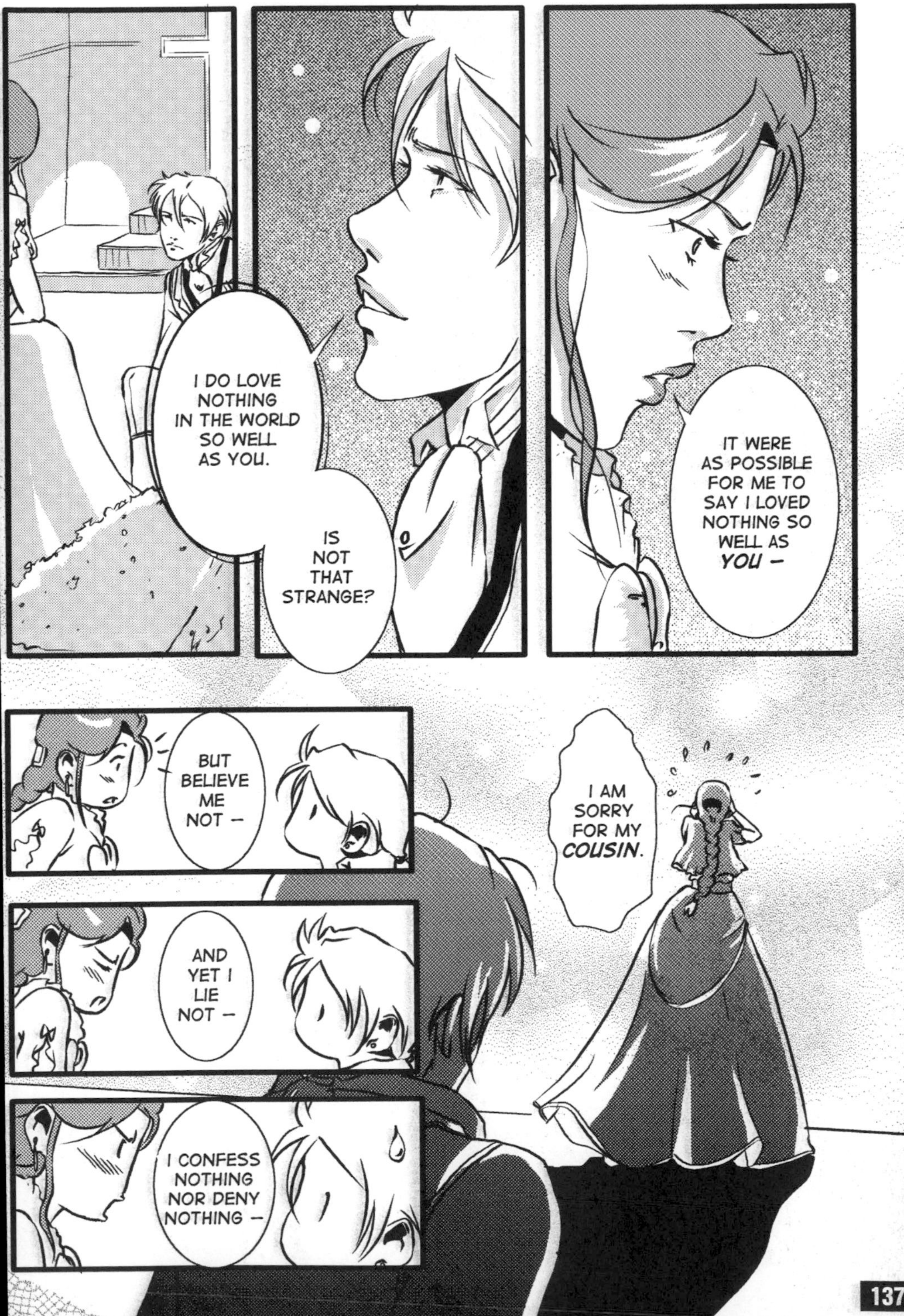
I DO LOVE NOTHING IN THE WORLD SO WELL AS YOU.
IS NOT THAT STRANGE?
IT WERE AS POSSIBLE FOR ME TO SAY I LOVED NOTHING SO WELL AS *YOU* –
BUT BELIEVE ME NOT –
AND YET I LIE NOT –
I CONFESS NOTHING NOR DENY NOTHING –
I AM SORRY FOR MY *COUSIN*.

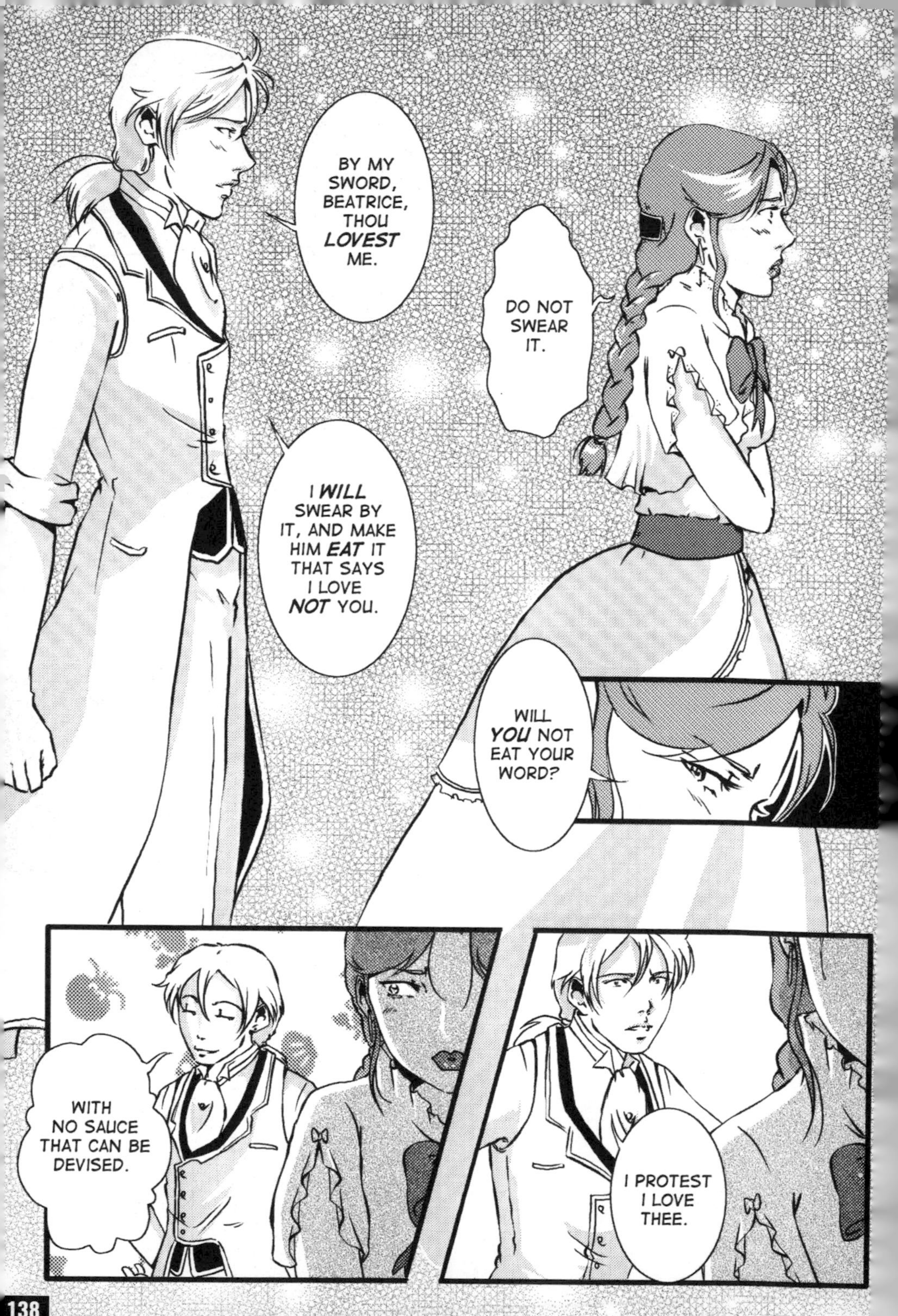
BY MY SWORD, BEATRICE, THOU *LOVEST* ME.
DO NOT SWEAR IT.
I *WILL* SWEAR BY IT, AND MAKE HIM *EAT* IT THAT SAYS I LOVE *NOT* YOU.
WILL *YOU* NOT EAT YOUR WORD?
WITH NO SAUCE THAT CAN BE DEVISED.
I PROTEST I LOVE THEE.

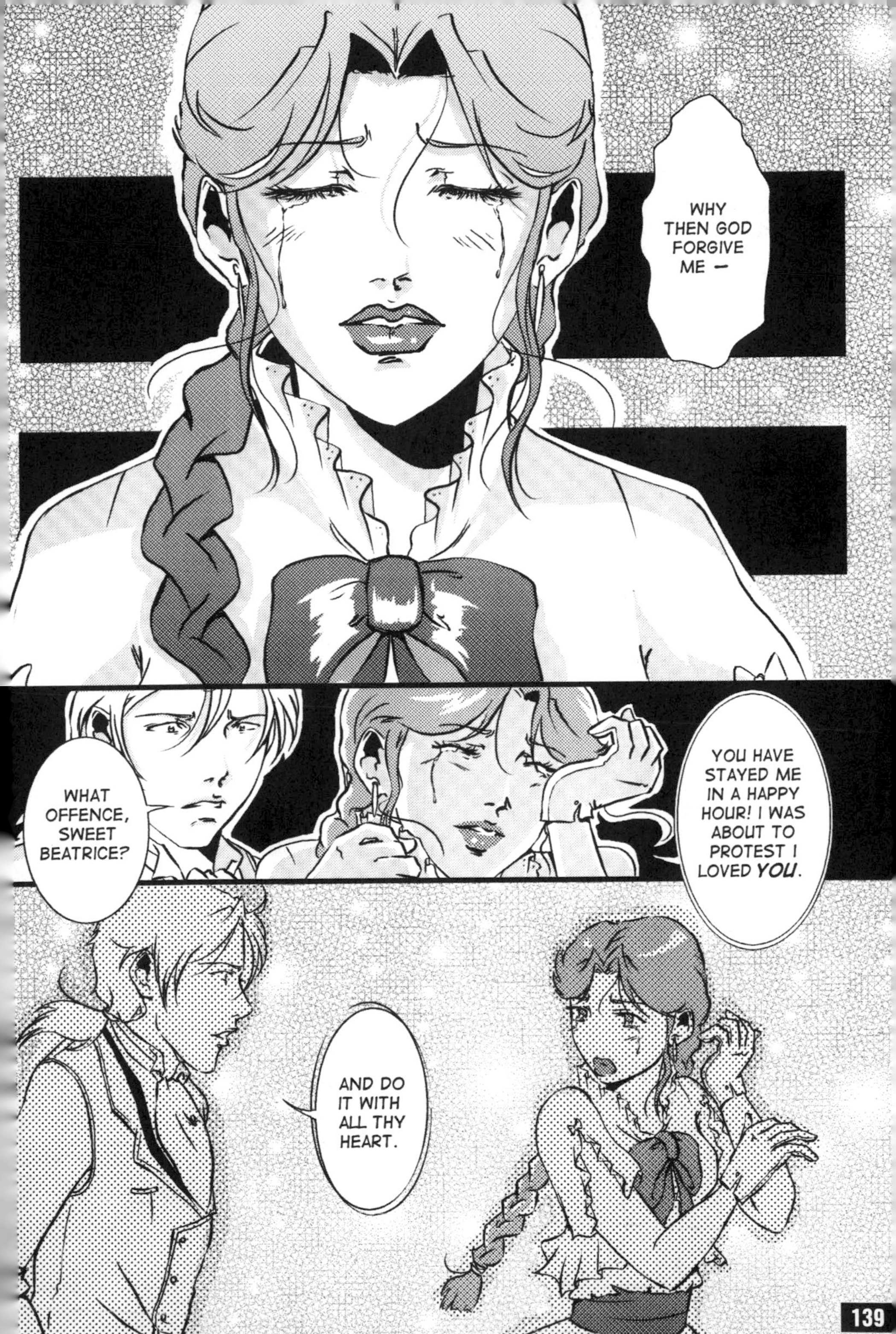
WHY THEN GOD FORGIVE ME —
WHAT OFFENCE, SWEET BEATRICE?
YOU HAVE STAYED ME IN A HAPPY HOUR! I WAS ABOUT TO PROTEST I LOVED *YOU*.
AND DO IT WITH ALL THY HEART.

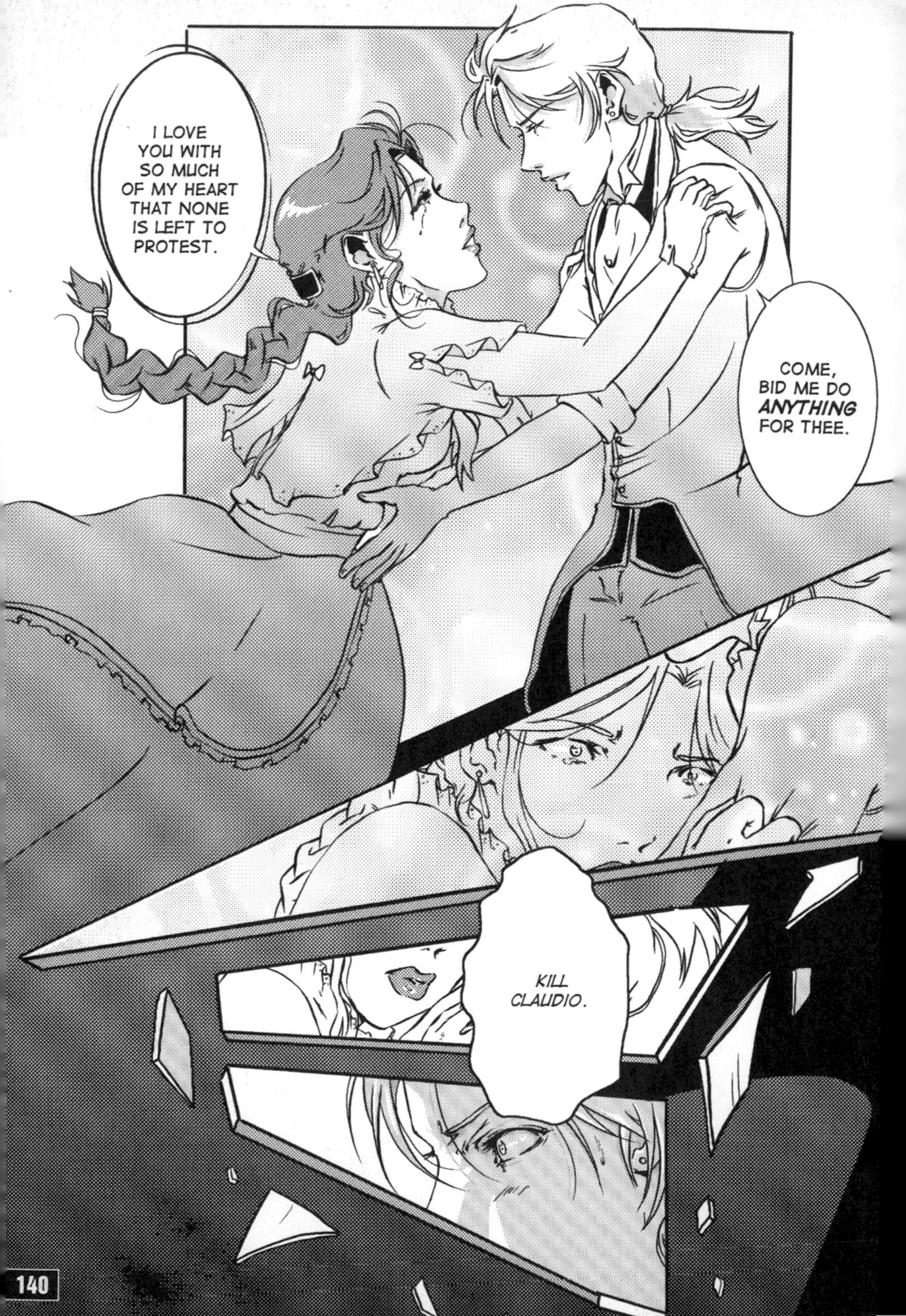
I LOVE YOU WITH SO MUCH OF MY HEART THAT NONE IS LEFT TO PROTEST.
COME, BID ME DO ***ANYTHING*** FOR THEE.
*KILL CLAUDIO.*

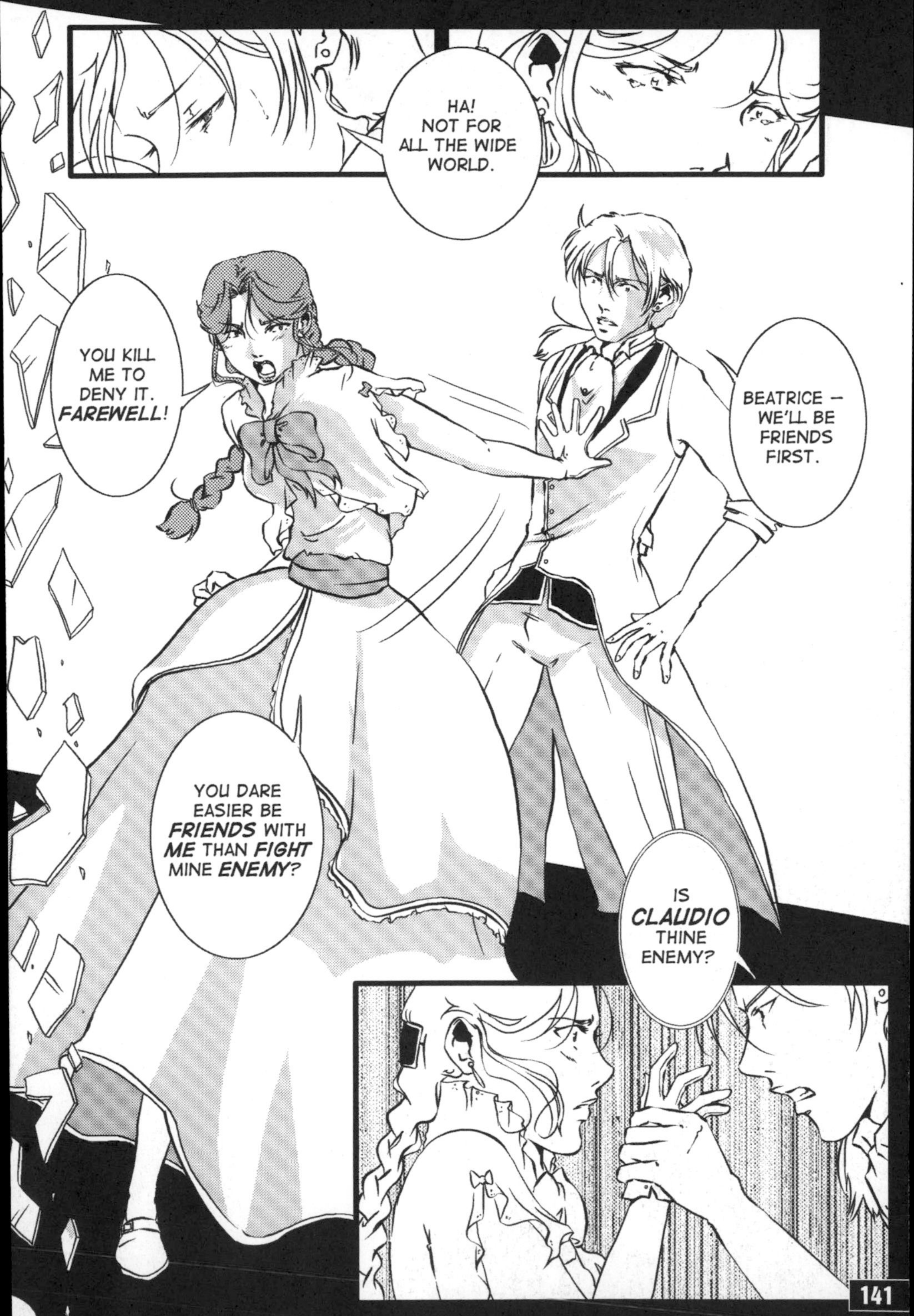
HA! NOT FOR ALL THE WIDE WORLD.
YOU KILL ME TO DENY IT. FAREWELL!
BEATRICE — WE'LL BE FRIENDS FIRST.
YOU DARE EASIER BE FRIENDS WITH ME THAN FIGHT MINE ENEMY?
IS CLAUDIO THINE ENEMY?

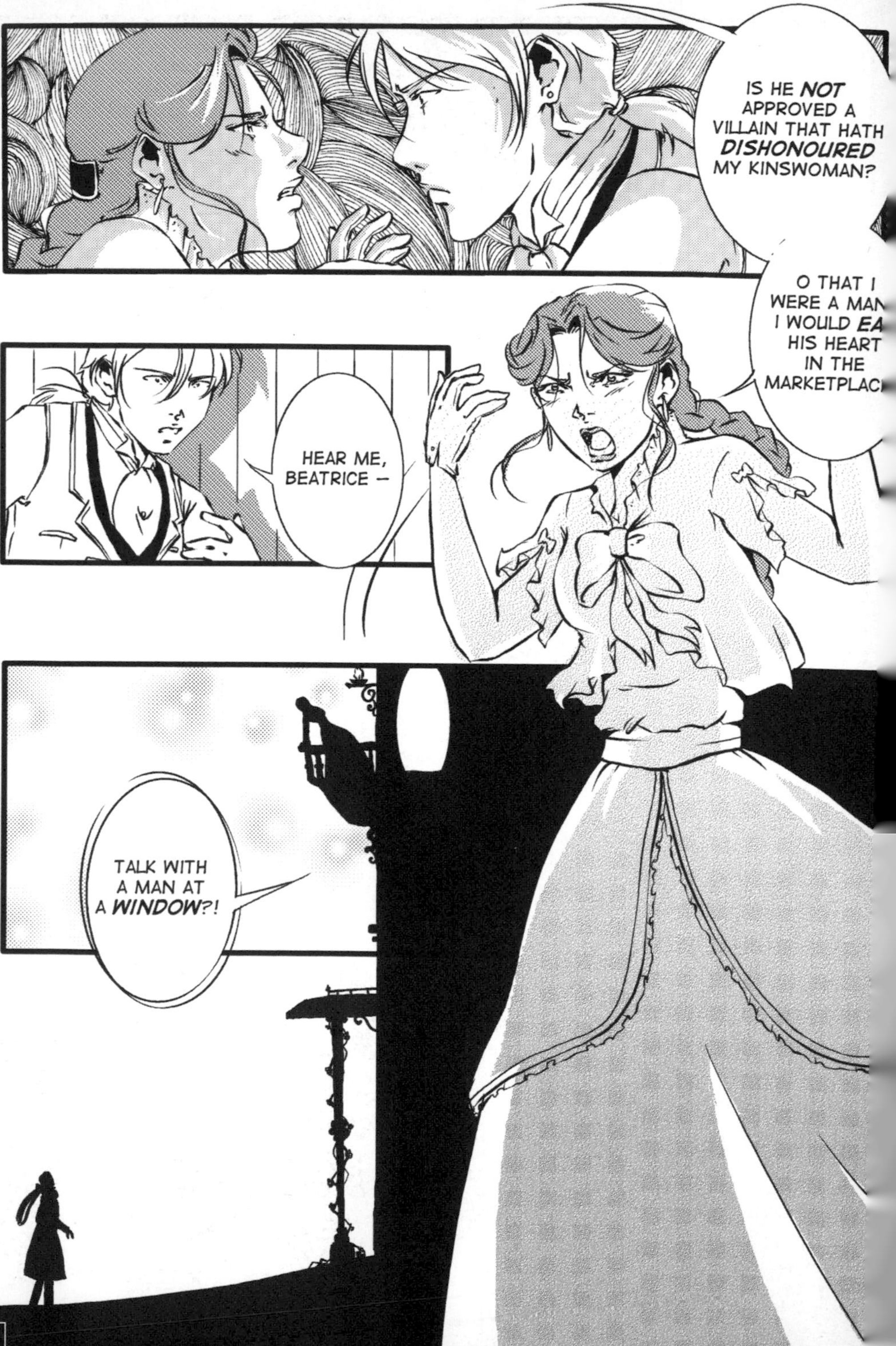

IS HE **NOT** APPROVED A VILLAIN THAT HATH **DISHONOURED** MY KINSWOMAN?
O THAT I WERE A MAN I WOULD **EA** HIS HEART IN THE MARKETPLAC
HEAR ME, BEATRICE –
TALK WITH A MAN AT A **WINDOW**?!

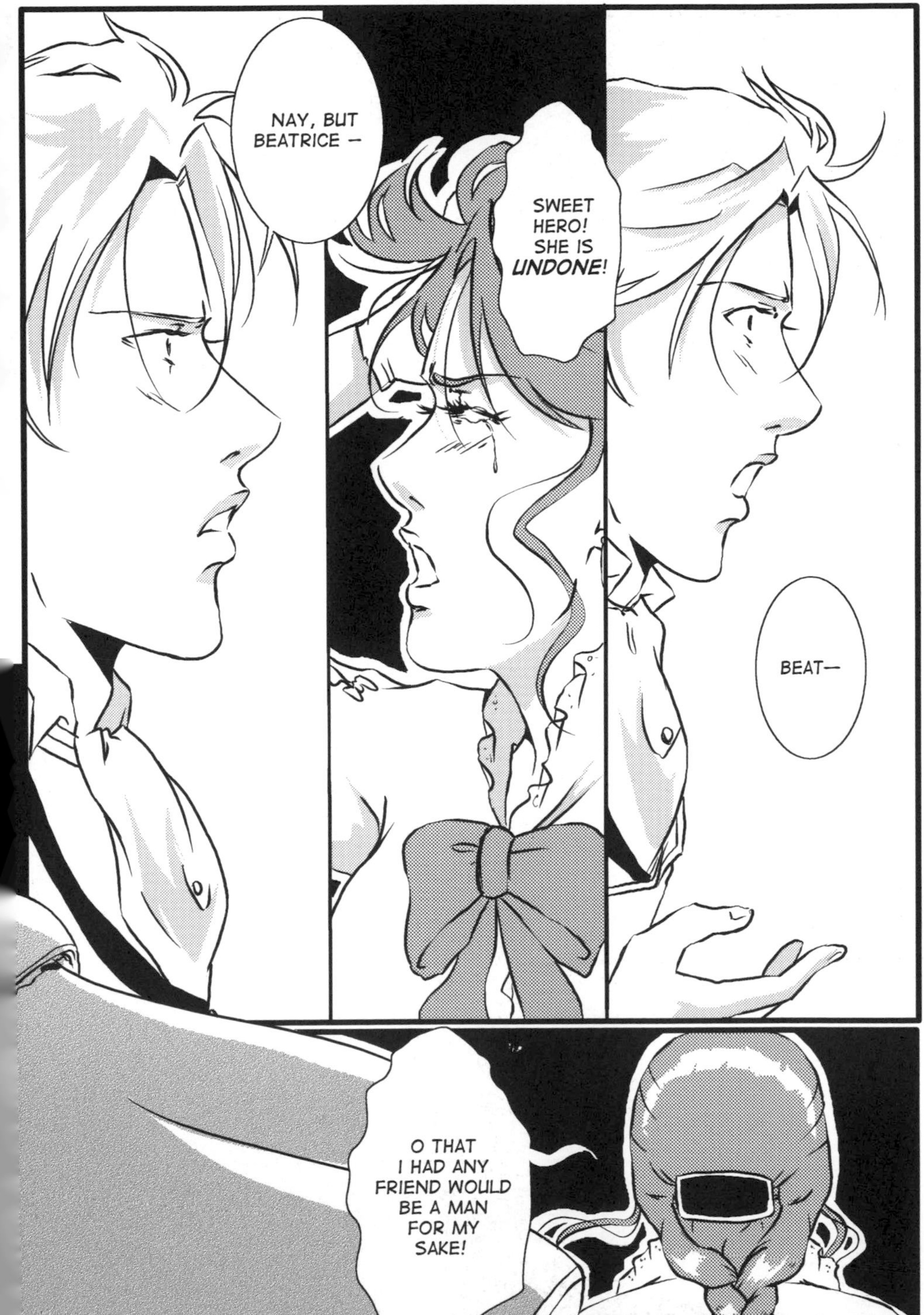
NAY, BUT BEATRICE –
SWEET HERO! SHE IS *UNDONE*!
BEAT—
O THAT I HAD ANY FRIEND WOULD BE A MAN FOR MY SAKE!

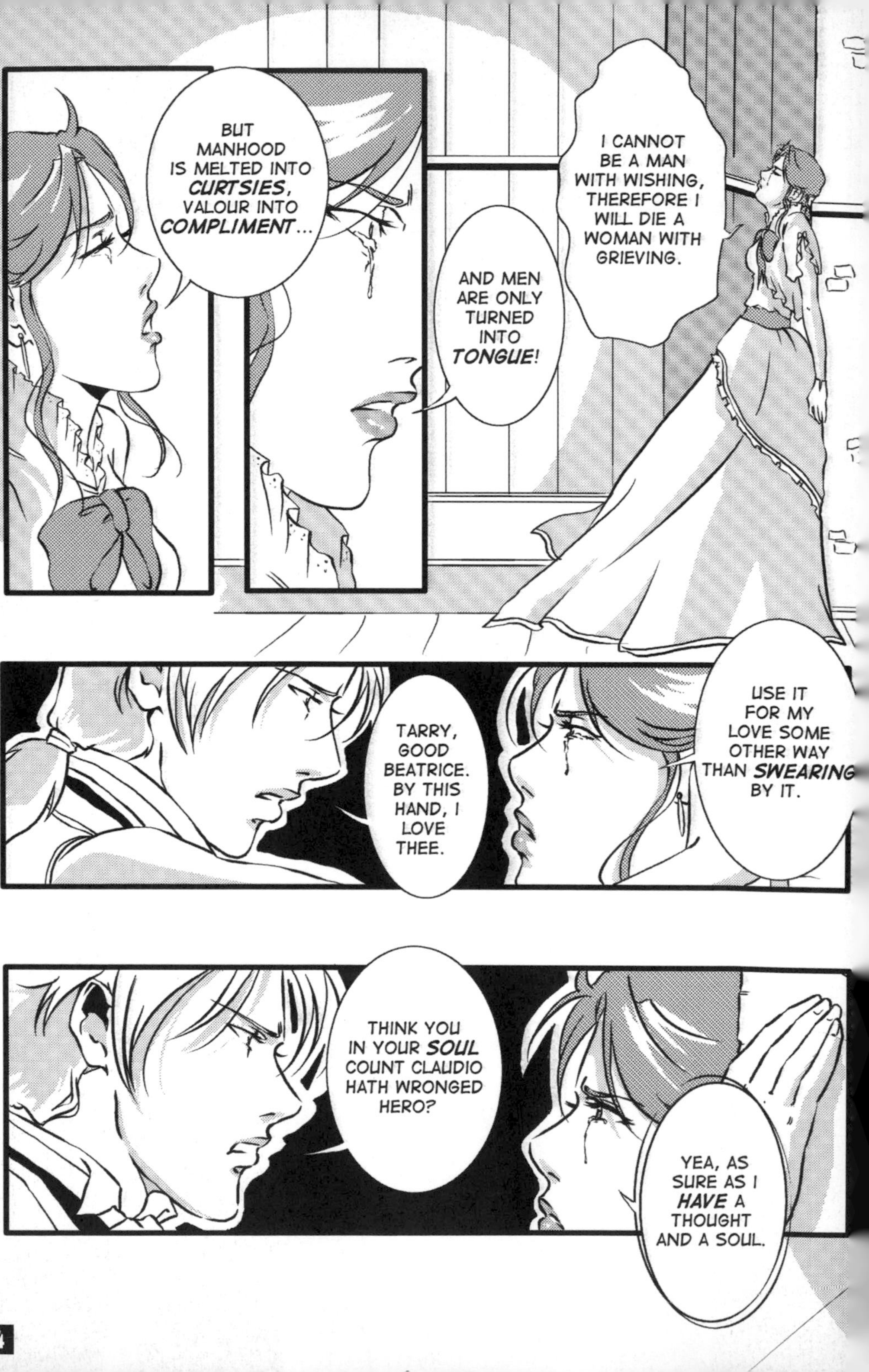
BUT MANHOOD IS MELTED INTO CURTSIES, VALOUR INTO COMPLIMENT...
AND MEN ARE ONLY TURNED INTO TONGUE!
I CANNOT BE A MAN WITH WISHING, THEREFORE I WILL DIE A WOMAN WITH GRIEVING.
TARRY, GOOD BEATRICE. BY THIS HAND, I LOVE THEE.
USE IT FOR MY LOVE SOME OTHER WAY THAN SWEARING BY IT.
THINK YOU IN YOUR SOUL COUNT CLAUDIO HATH WRONGED HERO?
YEA, AS SURE AS I HAVE A THOUGHT AND A SOUL.

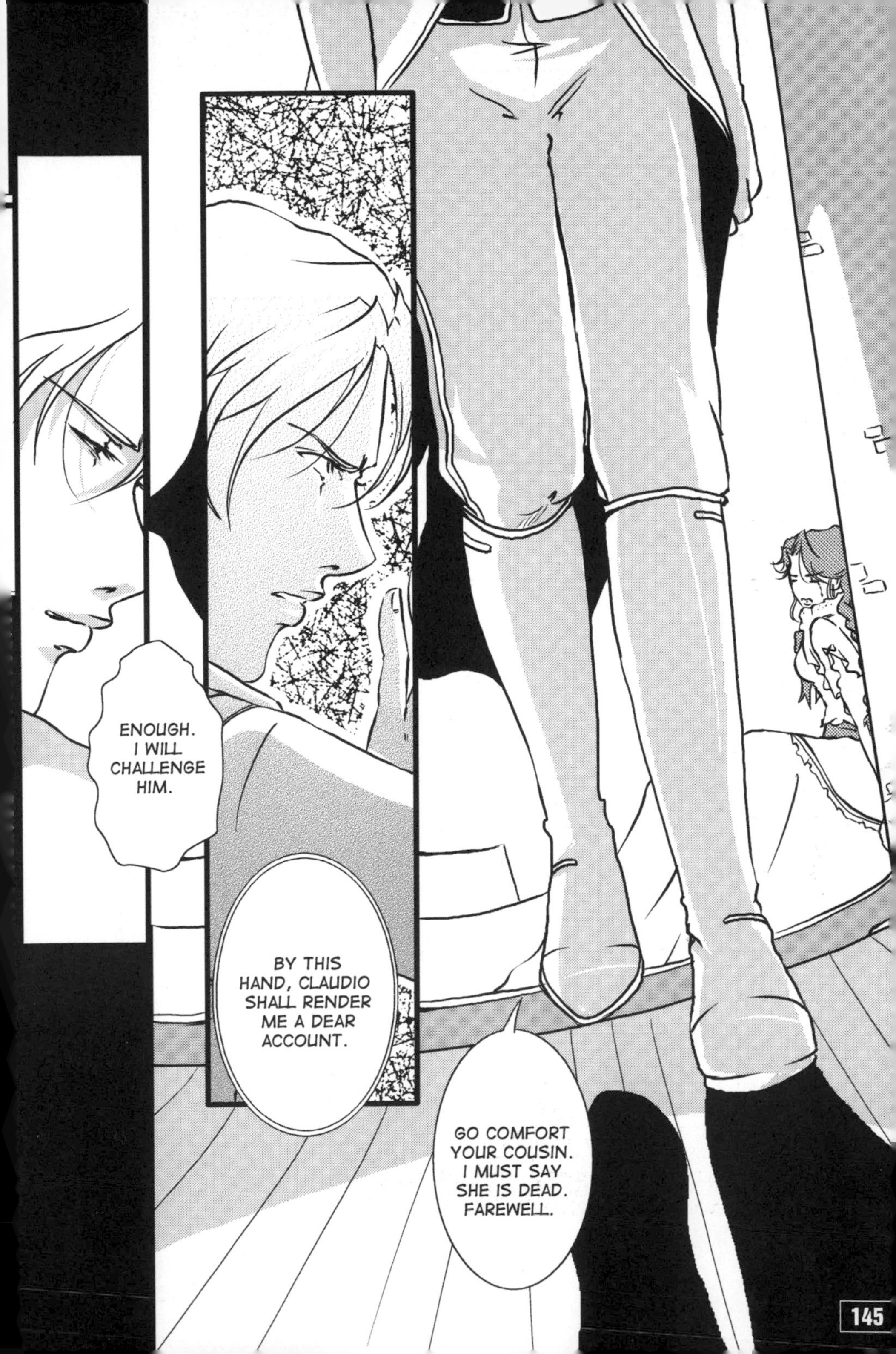
ENOUGH. I WILL CHALLENGE HIM.
BY THIS HAND, CLAUDIO SHALL RENDER ME A DEAR ACCOUNT.
GO COMFORT YOUR COUSIN. I MUST SAY SHE IS DEAD. FAREWELL.

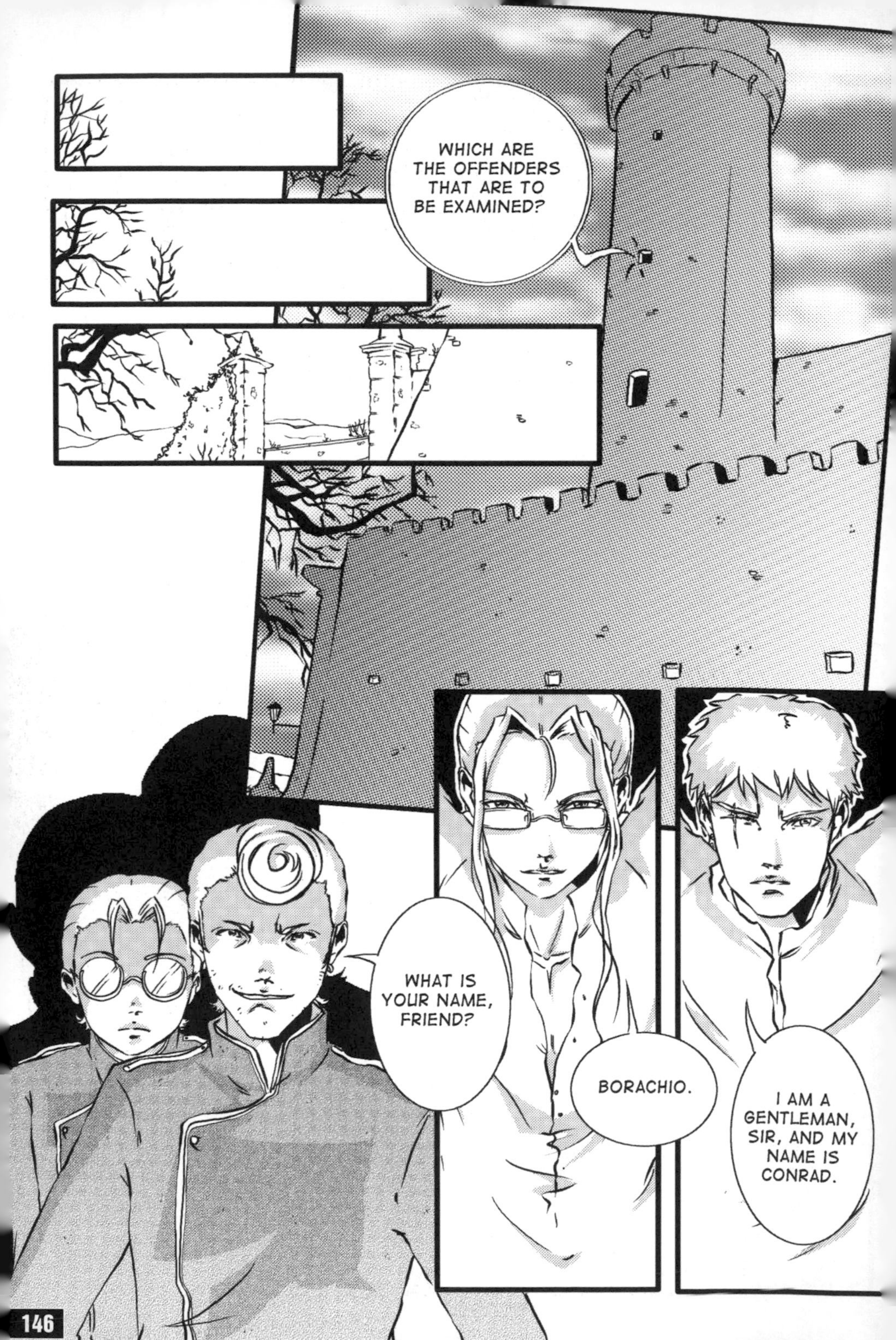
WHICH ARE THE OFFENDERS THAT ARE TO BE EXAMINED?
WHAT IS YOUR NAME, FRIEND?
BORACHIO.
I AM A GENTLEMAN, SIR, AND MY NAME IS CONRAD.

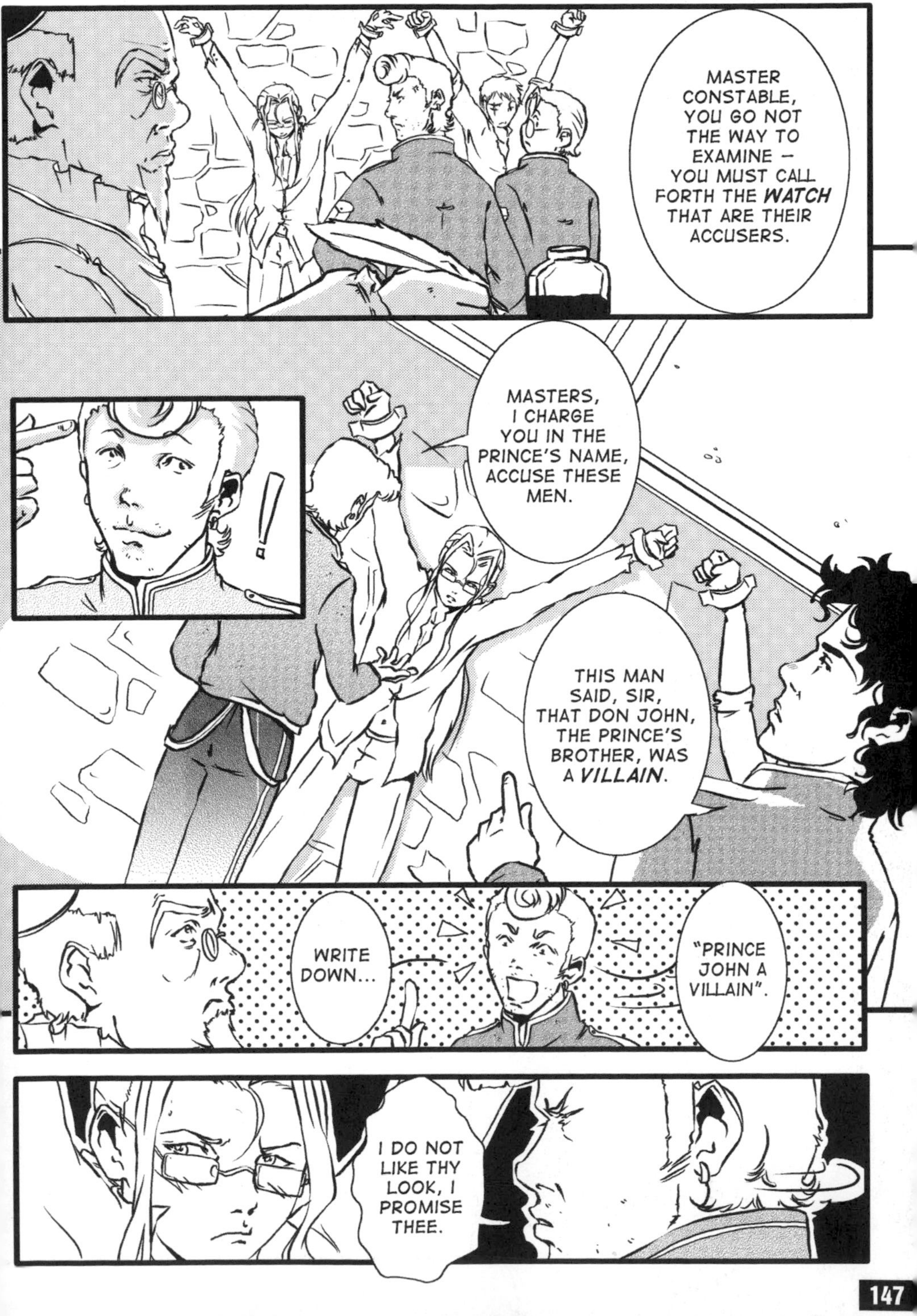
MASTER CONSTABLE, YOU GO NOT THE WAY TO EXAMINE – YOU MUST CALL FORTH THE **WATCH** THAT ARE THEIR ACCUSERS.
MASTERS, I CHARGE YOU IN THE PRINCE'S NAME, ACCUSE THESE MEN.
!
THIS MAN SAID, SIR, THAT DON JOHN, THE PRINCE'S BROTHER, WAS A **VILLAIN**.
WRITE DOWN...
"PRINCE JOHN A VILLAIN".
I DO NOT LIKE THY LOOK, I PROMISE THEE.

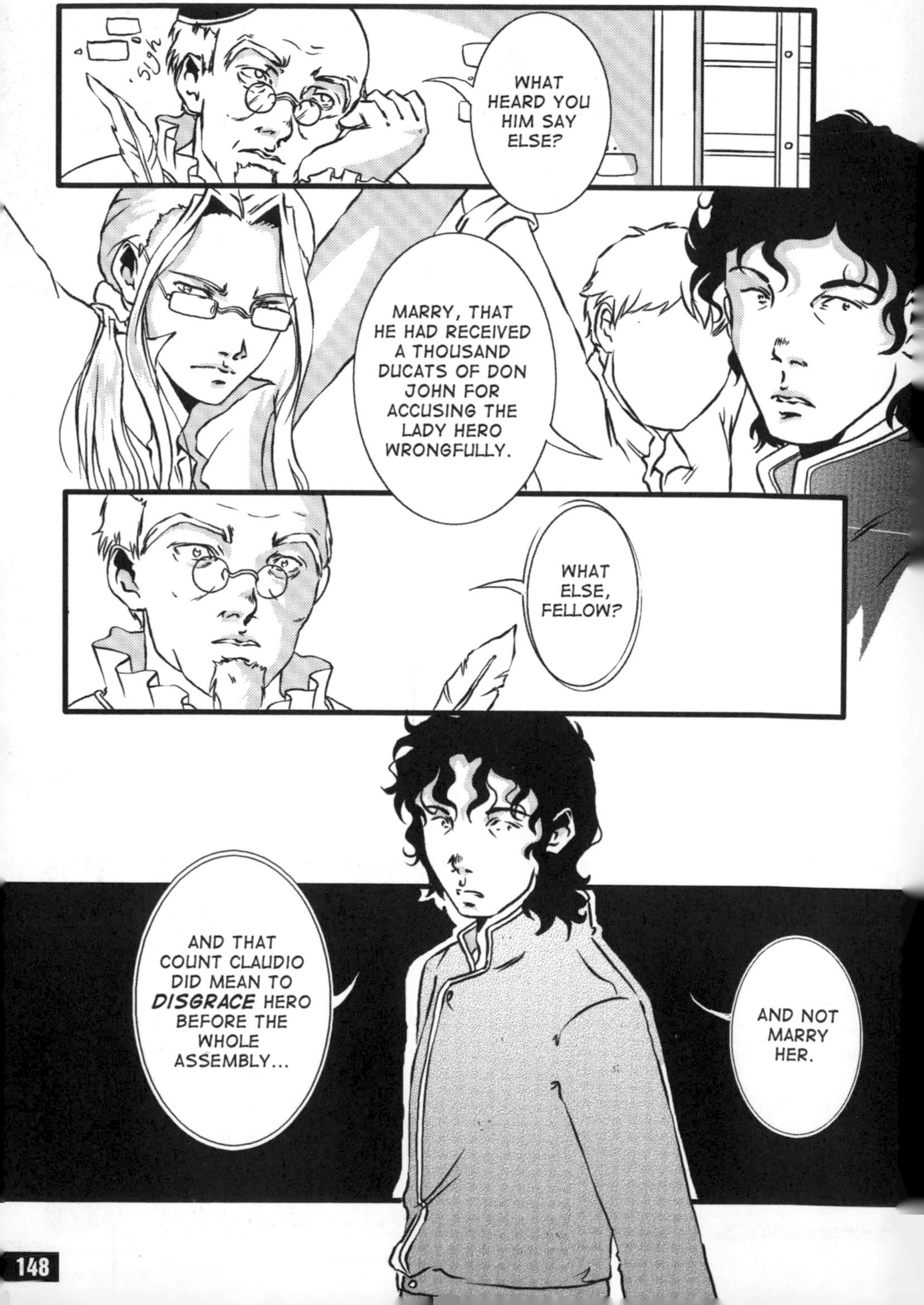
'sigh
WHAT HEARD YOU HIM SAY ELSE?
MARRY, THAT HE HAD RECEIVED A THOUSAND DUCATS OF DON JOHN FOR ACCUSING THE LADY HERO WRONGFULLY.
WHAT ELSE, FELLOW?
AND THAT COUNT CLAUDIO DID MEAN TO *DISGRACE* HERO BEFORE THE WHOLE ASSEMBLY...
AND NOT MARRY HER.

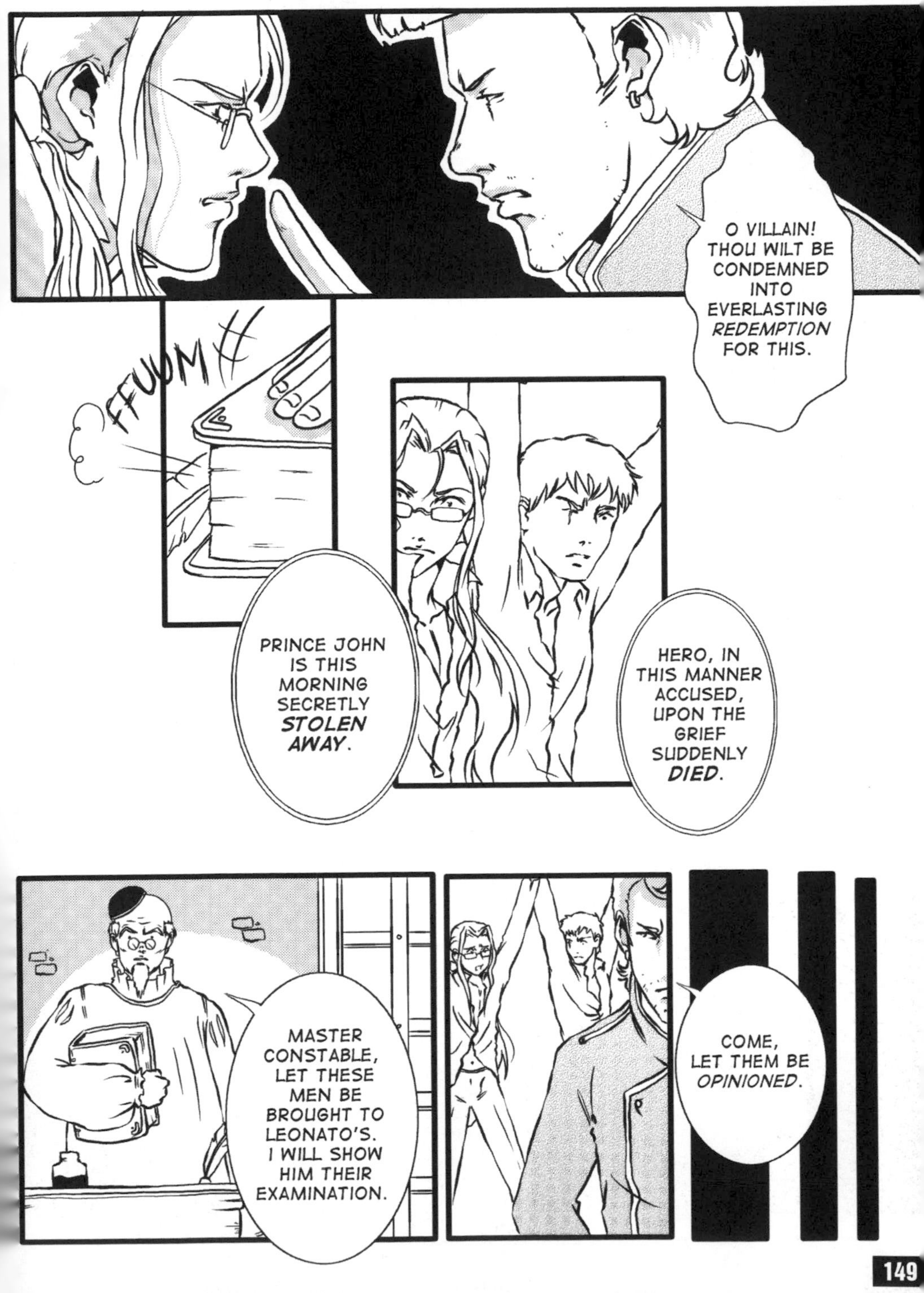
O VILLAIN! THOU WILT BE CONDEMNED INTO EVERLASTING *REDEMPTION* FOR THIS.
FFUUM
PRINCE JOHN IS THIS MORNING SECRETLY ***STOLEN AWAY***.
HERO, IN THIS MANNER ACCUSED, UPON THE GRIEF SUDDENLY ***DIED***.
MASTER CONSTABLE, LET THESE MEN BE BROUGHT TO LEONATO'S. I WILL SHOW HIM THEIR EXAMINATION.
COME, LET THEM BE *OPINIONED*.

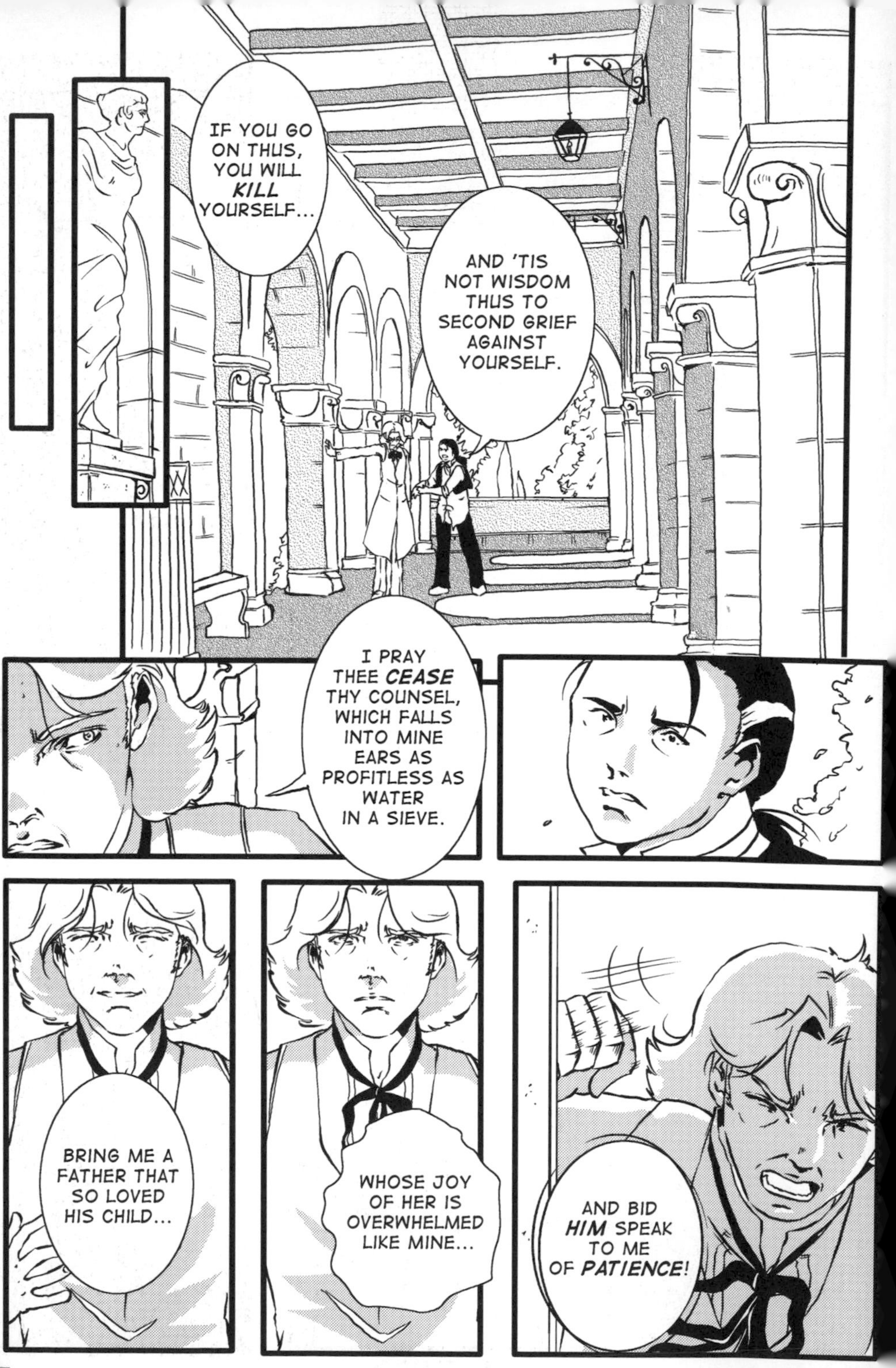
IF YOU GO ON THUS, YOU WILL KILL YOURSELF...
AND 'TIS NOT WISDOM THUS TO SECOND GRIEF AGAINST YOURSELF.
I PRAY THEE CEASE THY COUNSEL, WHICH FALLS INTO MINE EARS AS PROFITLESS AS WATER IN A SIEVE.
BRING ME A FATHER THAT SO LOVED HIS CHILD...
WHOSE JOY OF HER IS OVERWHELMED LIKE MINE...
AND BID HIM SPEAK TO ME OF PATIENCE!

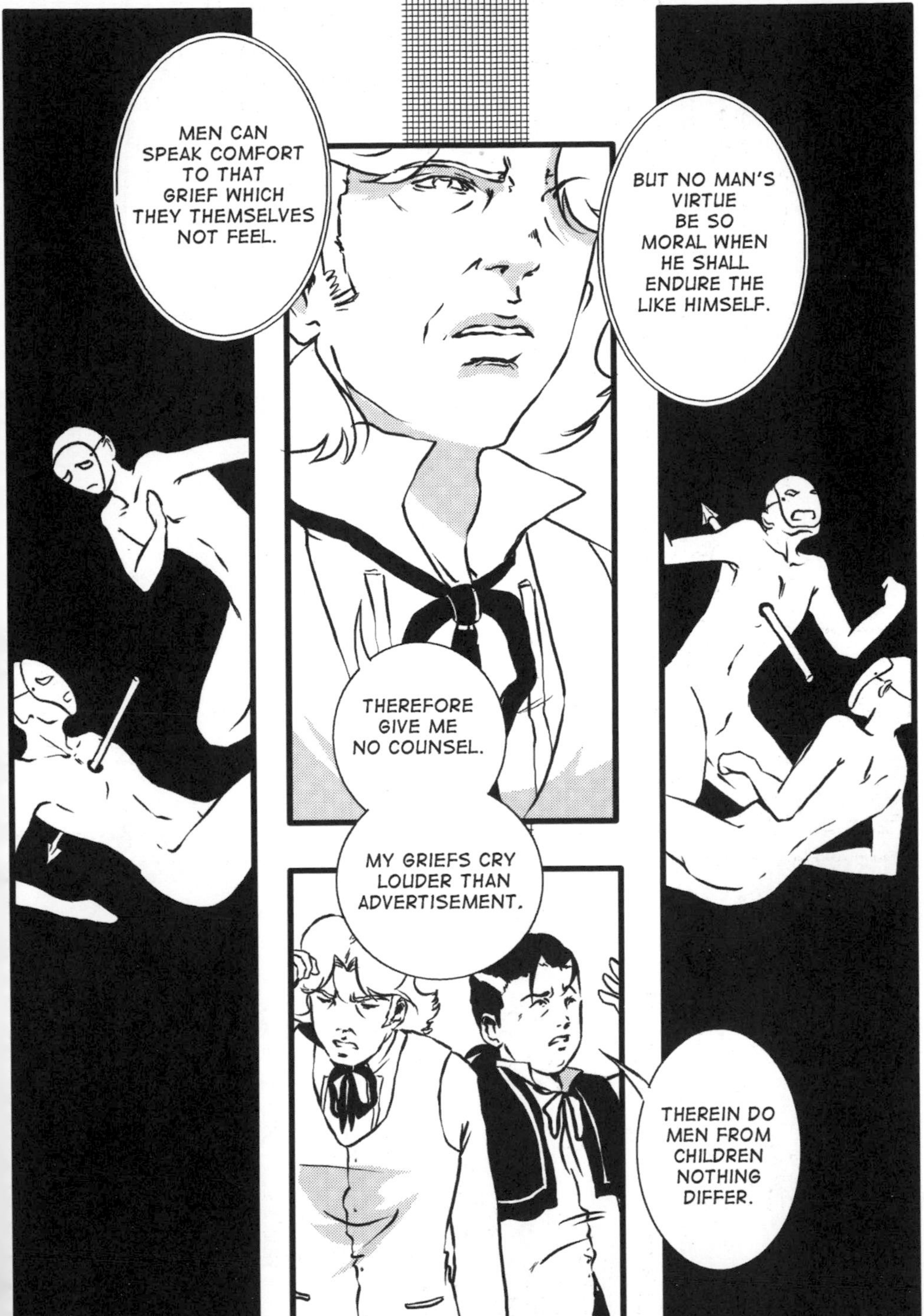
MEN CAN SPEAK COMFORT TO THAT GRIEF WHICH THEY THEMSELVES NOT FEEL.
BUT NO MAN'S VIRTUE BE SO MORAL WHEN HE SHALL ENDURE THE LIKE HIMSELF.
THEREFORE GIVE ME NO COUNSEL.
MY GRIEFS CRY LOUDER THAN ADVERTISEMENT.
THEREIN DO MEN FROM CHILDREN NOTHING DIFFER.

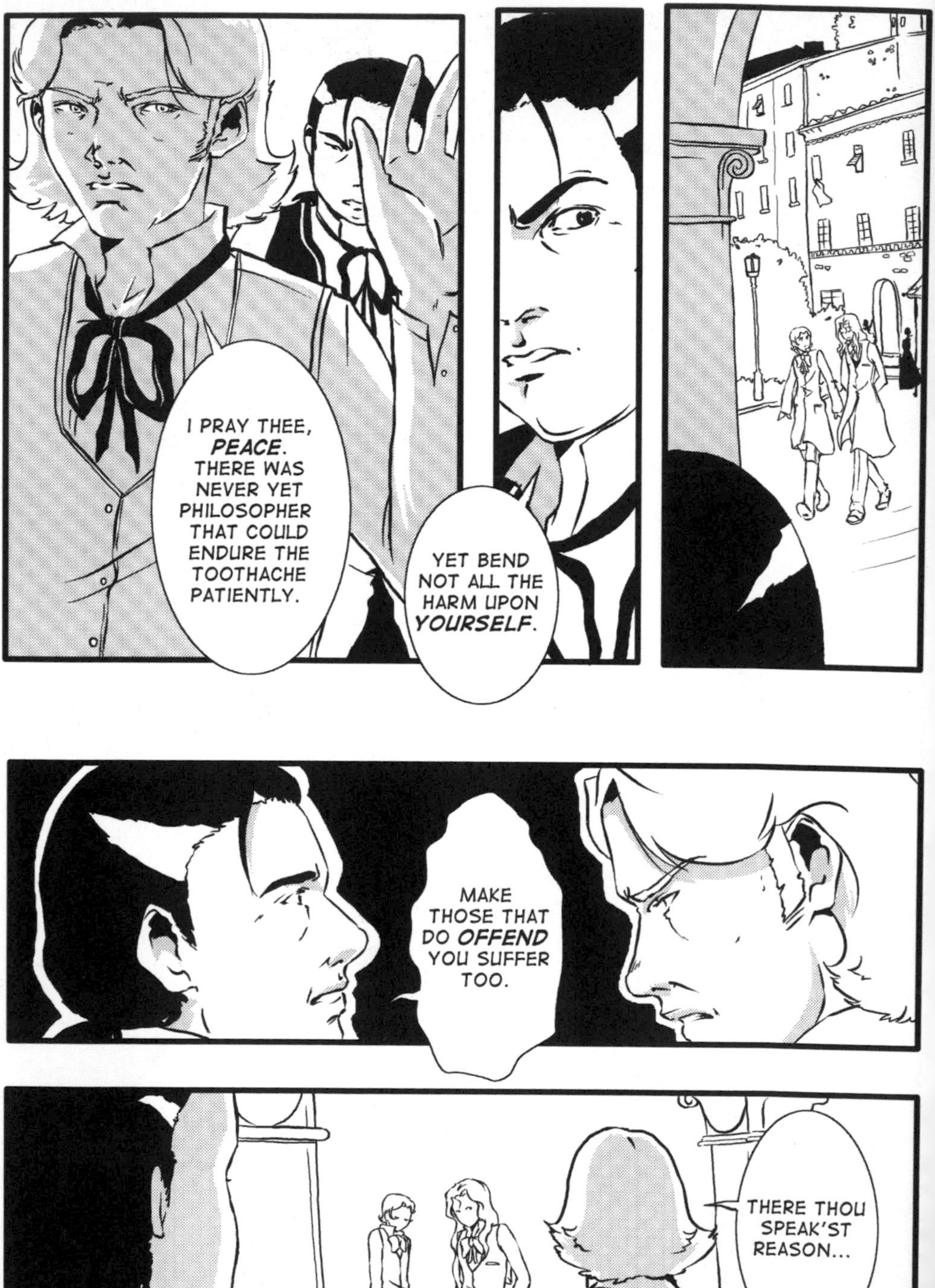
I PRAY THEE, *PEACE*. THERE WAS NEVER YET PHILOSOPHER THAT COULD ENDURE THE TOOTHACHE PATIENTLY.
YET BEND NOT ALL THE HARM UPON *YOURSELF*.
MAKE THOSE THAT DO *OFFEND* YOU SUFFER TOO.
THERE THOU SPEAK'ST REASON...

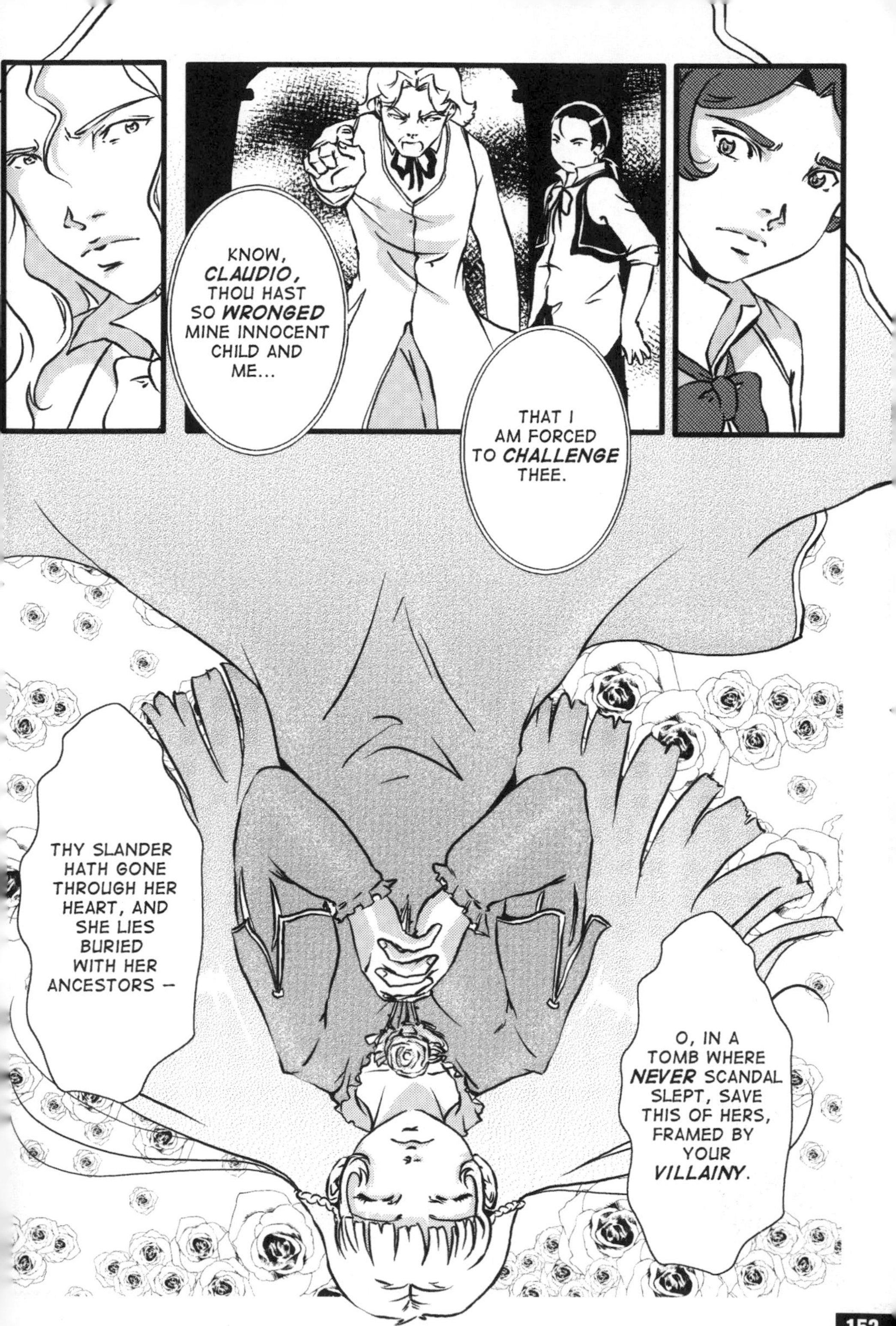
KNOW, CLAUDIO, THOU HAST SO WRONGED MINE INNOCENT CHILD AND ME...
THAT I AM FORCED TO CHALLENGE THEE.
THY SLANDER HATH GONE THROUGH HER HEART, AND SHE LIES BURIED WITH HER ANCESTORS --
O, IN A TOMB WHERE NEVER SCANDAL SLEPT, SAVE THIS OF HERS, FRAMED BY YOUR VILLAINY.

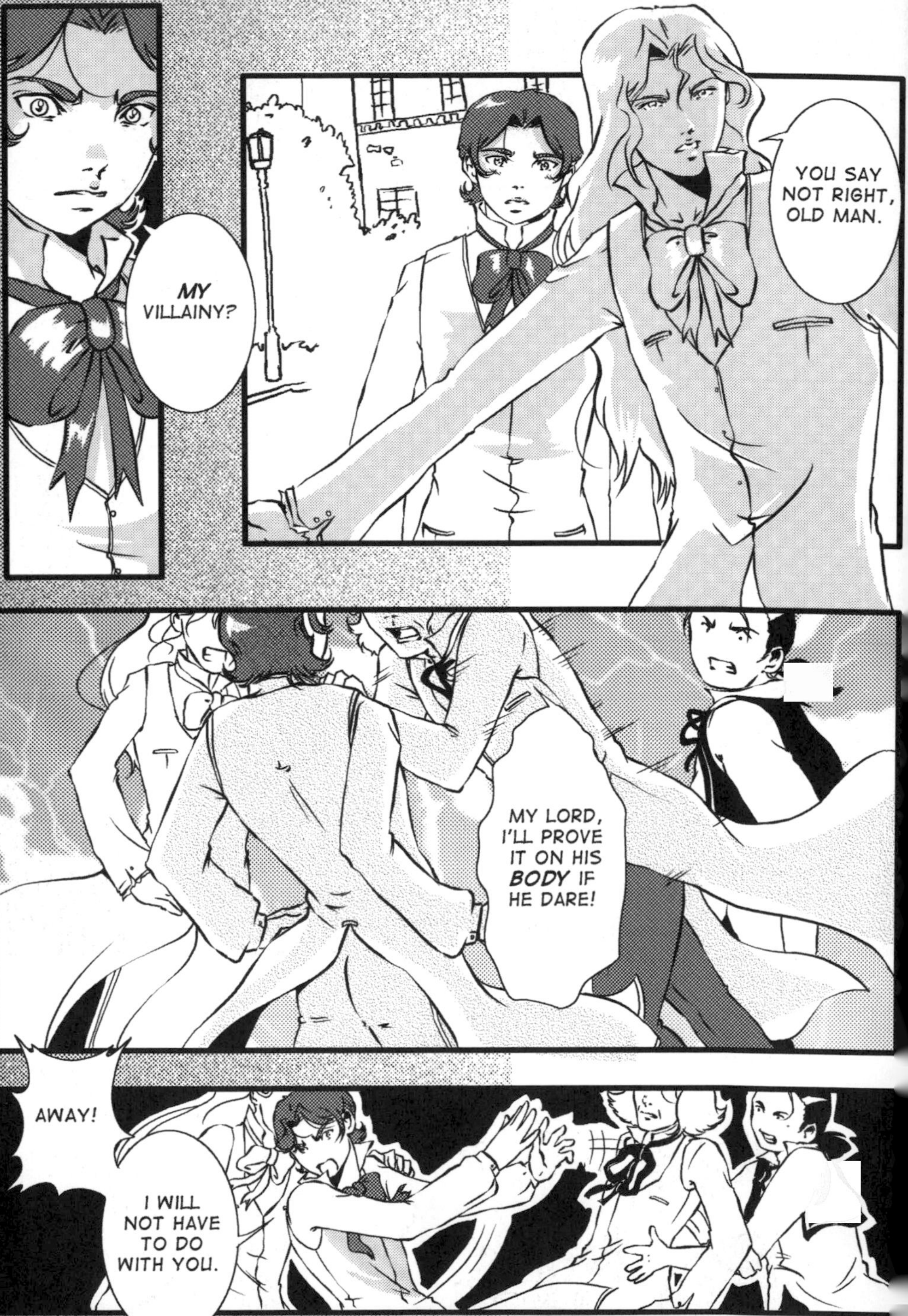
MY VILLAINY?
YOU SAY NOT RIGHT, OLD MAN.
MY LORD, I'LL PROVE IT ON HIS BODY IF HE DARE!
AWAY!
I WILL NOT HAVE TO DO WITH YOU.

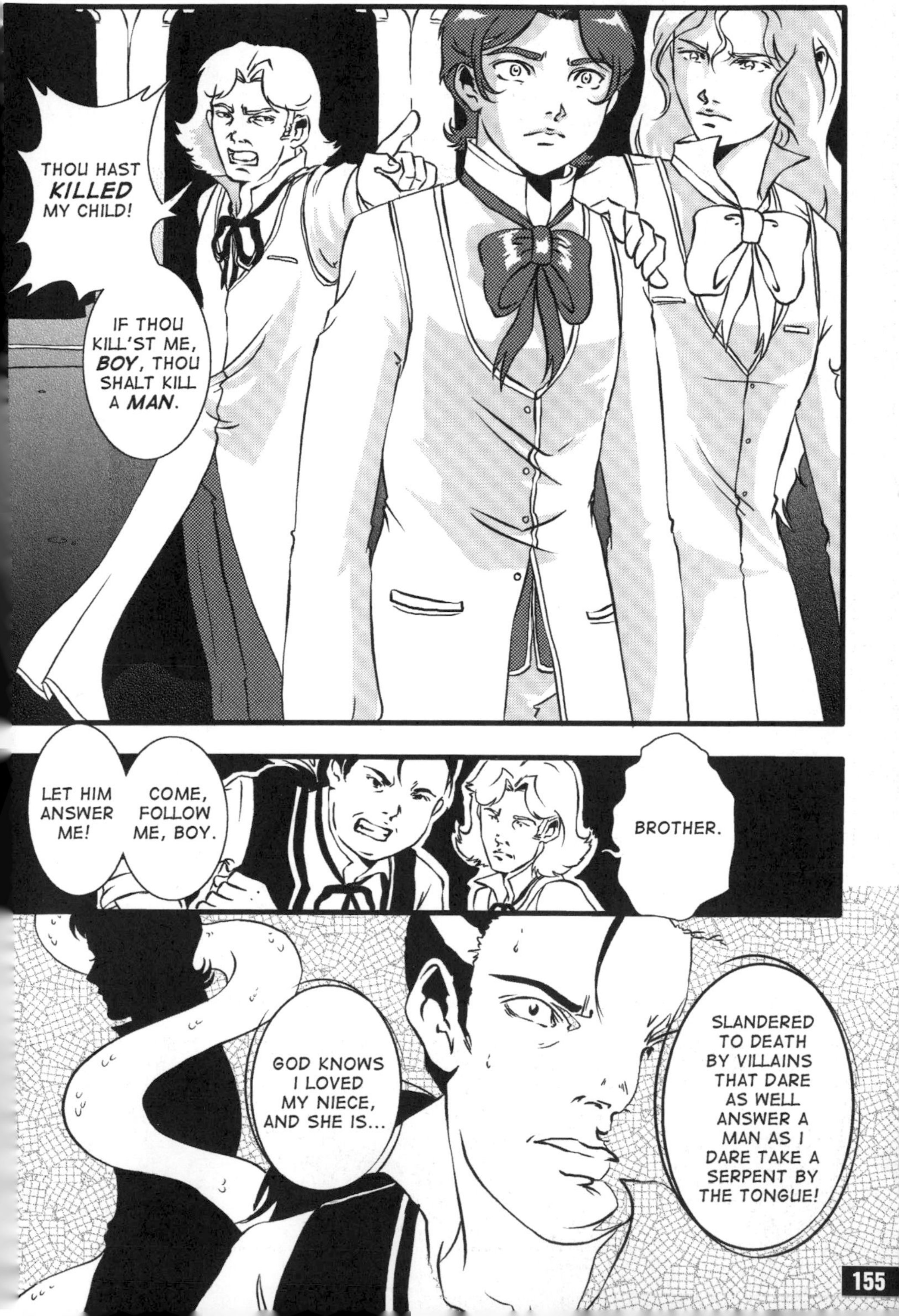

THOU HAST **KILLED** MY CHILD!
IF THOU KILL'ST ME, **BOY**, THOU SHALT KILL A **MAN**.
LET HIM ANSWER ME!
COME, FOLLOW ME, BOY.
BROTHER.
GOD KNOWS I LOVED MY NIECE, AND SHE IS...
SLANDERED TO DEATH BY VILLAINS THAT DARE AS WELL ANSWER A MAN AS I DARE TAKE A SERPENT BY THE TONGUE!

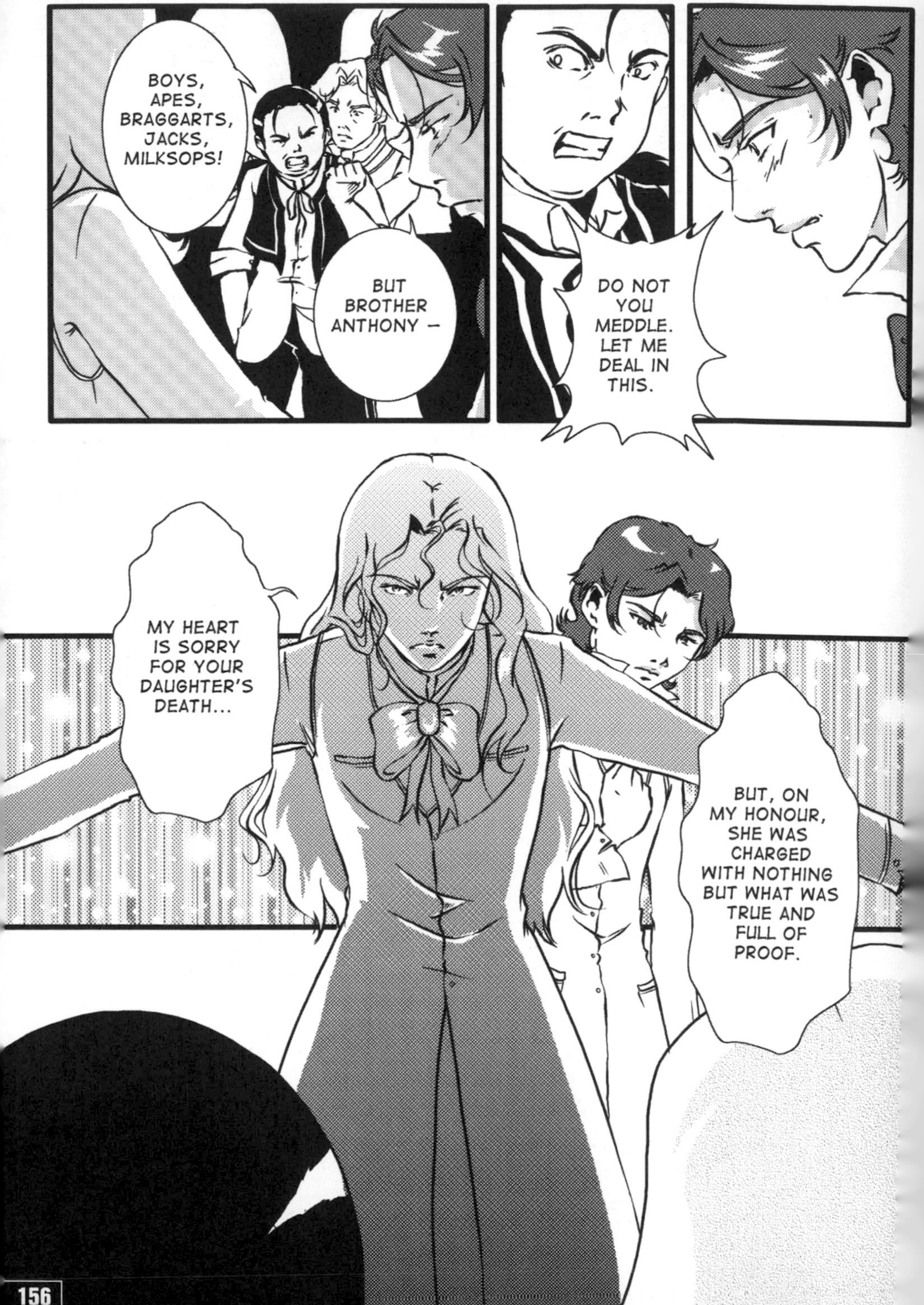
BOYS, APES, BRAGGARTS, JACKS, MILKSOPS!
BUT BROTHER ANTHONY –
DO NOT YOU MEDDLE. LET ME DEAL IN THIS.
MY HEART IS SORRY FOR YOUR DAUGHTER'S DEATH...
BUT, ON MY HONOUR, SHE WAS CHARGED WITH NOTHING BUT WHAT WAS TRUE AND FULL OF PROOF.

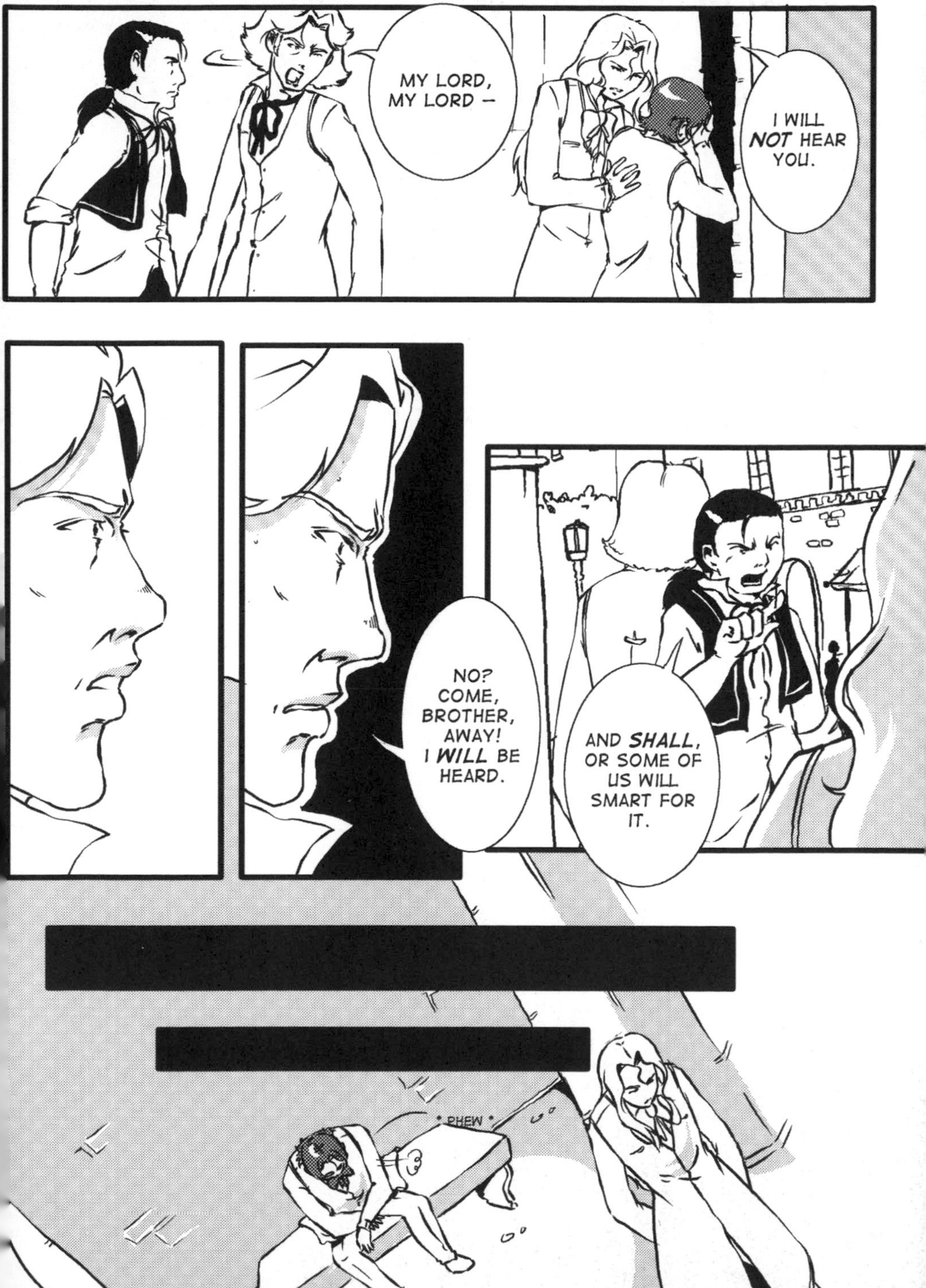
MY LORD, MY LORD –
I WILL *NOT* HEAR YOU.
NO? COME, BROTHER, AWAY! I *WILL* BE HEARD.
AND *SHALL*, OR SOME OF US WILL SMART FOR IT.
[redacted]
[redacted]
* PHEW *

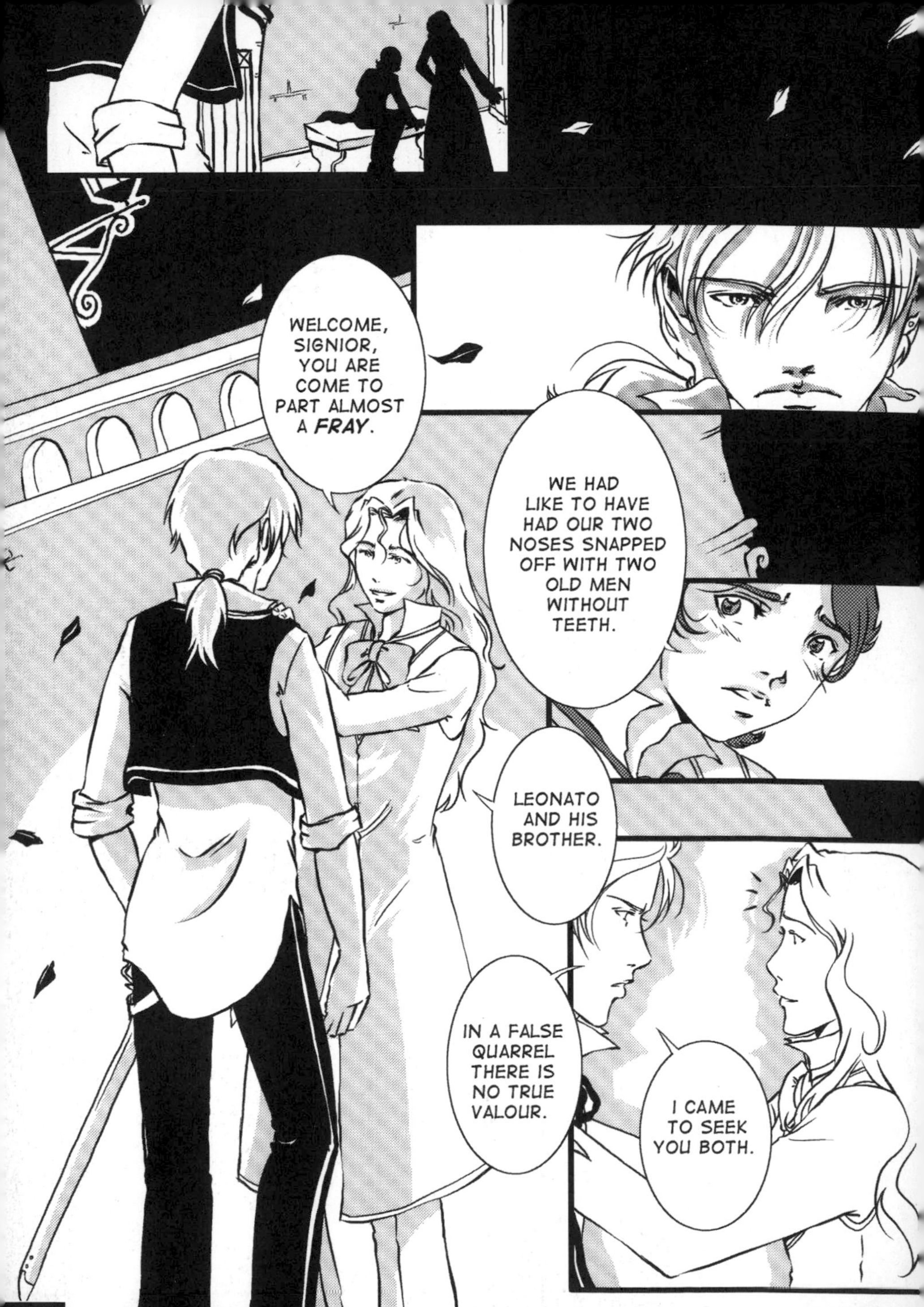
WELCOME, SIGNIOR, YOU ARE COME TO PART ALMOST A *FRAY*.
WE HAD LIKE TO HAVE HAD OUR TWO NOSES SNAPPED OFF WITH TWO OLD MEN WITHOUT TEETH.
LEONATO AND HIS BROTHER.
IN A FALSE QUARREL THERE IS NO TRUE VALOUR.
I CAME TO SEEK YOU BOTH.

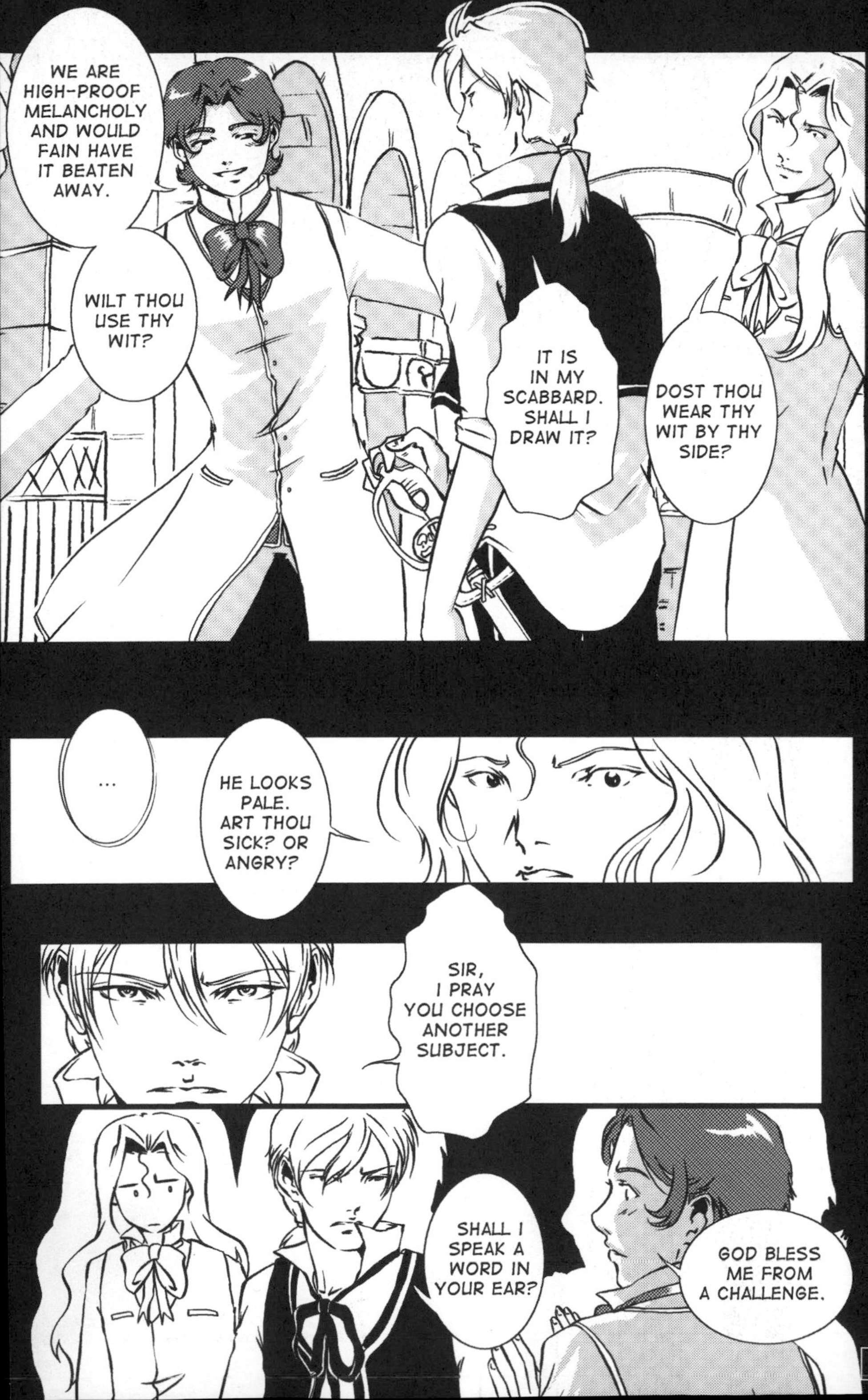

WE ARE HIGH-PROOF MELANCHOLY AND WOULD FAIN HAVE IT BEATEN AWAY.
WILT THOU USE THY WIT?
IT IS IN MY SCABBARD. SHALL I DRAW IT?
DOST THOU WEAR THY WIT BY THY SIDE?
...
HE LOOKS PALE. ART THOU SICK? OR ANGRY?
SIR, I PRAY YOU CHOOSE ANOTHER SUBJECT.
SHALL I SPEAK A WORD IN YOUR EAR?
GOD BLESS ME FROM A CHALLENGE.

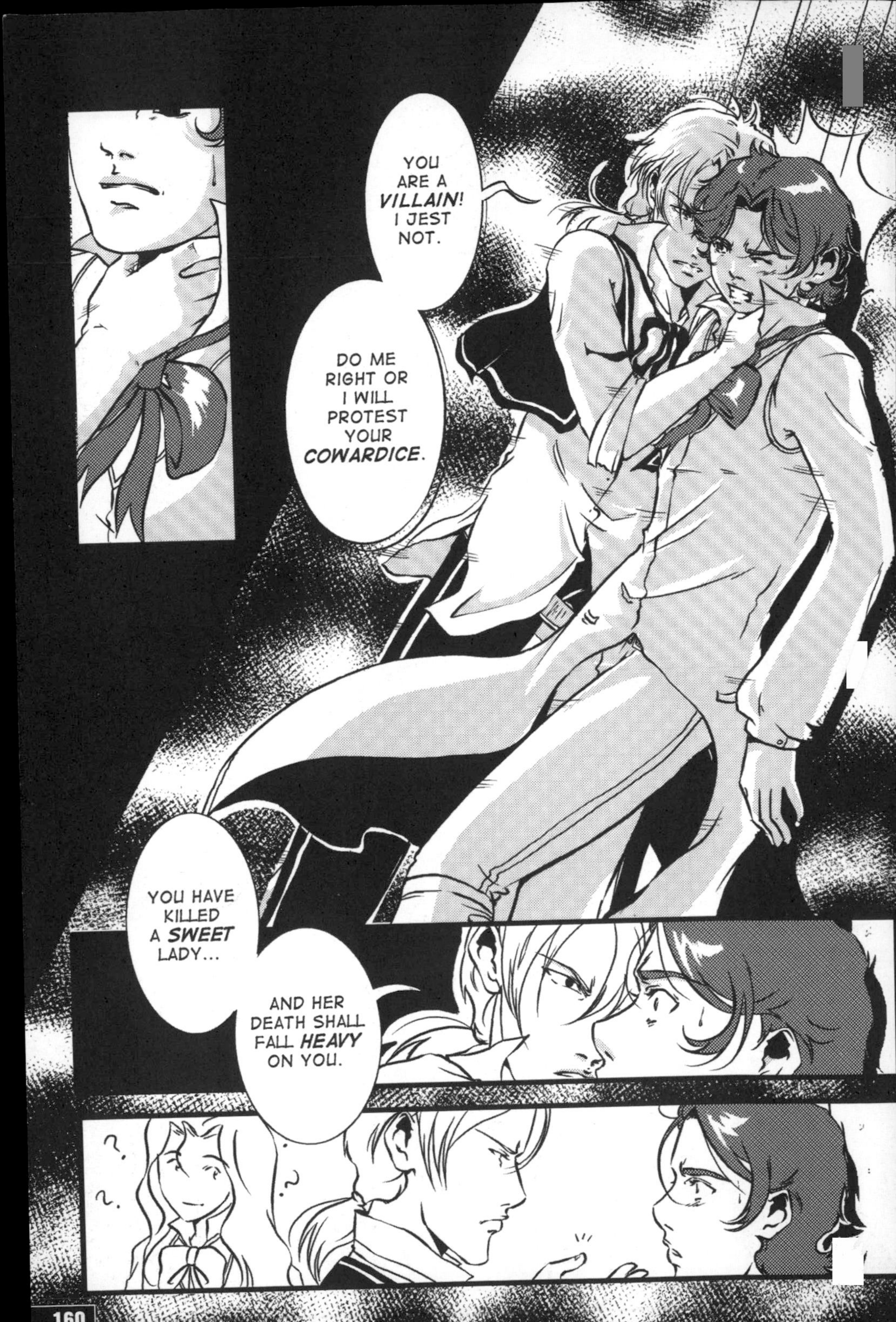

YOU ARE A VILLAIN! I JEST NOT.
DO ME RIGHT OR I WILL PROTEST YOUR COWARDICE.
YOU HAVE KILLED A SWEET LADY...
AND HER DEATH SHALL FALL HEAVY ON YOU.

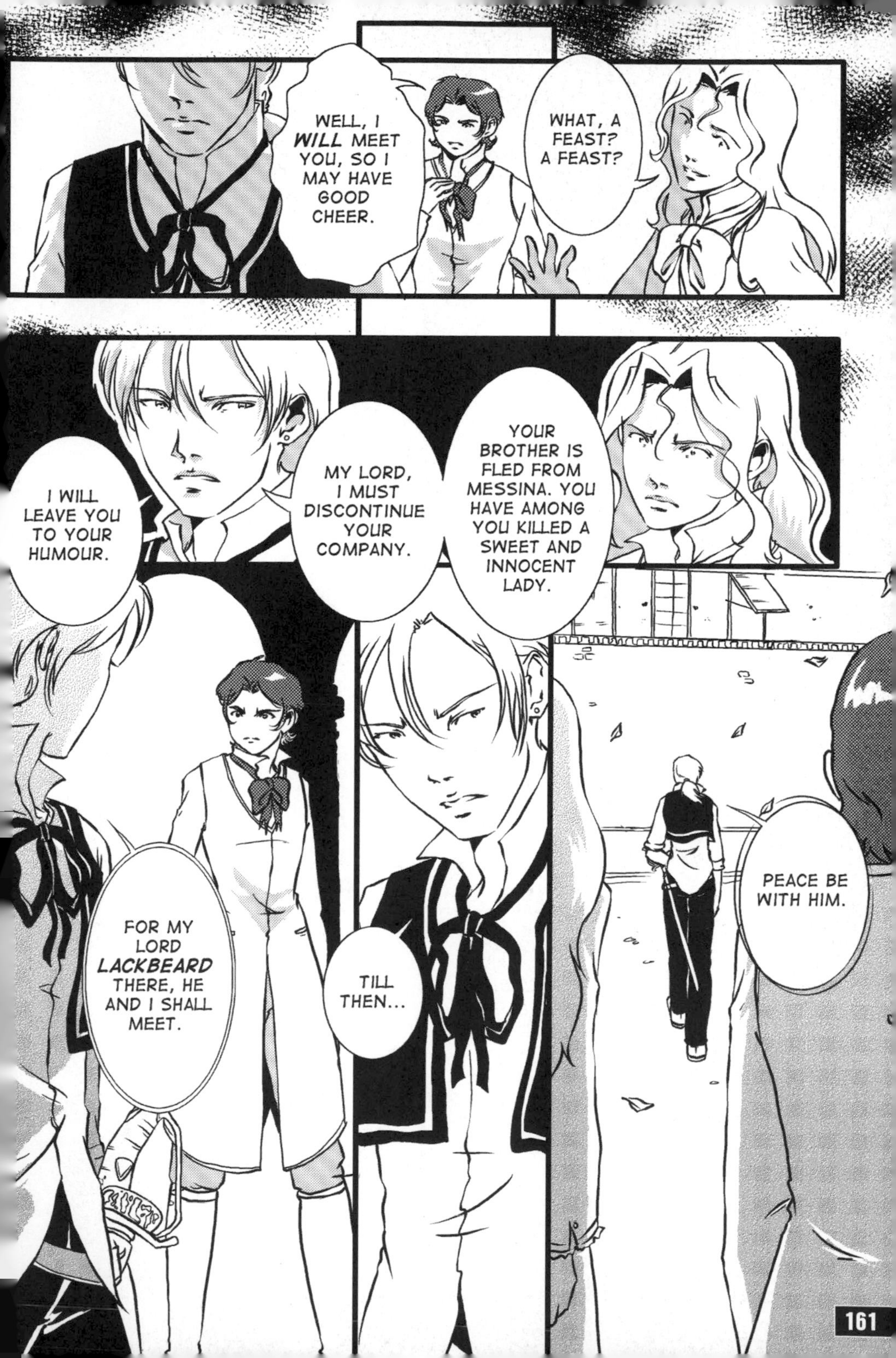
WELL, I *WILL* MEET YOU, SO I MAY HAVE GOOD CHEER.
WHAT, A FEAST? A FEAST?
I WILL LEAVE YOU TO YOUR HUMOUR.
MY LORD, I MUST DISCONTINUE YOUR COMPANY.
YOUR BROTHER IS FLED FROM MESSINA. YOU HAVE AMONG YOU KILLED A SWEET AND INNOCENT LADY.
FOR MY LORD *LACKBEARD* THERE, HE AND I SHALL MEET.
TILL THEN...
PEACE BE WITH HIM.

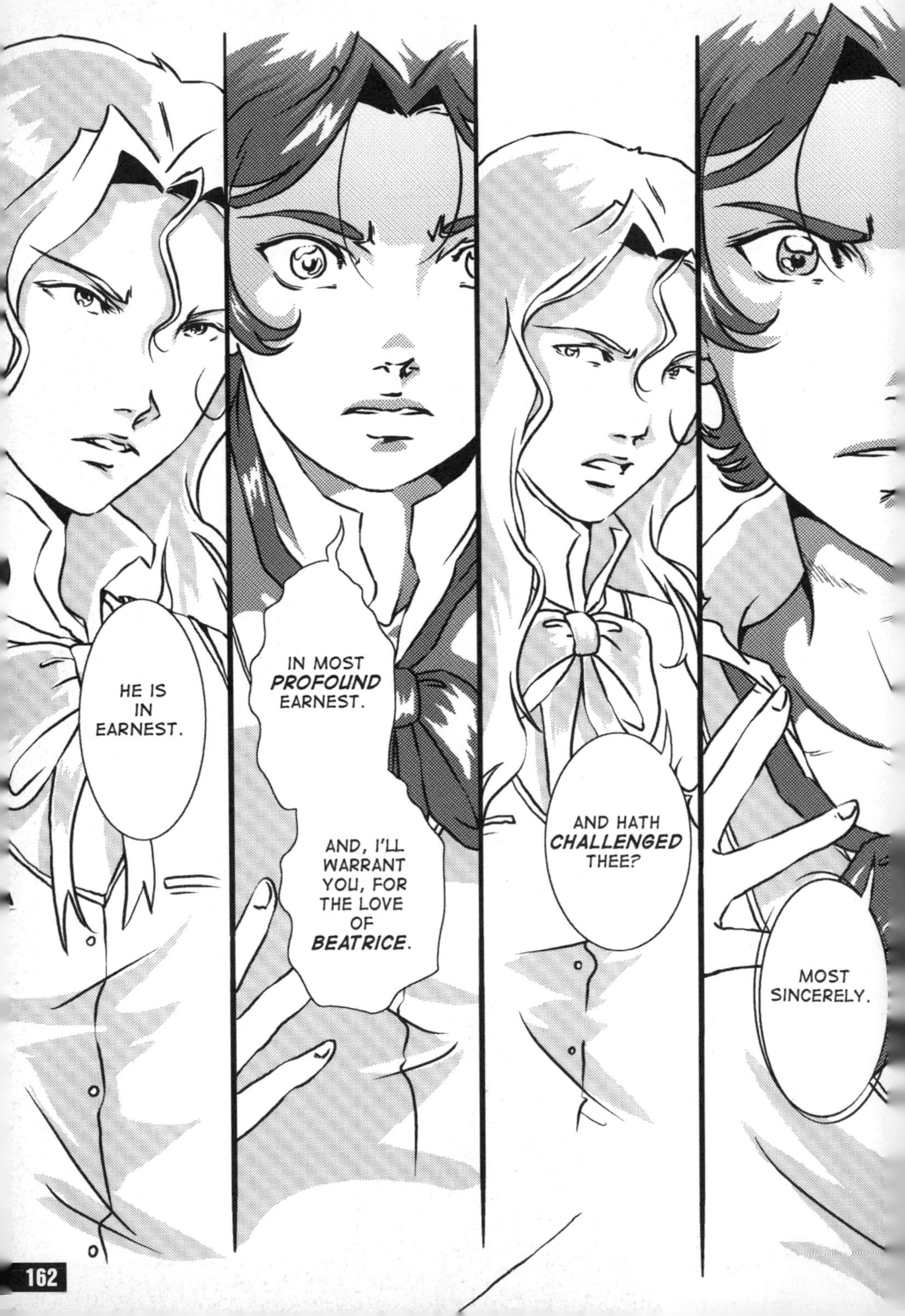
HE IS IN EARNEST.
IN MOST PROFOUND EARNEST.
AND, I'LL WARRANT YOU, FOR THE LOVE OF BEATRICE.
AND HATH CHALLENGED THEE?
MOST SINCERELY.

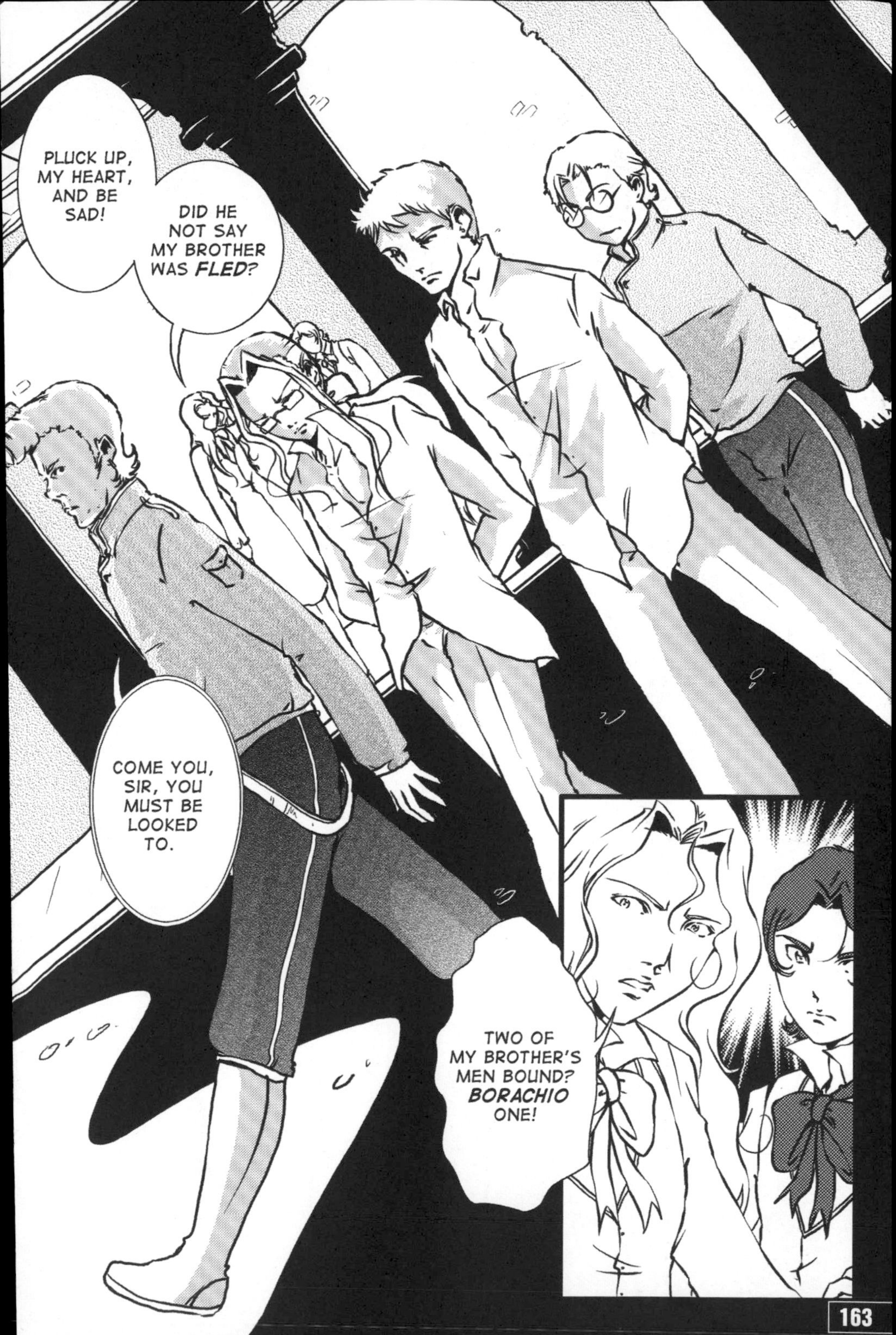
PLUCK UP, MY HEART, AND BE SAD!
DID HE NOT SAY MY BROTHER WAS **FLED**?
COME YOU, SIR, YOU MUST BE LOOKED TO.
TWO OF MY BROTHER'S MEN BOUND? **BORACHIO** ONE!

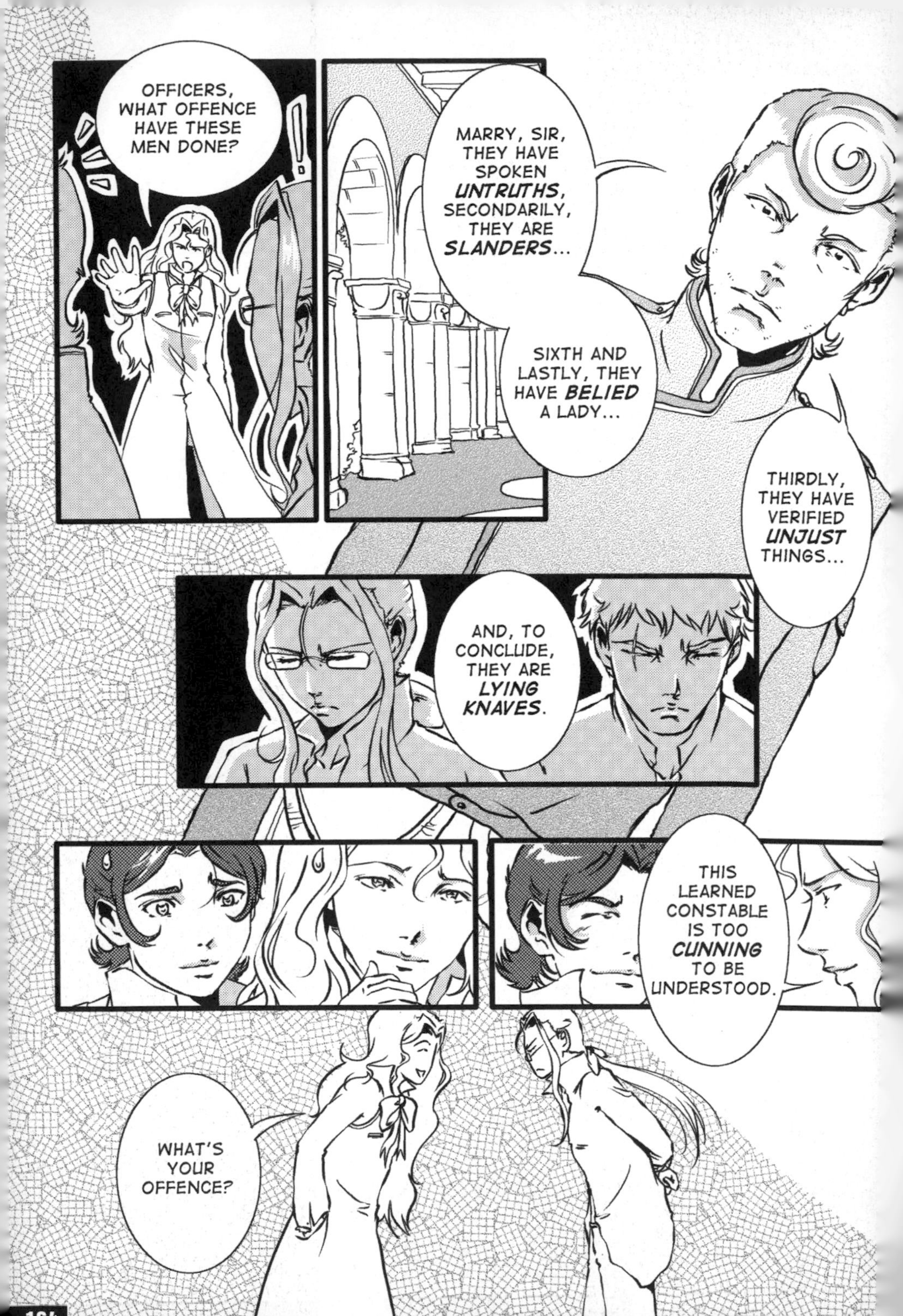

OFFICERS, WHAT OFFENCE HAVE THESE MEN DONE?
MARRY, SIR, THEY HAVE SPOKEN *UNTRUTHS*, SECONDARILY, THEY ARE *SLANDERS*...
SIXTH AND LASTLY, THEY HAVE *BELIED* A LADY...
THIRDLY, THEY HAVE VERIFIED *UNJUST* THINGS...
AND, TO CONCLUDE, THEY ARE *LYING KNAVES*.
THIS LEARNED CONSTABLE IS TOO *CUNNING* TO BE UNDERSTOOD.
WHAT'S YOUR OFFENCE?

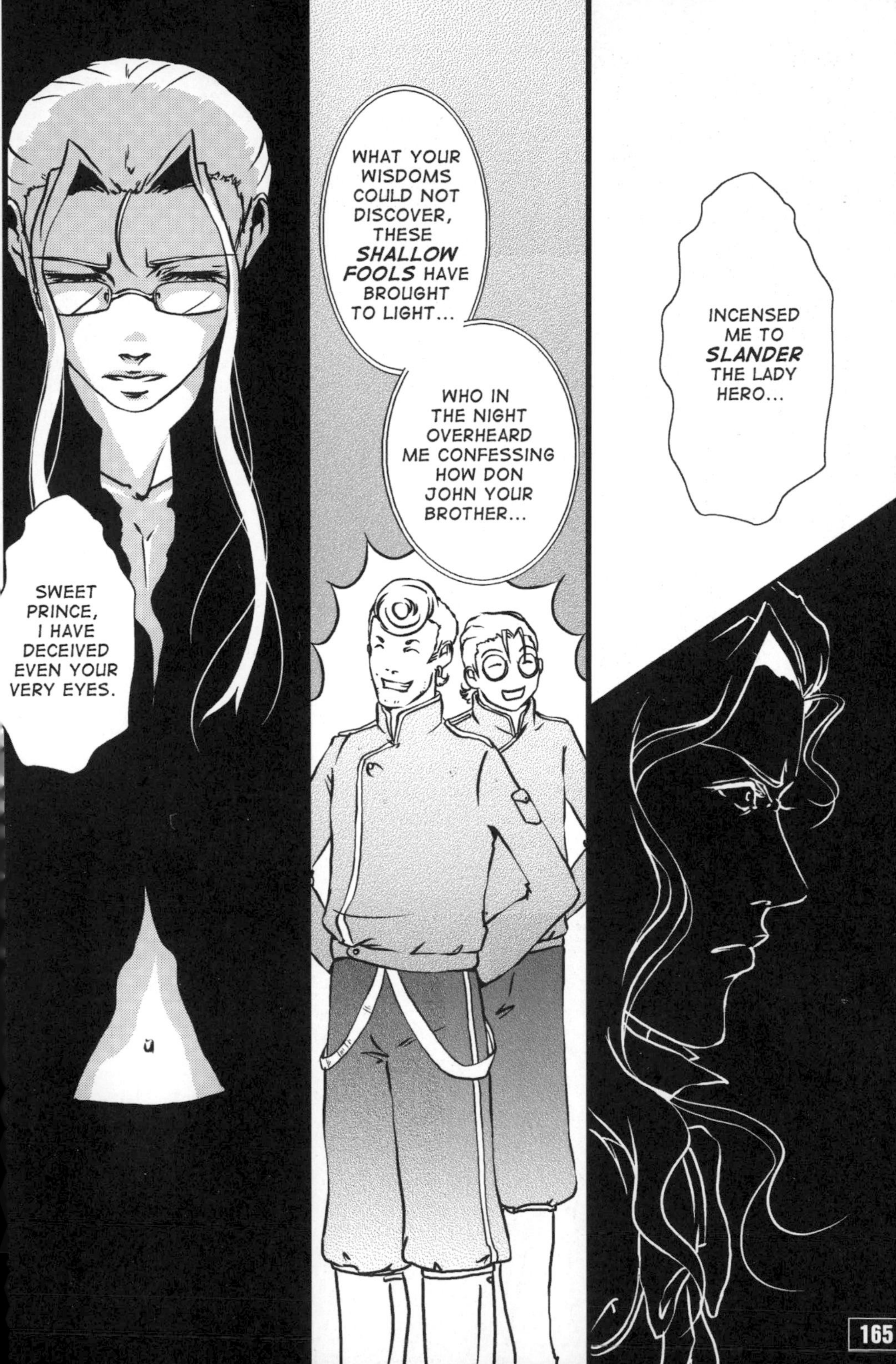
SWEET PRINCE, I HAVE DECEIVED EVEN YOUR VERY EYES.
WHAT YOUR WISDOMS COULD NOT DISCOVER, THESE SHALLOW FOOLS HAVE BROUGHT TO LIGHT...
WHO IN THE NIGHT OVERHEARD ME CONFESSING HOW DON JOHN YOUR BROTHER...
INCENSED ME TO SLANDER THE LADY HERO...

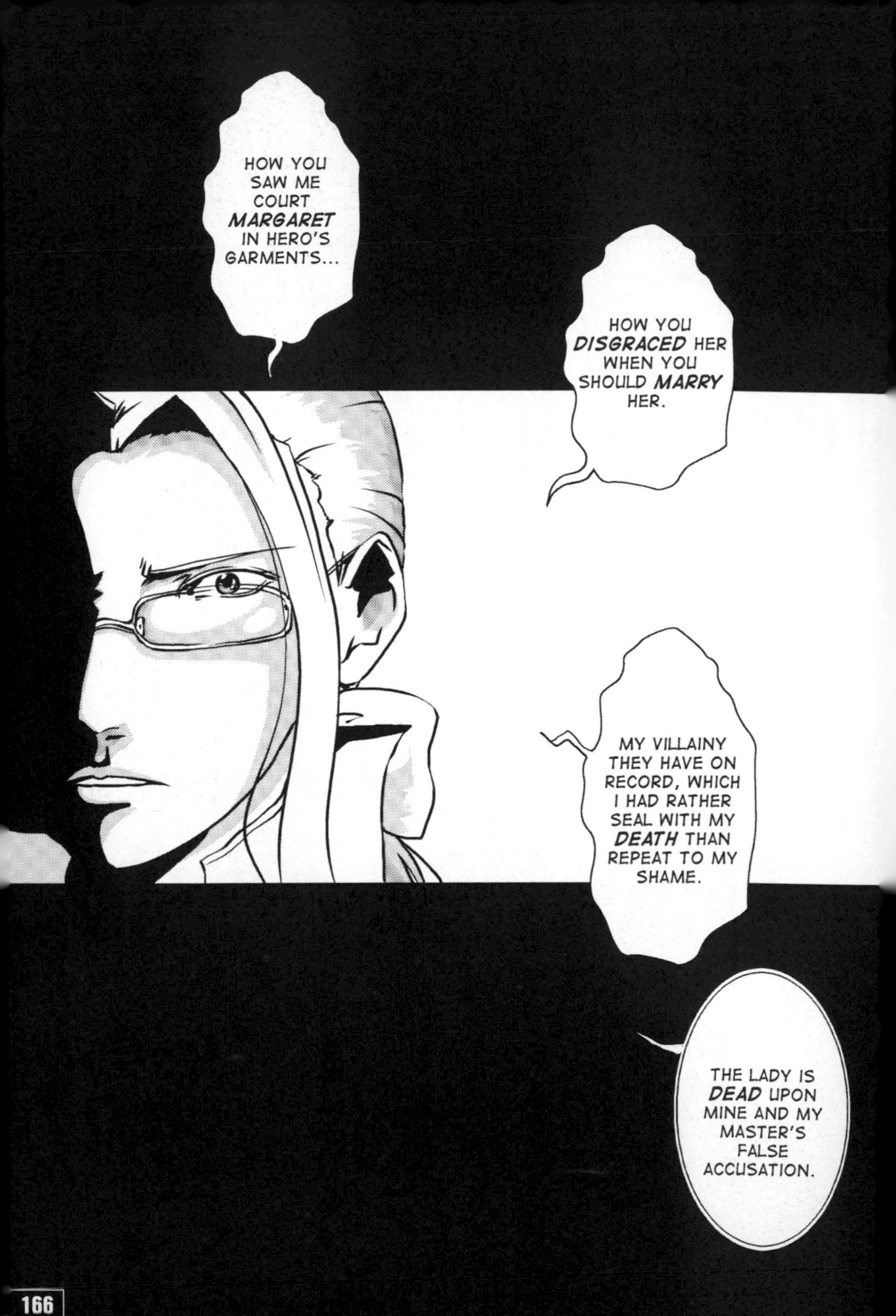
HOW YOU SAW ME COURT ***MARGARET*** IN HERO'S GARMENTS...
HOW YOU ***DISGRACED*** HER WHEN YOU SHOULD ***MARRY*** HER.
MY VILLAINY THEY HAVE ON RECORD, WHICH I HAD RATHER SEAL WITH MY ***DEATH*** THAN REPEAT TO MY SHAME.
THE LADY IS ***DEAD*** UPON MINE AND MY MASTER'S FALSE ACCUSATION.

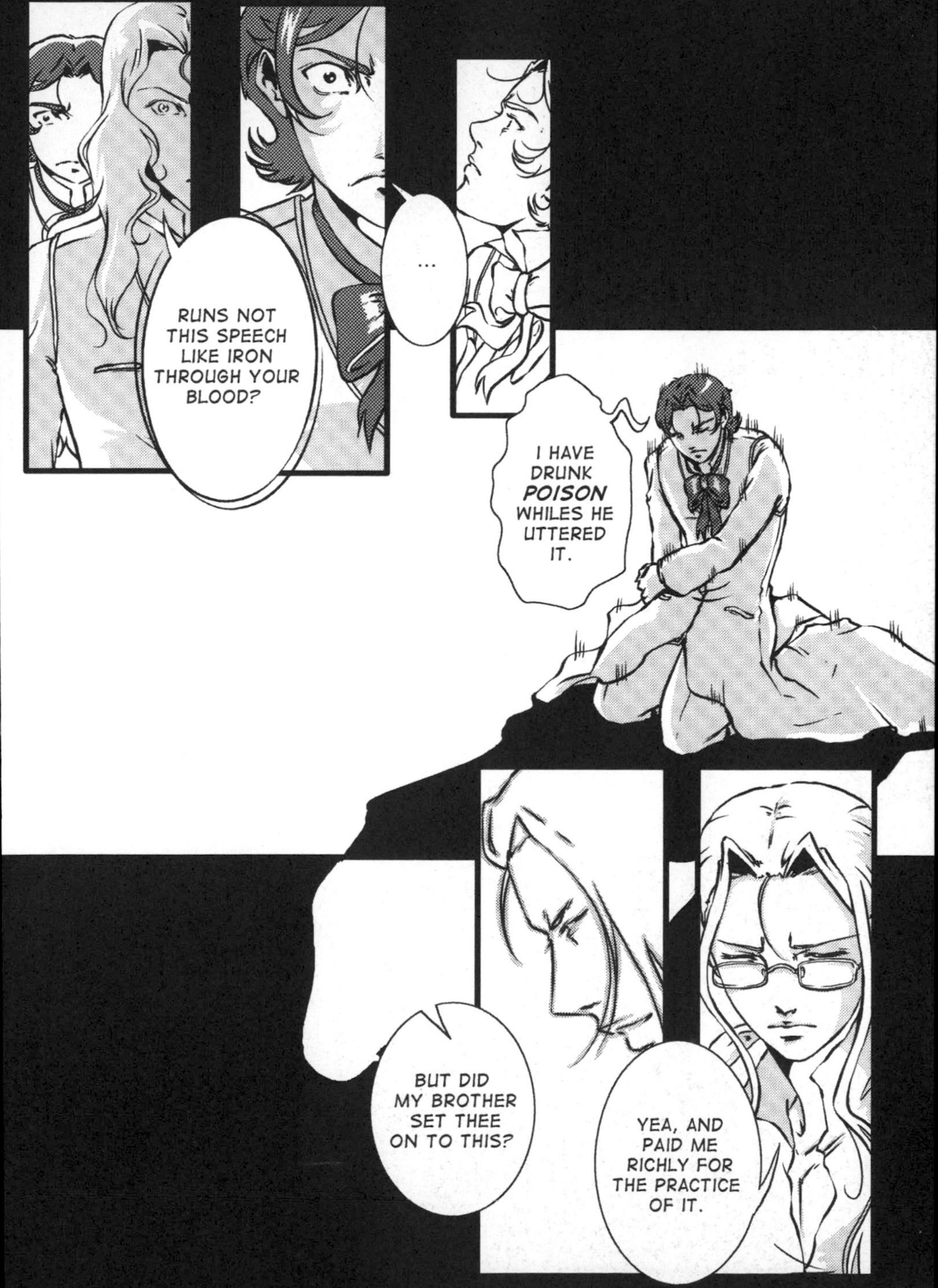
RUNS NOT THIS SPEECH LIKE IRON THROUGH YOUR BLOOD?
...
I HAVE DRUNK POISON WHILES HE UTTERED IT.
BUT DID MY BROTHER SET THEE ON TO THIS?
YEA, AND PAID ME RICHLY FOR THE PRACTICE OF IT.

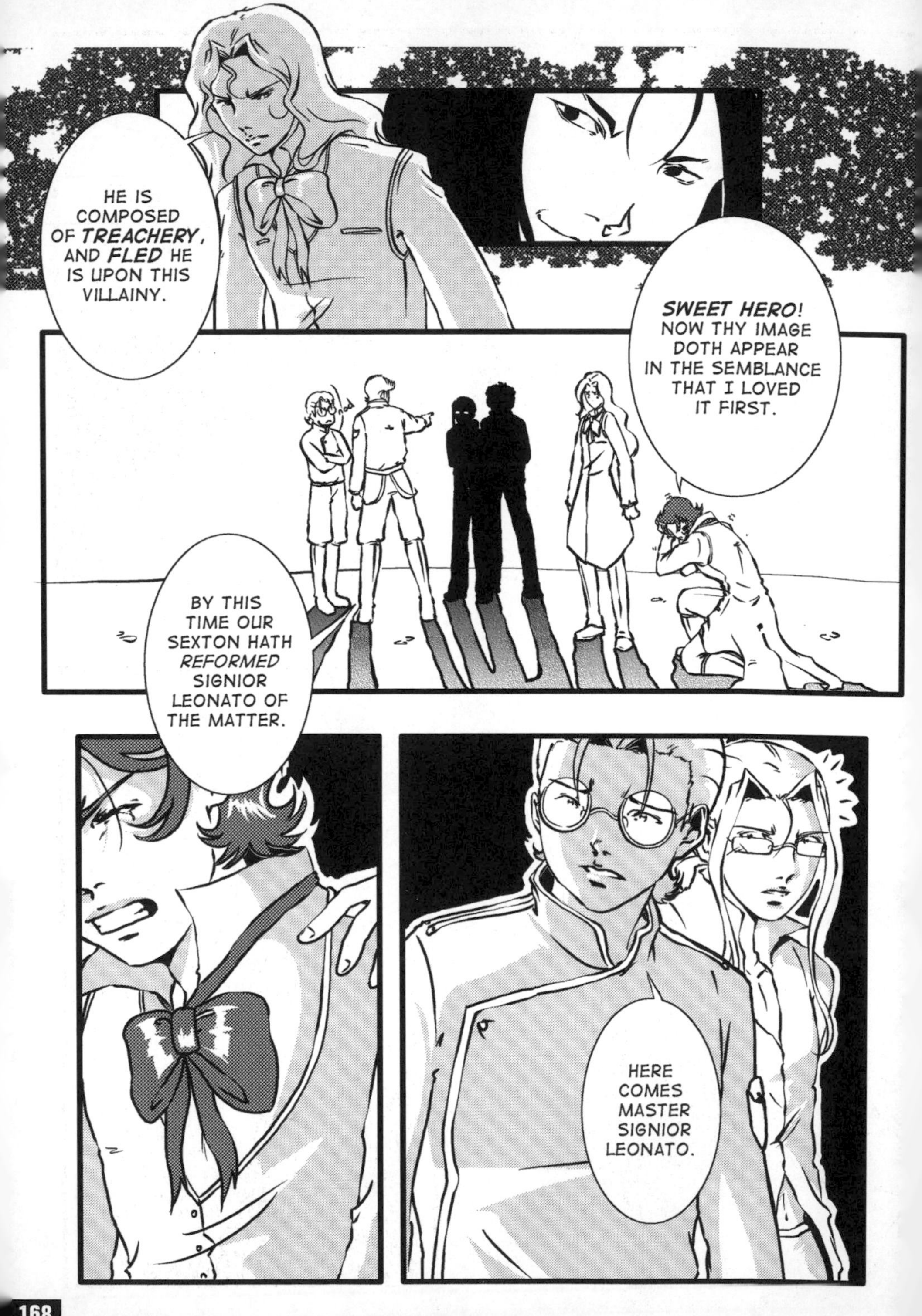
HE IS COMPOSED OF TREACHERY, AND FLED HE IS UPON THIS VILLAINY.
SWEET HERO! NOW THY IMAGE DOTH APPEAR IN THE SEMBLANCE THAT I LOVED IT FIRST.
BY THIS TIME OUR SEXTON HATH REFORMED SIGNIOR LEONATO OF THE MATTER.
HERE COMES MASTER SIGNIOR LEONATO.

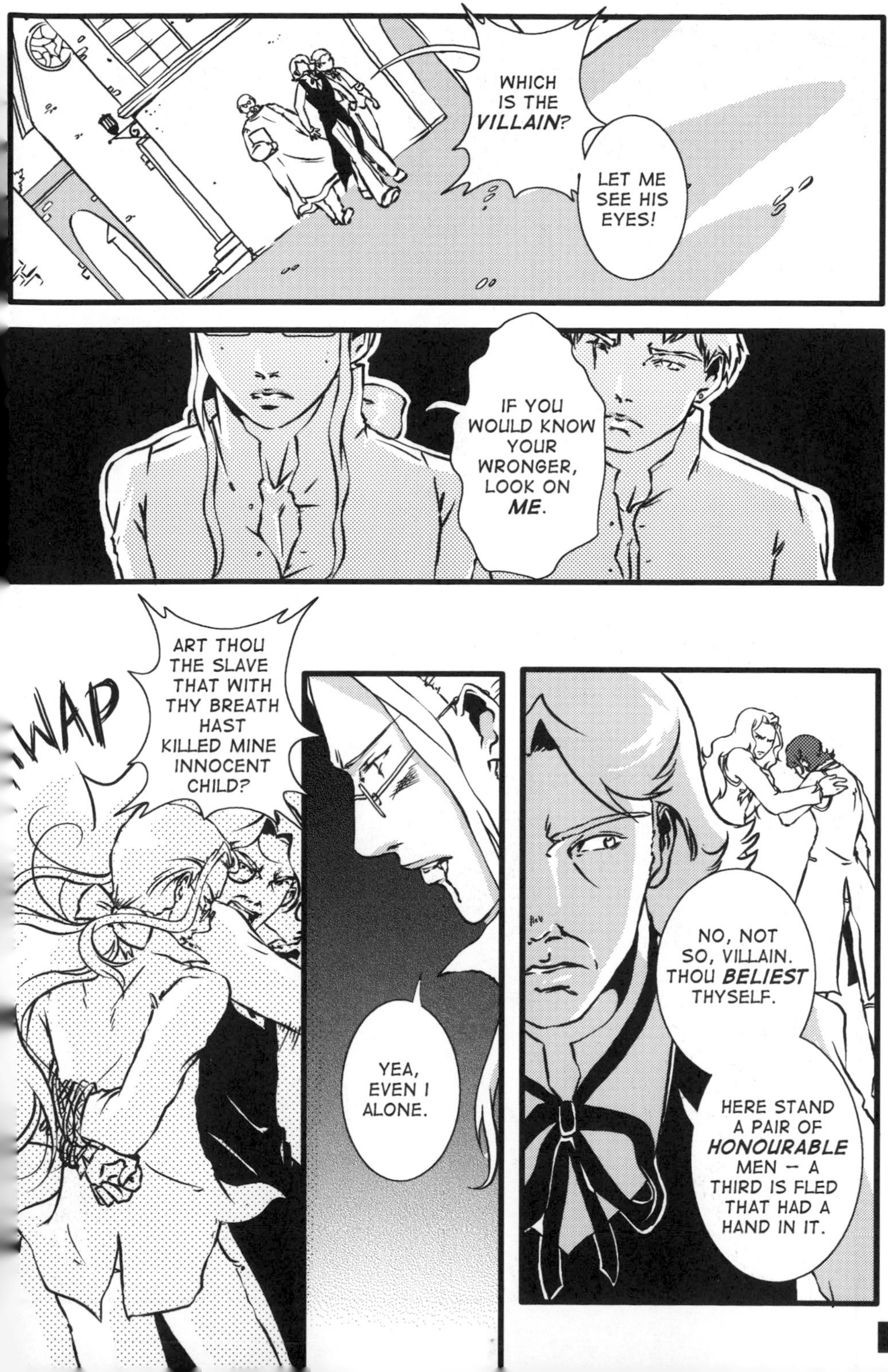
WHICH IS THE *VILLAIN*?
LET ME SEE HIS EYES!
IF YOU WOULD KNOW YOUR WRONGER, LOOK ON *ME*.
WAP
ART THOU THE SLAVE THAT WITH THY BREATH HAST KILLED MINE INNOCENT CHILD?
YEA, EVEN I ALONE.
NO, NOT SO, VILLAIN. THOU *BELIEST* THYSELF.
HERE STAND A PAIR OF *HONOURABLE* MEN -- A THIRD IS FLED THAT HAD A HAND IN IT.

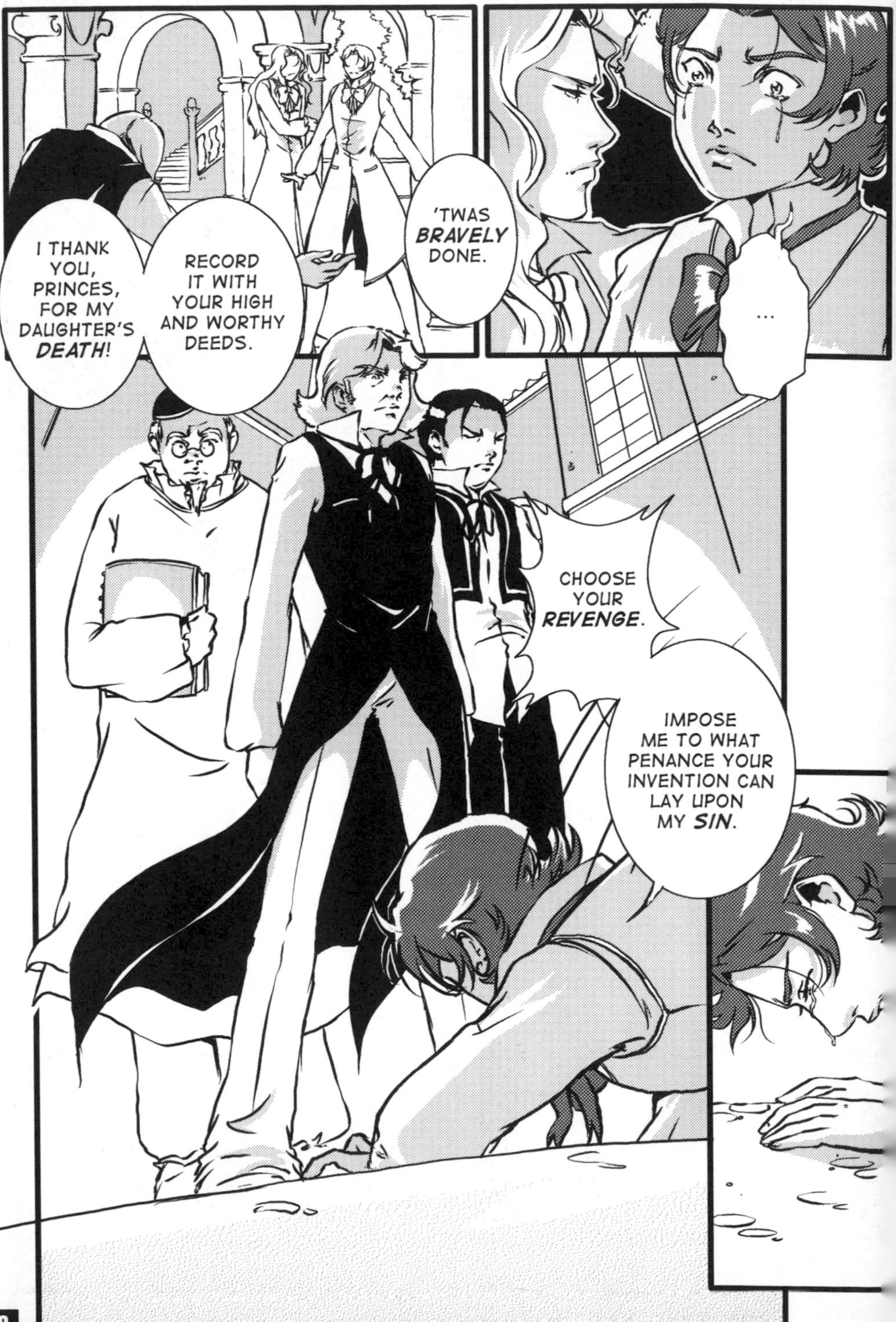
I THANK YOU, PRINCES, FOR MY DAUGHTER'S *DEATH*!
RECORD IT WITH YOUR HIGH AND WORTHY DEEDS.
'TWAS *BRAVELY* DONE.
...
CHOOSE YOUR *REVENGE*.
IMPOSE ME TO WHAT PENANCE YOUR INVENTION CAN LAY UPON MY *SIN*.

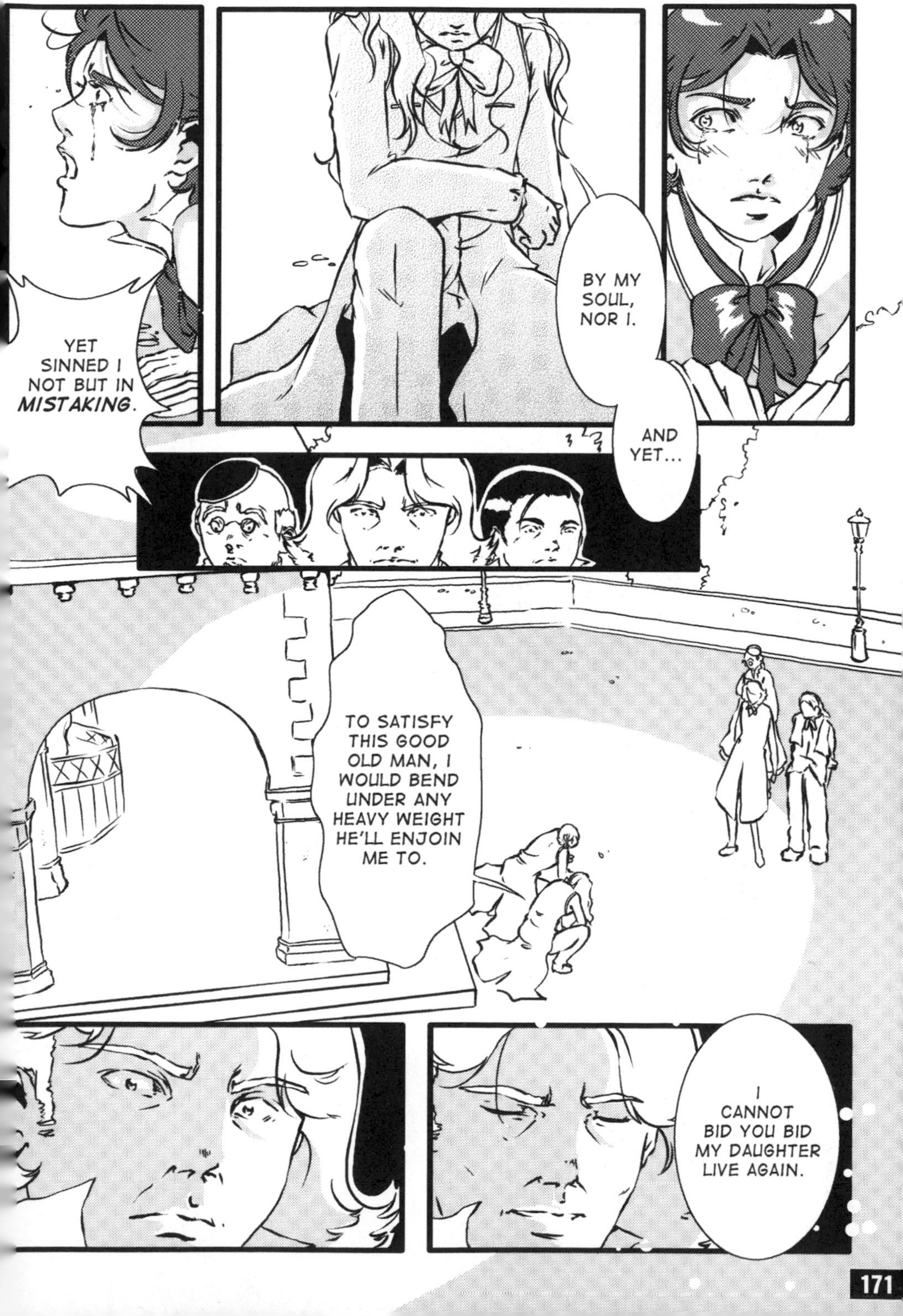
YET SINNED I NOT BUT IN *MISTAKING*.
BY MY SOUL, NOR I.
AND YET...
TO SATISFY THIS GOOD OLD MAN, I WOULD BEND UNDER ANY HEAVY WEIGHT HE'LL ENJOIN ME TO.
I CANNOT BID YOU BID MY DAUGHTER LIVE AGAIN.

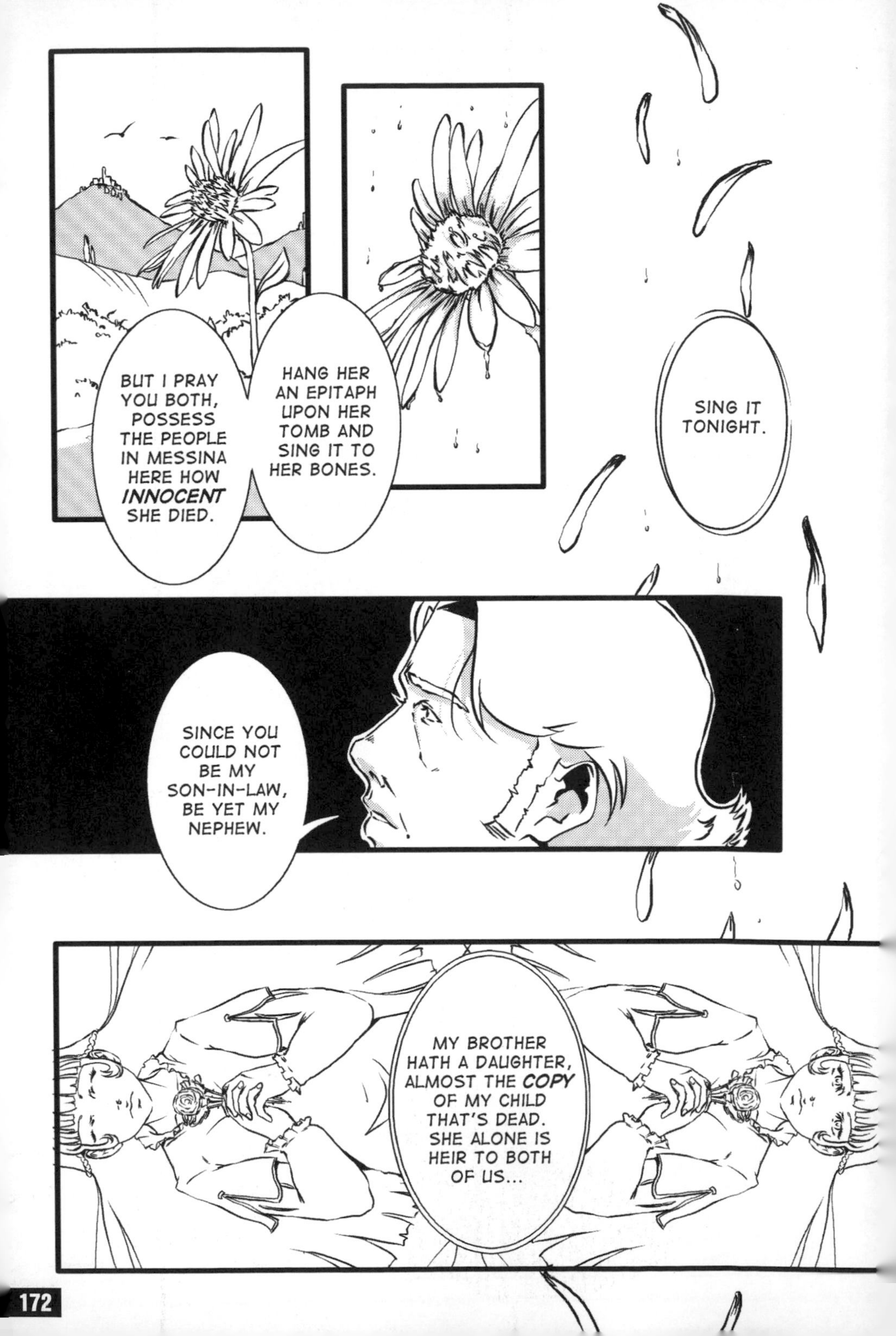
BUT I PRAY YOU BOTH, POSSESS THE PEOPLE IN MESSINA HERE HOW *INNOCENT* SHE DIED.
HANG HER AN EPITAPH UPON HER TOMB AND SING IT TO HER BONES.
SING IT TONIGHT.
SINCE YOU COULD NOT BE MY SON-IN-LAW, BE YET MY NEPHEW.
MY BROTHER HATH A DAUGHTER, ALMOST THE *COPY* OF MY CHILD THAT'S DEAD. SHE ALONE IS HEIR TO BOTH OF US...

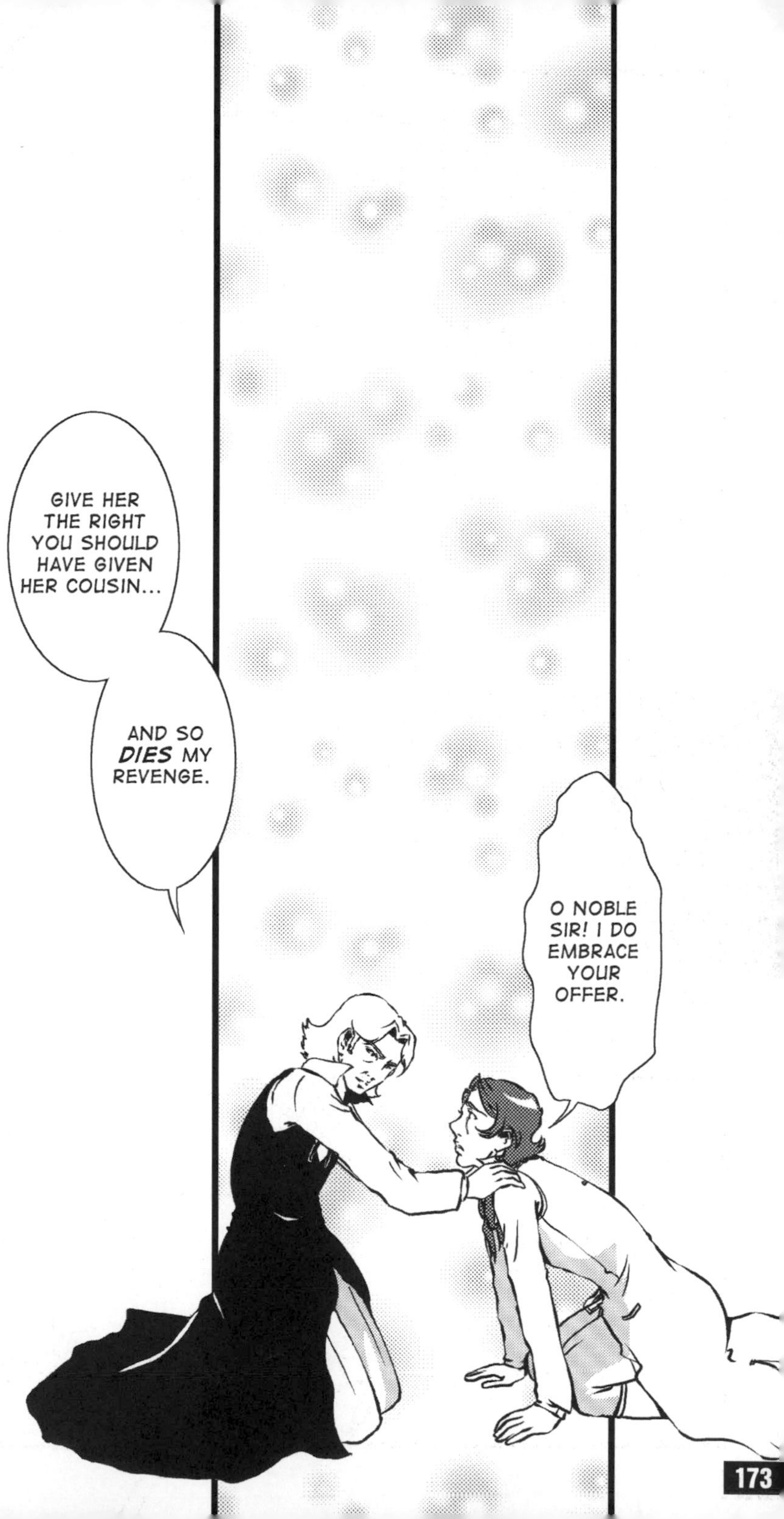
GIVE HER THE RIGHT YOU SHOULD HAVE GIVEN HER COUSIN...
AND SO *DIES* MY REVENGE.
O NOBLE SIR! I DO EMBRACE YOUR OFFER.

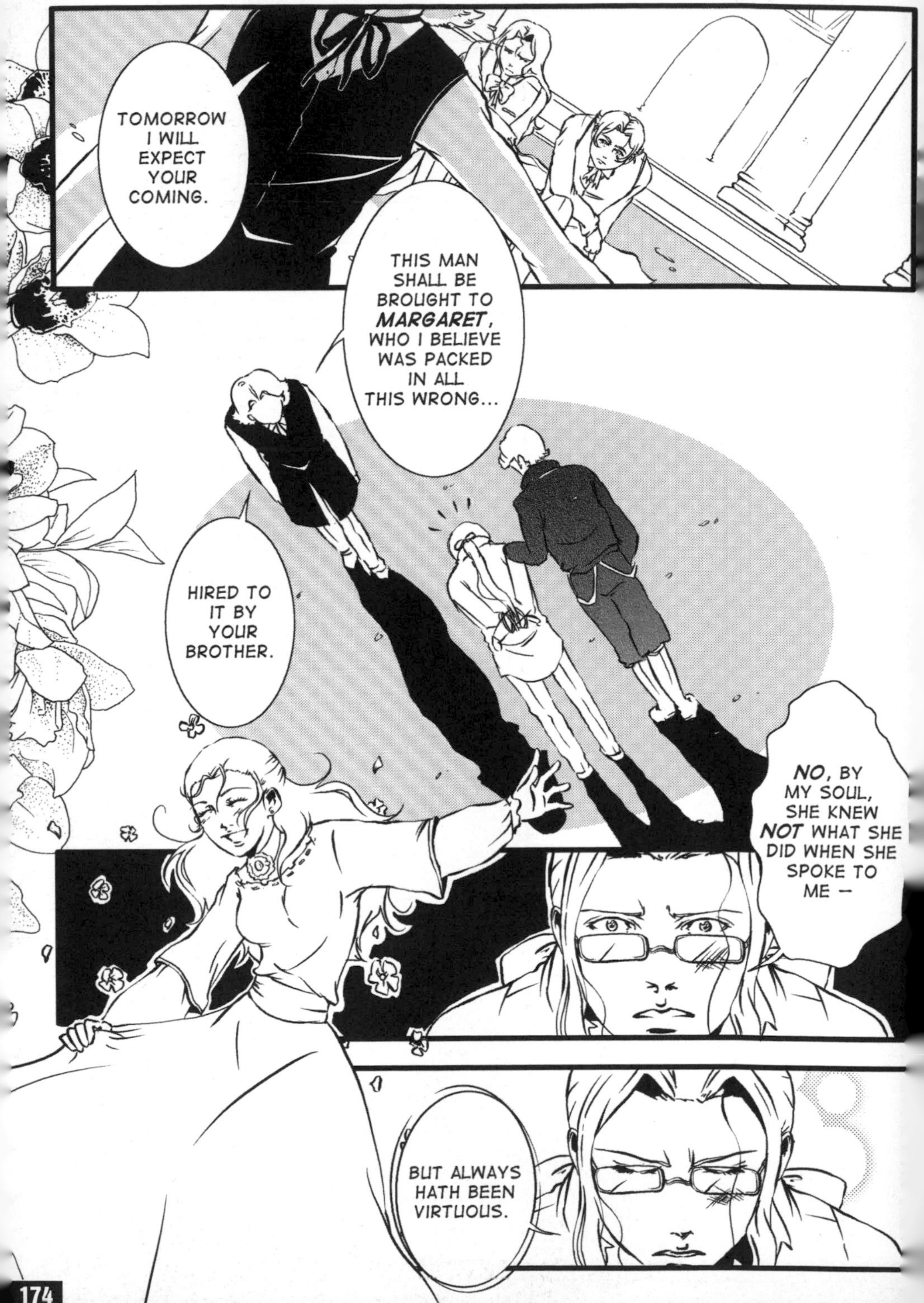
TOMORROW I WILL EXPECT YOUR COMING.
THIS MAN SHALL BE BROUGHT TO MARGARET, WHO I BELIEVE WAS PACKED IN ALL THIS WRONG...
HIRED TO IT BY YOUR BROTHER.
NO, BY MY SOUL, SHE KNEW NOT WHAT SHE DID WHEN SHE SPOKE TO ME –
BUT ALWAYS HATH BEEN VIRTUOUS.

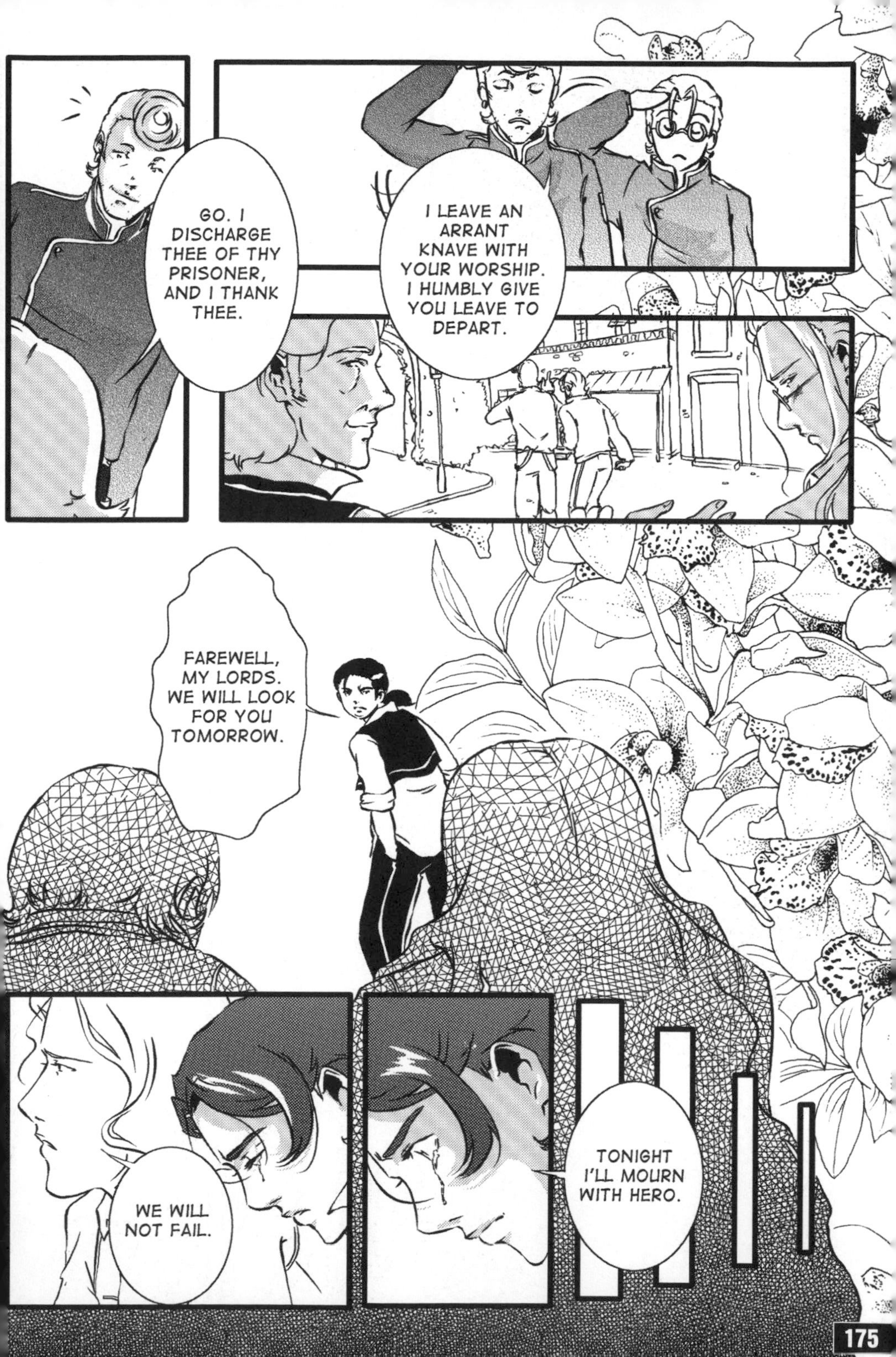
GO. I DISCHARGE THEE OF THY PRISONER, AND I THANK THEE.
I LEAVE AN ARRANT KNAVE WITH YOUR WORSHIP. I HUMBLY GIVE YOU LEAVE TO DEPART.
FAREWELL, MY LORDS. WE WILL LOOK FOR YOU TOMORROW.
WE WILL NOT FAIL.
TONIGHT I'LL MOURN WITH HERO.

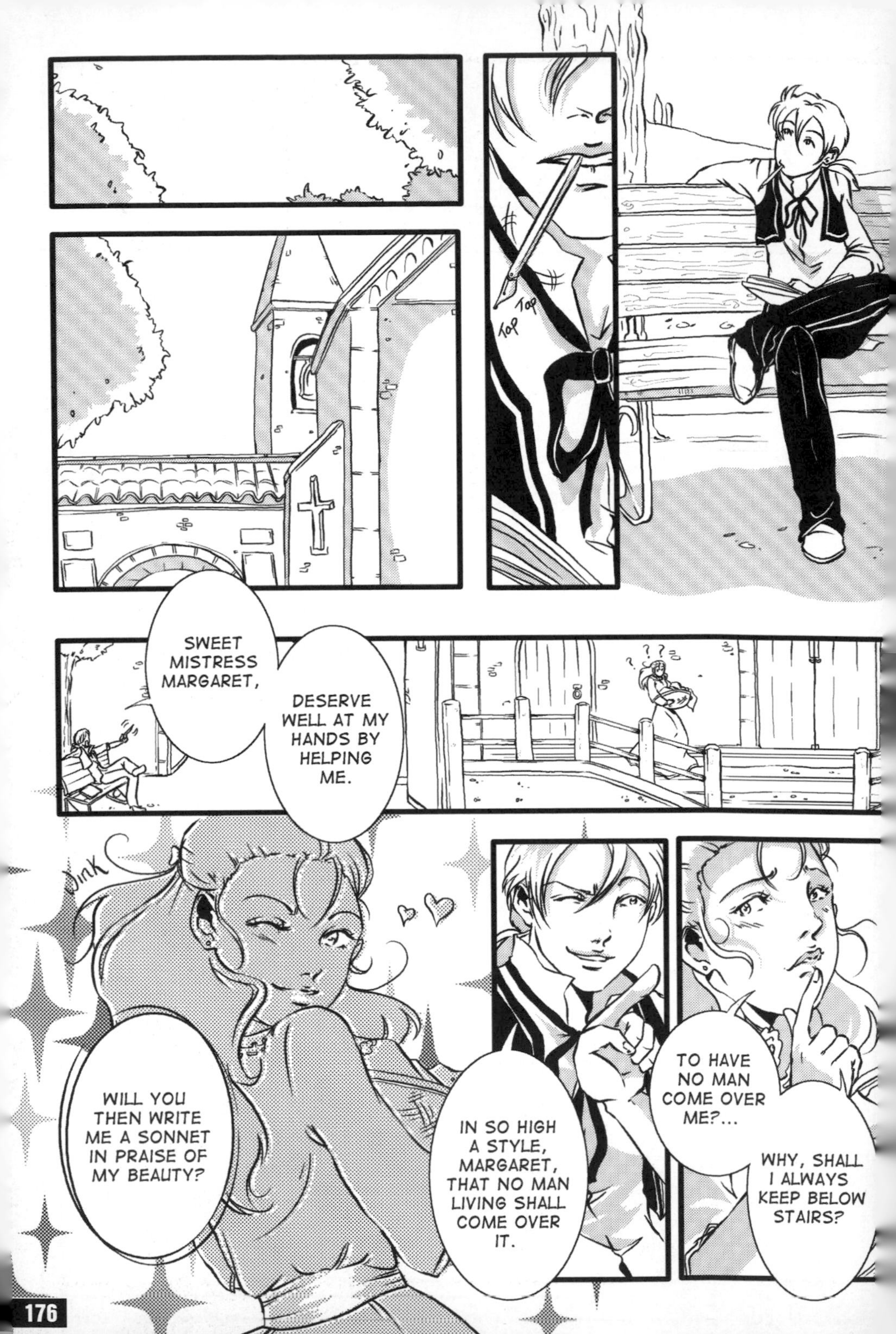

Tap Tap
SWEET MISTRESS MARGARET,
DESERVE WELL AT MY HANDS BY HELPING ME.
Wink
WILL YOU THEN WRITE ME A SONNET IN PRAISE OF MY BEAUTY?
IN SO HIGH A STYLE, MARGARET, THAT NO MAN LIVING SHALL COME OVER IT.
TO HAVE NO MAN COME OVER ME?...
WHY, SHALL I ALWAYS KEEP BELOW STAIRS?

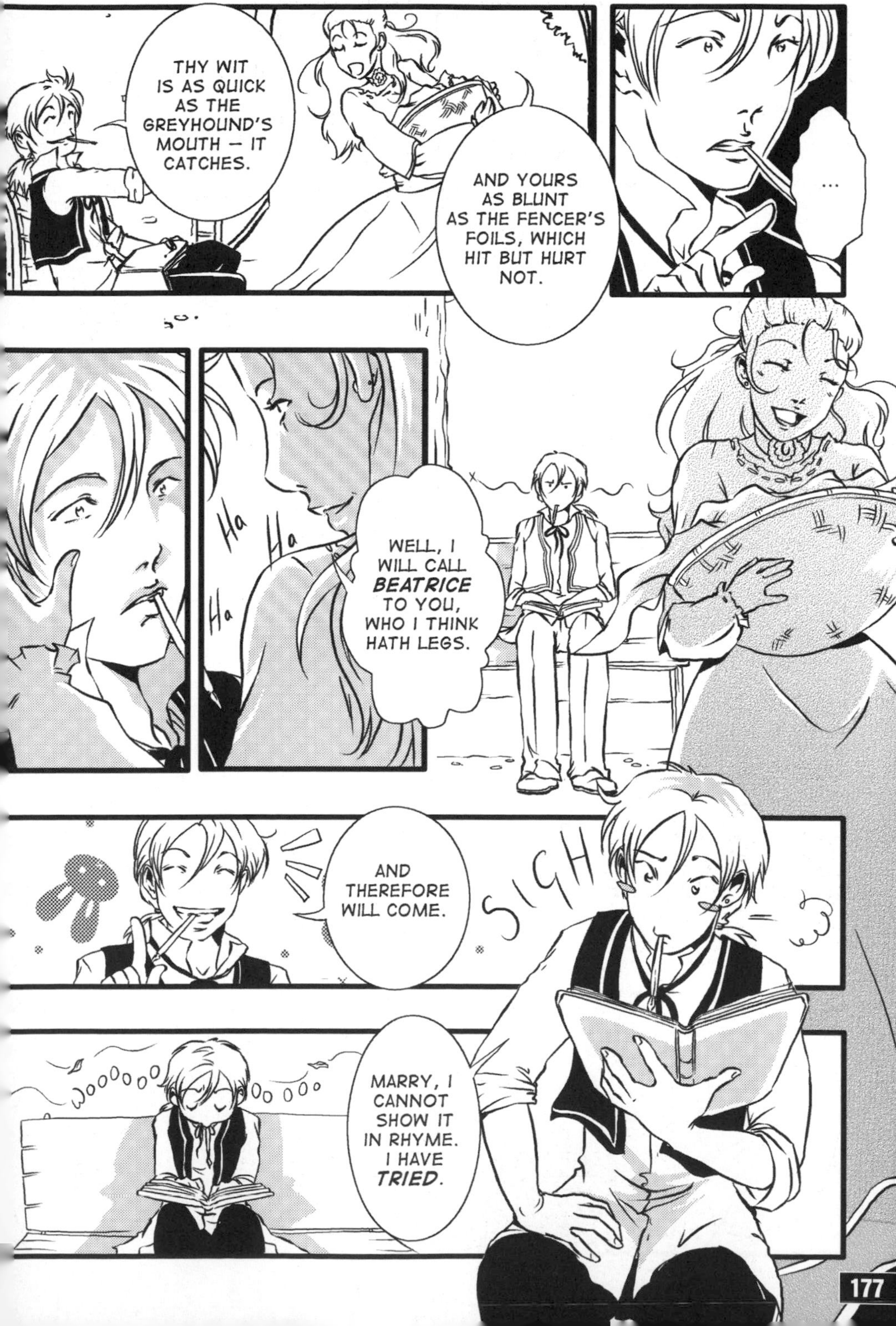
THY WIT IS AS QUICK AS THE GREYHOUND'S MOUTH — IT CATCHES.
AND YOURS AS BLUNT AS THE FENCER'S FOILS, WHICH HIT BUT HURT NOT.
...
Ha
Ha
Ha
WELL, I WILL CALL **BEATRICE** TO YOU, WHO I THINK HATH LEGS.
AND THEREFORE WILL COME.
wooooooo
oo ooo
MARRY, I CANNOT SHOW IT IN RHYME. I HAVE **TRIED**.
SIGH

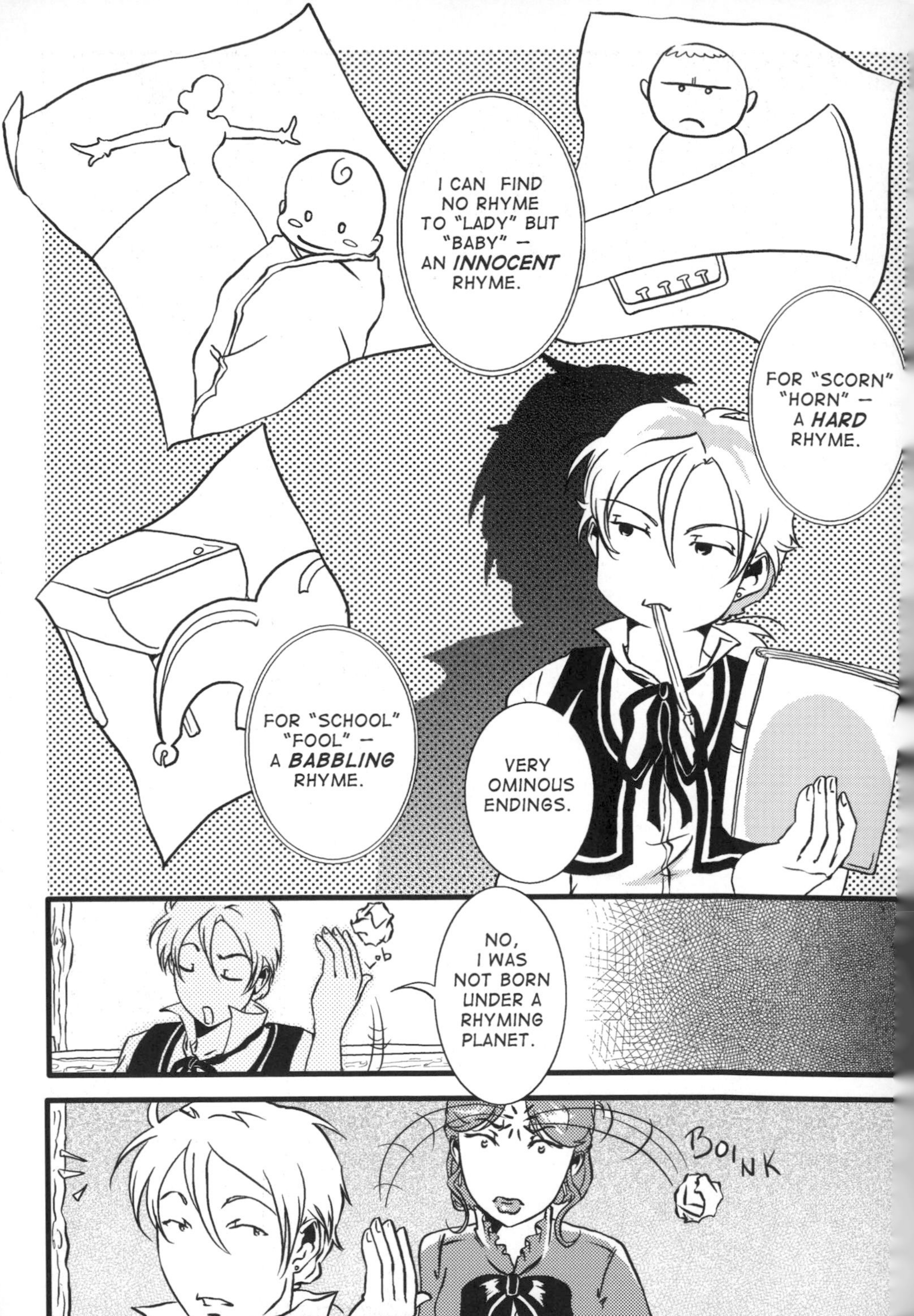
I CAN FIND NO RHYME TO "LADY" BUT "BABY" — AN *INNOCENT* RHYME.
FOR "SCORN" "HORN" — A *HARD* RHYME.
FOR "SCHOOL" "FOOL" — A *BABBLING* RHYME.
VERY OMINOUS ENDINGS.
Lob
NO, I WAS NOT BORN UNDER A RHYMING PLANET.
BOINK

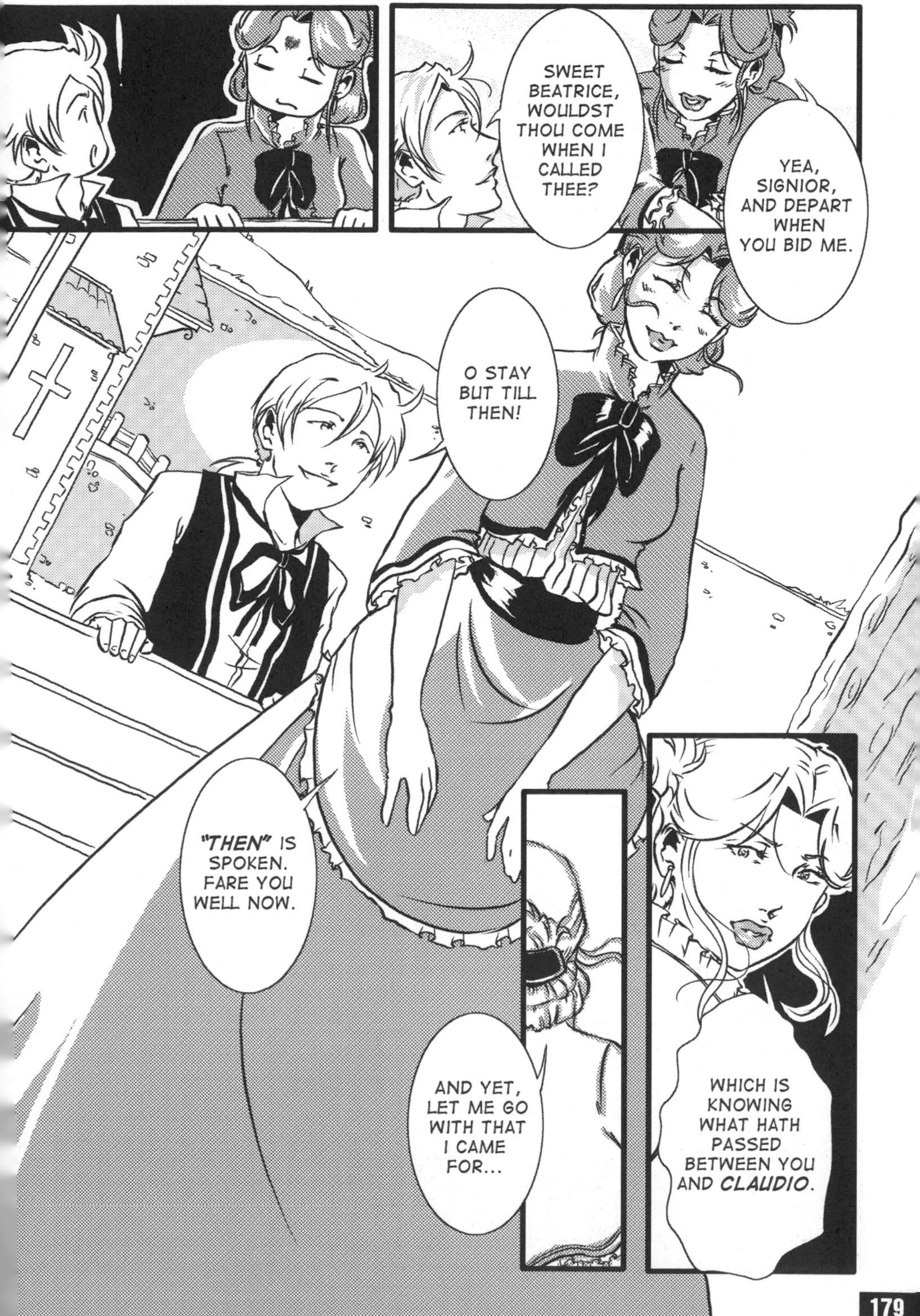
!
SWEET BEATRICE, WOULDST THOU COME WHEN I CALLED THEE?
YEA, SIGNIOR, AND DEPART WHEN YOU BID ME.
O STAY BUT TILL THEN!
"THEN" IS SPOKEN. FARE YOU WELL NOW.
AND YET, LET ME GO WITH THAT I CAME FOR...
WHICH IS KNOWING WHAT HATH PASSED BETWEEN YOU AND CLAUDIO.

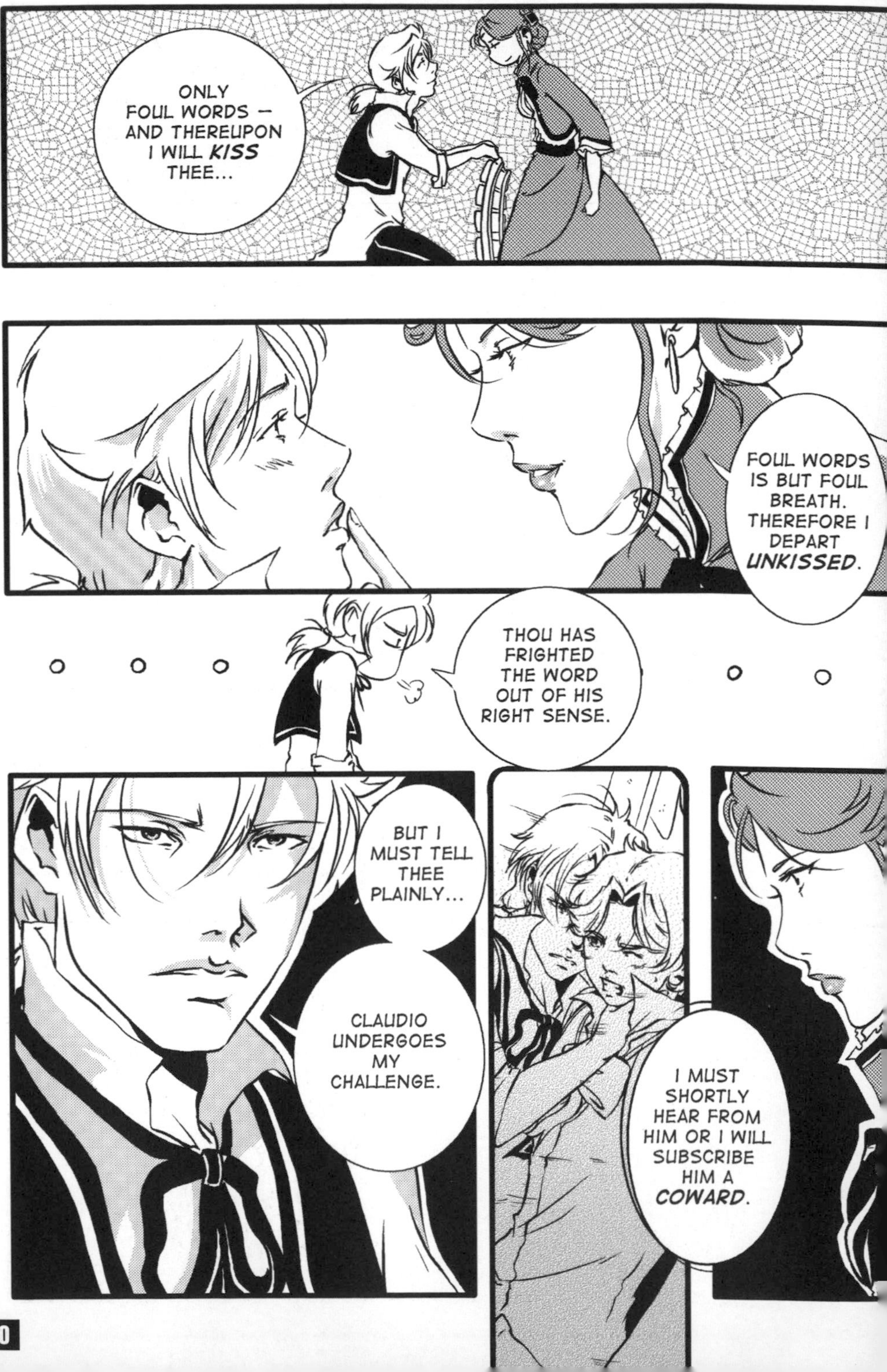

ONLY FOUL WORDS — AND THEREUPON I WILL KISS THEE...
FOUL WORDS IS BUT FOUL BREATH. THEREFORE I DEPART UNKISSED.
THOU HAS FRIGHTED THE WORD OUT OF HIS RIGHT SENSE.
BUT I MUST TELL THEE PLAINLY...
CLAUDIO UNDERGOES MY CHALLENGE.
I MUST SHORTLY HEAR FROM HIM OR I WILL SUBSCRIBE HIM A COWARD.

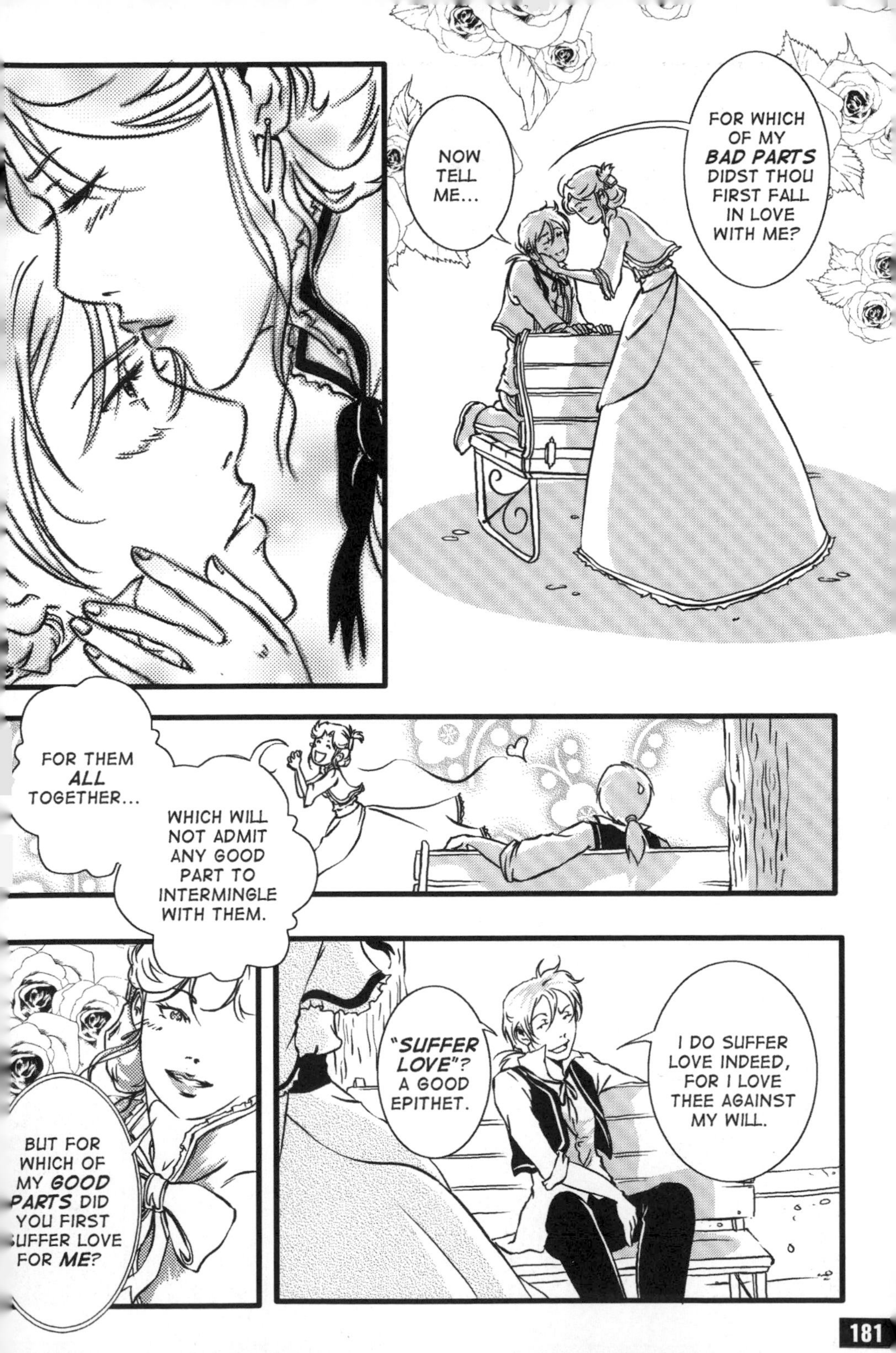
NOW TELL ME...
FOR WHICH OF MY **BAD PARTS** DIDST THOU FIRST FALL IN LOVE WITH ME?
FOR THEM **ALL** TOGETHER...
WHICH WILL NOT ADMIT ANY GOOD PART TO INTERMINGLE WITH THEM.
BUT FOR WHICH OF MY **GOOD PARTS** DID YOU FIRST SUFFER LOVE FOR **ME**?
"**SUFFER LOVE**"? A GOOD EPITHET.
I DO SUFFER LOVE INDEED, FOR I LOVE THEE AGAINST MY WILL.

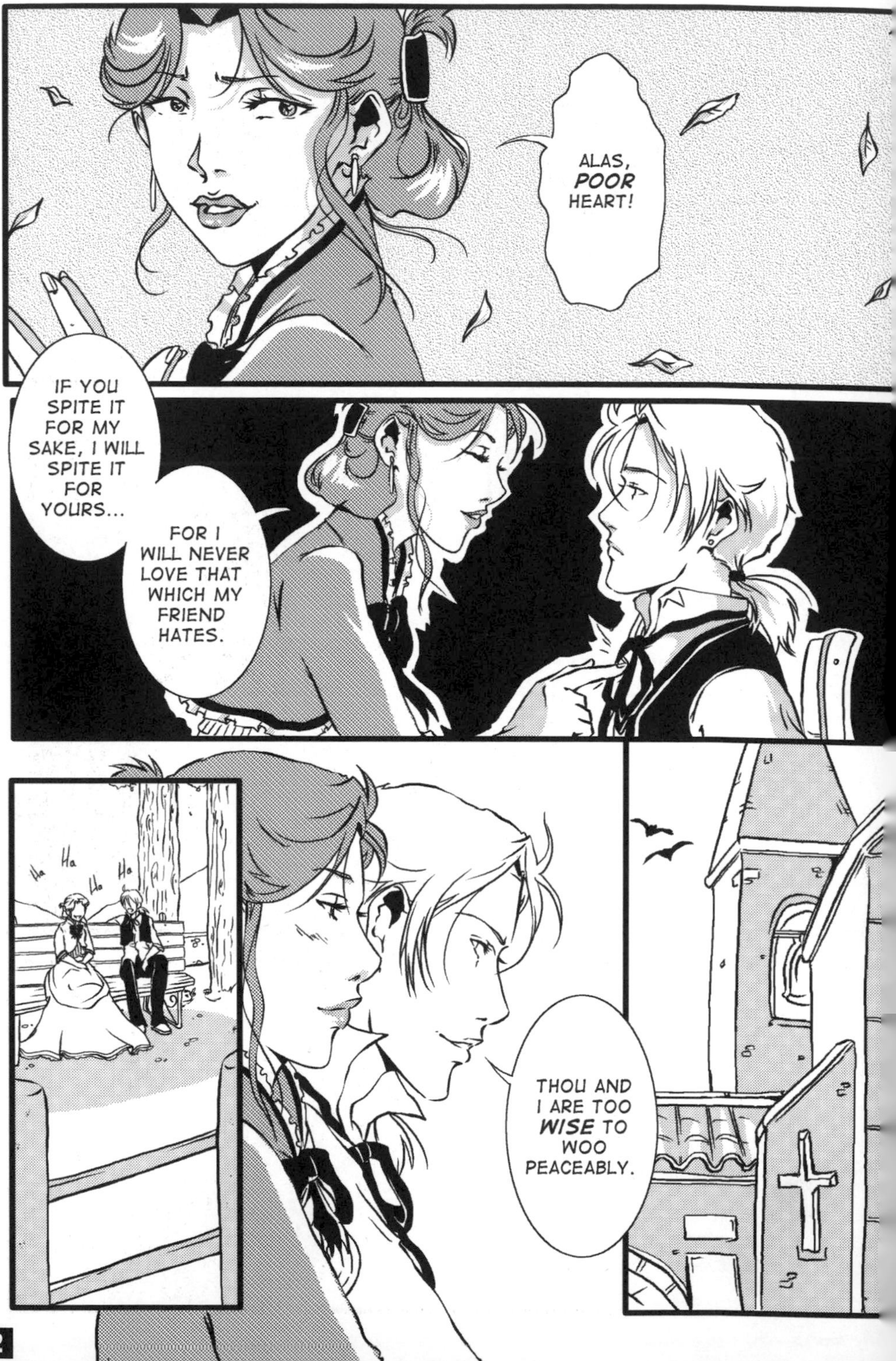
ALAS, **POOR** HEART!
IF YOU SPITE IT FOR MY SAKE, I WILL SPITE IT FOR YOURS...
FOR I WILL NEVER LOVE THAT WHICH MY FRIEND HATES.
Ha Ha Ha Ha
THOU AND I ARE TOO **WISE** TO WOO PEACEABLY.

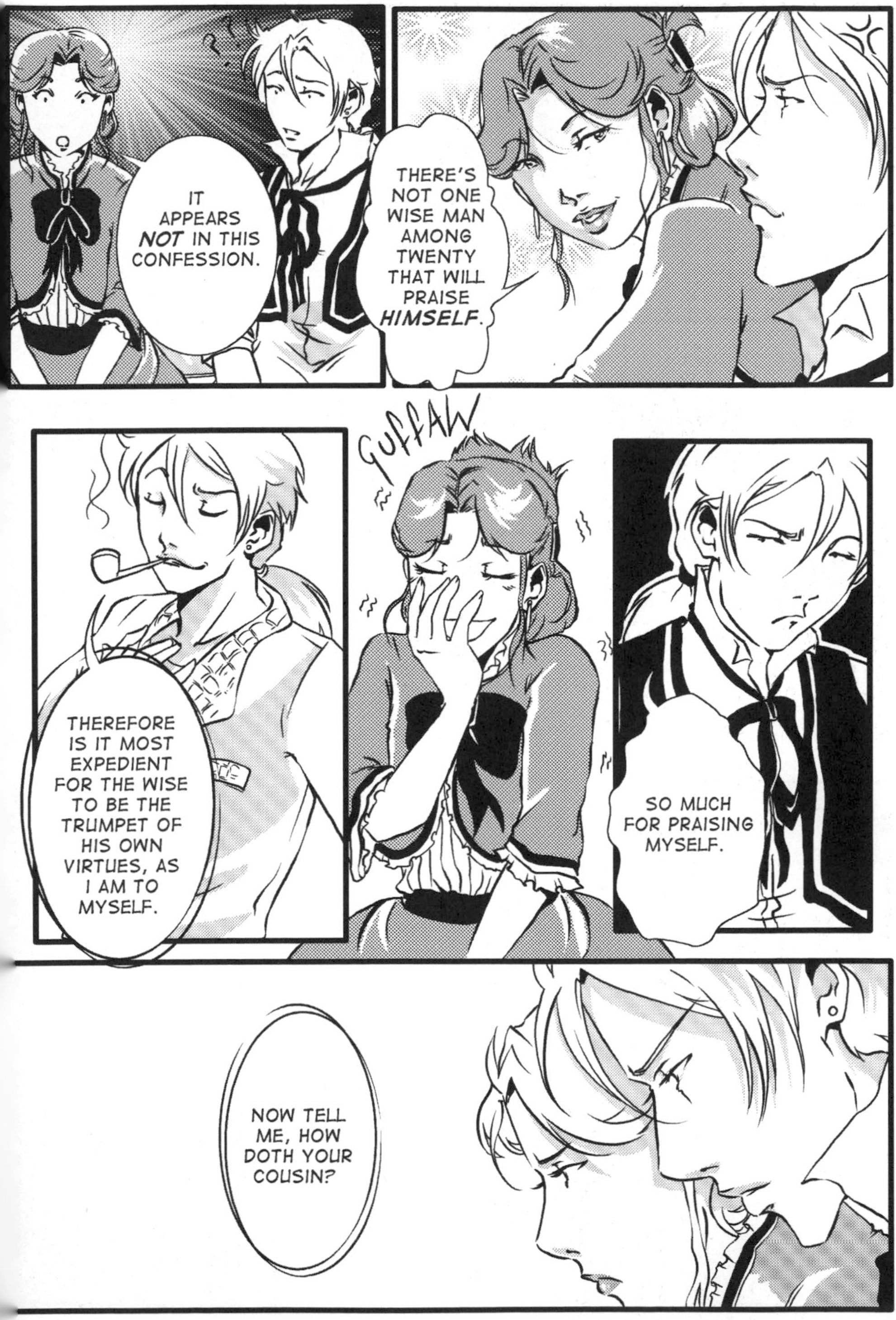
IT APPEARS NOT IN THIS CONFESSION.
THERE'S NOT ONE WISE MAN AMONG TWENTY THAT WILL PRAISE HIMSELF.
THEREFORE IS IT MOST EXPEDIENT FOR THE WISE TO BE THE TRUMPET OF HIS OWN VIRTUES, AS I AM TO MYSELF.
GUFFAW
SO MUCH FOR PRAISING MYSELF.
NOW TELL ME, HOW DOTH YOUR COUSIN?

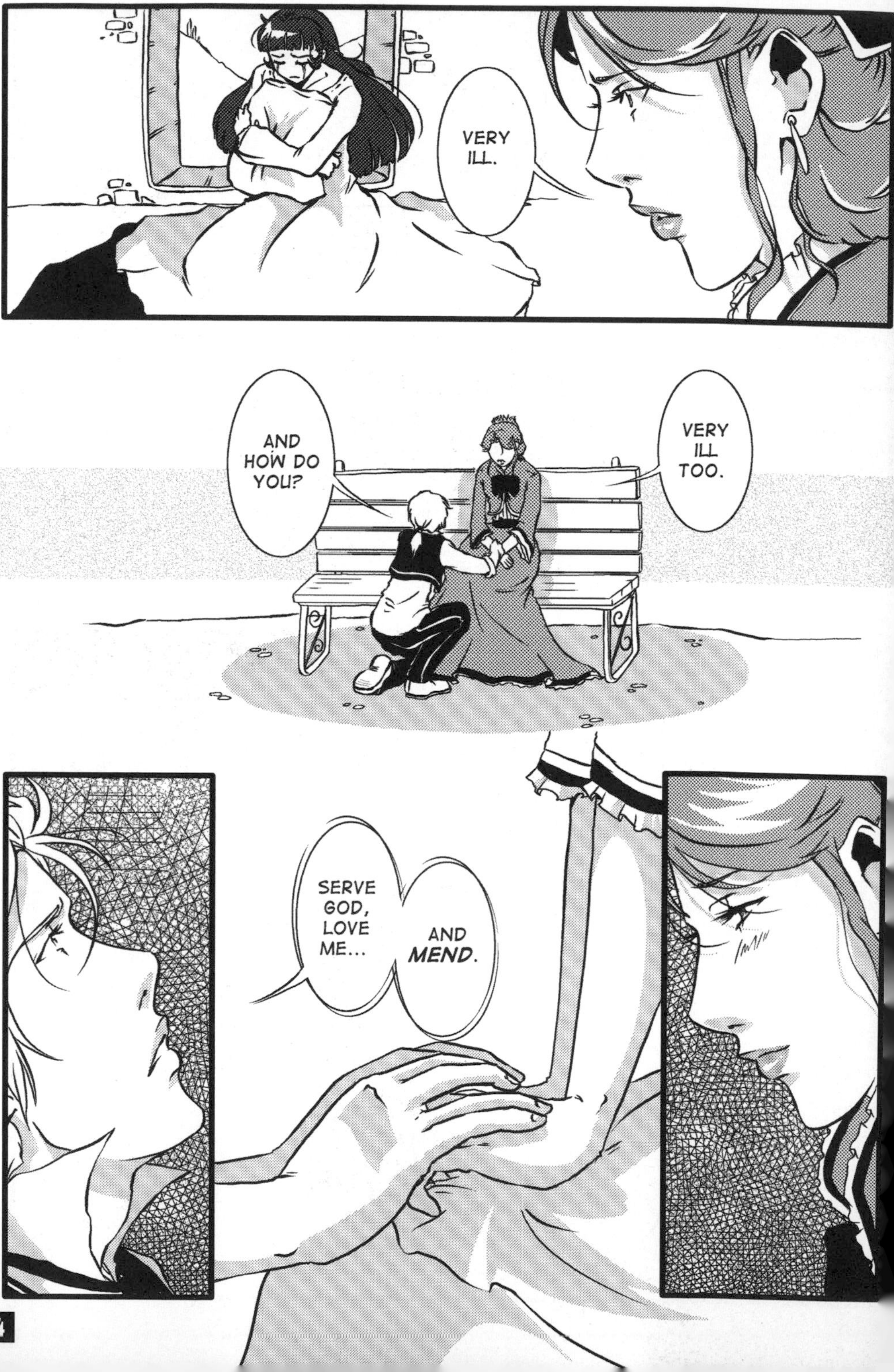
VERY ILL.
AND HOW DO YOU?
VERY ILL TOO.
SERVE GOD, LOVE ME...
AND *MEND*.

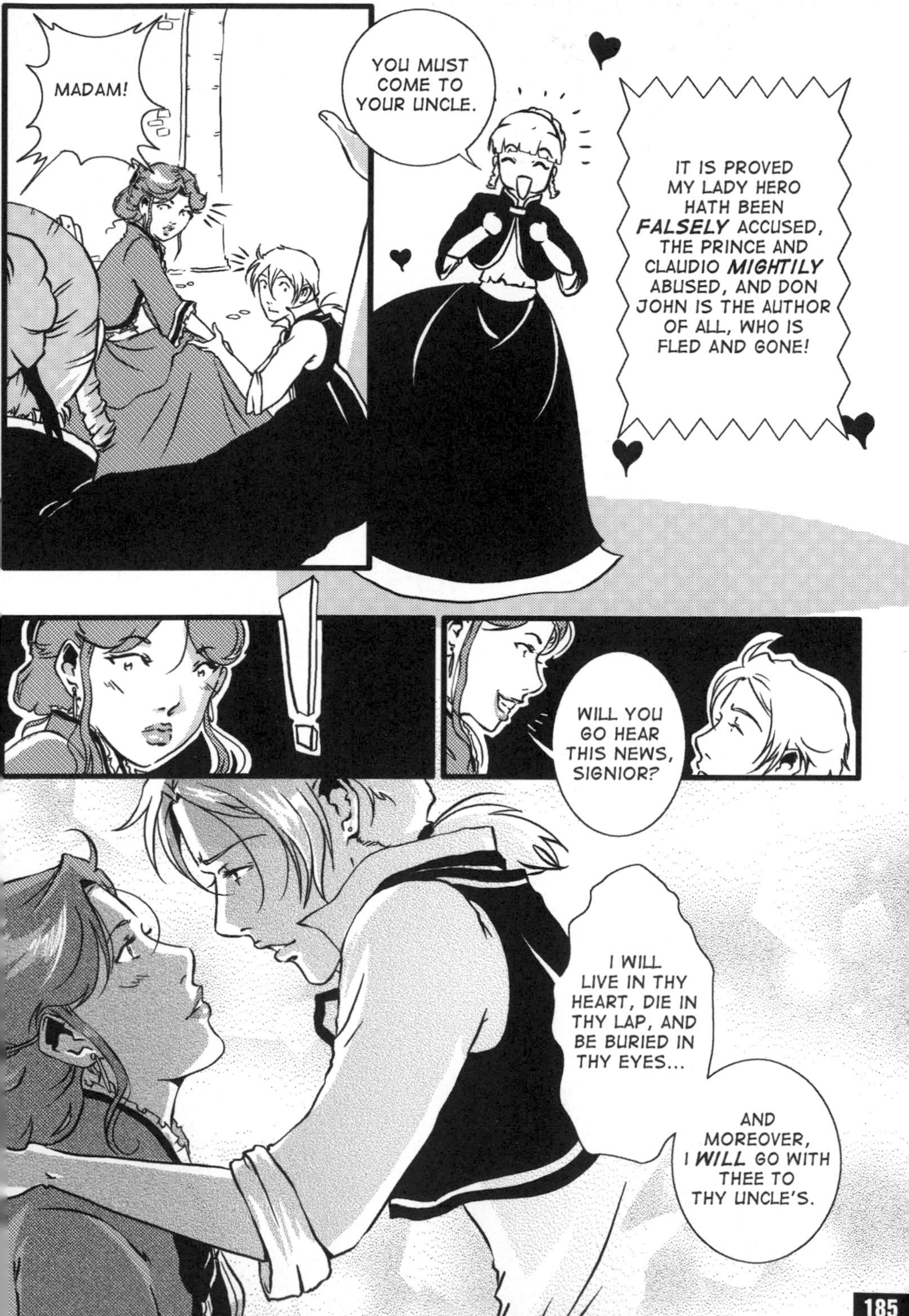
MADAM!
YOU MUST COME TO YOUR UNCLE.
IT IS PROVED MY LADY HERO HATH BEEN **FALSELY** ACCUSED, THE PRINCE AND CLAUDIO **MIGHTILY** ABUSED, AND DON JOHN IS THE AUTHOR OF ALL, WHO IS FLED AND GONE!
WILL YOU GO HEAR THIS NEWS, SIGNIOR?
I WILL LIVE IN THY HEART, DIE IN THY LAP, AND BE BURIED IN THY EYES...
AND MOREOVER, I **WILL** GO WITH THEE TO THY UNCLE'S.

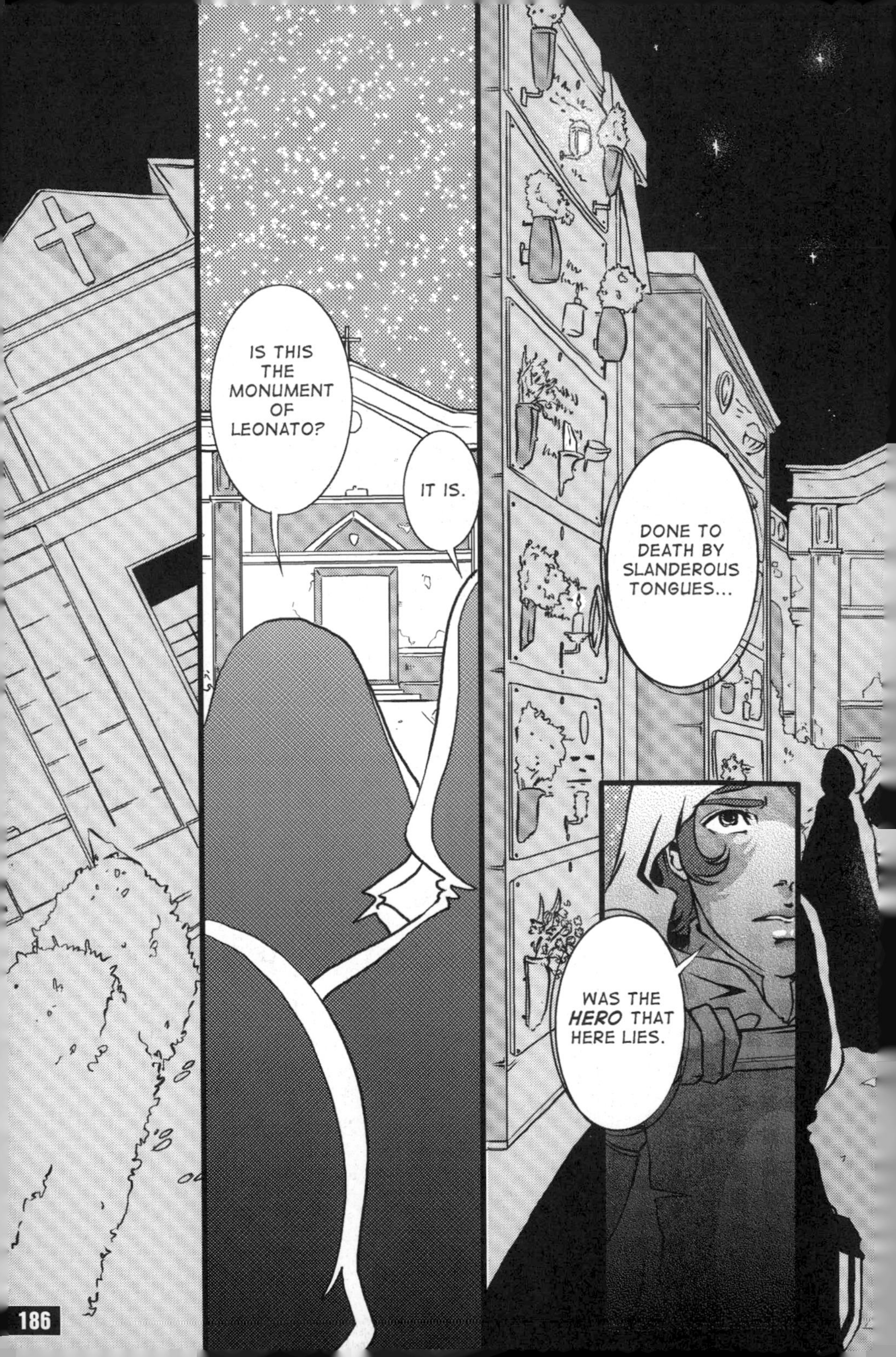
IS THIS THE MONUMENT OF LEONATO?
IT IS.
DONE TO DEATH BY SLANDEROUS TONGUES...
WAS THE HERO THAT HERE LIES.

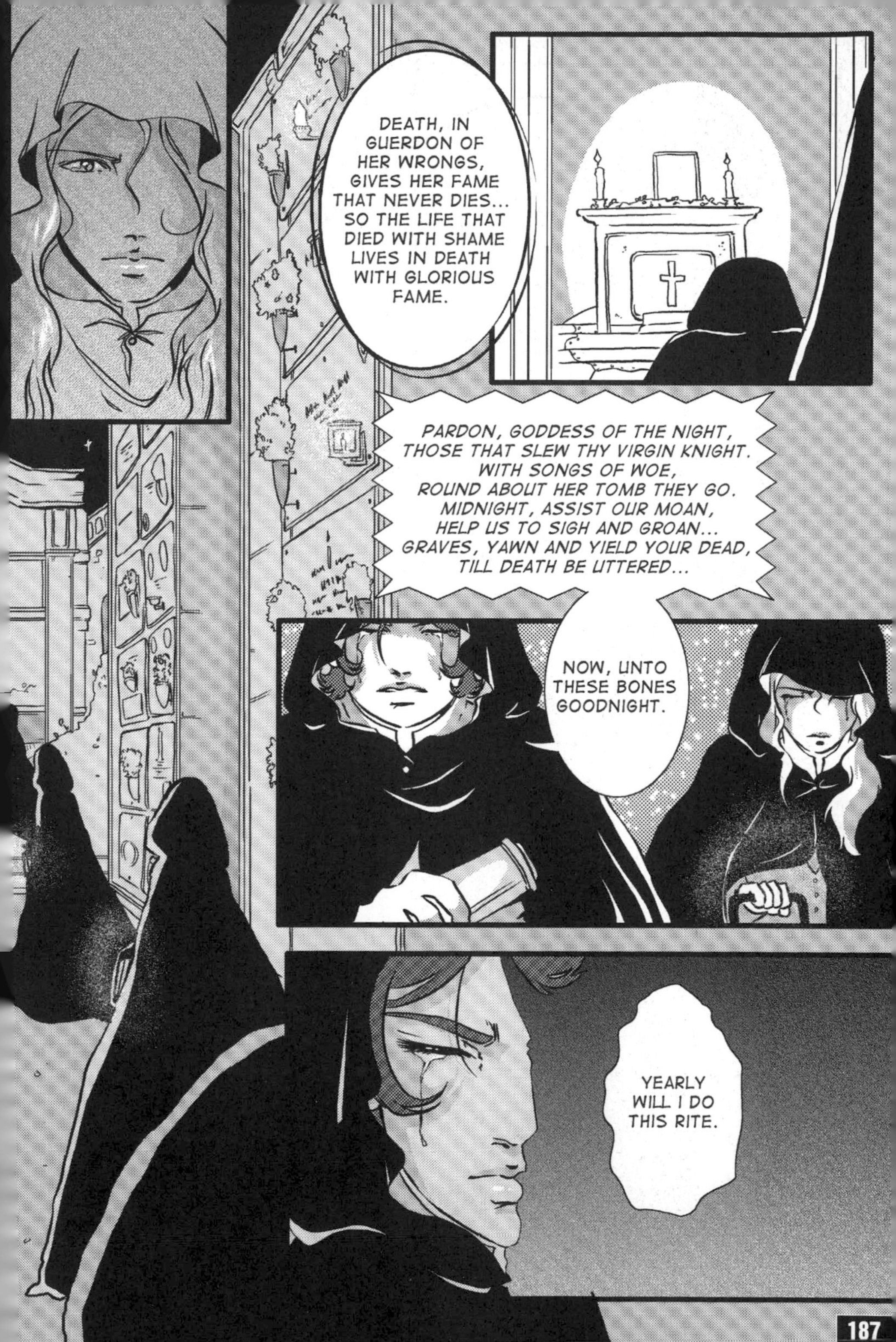
DEATH, IN GUERDON OF HER WRONGS, GIVES HER FAME THAT NEVER DIES... SO THE LIFE THAT DIED WITH SHAME LIVES IN DEATH WITH GLORIOUS FAME.
PARDON, GODDESS OF THE NIGHT, THOSE THAT SLEW THY VIRGIN KNIGHT. WITH SONGS OF WOE, ROUND ABOUT HER TOMB THEY GO. MIDNIGHT, ASSIST OUR MOAN, HELP US TO SIGH AND GROAN... GRAVES, YAWN AND YIELD YOUR DEAD, TILL DEATH BE UTTERED...
NOW, UNTO THESE BONES GOODNIGHT.
YEARLY WILL I DO THIS RITE.

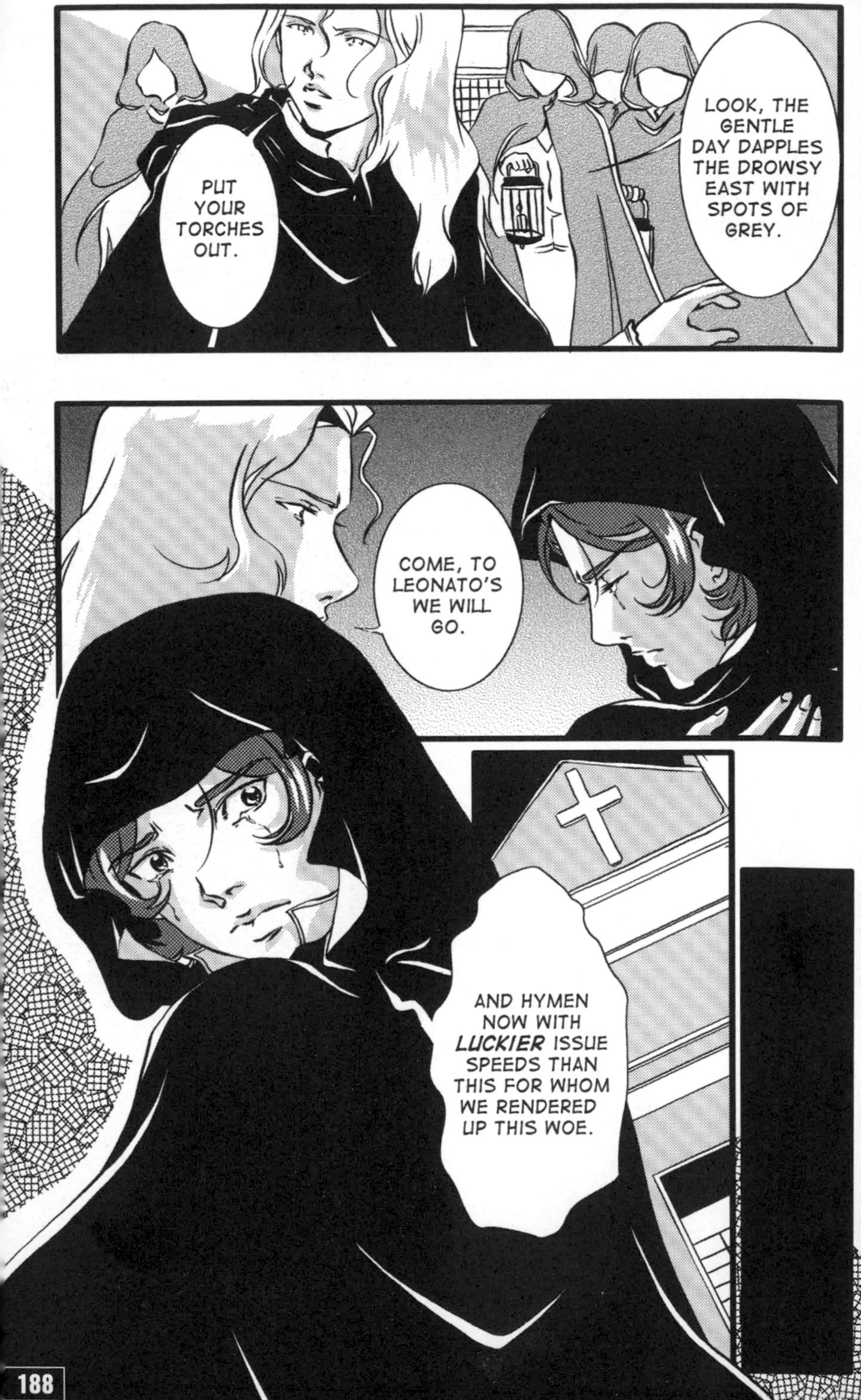
PUT YOUR TORCHES OUT.
LOOK, THE GENTLE DAY DAPPLES THE DROWSY EAST WITH SPOTS OF GREY.
COME, TO LEONATO'S WE WILL GO.
AND HYMEN NOW WITH *LUCKIER* ISSUE SPEEDS THAN THIS FOR WHOM WE RENDERED UP THIS WOE.

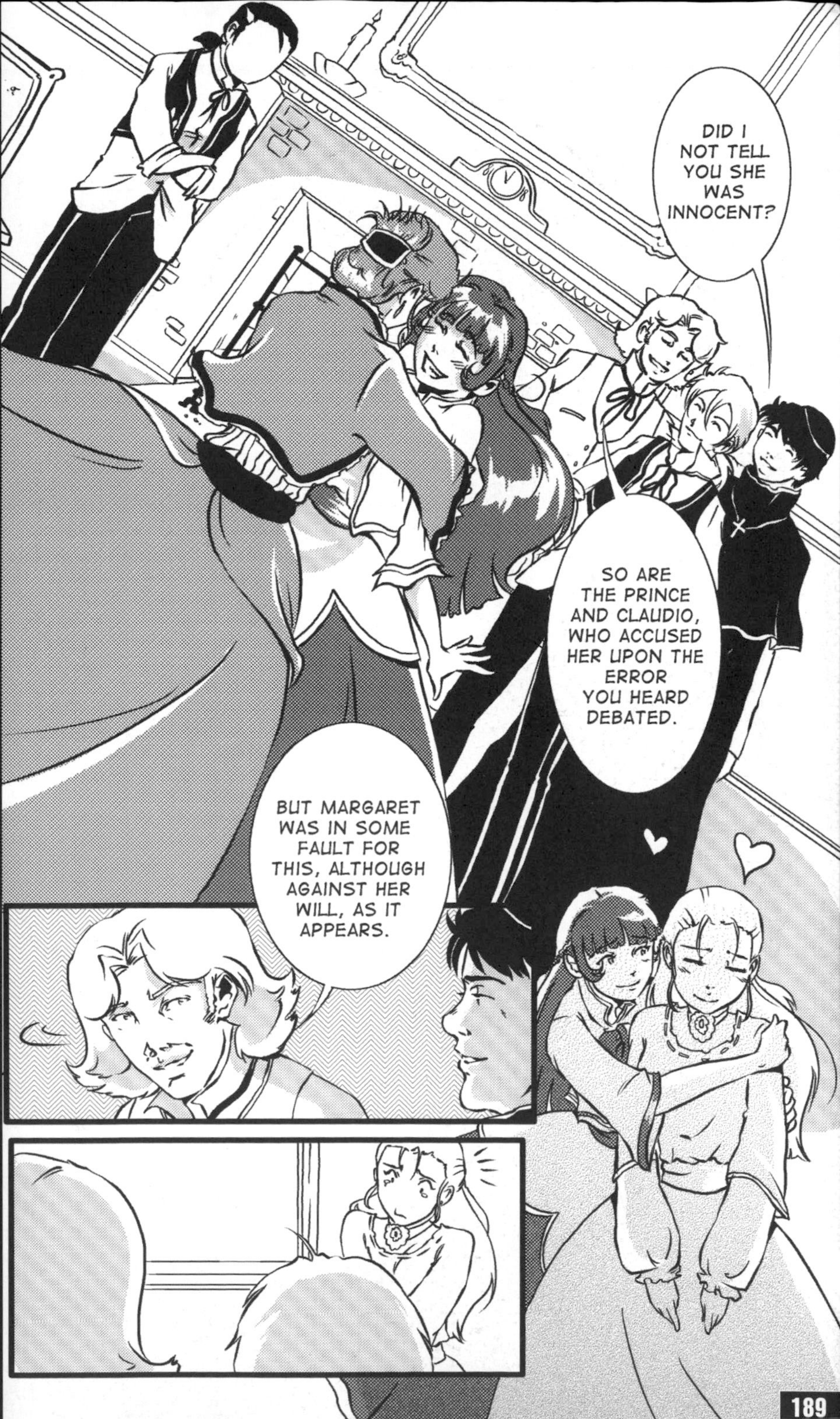
DID I NOT TELL YOU SHE WAS INNOCENT?
SO ARE THE PRINCE AND CLAUDIO, WHO ACCUSED HER UPON THE ERROR YOU HEARD DEBATED.
BUT MARGARET WAS IN SOME FAULT FOR THIS, ALTHOUGH AGAINST HER WILL, AS IT APPEARS.

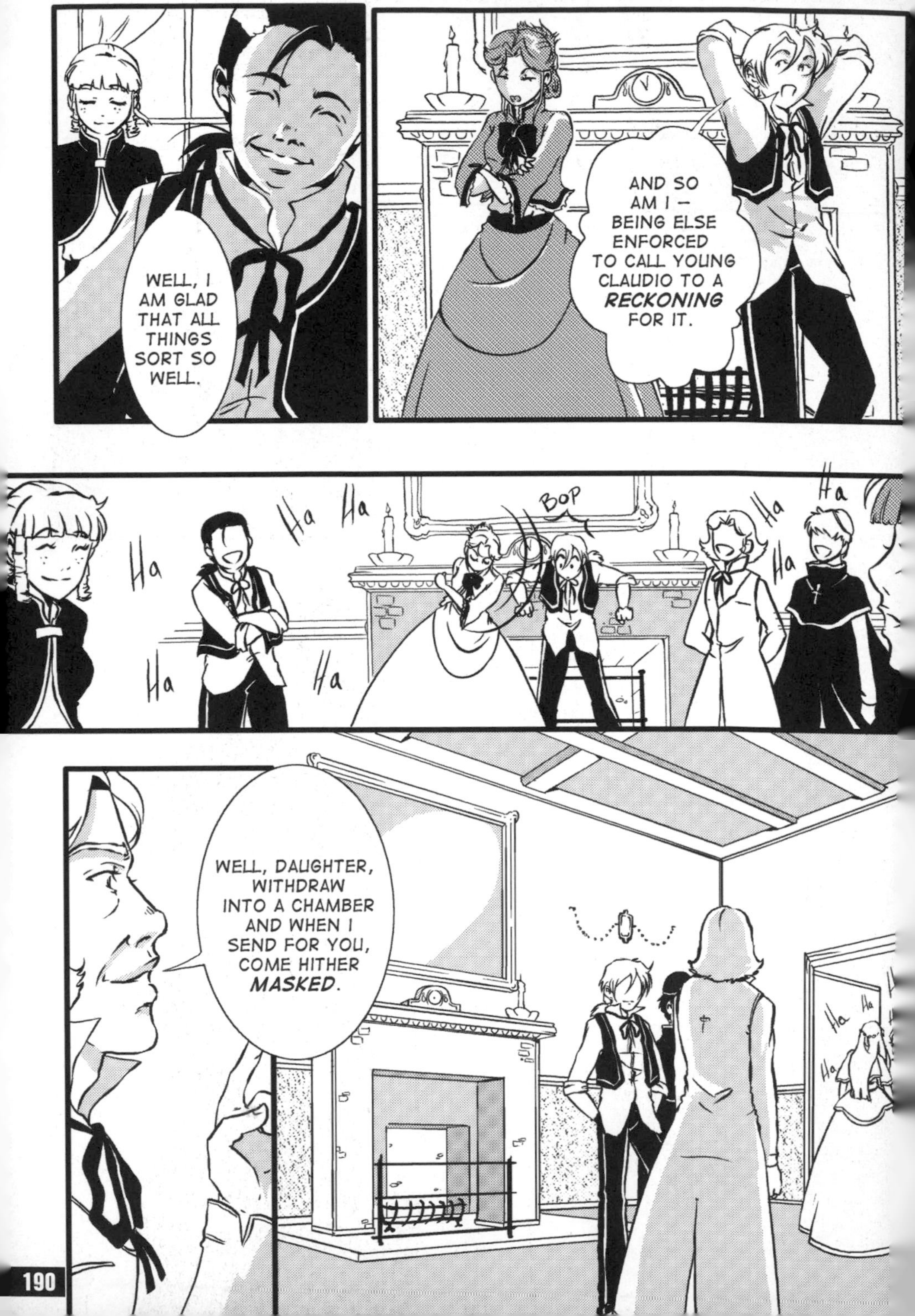
WELL, I AM GLAD THAT ALL THINGS SORT SO WELL.
AND SO AM I — BEING ELSE ENFORCED TO CALL YOUNG CLAUDIO TO A *RECKONING* FOR IT.
Ha
Ha
Ha
Ha
Ha
BOP
Ha
Ha
Ha
WELL, DAUGHTER, WITHDRAW INTO A CHAMBER AND WHEN I SEND FOR YOU, COME HITHER *MASKED*.
Ha
Ha
Ha

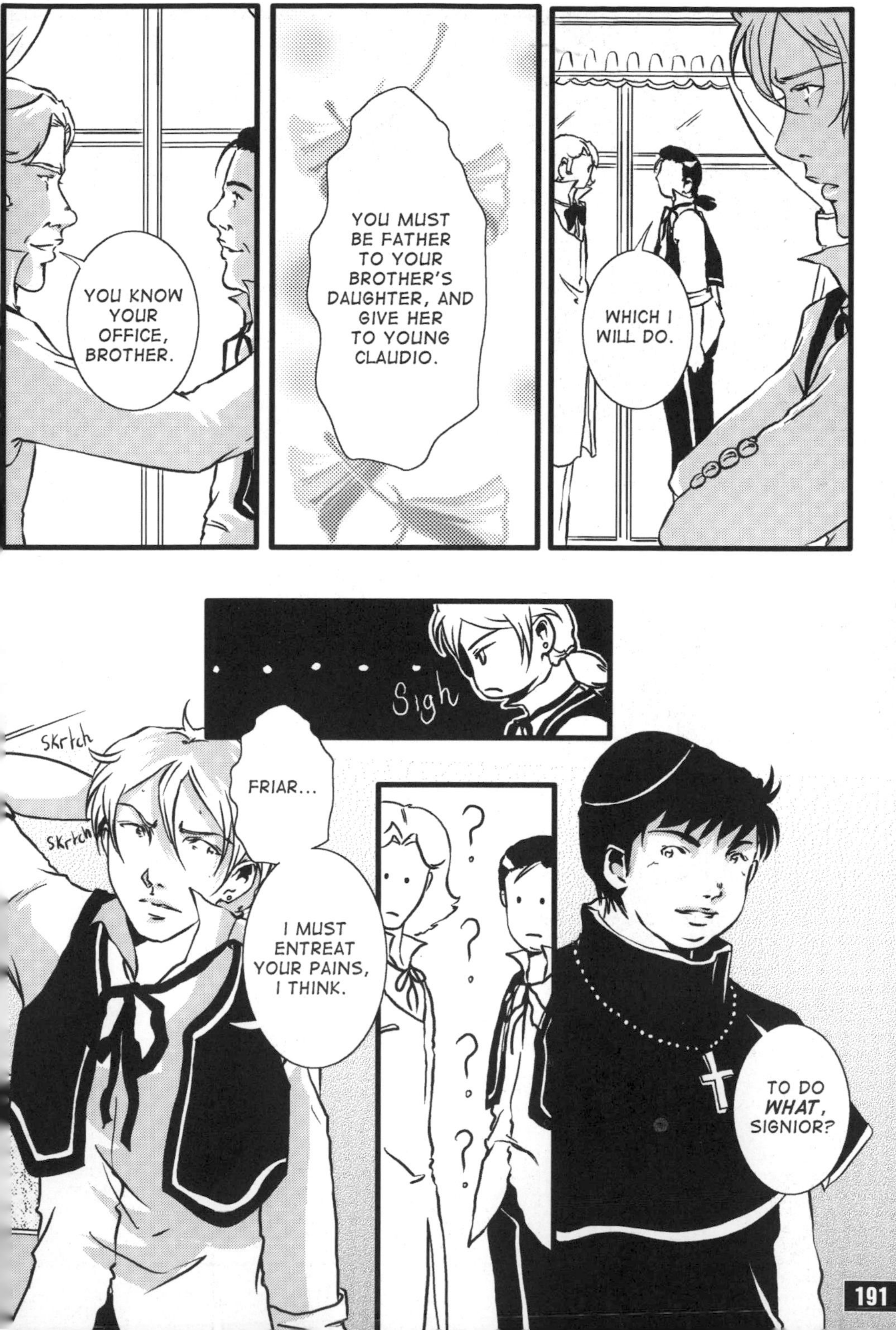

YOU KNOW YOUR OFFICE, BROTHER.
YOU MUST BE FATHER TO YOUR BROTHER'S DAUGHTER, AND GIVE HER TO YOUNG CLAUDIO.
WHICH I WILL DO.
. . . . . .
Sigh
Skrtch
Skrtch
FRIAR...
I MUST ENTREAT YOUR PAINS, I THINK.
TO DO ***WHAT***, SIGNIOR?

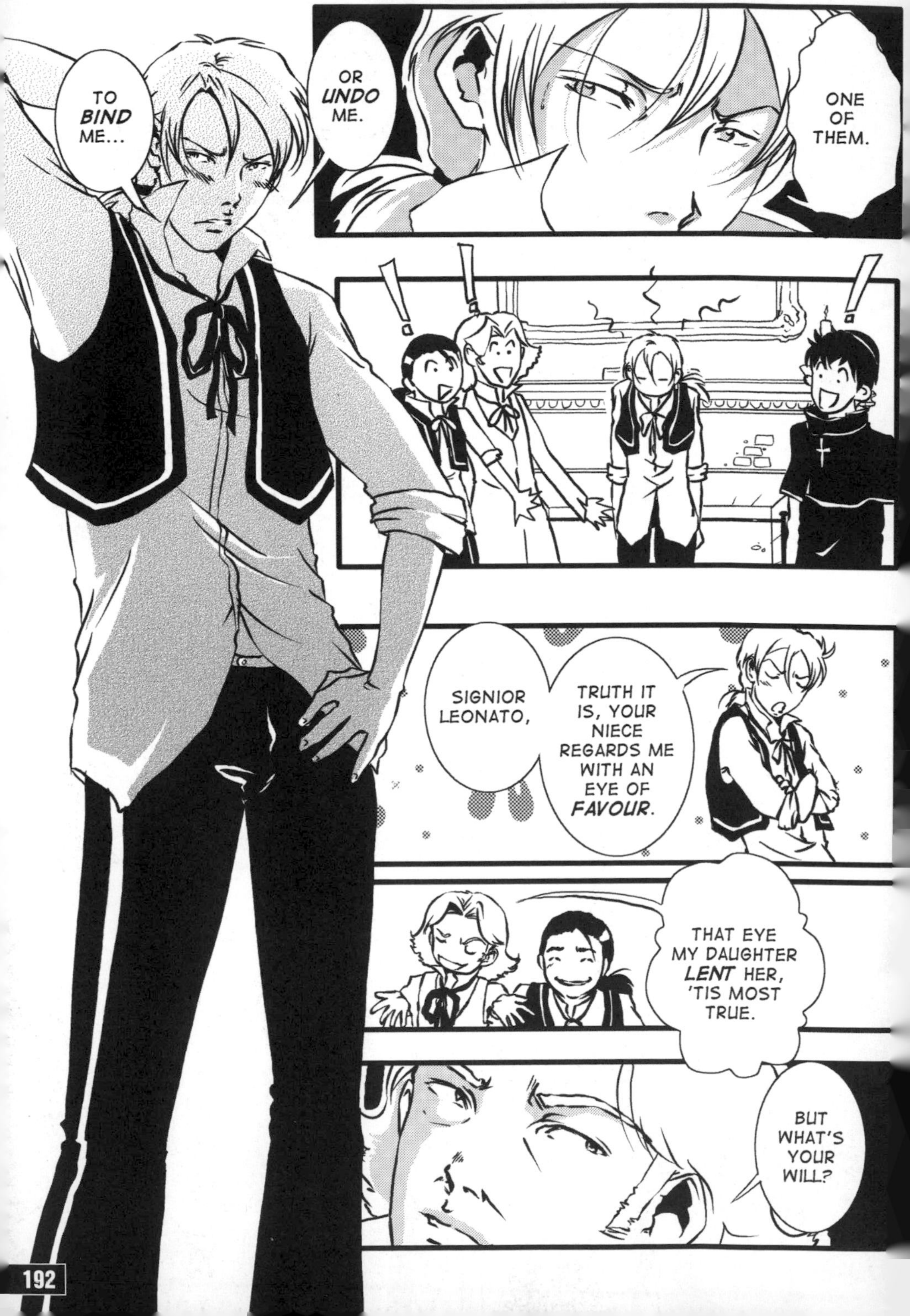
TO BIND ME...
OR UNDO ME.
ONE OF THEM.
SIGNIOR LEONATO,
TRUTH IT IS, YOUR NIECE REGARDS ME WITH AN EYE OF FAVOUR.
THAT EYE MY DAUGHTER LENT HER, 'TIS MOST TRUE.
BUT WHAT'S YOUR WILL?

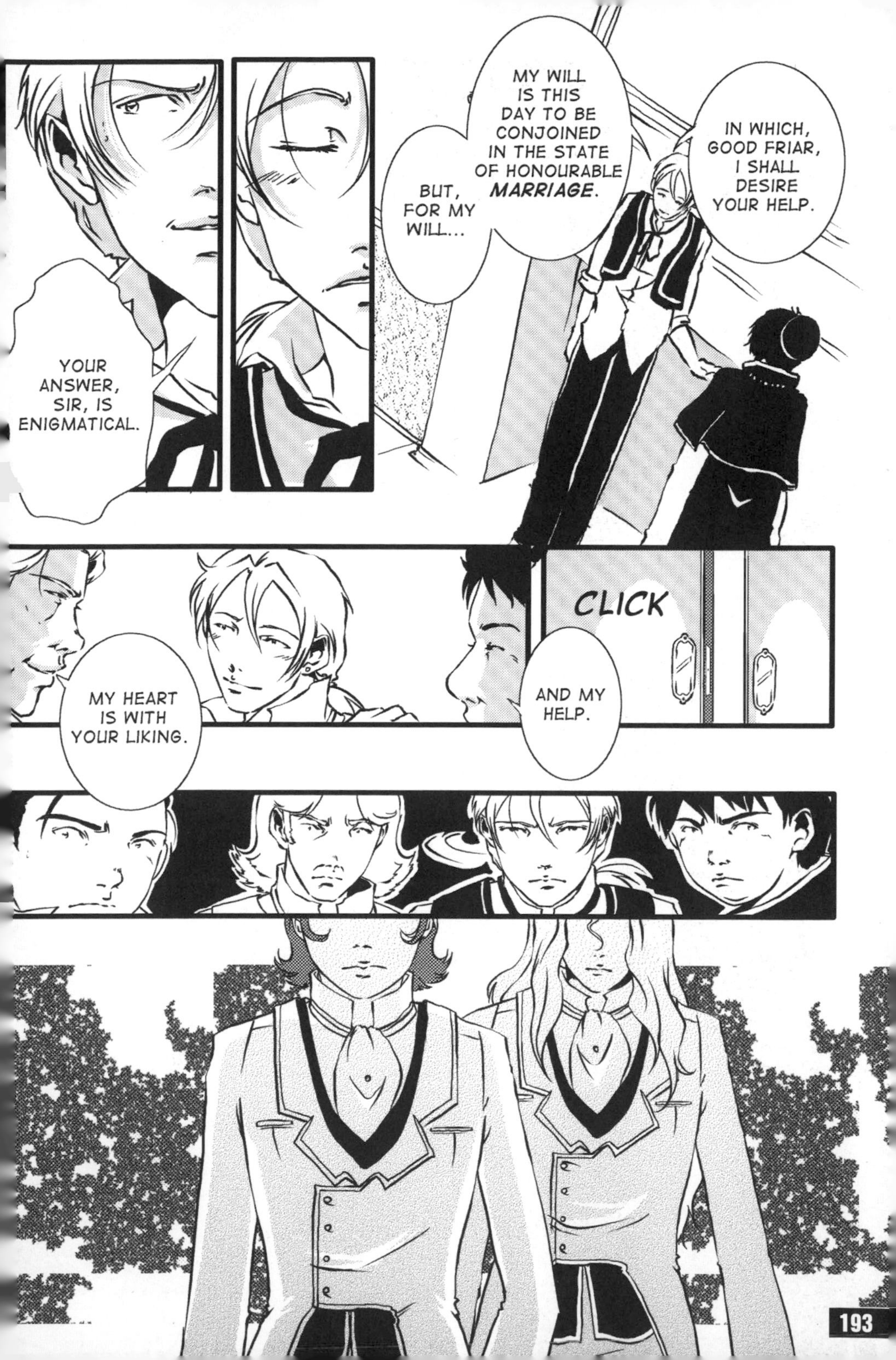
YOUR ANSWER, SIR, IS ENIGMATICAL.
BUT, FOR MY WILL...
MY WILL IS THIS DAY TO BE CONJOINED IN THE STATE OF HONOURABLE MARRIAGE.
IN WHICH, GOOD FRIAR, I SHALL DESIRE YOUR HELP.
MY HEART IS WITH YOUR LIKING.
AND MY HELP.
CLICK

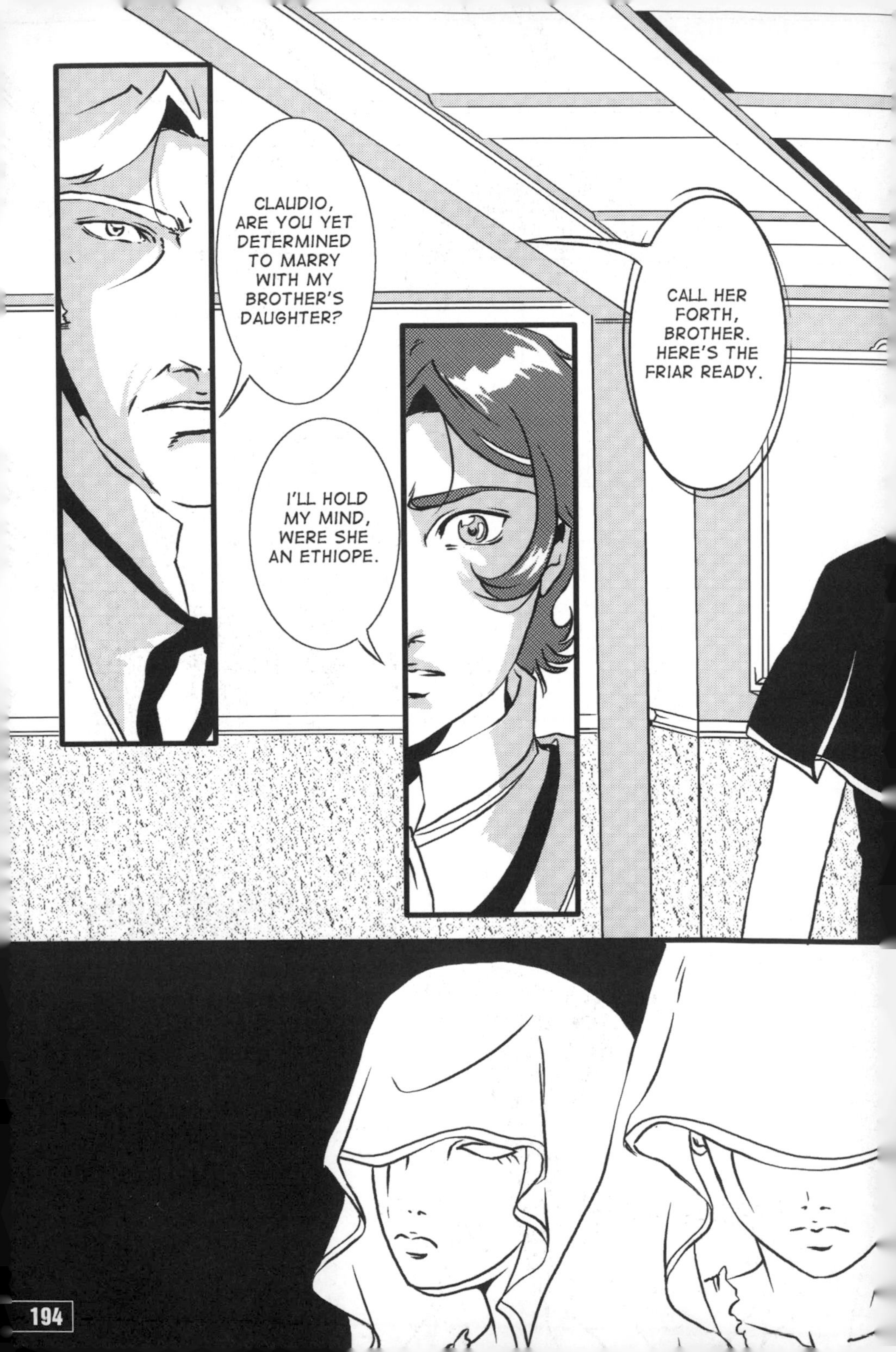

CLAUDIO, ARE YOU YET DETERMINED TO MARRY WITH MY BROTHER'S DAUGHTER?
I'LL HOLD MY MIND, WERE SHE AN ETHIOPE.
CALL HER FORTH, BROTHER. HERE'S THE FRIAR READY.

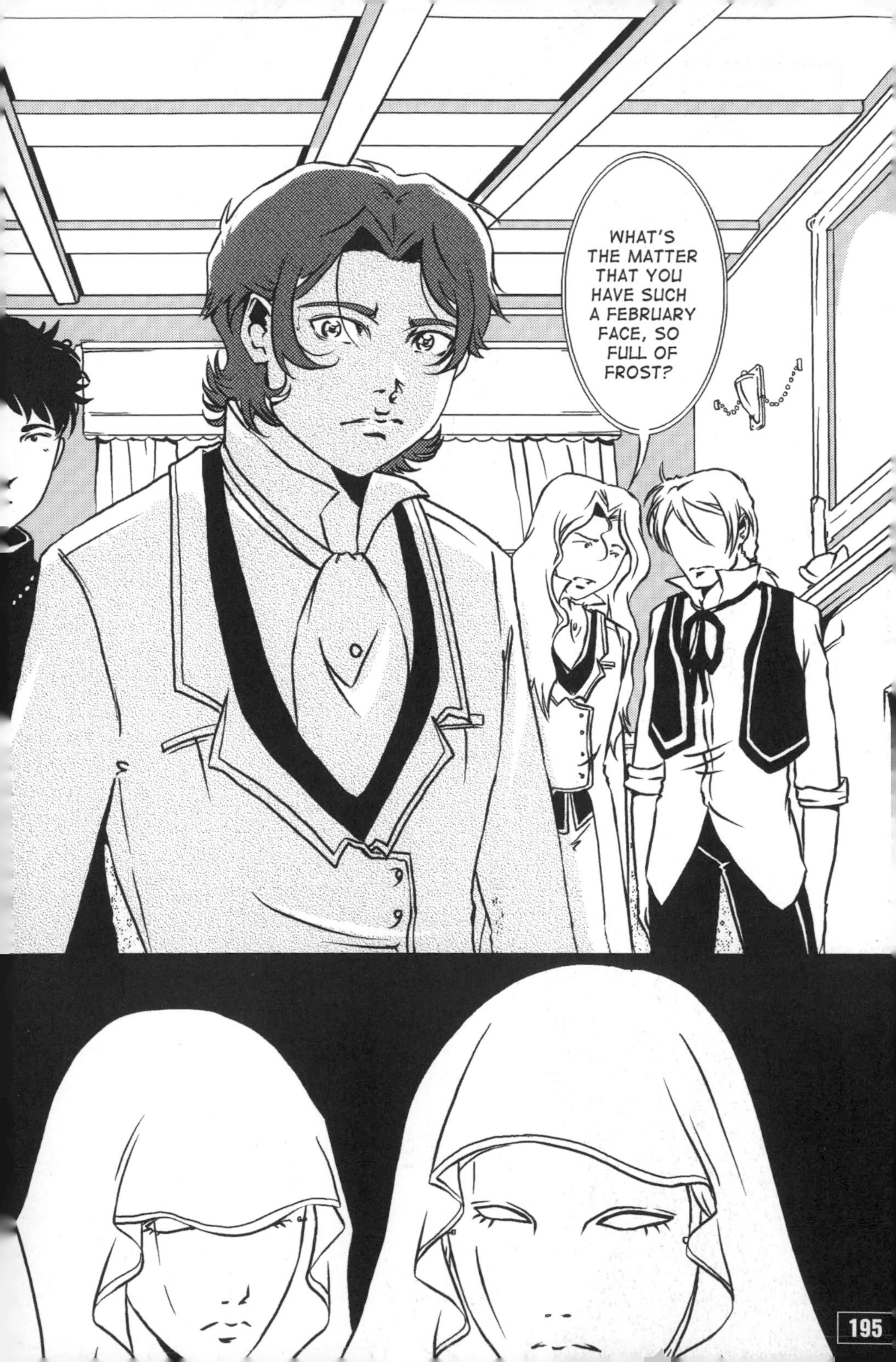
WHAT'S THE MATTER THAT YOU HAVE SUCH A FEBRUARY FACE, SO FULL OF FROST?

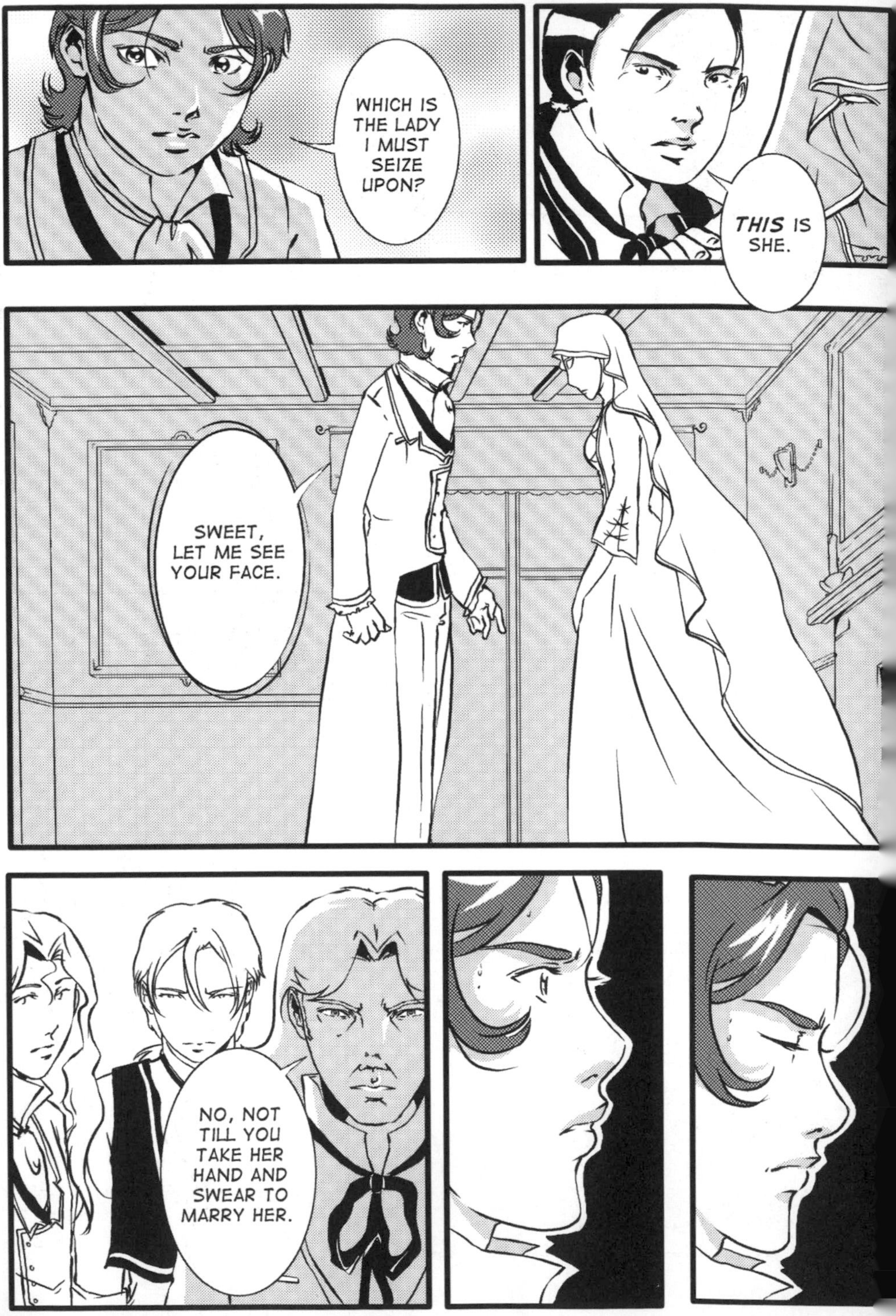
WHICH IS THE LADY I MUST SEIZE UPON?
THIS IS SHE.
SWEET, LET ME SEE YOUR FACE.
NO, NOT TILL YOU TAKE HER HAND AND SWEAR TO MARRY HER.

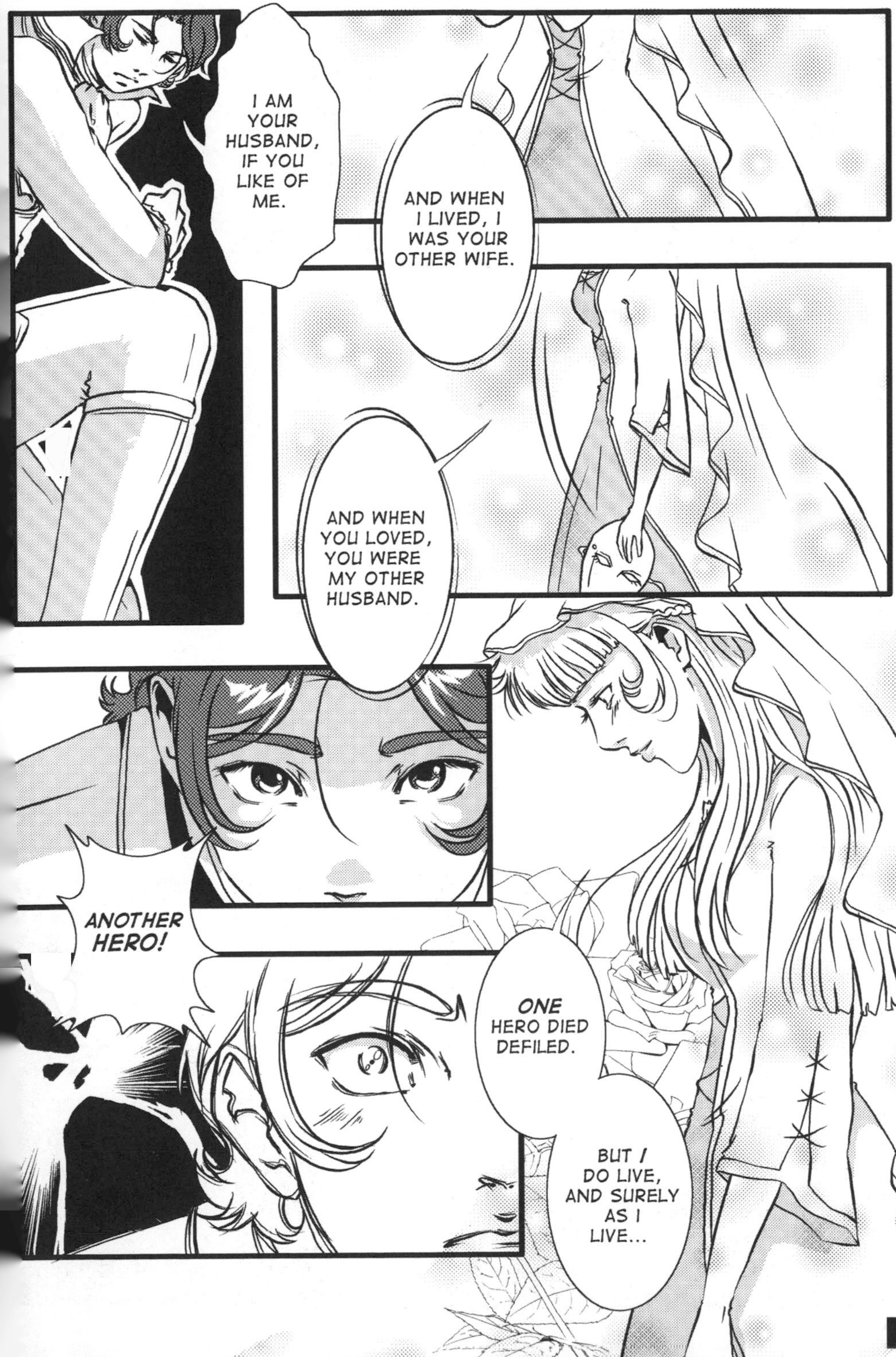
I AM YOUR HUSBAND, IF YOU LIKE OF ME.
AND WHEN I LIVED, I WAS YOUR OTHER WIFE.
AND WHEN YOU LOVED, YOU WERE MY OTHER HUSBAND.
ANOTHER HERO!
ONE HERO DIED DEFILED.
BUT I DO LIVE, AND SURELY AS I LIVE...

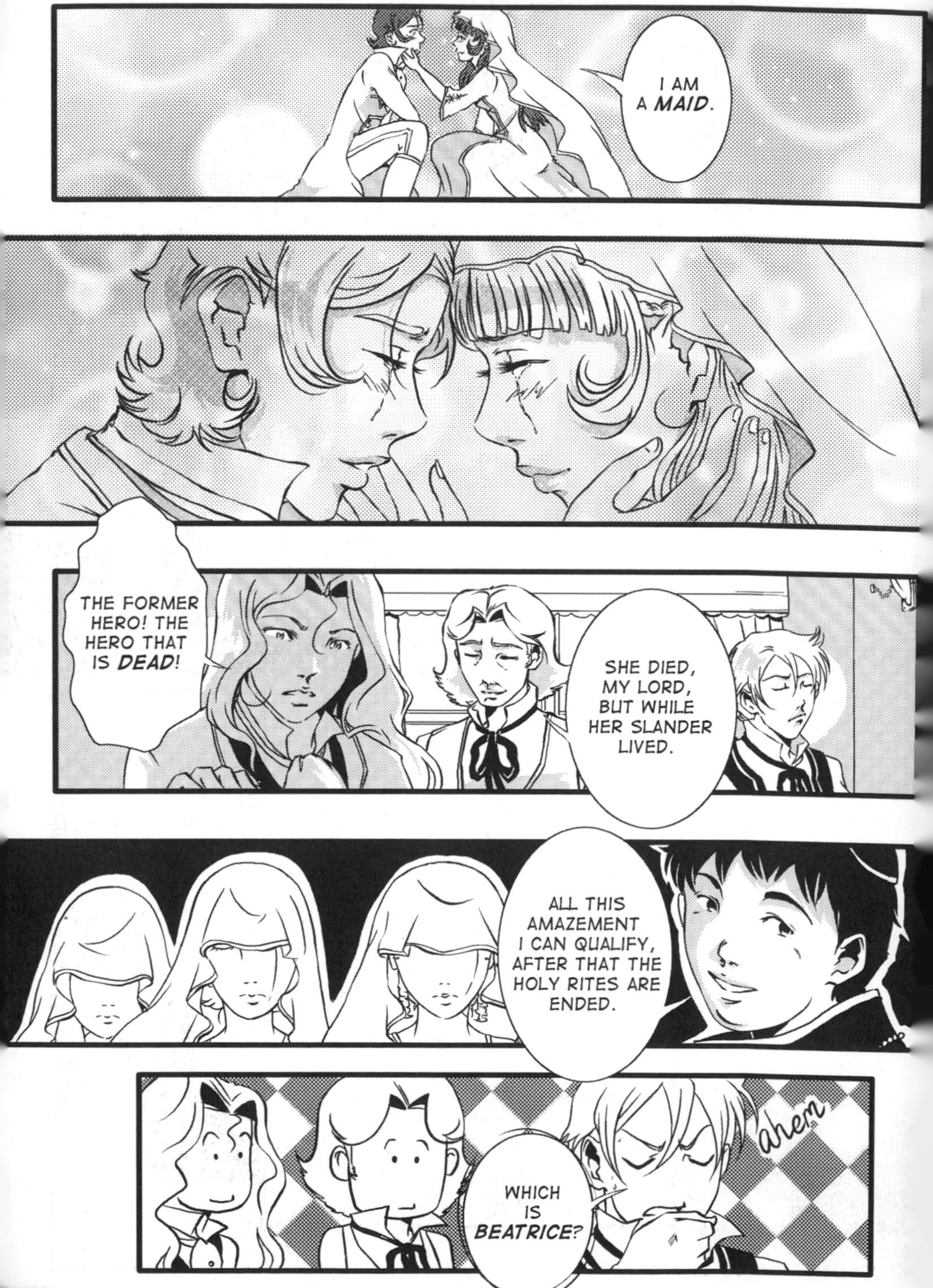
I AM A *MAID*.
THE FORMER HERO! THE HERO THAT IS *DEAD*!
SHE DIED, MY LORD, BUT WHILE HER SLANDER LIVED.
ALL THIS AMAZEMENT I CAN QUALIFY, AFTER THAT THE HOLY RITES ARE ENDED.
WHICH IS *BEATRICE*?
ahem

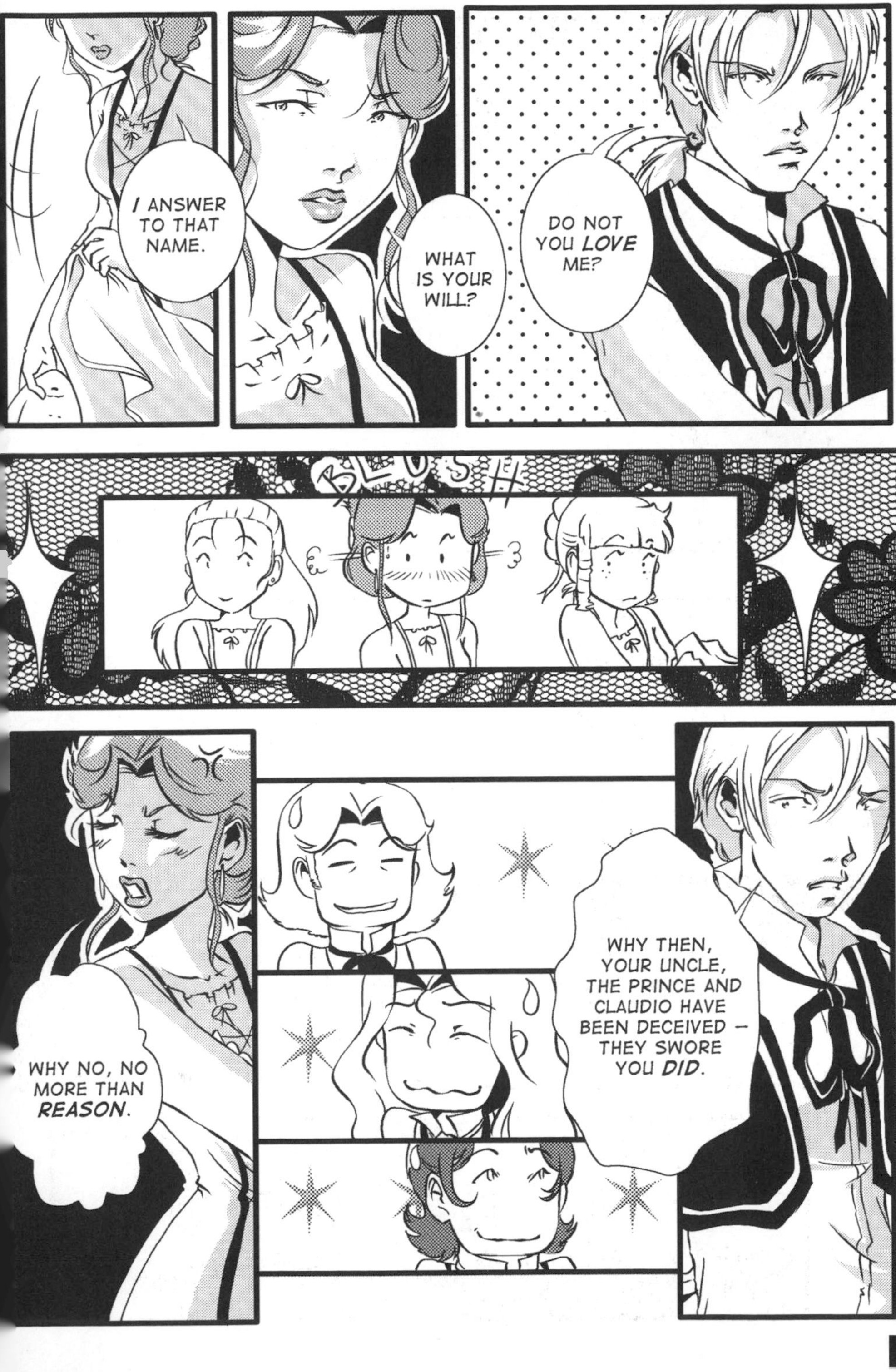
I ANSWER TO THAT NAME.
WHAT IS YOUR WILL?
DO NOT YOU LOVE ME?
BLUSH
WHY NO, NO MORE THAN REASON.
WHY THEN, YOUR UNCLE, THE PRINCE AND CLAUDIO HAVE BEEN DECEIVED – THEY SWORE YOU DID.

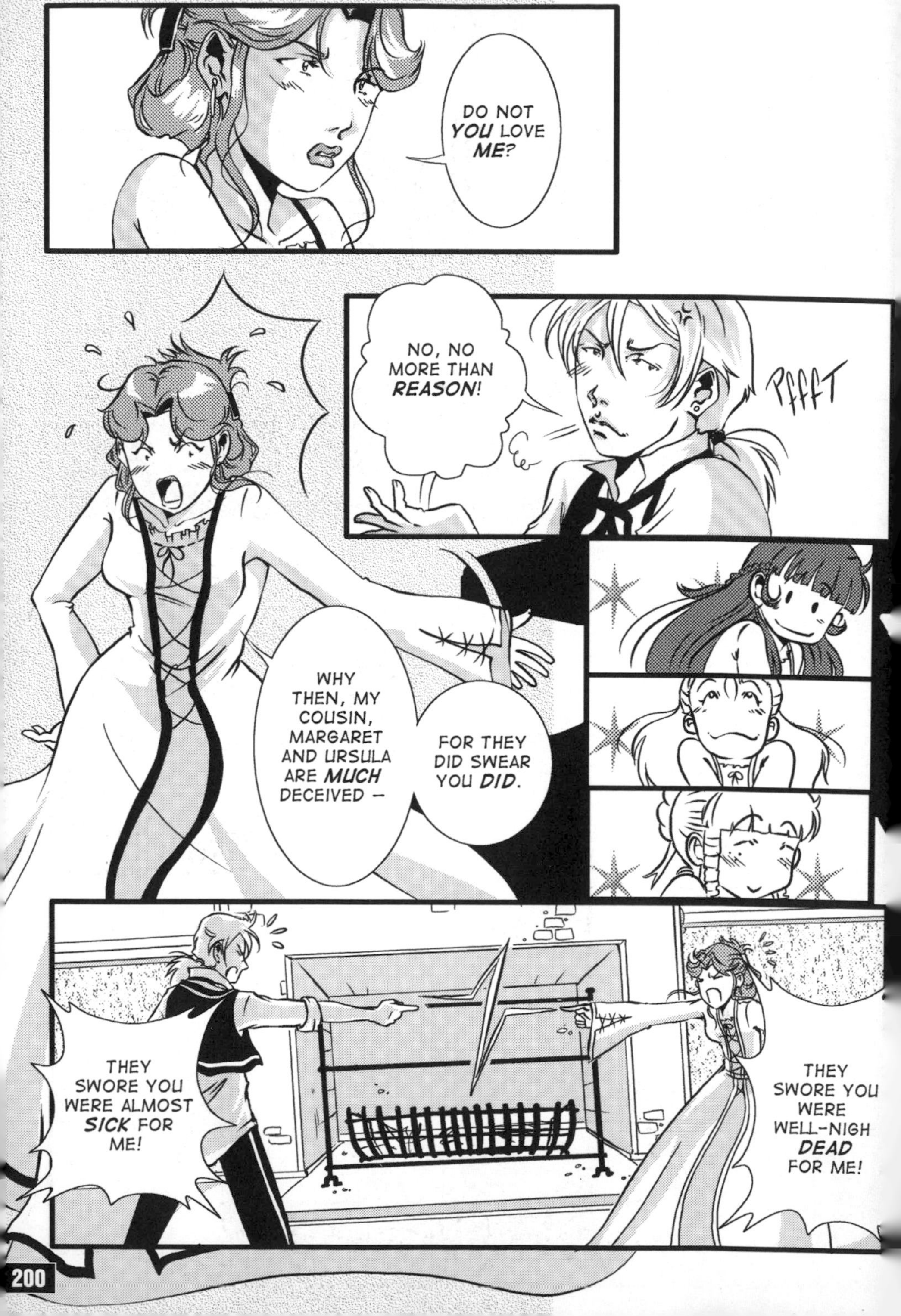

DO NOT *YOU* LOVE *ME*?
NO, NO MORE THAN *REASON*!
PFFFT
WHY THEN, MY COUSIN, MARGARET AND URSULA ARE *MUCH* DECEIVED –
FOR THEY DID SWEAR YOU *DID*.
THEY SWORE YOU WERE ALMOST *SICK* FOR ME!
THEY SWORE YOU WERE WELL-NIGH *DEAD* FOR ME!

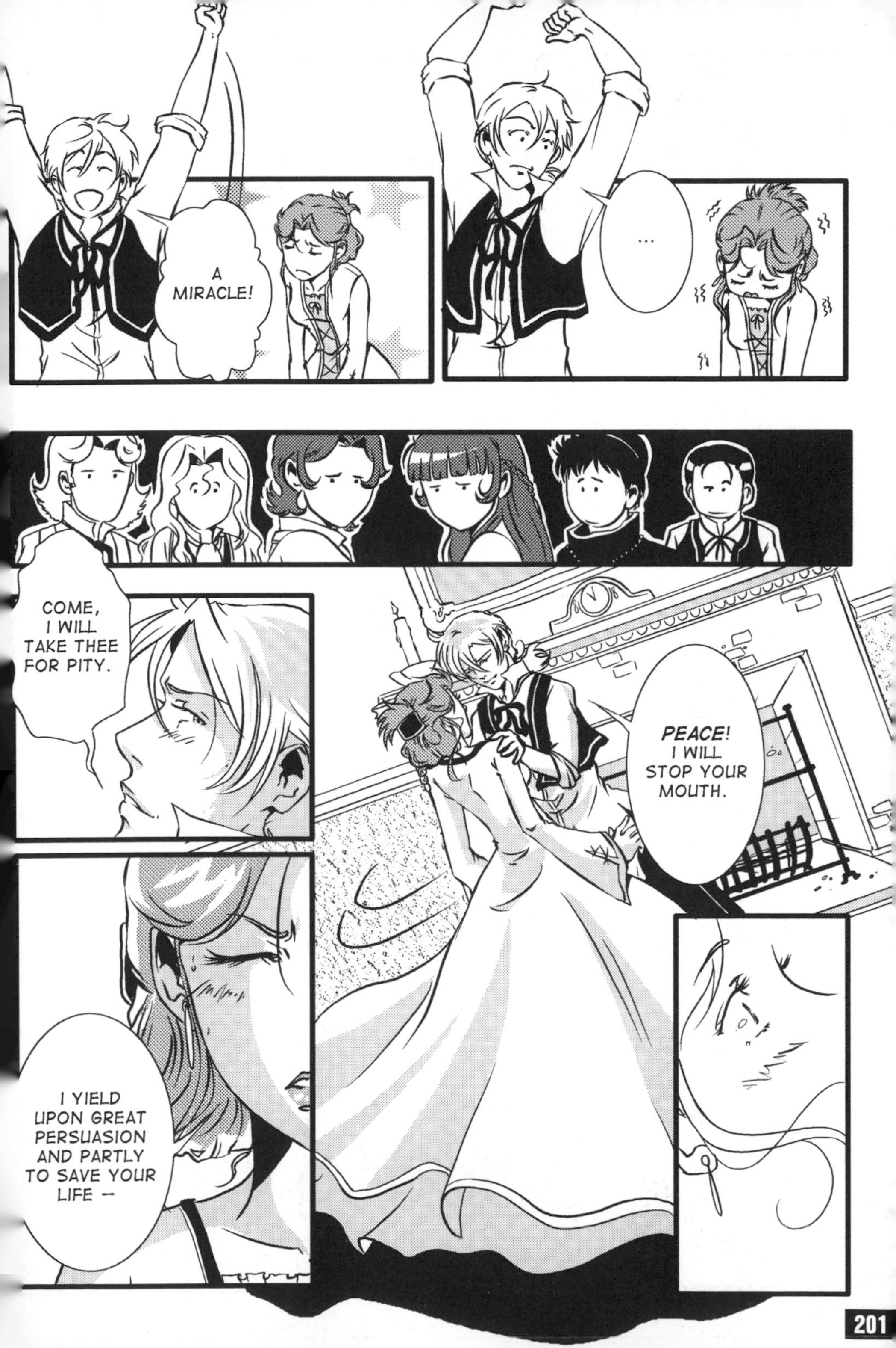
A MIRACLE!
...
COME, I WILL TAKE THEE FOR PITY.
PEACE! I WILL STOP YOUR MOUTH.
I YIELD UPON GREAT PERSUASION AND PARTLY TO SAVE YOUR LIFE –

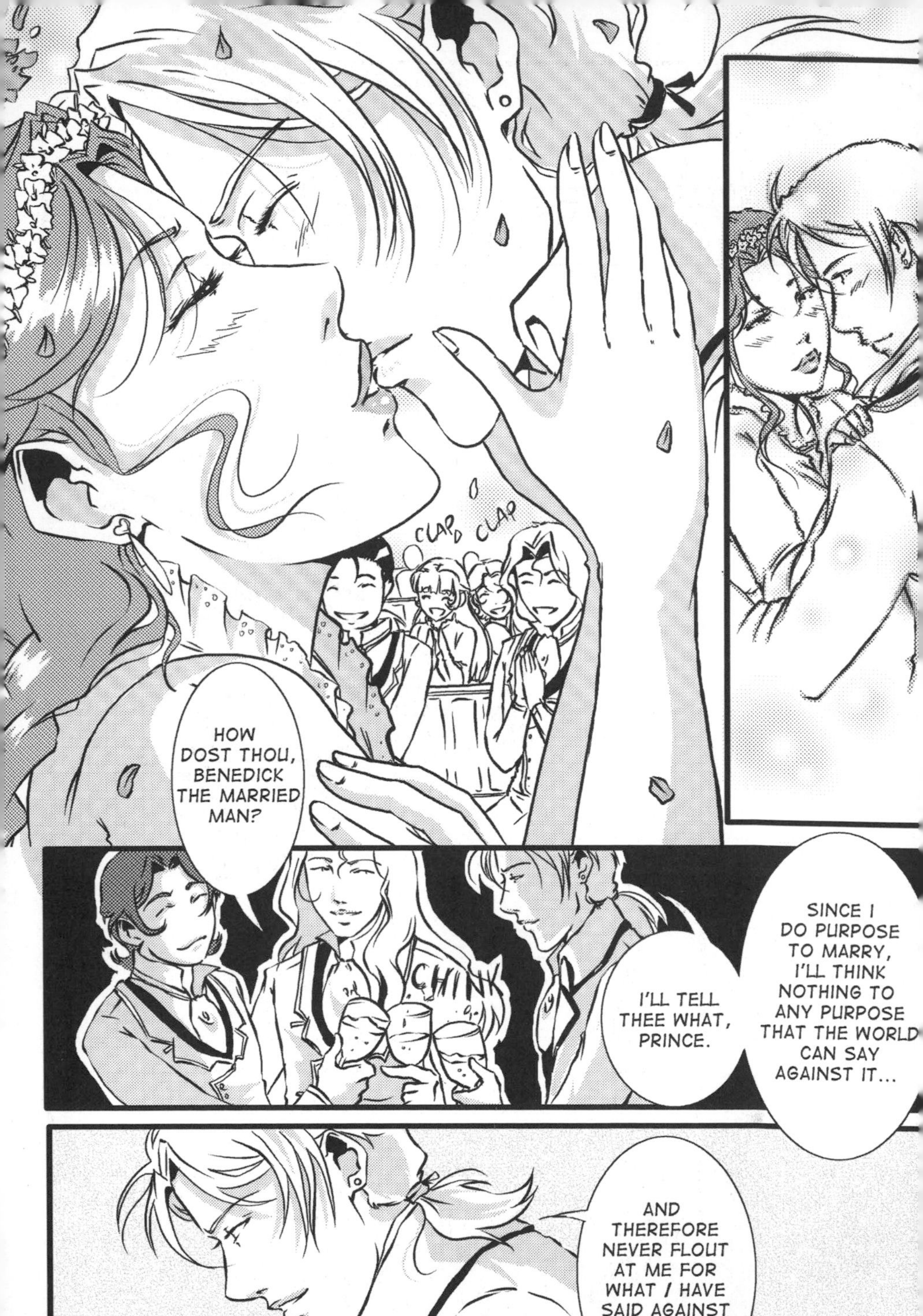
CLAP CLAP
HOW DOST THOU, BENEDICK THE MARRIED MAN?
CHINK
I'LL TELL THEE WHAT, PRINCE.
SINCE I DO PURPOSE TO MARRY, I'LL THINK NOTHING TO ANY PURPOSE THAT THE WORLD CAN SAY AGAINST IT...
AND THEREFORE NEVER FLOUT AT ME FOR WHAT I HAVE SAID AGAINST IT.

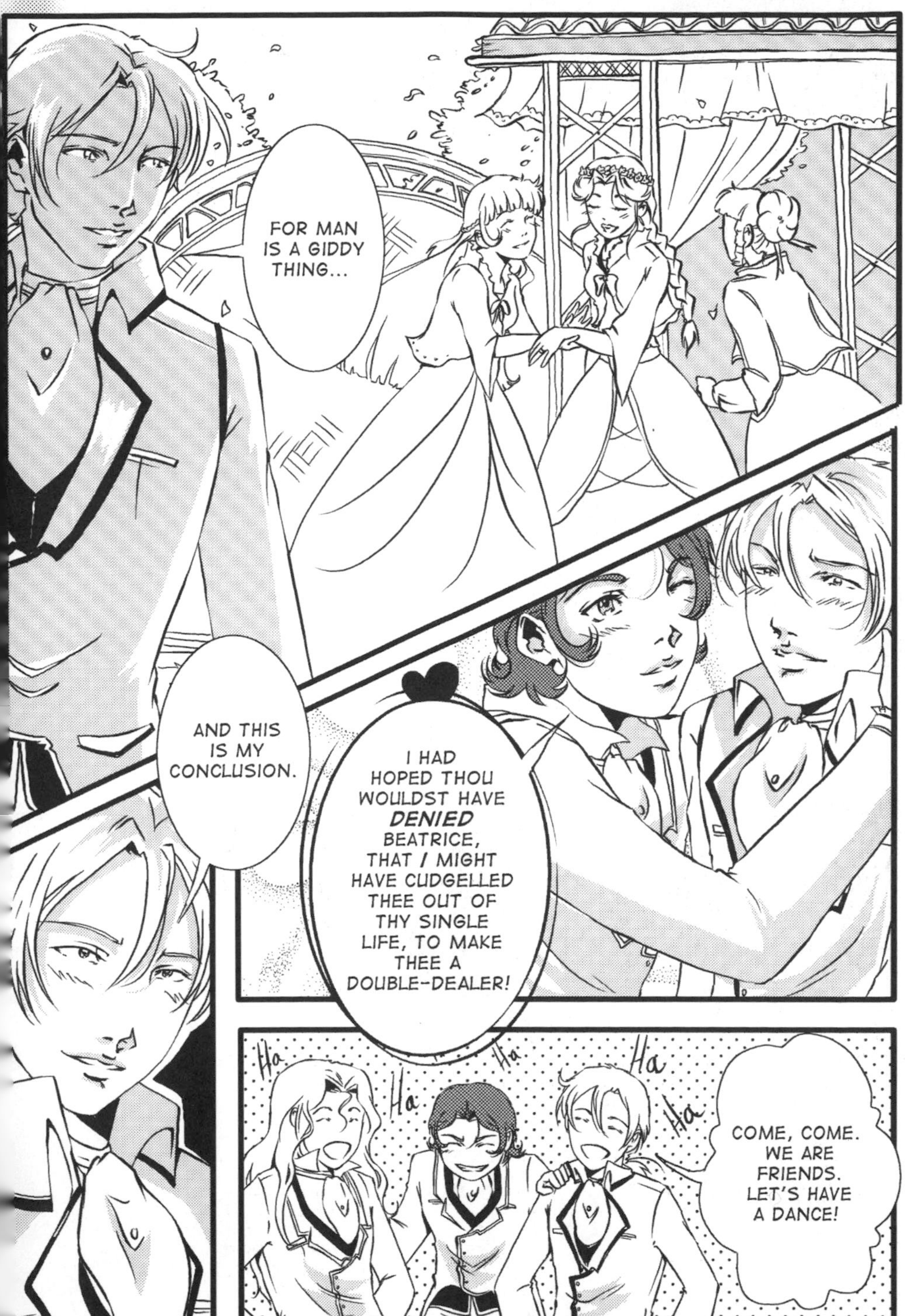
FOR MAN IS A GIDDY THING...
AND THIS IS MY CONCLUSION.
I HAD HOPED THOU WOULDST HAVE ***DENIED*** BEATRICE, THAT *I* MIGHT HAVE CUDGELLED THEE OUT OF THY SINGLE LIFE, TO MAKE THEE A DOUBLE-DEALER!
Ha
Ha
Ha
Ha
Ha
COME, COME. WE ARE FRIENDS. LET'S HAVE A DANCE!

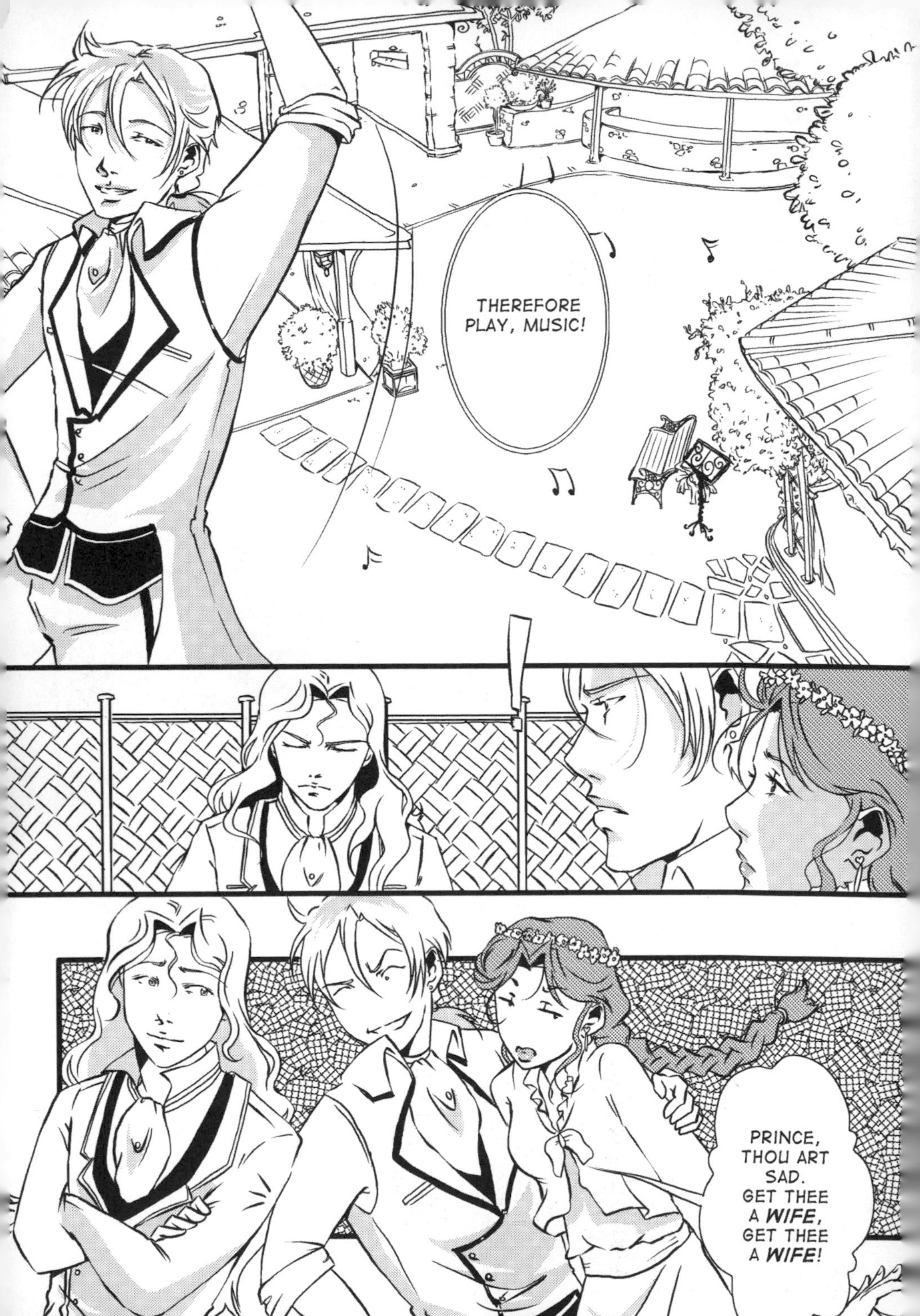
THEREFORE PLAY, MUSIC!
PRINCE, THOU ART SAD. GET THEE A **WIFE**, GET THEE A **WIFE**!

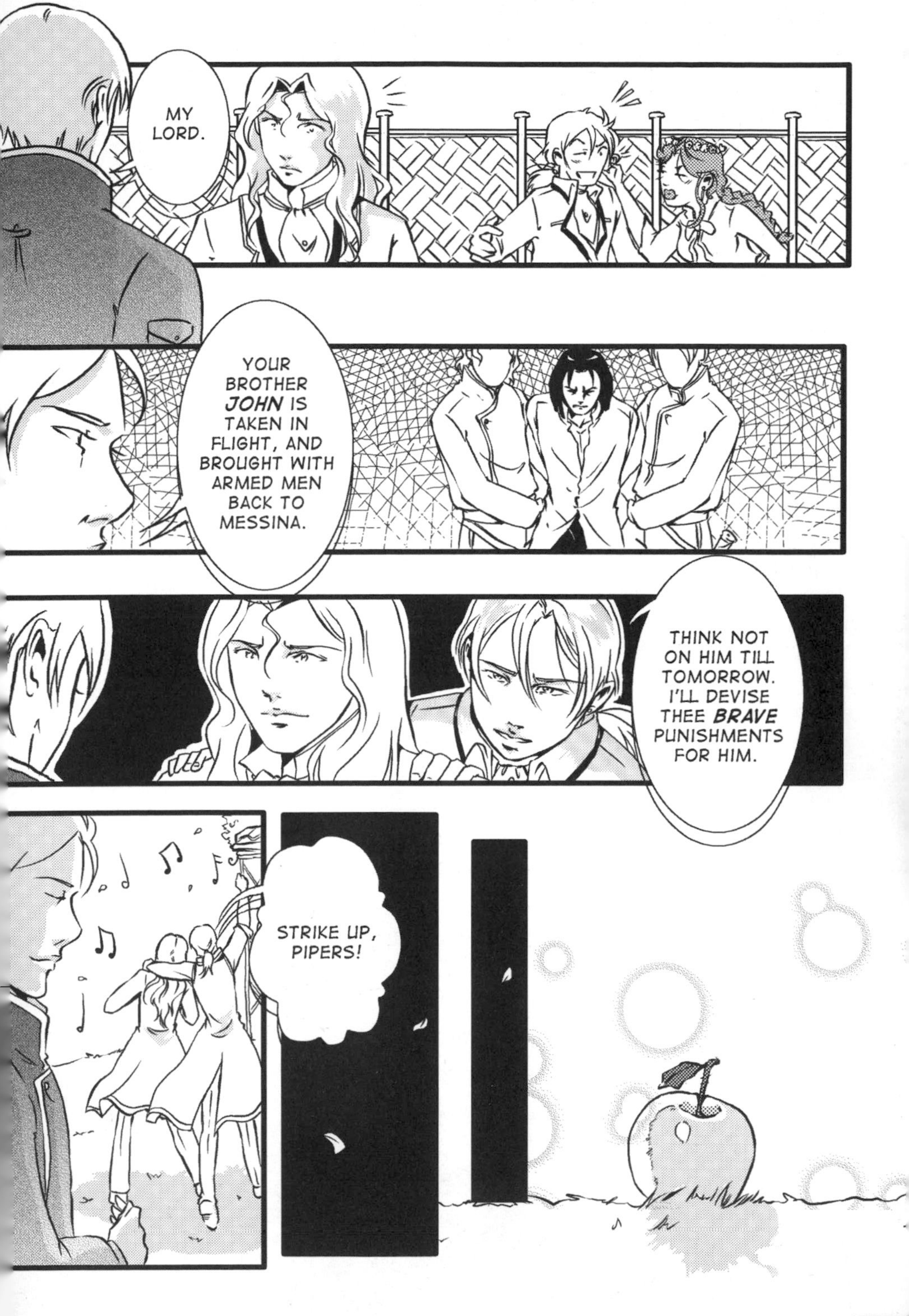
MY LORD.
YOUR BROTHER JOHN IS TAKEN IN FLIGHT, AND BROUGHT WITH ARMED MEN BACK TO MESSINA.
THINK NOT ON HIM TILL TOMORROW. I'LL DEVISE THEE BRAVE PUNISHMENTS FOR HIM.
STRIKE UP, PIPERS!

# PLOT SUMMARY OF MUCH ADO ABOUT NOTHING

News comes to Leonato, Governor of Messina, of Don Pedro the Prince of Aragon's imminent arrival from the wars in which two brave gentlemen have earned their spurs: Claudio and Benedick. Leonato's niece Beatrice remains unimpressed – she and Benedick are old flames, nowadays exchanging barbed witticisms in their own "merry war". On one thing, though, they are agreed: they are perfectly happy being single. But why is Leonato's daughter (Beatrice's cousin) Hero staying so quiet? Because – as Benedick's merciless teasing reveals – Claudio has fallen hopelessly in love with her. Don Pedro takes more pity on Claudio's shyness: he will pose as Claudio at that evening's masked ball, and woo Hero on Claudio's behalf.

The plan works, Pedro winning Hero's hand for Claudio at the ball – where the mischievous deceptions multiply. Beatrice, pretending not to recognize Benedick, ridicules him to his own (masked) face; while Pedro's villainous half-brother Don John (supported by his cronies Borachio and Conrad) spitefully pretends to mistake Claudio for Benedick, telling him that Pedro is genuinely in love with Hero. This throws Claudio into a fit of jealous rage, only defused when Pedro unites the happy couple. Before Hero and Claudio can marry, however, two more convoluted schemes emerge and play out – one warmly comic, the other chillingly malevolent. Firstly, with Claudio's connivance, Benedick is tricked into believing that Beatrice, for all her spiky hostility, is

actually in love with him; next, with Hero's connivance, Beatrice is identically tricked into believing that Benedick in fact loves her just as deeply. (The trick works, of course, because Benedick and Beatrice discover that they really *are* helplessly in love with each other!) The second plot, implemented by Don John, is altogether more sinister. Using the same stage-managed eavesdropping that brings Benedick and Beatrice together, Borachio drives Claudio and Hero apart: Pedro and Claudio overhear a contrived liaison during which Borachio passionately addresses his girlfriend Margaret (Hero's waiting-gentlewoman) by Hero's name...

Hero is violently jilted at the altar by Claudio; even her father Leonato doubts her honesty; and a black cloud descends over Beatrice and Benedick's newly tender relationship: the first test of his love she sets him is to "kill Claudio". Disaster is finally averted thanks to Friar Francis (the canny priest who believes in Hero's innocence) and Constable Dogberry (the dim policeman who eventually foils Borachio's plot). It is Friar Francis who devises the story's last piece of deception. It is announced that Hero has been "slandered to death by villains": shamed into remorse, Claudio agrees instead to marry the daughter of Leonato's brother, Antonio. But when this mystery bride unveils at the altar, she is of course... Hero herself. As the wedding music strikes up for the two couples, news comes of Don John's capture.

# A BRIEF LIFE OF WILLIAM SHAKESPEARE

Shakespeare's birthday is traditionally said to be the 23rd of April – St George's Day, patron saint of England. A good start for England's greatest writer. But that date and even his name are uncertain. He signed his own name in different ways. "Shakespeare" is now the accepted one out of dozens of different versions.

He was born at Stratford-upon-Avon in 1564, and baptized on 26th April. His mother, Mary Arden, was the daughter of a prosperous farmer. His father, John Shakespeare, a glove-maker, was a respected civic figure – and probably also a Catholic. In 1570, just as Will began school, his father was accused of illegal dealings. The family fell into debt and disrepute.

Will attended a local school for eight years. He did not go to university. The next ten years are a blank filled by suppositions. Was he briefly a Latin teacher, a soldier, a sea-faring explorer? Was he prosecuted and whipped for poaching deer?

We do know that in 1582 he married Anne Hathaway, eight years his senior, and three months pregnant. Two more children – twins – were born three years later but, by around 1590, Will had left Stratford to pursue a theatre career in London. Shakespeare's apprenticeship began as an actor and "pen for hire".

He learned his craft the hard way. He soon won fame as a playwright with often-staged popular hits.

He and his colleagues formed a stage company, the Lord Chamberlain's Men, which built the famous Globe Theatre. It opened in 1599 but was destroyed by fire in 1613 during a performance of *Henry VIII* which used gunpowder special effects. It was rebuilt in brick the following year.

Shakespeare was a financially successful writer who invested his money wisely in property. In 1597, he bought an enormous house in Stratford, and in 1608 became a shareholder in London's Blackfriars Theatre. He also redeemed the family's honour by acquiring a personal coat of arms.

Shakespeare wrote over 40 works, including poems, "lost" plays and collaborations, in a career spanning nearly 25 years. He retired to Stratford in 1613, where he died on 23rd April 1616, aged 52, apparently of a fever after a "merry meeting" of drinks with friends. Shakespeare did in fact die on St George's Day! He was buried "full 17 foot deep" in Holy Trinity Church, Stratford, and left an epitaph cursing anyone who dared disturb his bones.

There have been preposterous theories disputing Shakespeare's authorship. Some claim that Sir Francis Bacon (1561–1626), philosopher and Lord Chancellor, was the real author of Shakespeare's plays. Others propose Edward de Vere, Earl of Oxford (1550–1604), or, even more weirdly, Queen Elizabeth I. The implication is that the "real" Shakespeare had to be a university graduate or an aristocrat. Nothing less would do for the world's greatest writer.

Shakespeare is mysteriously hidden behind his work. His life will not tell us what inspired his genius.